R.L. PEREZ

CROWN OF POISON

A SNOW WHITE RETELLING

CROWNS OF THE FAE

CROWN OF POISON

Copyright © 2026 R.L. Perez

All rights reserved.

Published by Willow Haven Press 2026

United States of America

No parts of this publication may be reproduced, stored in a retrieval system, or transmitted in any form or by any means, electronic, mechanical, photocopying, recording, or otherwise, without the prior written permission of the copyright owner.

This book is sold subject to the condition that it shall not, by way of trade or otherwise, be lent, resold, hired out, or otherwise circulated without the publisher's prior consent in any form of binding or cover other than that in which it is published and without a similar condition including this condition being imposed on the subsequent purchaser. Under no circumstances may any part of this book be photocopied for resale.

This is a work of fiction. Any similarity between the characters and situations within its pages and places or persons, living or dead, is unintentional and coincidental.

Cover Art by Blue Raven Book Covers

Edited by Allison Rose

ISBN: 978-1-955035-76-7

www.rlperez.com

For the readers who loved Sheriff Graham from Once Upon a Time.

He deserved better.

THE SEVEN PROVINCES OF THE WINTER COURT

AUTHOR'S NOTE

This novel contains content that may be triggering. There is a scene of child endangerment and threat of harm (no children are actually harmed), brief mentions of animal deaths off-page, mild animal violence, and one scene of mild dub-con.

In addition, the story includes graphic violence and graphic sexual content (consensual).

Please be mindful of your triggers and mental health before you read.

The Princess

The queen was hiding something.

And I was determined to uncover her secret.

I crept down the corridor toward her chambers, wrapping my magic around myself like a cloak. Invisibility tingled over my skin, the cool whisper of power making me shudder.

Very few knew about my fae magic. In the Winter Court, fae and humans mingled together, but humans were considered the lesser, weaker species. So, as the half-human princess, I was the scum of the court and was often scorned for my "tainted" bloodline. Most people wanted nothing to do with me.

They didn't bother to ask whether my fae blood meant I possessed any gifts.

I thought of my father, who had been the only one to truly see me. He had died a year ago. I always suspected Calista had something to do with it, but I never found proof.

I hoped I would find it tonight.

A pair of maids shuffled past me, their arms full of folded linens, as they giggled together. I flattened myself against the wall, holding perfectly still. My invisibility was useful, but it didn't stop me from making sounds or running into people.

As the maids rounded the corner, their laughter echoing in the hall, I eased off the wall and continued my trek toward Queen Calista's rooms. I knew they were empty because she was currently dining with Sir Quinton and his wife. The two nobles had recently arrived in the Winter Court, and Sir Quinton was renowned for his fae gift of foresight. No doubt Calista wanted to dig in her claws and utilize his power for her own gain.

Calista's fae gift was terrifying. With a single drop of a person's blood, she had the power to control them. I had seen it firsthand.

Which was one of the reasons why she kept me locked away. She didn't want me exposing her manipulative powers to the public.

Not that anyone would believe me, the human princess who was so loathsome that the queen kept her hidden from the kingdom.

I thanked the gods that Calista didn't know about my fae magic; otherwise, she would have drawn my blood years ago and tried to control me. But there were benefits to being perceived as useless. It kept her away from me.

Holding my breath, I inched closer to her bedchamber door and rattled the doorknob.

Locked, of course. But I was prepared.

"Sybelle?" I whispered. Though my voice was only a breath, it still seemed to ring around me like a beacon alerting the world to my presence. I flinched, cramming my eyes shut, then waited.

A moment passed. Then another.

At long last, my friend's voice brushed against my ear. "I'm here."

I jumped, my gaze darting around the corridor in search of her. Squinting, I made out a faint, shadowy outline to my right. If I hadn't been searching for it, I wouldn't have noticed it at all. Sybelle stood next to me, her body camouflaged, allowing her to blend in completely with the stone wall behind her.

"Incredible," I murmured, reaching out a hand to brush her arm. Everything from the color of her skin to the texture of her tunic resembled the wall.

She chuckled. "Not as incredible as your invisibility. I can't see you at all."

"Do you have the lock stone?" I asked.

The clinking of stones told me she was sifting through her pouch of gems. Sybelle, like me, was half fae and half human. Her fae magic allowed her to wield all kinds of powers depending on which gemstone she was holding. She recently told me she had discovered a black diamond that could open any lock.

"It's here," Sybelle said softly, then inched closer to Calista's door. My heart thundered in my chest as she pressed the dark stone to the door handle. Metal shifted, and with a *click*, the lock released. Sybelle tugged on the handle, then eased the door open, revealing a dark chamber.

My breath shuddered as I peered inside. The curtains were drawn, shrouding the room in darkness. Not even a candle was lit.

Oh yes, this place was certainly full of secrets.

"Thank you," I whispered to Sybelle. "You should leave now."

"Eira—"

I turned to face her, dropping my invisibility for a moment so she could see my intent gaze. "I *mean* it. My stepmother cannot catch you here. It's dangerous enough with you helping me. But if I'm caught, and the servants see you in your chambers, you'll be absolved of any guilt. I can't bring trouble to your court, Sybelle."

She exhaled slowly. Though I couldn't see her face, I knew her brows were drawn together in concern. She was the Queen of the Shadow Court. The only reason she was a welcome guest here at all was because her husband was one of the most powerful unseelie fae in the realm.

"I can handle trouble in my court," she insisted.

But I shook my head. "This is my problem. Not yours. I don't even know for sure if Calista is hiding anything. And even if she is, it could be something ridiculous like harboring a collection of dried-up fingernails."

Sybelle snorted.

"Don't risk yourself for *my* curiosity," I went on. "Please."

Sybelle sighed, her frame drooping slightly. "Fine. But if you run into trouble, Azure is just outside. She can help."

I smiled at the thought of Sybelle's mighty blue dragon. "Thank you."

"I'm here for you, Eira. No matter what."

I squeezed her arm, and she squeezed back. She whispered a quick, "Be careful," before she disappeared down the hall. I stared after her, listening to her soft footsteps fade away.

Now I was well and truly alone.

Unease rippled over me like an icy chill, but I swallowed my fear. With a deep breath, I inched inside the room, my shuffling steps echoing in the vast space. Squinting, I struggled to make out any details within the chamber. With my half-human senses, my eyesight wasn't nearly as keen as Calista's.

My steps were clumsy as I fumbled my way to the bedside table, then lit a lantern with trembling fingers. Warm amber light illuminated the chamber, and I stifled a gasp.

A wall of shelves stood before me, stocked with rows and rows of vials. Each one contained a dark liquid—some crimson, others black like ink.

I knew exactly what this was: her stores of blood. This was where she kept the blood of those she wanted to control. There was the red blood of the seelie fae, and the black blood of the unseelie.

My stomach twisted as I glanced over each glass.

They were labeled. I wasn't sure I wanted to know who she had control over. I knew for sure my blood wasn't there.

It probably wouldn't hurt to check, just in case. Perhaps I could even smash a few vials to free as many people as I could from Calista's magic.

I strode forward, but footsteps in the hall made me freeze. I held my breath, ensuring my magic was draped over me, then held perfectly still.

The footsteps came and went, fading as whoever it was continued down the hall.

Biting my lip, I shook my head. I didn't have time for distractions. I needed to find proof of Calista's treachery and then get out before she caught me.

The most important thing was finding evidence of her hand in Father's death. But if I couldn't find that, I would settle on anything else incriminating: details of her court schemes, a list of nobles whose blood she was after... anything to condemn her so I could free this court from her greedy clutches.

I had remained hidden in the shadows for far too long.

My eyes fell on the large vanity on the opposite side of the room. I moved toward it and eased open drawers. As I sifted through papers, I found old maps, a list of potion breweries in the province, and a parchment with several cities written on it. Squinting, I glanced over the list, unable to make sense of what these cities had in common.

With a curse, I ensured everything was back in place before shutting the drawer. Something within made a *thunk* when it closed.

I froze. There hadn't been anything particularly heavy in the drawer. So what had made the noise?

I opened it again, inserting my hand to the very back of the drawer. Still nothing but papers. I pressed my fingertips along the bottom of the drawer until the wood gave way, revealing a false bottom.

My heart lurched as I inspected the secret chamber. It only held two things: an ornate silver hand mirror and a crumpled piece of parchment.

Carefully, I lifted the parchment, which had small crimson splotches on it. Was that... blood?

My stomach dropped. It was in my father's handwriting, and it was addressed to his guard captain.

Victor,

I have seen her. I have seen my wife's true nature, and it is horrifying. You must alert the court at once before it's too late.

I think she suspects me. I have been trying to get closer to find evidence so I can expose her true nature. In case something happens to me, please tell everyone you can that she is not who she appears to be. And if I cannot expose her true nature, then I pray to the gods that someone else can.

Judas

My blood chilled as I read over the letter a second time. Then my eyes snagged on the date scrawled at the top.

The day before my father's death.

My hands shook, and my fingers started to tingle. I stared in horror at the red splotches on the parchment. Blood and ice, was this *my father's* blood?

Bile crept up my throat. No, no, no…

I was going to be sick.

My heart felt like it was about to burst out of my chest. For a moment, I thought I might faint.

I gave my head a firm shake and gritted my teeth. *This is why you're here, Eira. This is the evidence you were looking for.*

Blinking back tears, I kept the letter clutched in one hand and eased the hand mirror out of its hiding spot with the other.

What was so special about a hand mirror? Why did she have it hidden? It was unsettling, to look into a mirror and see nothing but a darkened room reflected back at me. My invisibility was still cloaking me, concealing me even from the mirror.

But as I gazed at it, a strange fog clouded over the glass. Words appeared in the fog, as if an invisible person were writing letters on the misty glass with their finger.

I murmured the words softly as I read them. *"Magic mirror, whose glass I see, reveal and reflect the truth unto me."*

The mirror began to tremble in my hand. I almost dropped it in surprise. The handle grew hot, and I hissed in pain, prepared to set it down until I noticed a white glow forming around the glass. It ignited the room, and I sucked in a sharp breath, my heart hammering loudly in my chest. The light burned against my eyes, making me squint.

Gradually, the glow faded, and I nearly yelped in surprise at the sight of my own pale face reflected back at me. My black tresses almost blended in with the darkness of the room around me.

And I had a pair of pointed fae ears.

My breath hitched, and I quickly ran my fingers over each ear. They were round, just as they always were. Round like a human's.

And yet, this mirror was showing what I would look like as a full-blooded fae. I blinked slowly, entranced by the vision. My skin looked softer, my eyes a brighter shade of blue instead of the pale icy color I was accustomed to. My hair was shinier, the curls a bit tighter and neater than my usual messy waves.

Never before had I looked like this, though I had often dreamed of it. My life would have been so much easier if I looked like all the other fae nobles. I would not have been scoffed at or mocked. I would have been like everyone else.

I swallowed hard, struggling to remember the task at hand. I was here to find evidence, not daydream of a life that would never be.

But curiosity burned within me. Why did Calista have this mirror? It clearly showed visions, but did it do anything else? And most importantly—why did she have it hidden under the false bottom of a drawer?

It had to be damning somehow. It had to be important.

Perhaps it had to do with my father's death. Did she use this magic mirror to kill him?

I was so focused on the mirror that I didn't hear the soft creak of the door opening behind me. During the shock of seeing my altered reflection, I had also dropped my invisibility.

It wasn't until a thick black mist pooled into the room that I went completely rigid, horror washing over me like a bucket of ice water. A foul odor filled my nostrils. It smelled like the decaying flesh of a dead animal.

I was not alone.

"Little thief," hissed a familiar voice. "That belongs to *me*."

I froze with terror, my eyes wide as I stared at the mirror's reflection. Behind me stood a creature who was both familiar and foreign all at once. It was my stepmother—the same blood-red lips, pointed ears, and bronze hair. But long, sharp fangs were visible between her parted lips. The whites of her eyes were gone, leaving nothing but a red abyss. Deadly claws extended from her fingers. Her skin, usually as pale as mine, was now leathery and gray.

I remembered the tales—the bedtime stories told to me as a child.

The fae who had dabbled in black magic were twisted and transformed into something horrific and unrecognizable.

Demon Fae.

With a shriek, I whirled to face her, only to find her completely normal. She wore a regal crimson gown, and her skin was ivory like normal. Her eyes were the usual brown. No fangs. No claws.

"B-But... I..." I sputtered, unable to form words. My heart slammed against my rib cage, making it hard for me to breathe.

She inched closer, her eyes flashing with lethal intensity. Her movements were so smooth and graceful, like a predator. My skin prickled, every instinct screaming at me to *run*. "How did you find that, Eira?" Each word was sharp and precise. "In fact, I'm fairly certain my chambers were locked. You shouldn't have been able to get in at all."

My throat went bone dry. I held up the mirror, then glanced at the reflection again, angling it so it was facing her.

That beastly creature stared back at me, baring her fangs.

I flinched, and Calista hissed, "Give it to me!"

I darted backward just as she lunged. The black mist in the room thickened, concealing the floor from view. I tried to stumble away, but I tripped over something. Pain ricocheted up my body, and I crashed to my knees with a loud cry.

A low growl echoed, making my skin crawl. Blood and ice, what *was* that? Did she have an animal with her?

Or had the sound come from the queen herself?

Shivering bones, she was going to *kill* me.

Light gleamed in my peripheral vision, and I glimpsed the open door of her bedchamber. The faint lantern light from the corridor beckoned. My only chance to escape.

I moved toward it, but I was hit by something heavy and solid, my body crumpling from the impact. Dizzy, I staggered to my feet, only to gape in horror at the sight before me.

Calista stood nearly as tall as the ceiling, her skin gray and leathery, with great black wings stretched behind her.

She looked exactly like the vision in the mirror. Her all-red eyes blazed as she bared her fangs at me. She was positively monstrous. A creature from my nightmares.

Pure, blood-chilling terror clawed its way through me, coiling so tightly that I felt like I was choking.

"Give me the mirror!" she screeched. She swiped her arm, claws slashing. A sudden rush of adrenaline flooded my body, and I ducked just in time. On instinct, I draped my invisibility over myself, backing slowly away from this beast that was my stepmother. I heard Calista's sharp intake of breath as I vanished from view.

Where were the guards? Her door was wide open. Why weren't they coming? Surely, the people had to see this. They had to know who their queen truly was.

All this time, she *had* been harboring a secret. But the evidence wasn't hidden in her chambers. It was what lay underneath her powerful glamour.

Father had said Calista's true nature was horrifying. *This* was what he'd meant.

She was a Demon Fae.

"Where are you, you vile vermin?" Calista shrieked, her head swinging back and forth as she searched for me.

Thanking the gods I had managed to hide my invisibility from her all these years, I stumbled toward the open door, desperate to escape, to survive. If I was the only one who knew about Calista's true form, it was my duty to the people to expose her. I had to—

My thoughts were silenced by a sharp pain, followed by white-hot fire scorching my veins. Calista had been wildly slicing her claws through the air in her efforts to cut me.

And she had succeeded.

I tried to scream, but no sound came out. Gods, the pain was blinding. I couldn't see. I couldn't feel my body at all.

I let out a low groan as my head started to spin.

Calista's eyes narrowed as she turned her head in my direction.

"What is this?" she hissed.

I froze, alarm coursing within me. Had she seen me?

Quick as lightning, her claws lashed out. I screamed, thinking she had sliced into me again. The sound of paper ripping made my blood chill.

"I had meant to destroy that letter," she said smugly. "Thank you for reminding me. It's a shame Judas never got to send it."

Oh no... In my haste to escape, I had dropped my father's letter.

It now lay in tattered pieces on the floor.

Rage boiled within me, and my fingers curled into fists. I wanted to kill her. I wanted to *destroy* her.

My vision blurred, and I swayed on my feet. The wound in my arm burned as if someone had branded me with a hot iron.

Calista drew nearer. If she had seen the letter, then she knew I had to be close.

Move! I thought. *You have to keep moving!*

Something hot and liquid dripped down my arm. Numbly, I glanced at it, only to find a bloody gash just below my shoulder. Bubbling green liquid formed around the exposed wound.

Shit, shit, *shit*.

She had cut me.

She had my blood.

But I didn't have time to clean it off. If I lingered, she would kill me.

I had to risk it.

"Ah..." Calista inhaled deeply, a slow, cruel smile spreading on her face. "You're bleeding." Her eyes fixed on the droplets of my blood staining the floor, which led to precisely where I was standing.

In a flash, her hand darted out, clawed fingers wrapping around my arm.

"I've got you, foul brat," she hissed, drawing me closer. I wriggled in her grip, but her fingers clutched me more firmly. Blood continued to gush from my wound, making me see stars.

Shivering bones, if I didn't get out of here now, I would faint from blood loss. And then she would have her way with me.

I had to fight. I had to *survive*.

With a grunt, I elbowed her in the ribs, then stomped on her feet. She snarled, her grip on me loosening.

It was just enough for me to duck down low, where she wouldn't expect to find me. On all fours, I wriggled toward the opposite side of the room, knowing I wouldn't be able to get past her to the door.

Fine. If she blocked that path, I would take another.

Calista let out a roar of fury as I crawled toward the balcony doors. When I reached them, I staggered to my feet and threw them open.

"Help me!" I screamed into the chilled night air. My voice echoed around me.

Calista chuckled, drawing closer. "No one is out there to save you, child. You're mine now."

In the distance came the whooshing of heavy wing beats.

I faced Calista and dropped my invisibility, then gave her a savage smile. "Think again."

Her face slackened in surprise, and I tumbled over the balcony wall. She let out another deafening roar that pierced the night. I was careening, tumbling to my death, the icy wind burning against my skin. My stomach hollowed, and my scream was drowned out by the frigid wind.

A blur of midnight blue appeared, and I landed hard on a patch of firm scales. Gasping, my eyes moist with tears, I righted myself on Azure's back and let out a trembling sigh of relief. Sybelle's dragon arced around the castle, a low grumble quivering through her body.

I interpreted that as admonishment. She didn't like being summoned like some pack mule.

"Sorry, friend," I murmured to her, patting her scaly back. The dark blue scales blended in with the night sky. The muscles of her shoulders flexed with each beat of her wings, shifting underneath me. "Just get me out of the city and you can return for Sybelle."

I pressed a hand to the wound in my arm, trying to staunch the flow of blood. Anxiety coursed through me as I glanced up at the castle spires we were leaving behind. From the folds of my dress, I felt the solid weight of Calista's small hand mirror. She had been fooling the court for *years* with her glamour. But this mirror seemed to reveal her true nature.

I had to find a way to use it to expose her for who she really was. I only hoped it would be enough to destroy her.

Five Years Later

The cool, wintry air swirled around me, capturing stray strands of my black hair and coiling them around my cheeks. But it didn't matter. My magic cloaked me completely, so no matter how my hair billowed around me, no one would notice.

I waited at the edge of the forest, watching patrons enter and exit the pub, searching for one man in particular. The icy air nipped at my arms, but it wasn't unpleasant. Sometimes, when I focused hard enough, I could pretend I was impervious to the cold. That my magic provided a shield for me, even if it didn't.

It made me feel as if I truly *were* invisible. As if I didn't exist at all.

An aching hollowness filled my chest, threatening to cave inward as I was reminded of being invisible in the palace of the Winter Court. Once my father married Calista, it was as if I no longer existed. I was an outsider. Unwanted. Unloved.

Even after the Snow Princess mysteriously disappeared, no one at court seemed to care.

No one except Calista, of course. She had been hunting me nonstop.

Everyone else in the kingdom had been perfectly content to let my stepmother rule, oblivious to the monstrous secret she was hiding.

A renewed sense of focus and determination had me straightening my spine. This was why I was here: to take back my kingdom and rid the people of Calista's tyranny for good.

A tall, wiry fellow with bright red hair entered the pub, his swagger and smug expression telling me everything I needed to know. He was a fae lord. A wealthy one. Exactly who we were looking for.

"I see him," I whispered. The wind washed away my words, but I knew Frisk would hear me. His keen fox hearing never failed.

A small chitter sounded next to me, followed by a low chuckle as Frisk's furry ears twitched. "The fool won't know what hit him."

I couldn't suppress my grin. Frisk always loved these missions. It was part of the reason I always brought him.

That, and his knack for stealth.

A burst of icy wind tickled my arm as Kendra twined her long white tail around me. Her all-blue eyes blinked balefully up at me. "Can I blast this one?" she asked.

I frowned at the tiny dragon wrapped around my arm like a cuff. With my invisibility, she looked like she was floating in the air. "And what happens when he grabs you?"

"I blast him again."

I snorted. "Not a chance, Kendra. You're with me."

She huffed, exhaling another cold blast. "But I—"

"You are *too valuable*," I insisted. "Besides, I need your help. Stay with me, please?"

She blinked at me again, and I offered her my sweetest smile. Her brilliant eyes could always see right through my invisibility, thanks to her dragon blood. All Crystal Icebolts had otherworldly all-blue eyes that could see through glamours.

Which made her a valuable asset that scumbags like the red-haired fae lord might want to exploit.

But her pride wouldn't let her stay behind, so I had to remind her how much *I* needed her.

"Fine," she said with a heavy sigh. "Go on then, Frisk."

"With pleasure," Frisk said.

A blur of motion shot forward. If I hadn't been looking for it, I wouldn't have noticed the ripple in the snow. Frisk was an arctic fox, and he blended into the surroundings almost as well as I did. It didn't take long for his form to vanish entirely, leaving me squinting through the flurries, awaiting his signal.

A few moments later, a high-pitched chitter rang out.

With Kendra on my arm, I sprang forward, circling the pub to find the lord's carriage, his driver flat on his back with Frisk sitting calmly atop him.

I scoffed and put my hands on my hips, even knowing Frisk couldn't see me. "Is that really necessary?"

"What?" Frisk blinked his wide, dark eyes—the picture of innocence.

Stifling a laugh, I muttered, "Keep watch, will you?" and flung open the carriage doors.

It appeared empty at first glance, but I knew better. The queen had gotten crafty with her methods. No doubt my thievery had her growing more and more paranoid. A smile formed on my lips at the thought of mighty Calista wringing her hands in frustration and anxiety.

But no. That wasn't my stepmother. She was much more likely to kill someone instead of fret.

All life is precious, my father had once said. *We must protect our own. Especially those who cannot protect themselves.*

That was why I was here: for the humans. For the people of this court who suffered under Calista's rule.

"There," came Kendra's soft voice. She pointed her elongated snout toward the cushioned seat. "It's glamoured."

I pressed down on the seat. A low creak echoed, and I pushed harder, feeling around the outer edges of the seat until I found a small lever. I pulled it, and the mechanism released a tiny compartment underneath.

"Wow," I murmured. "Fae glamour *and* a hidden mechanism? The false queen must be worried about bandits or something."

Kendra snorted. "Rightfully so."

I peered into the compartment and gasped. Piles and piles of gold, some in pouches and some simply spilled over as if the lord had been in a hurry. He likely wanted to down a few more drinks before he had to report back to court. What a gluttonous goat.

"See anything good?" Frisk called out.

"Hush!" I hissed. "You're just an ordinary fox, remember?"

An innocent chitter followed my words, and I laughed. Not many fae folk knew of the faerie creatures that roamed the woods of the Winter Court. Most dismissed them as children's tales, but I knew better. I lived in these woods, and the faerie creatures were my closest friends. Some were ordinary animals, but others were sentient. Some even had magic, just like the fae folk.

I opened my sack and started scooping coins into it, wincing as they jingled loudly. But there was nothing but the quiet, frigid air behind me. Even so, I didn't want to push my luck. My movements were quick as I shoveled more and more coins into my sack. I was almost finished when Frisk gave a low bark. I went rigid.

Damn. Out of time.

I bit my lip and gazed at the pile of coins that still remained, knowing it could help fund the rebel cause. How could I just leave this gold sitting here?

"Eira," Kendra hissed in warning.

Ignoring her, I swiped one last handful just as someone grabbed my cloak from behind.

"Who's this, eh?"

Kendra skittered up my arm, burrowing herself in my hood to stay out of sight. I wriggled, struggling to free myself. Too late, I realized I'd let my invisible glamour fall in my haste to grab more coins. I couldn't risk using it now; very few people knew the extent of my magic, and I wanted to keep it that way.

Someone yanked me out of the carriage and spun me around. It was the red-haired lord. He raised an eyebrow, his lips curling into a cruel smile. "Ah. You're a looker, aren't ye?" His bloodshot eyes drifted to my rounded ears, and his eyebrows lifted. "And *human*."

People often mistook me for a full-blooded human, even though I was half fae. My ears were both a gift and a curse in that sense.

I knew how to get myself out of this situation. But I hated playing the damsel.

I pretended to gasp. "Oh please, good fae lord, please let me go! I didn't mean any harm!" As part fae, I couldn't lie, but I had plenty of practice skirting the truth. In all honesty, I *didn't* mean any harm; generally, we tried to steal without hurting anyone.

"Save it, lass, I can see the gold gleaming in your pack," the lord spat. "I think the queen will be pleased I've finally caught one of the Snow Princess's thieves."

So he didn't know it was me, then. Relief swelled inside me. One of the benefits to being an invisible and unloved princess was that no one recognized my face. I released an anguished wail and covered my face with my hands. "Please. *Please!* There must be *something* I can do to make it right. Name your price."

The man's hold on my cloak loosened slightly. "Any price, eh?" The dark hunger stirring in his eyes told me all I needed to know.

Blood and ice, this man was foul. I would enjoy beating him senseless.

"Yes, yes," I urged, layering my voice with more desperation and sobs. "*Anything* you want." I widened my eyes so he would understand my meaning.

His foul grin widened, his arm dropping and releasing me completely. He leaned forward, and I did, too, holding my breath so I wouldn't have to smell the nasty stench of his inebriation. In a flash, I unsheathed my dagger and raised it to his throat.

"Step away from me," I said, dropping all pretenses. "*Now.*"

The man's face slackened in shock, then turned a deep red, anger boiling in his eyes. "You little bitch."

I cocked my head and smiled. "Go ahead and test me. I

haven't gotten this knife dirty in a while, and I miss the feeling."

His eyes darted to the gleaming silver blade, and his expression faltered. It wasn't made of iron, but it would still do some damage. "You wouldn't. A fine lass like you—"

I sliced hard, nicking the sleeve of his tunic. He swore loudly, cradling his arm as a drop of blood fell on the ground, leaving a large, crimson stain in the snow.

Frisk let out another loud bark.

I groaned and slammed the hilt of my dagger into the man's skull. With a grunt, he collapsed, and I easily stepped over him, my boots crunching in the snow. I secured my glamour back in place before stepping away from the carriage and the unconscious scumbag still lying on the ground.

"You all right?" I asked Kendra.

"Yes, I'm fine!" Kendra's voice was a bit higher pitched than normal. She was still buried in the hood of my cloak, and I could feel her trembling.

Despite her bravado, most altercations terrified her. And I couldn't blame her. That fae lord had been a downright bastard.

From the pub emerged several other men, their shouts loud and echoing as they drew closer.

"Let's dash, shall we?" Frisk asked.

Together, we darted off toward the woods. "I didn't even get to toy with him," I lamented.

Frisk chuckled as he scampered alongside me. "Next time, Princess, I'll let you torment all the queen's lackeys to your heart's content."

Once we reached the cover of the trees, we slowed our

pace, veering west toward the rendezvous point. A soft nicker told me Stella was already waiting with the horses.

"We should have brought Mauro," Frisk said with a sniff. "He's faster."

"He can't carry all of us," I argued. "Besides, he gets grumpy if we ask for too many favors." Mauro was a stag—a fae creature, like Frisk. The fox was right; Mauro *was* faster, but he had a grouchy disposition. We had to tread carefully around him.

We edged around a particularly large pine tree, and then I caught sight of my friend, who stood next to two chestnut horses. Stella's pale blonde hair almost blended in with the snowy forest. She was biting her lip in worry, her blue eyes scanning the woods until they locked onto me. Relief filled her face.

I grinned and held up my sack, shaking it so she could hear the jingle of coins. "Good haul this time."

Stella laughed. "Excellent. No trouble, I presume?" She glanced over me as if to search for injuries.

I pressed a hand to my chest. "You wound me, Stella. Of course there wasn't trouble."

"Well, the fae lord *did* nearly catch her," Frisk said slyly.

Stella's grin fell. "Eira…"

"I said no trouble, and I can't lie," I said, shooting a glare at Frisk. "I had it handled, and I barely spilled any blood."

Stella massaged her temples. "You stabbed him?"

"I *nicked* him."

Stella's brows knitted together. "Eira, if you're going to continue to be reckless like this, the others will insist you stay behind. You are too valuable to risk getting captured or killed. Our entire rebellion depends on *you*."

A hard lump formed in my throat, but I swallowed

around it, forcing a smile. "I know that. Like I said, I knew what I was doing."

Stella looked up at me and squeezed my shoulder, her face softening. Though she stood shorter than me, I often looked at her as an older, protective sister. She was stern when I was playful, and her concern was often warranted.

"I have no problem with you going on missions," Stella said quietly. "I'm just saying, the others will. You need to be careful."

I thought of Huck, the strictest member of our little band of rebels. He was the most vocal about his objection to these missions, especially when I was the one heading them.

Not to mention Denton… He often had his reservations where I was concerned, but that was for a whole different reason.

I shook my head, trying to clear it. "It'll be fine. We got a good stash of coin this time. Hopefully, this will be enough."

Stella smiled again, and a dimple appeared in her right cheek. She looked me over once more. "Where's Kendra?"

"She's hiding."

"I am *not* hiding," Kendra objected, though she did not emerge from within my hood.

Stella and I exchanged knowing looks. Fae creatures couldn't lie, but for some reason, dragons could.

And everyone here knew Kendra was lying.

"Aren't you excited to see Rogun again?" I asked.

Kendra's quivering stopped for a moment, and her snout came out as she sniffed. "Is he here?" Kendra had a soft spot for the big dragon that often slept in the woods near my cottage.

"No, but I'm sure he's waiting for you."

Her head popped out, her blue eyes gleaming. "Yes, I suppose I *am* eager to see him."

"Then, you'd better stop *not-hiding*; otherwise, he won't know where you are. You don't want to worry him, do you?"

Kendra's wings unfurled as they slid out of my cloak. She shook her head, her tail curling outward as she stretched. "I am *not hiding*," she said again, more vehemently.

Stella handed me the reins of one of the horses, shaking her head as she chuckled silently. She climbed atop her mount, and I followed suit. Together, we urged the horses into a trot, weaving our way through the woods as we journeyed back home.

The Hunter

The sun beat down on me like the brutal lashings of a whip. The heat was a relentless force that seemed to melt my very skin from its bones, making me yearn for the chilled wintry air of my home. The silent stillness of an icy forest. The whisper of frosty wind.

But no. I was bound to the Winter Queen, and, unfortunately for me, my current prey lived in the Sun Court.

Sweat beaded along my brow, stinging the corners of my eyes. My fae body was built for endurance, but I'd been crouching in the green foliage for hours. Not even my fae blood could endure this damned heat.

He should arrive at any moment, I told myself. *Soon, you'll trap him and be done with this assignment.*

I tried not to let my thoughts roam to the forested landscape where my cabin was tucked away in the mountains of the Winter Court, isolated and undisturbed. The queen had promised I would be granted a lengthy holiday after this mission was fulfilled. And fae bargains were binding. She would have no choice but to let me take my leave.

Later, I thought. *You can daydream later. For now, focus on the task at hand.*

I clutched my crossbow, my hands slick with sweat. It was already loaded, the sharpened point of the iron-studded arrow ready to burrow into my target's neck. Once he appeared, I didn't want to waste time loading my weapon and potentially alerting him to my presence. My head throbbed from the strain of maintaining my glamour for this long. I was currently masked, the color of my skin a vibrant green that blended in perfectly with the leafy surroundings. But the energy required to keep myself camouflaged was wearing on me. If the bastard didn't show up soon, I would have to leave and recharge my magic.

A twig snapped nearby, and my skin prickled with awareness. Someone—or something—was approaching. It was too big to be an animal, unless it was a large predator. As bored as I was, I almost would have welcomed the distraction of wrestling one of the dreaded fae beasts.

Almost.

I held perfectly still, waiting for the visitor to reveal itself.

There he was. My mark.

Sir Ethan Bloodwright of the Sun Court, heir apparent and next in line to the throne as soon as his uncle, the king, passed away. He'd made his disdain for the Winter Court quite clear in all his political dealings. The queen had no doubts that he would declare war on our court the instant he was crowned.

I believed it, too, though I was never one to follow politics. I only followed orders. Nothing more. The bitterness of my situation swept through me, and I felt myself scowling.

But now was not the time to grumble about my circumstances. I had work to do.

Ethan drew nearer, his steps slow and careful. He glanced

over his shoulder as if nervous he would be spied upon. I smirked. Little did he know...

My blood chilled as a second figure appeared—a woman.

Oh, shit.

"I told you we had to stop meeting like this," the woman whispered. She had long, curly brown hair that fell to her waist and doe-like caramel eyes that gazed pleadingly at Ethan.

But my attention was fixed on her ears. They were curved, not pointed.

She was human.

Well, son of a bitch, I thought. Not only was Ethan cavorting with a woman in secret, but a *human* woman, no less. The one thing most courts agreed on was that humans were the lesser species. Though fae allegedly lived peacefully with humans, there was still a clear division between the two, especially in the Winter Court.

I didn't know much about it. Aside from my isolated cottage in the woods, my dealings were only with courtiers and those who worked within the palace—all fae. I'd only encountered humans in my travels.

"This is the only spot where Uncle Moorland won't find me," Ethan murmured, clutching the woman's hands in his own and pressing soft kisses to her knuckles.

"These woods frighten me," the woman whimpered. "What if a fae beast comes along?"

Ethan laughed. "Don't believe all the stories they tell you about fae creatures."

My eyebrows lifted. What a fool. The girl *should* believe in the stories, and fear them, too. I'd encountered my fair share of fae beasts, and they were just as horrifying as the stories made them seem. They had Demon Fae blood, which meant they were wild, feral, and unpredictable.

"Besides," the woman said, lifting her chin, "I thought you said you would announce our engagement to your uncle this week."

"Ah. Right." Ethan rubbed the back of his neck, looking chagrined. "Uncle is overwhelmed with court dealings this week. It's too chaotic. I would rather approach him with this when his mind isn't as preoccupied."

The woman frowned, now resembling a pouting toddler. "Ethan…"

"I swear, I will do it soon. I love you, Ryla."

Ryla's expression softened as Ethan leaned in to brush her lips with his.

I raised my crossbow. Now would be the perfect time to strike.

But the woman wrapped her arms fully around him, drawing him closer so their bodies pressed together.

I hesitated. Ryla wasn't my target. If I shot now, I would risk hitting her instead. Not only would that alert Ethan to the threat, but it would leave her blood on my hands as well.

Not that they weren't bloody enough already.

But I tried my damnedest to only kill my assignments. I was still a cold-blooded killer, but at least that much decency I could manage. Even if the woman was a lowly human, I still didn't want to kill her if I could help it.

"Ethan," Ryla moaned as his mouth trailed down her throat.

Shivering bones, if I didn't make my move soon, I would have to witness their lovemaking. Gritting my teeth, I took aim just as Ryla wrapped her legs around him. Ethan turned to grasp her ass more fully, and I had a perfect shot between his shoulder blades.

I would have to be quick. No time to ensure I hit my mark, because Ryla's scream would no doubt alert anyone nearby of the murder.

But no matter. I never missed.

This time was no exception.

The bolt struck true, straight between his shoulder blades. Ethan stiffened as blood bubbled from the wound. For a moment, Ryla didn't notice, still writhing against him and moaning with pleasure.

Then, his body slumped, taking her with it.

"Ethan, what—"

By the time she realized he was dead and her scream cut through the forest, I was already gone.

"Tell me," Queen Calista commanded.

The man's screams reverberated against the massive throne room walls. I stood, shoulders squared and spine straight, watching impassively as the Queen of the Winter Court tortured the mayor of the Quinton Province. He was a small, portly man with graying hair and a short brown beard. His rounded ears marked him as human. Sweat beaded along his brow, and blood trickled from his nose.

"Please," he rasped. "Your Majesty, *please*."

"Answer my question, and the pain stops," Calista said calmly. She sat atop her pale stone throne, which blended in with the silver carpet stretched across the white marble floors. Enormous glass panes illuminated the room from the ceiling. Light danced from the chandelier, giving the throne room the appearance of a sparkling, crystalline field of snow.

"I—I *can't*," the man whispered.

"Very well." Calista lifted a small vial and poured a drop of crimson liquid onto her finger.

The man's eyes widened as Calista pressed her finger to her mouth. "No. No, *please*—" His words cut off with another piercing scream. His back arched, his arms jutting at odd angles as Calista's magic tormented him. I shuddered as I watched, knowing firsthand how painful her blood magic could be.

The man collapsed to the ground, writhing on the floor as he tried to escape the pain that would not end.

Calista's red lips spread into a thin smile as she watched the man's eyes bulge, more blood leaking from his nose.

His shouts became unintelligible, his words mangled. But Calista clearly heard something important. She sat up straighter, and the man's cries abruptly ceased.

"What was that?" she prompted.

With a shuddering sob, the man went limp on the floor, his eyes closed as tears ran down his face. "C-Courthouse. There is... a chest hidden... in the floorboards... of the courthouse."

Calista looked at one of the soldiers stationed against the wall and nodded once. In an instant, the guard exited the throne room, no doubt to travel to Quinton and take the chest of coins the mayor had hidden in his courthouse.

"Well done, Hector," Calista said, her smile serpentine. "I assure you I will put your city's funds to good use."

"Please, Your Majesty," Hector wheezed, his body still convulsing. "My people... *need* those coins. We must... eat. The children... are starving."

I swallowed down bile, my nostrils flaring. I had traveled through enough of the Winter Court to know Hector spoke the truth. Many villages, especially the smaller ones, were suffering because of the queen's taxes.

But Hector's village consisted mostly of humans, which meant Calista cared little for them.

Calista waved a hand, her expression bored. "Enough of your blathering. I am finished with you. Berrick?"

I inwardly flinched as another soldier peeled off the wall and drew his sword. I held my breath as Berrick sliced off the man's head, the squelching sound echoing in the throne room. I didn't care much for humans, but that didn't mean I enjoyed watching them get beheaded.

When it was finished, I stared numbly at the man's corpse. His head rolled along the floor, leaving a trail of blood.

"Clean this up," Calista ordered the servants to her left.

Attendants scurried forward with buckets and cloths at the ready, as if they had been standing there waiting for a man to lose his head.

The people in this court were accustomed to blood staining the floors.

I hated this. I hated working for a queen who was so cruel and murderous. But I had no choice. Thanks to my father, I was trapped in a contract with her.

No, I firmly told myself. *You* will not *think about that horrible man.*

Ever since my father died, I vowed never to think of him again.

He wasn't worth it.

I pushed him from my mind and swallowed hard. Taking

a deep breath, I tried to prepare myself for my turn to face the queen.

When the floor was spotless once more, Calista's dark eyes fixed on me. "Come, Theron."

I obediently strode forward until I stood where Hector had been moments before. I could still smell his blood and sweat in the air.

"Report," she commanded.

I briefly went over the details of my mission, explaining how I killed Sir Ethan Bloodwright without being spotted or suspected.

"I'm impressed, Theron," Calista said, her thin eyebrows lifted and her blood-red lips curling into the cruel smile I knew so well. "You've never completed an assignment this quickly before. You must be anxious to take your leave."

Queen Calista often teased me, trying to get under my skin, but I never acquiesced. Years of hunting and killing had taught me how to brush off the pointed barbs of an opponent.

"But I must admit," she went on when I made no response, "I'm a bit disappointed. You did not bring me the man's heart, as I requested."

"He was not alone, my queen. To stay and carve out his heart would have exposed me to witnesses and jeopardized the mission."

Calista's lips grew even thinner until they practically disappeared into her face. Her sharp, angular cheekbones gave her quite a skeletal look as she surveyed me. She almost resembled a terrifying fae beast. But the pointed ears that supported her glistening silver crown marked her as a full-blooded seelie fae.

"I understand the risk," she said coldly as she rose from

her throne, her midnight blue skirts swishing behind her. Along the walls, several of her most trusted guards straightened as if sensing the lethal edge to her voice.

I sensed it, too. I went perfectly still, treating the queen as the predator she was.

"If there were witnesses, they might have marked you as a member of my court," Calista went on, drawing closer to me. I stood more than a head taller than her, but her powerful presence still made my skin quiver. "And we can't have that. However..." Her sharp eyes drilled into me. "There is another solution that I'm shocked you didn't consider."

"You mean killing the witness," I said impassively.

She smirked again. "Yes. You are, after all, a killer. And a good one at that. It's why I have you in my employ."

If she only knew the witness had been a human. Humans were lesser than dirt, especially in the queen's eyes. She would have been outraged to know I had let one live. "The witness was not my target," I said. "If you wanted me to kill Sir Ethan and any surrounding civilians, you should have specified."

The queen went rigid, her eyes flaring with rage.

Shit. Too late, I realized my mistake. I bowed my head in subservience, sinking to my knees before her.

But the damage had been done. Even the soldiers lining the walls shifted their weight in discomfort.

"Give me your hand, Theron," the queen whispered, her voice soft and dangerous.

I extended my wrist obediently, my body stiff with apprehension. I clenched my teeth hard as one of her long fingernails struck the back of my hand, drawing blood. Pain burst within my skin as my blood boiled from the contact. My magic swelled, rising to my defense, but I pushed it down.

This was a fight I would not win.

Calista lifted her hand, surveying the drop of my blood coating her nail. "Such a small drop yields so much power," she mused, bringing her finger to her mouth and sucking the droplet. She smacked her lips and shot me a feral grin.

Agony exploded within me, coursing mercilessly through my veins. I cried out, my limbs going stiff, my back bowing under the intensity of her power. Darkness filled my vision, and I groaned, my arms shaking. Her magic sliced into my bones, my organs, my very soul...

"I own you, Theron," the queen hissed. "Your blood belongs to me. Never forget that."

With a wave of her hand, she released her hold on me, and I crumpled to the marble floor, panting and covered in sweat. I struggled to catch my breath as she resumed her perch on her throne.

"I apologize, my queen," I rasped, slowly rising to my feet, my chest heaving. "I am at your complete disposal."

"That's right," she said smugly. "For your insolence, I require one last assignment from you."

My nostrils flared. She wouldn't—she *couldn't*—

"Ah, I see the look of defiance on that handsome face," she crooned, the delight in her eyes revealing just how much she enjoyed my torment. "You think I mean to break my bargain with you. But I believe the official wording of our deal was, *'If you bring me Sir Ethan's heart, then you will be free to take your leave for the season.'* So, our bargain is not fulfilled, as you refused to bring me his heart."

I stilled, digging through my memories to recall the exact terms of our bargain.

Shivering bones, she was right. The agreement was for me to bring her his heart. How could I have been so foolish?

If I had made a verbal vow to do so, I would be dead right now. The fae magic would have claimed my life as soon as I'd left Sir Ethan in the woods. Luckily, only Calista had spoken the words.

Which now meant she was no longer bound to let me take my leave.

Calista laughed, her smile widening to reveal her perfectly white teeth. I was half surprised she didn't have fangs glistening with my blood.

"Who is the target?" I asked tightly.

"Princess Eira. My stepdaughter."

My eyes widened. "The Snow Princess?" I'd never met the princess, as she had been banished years ago. But there were whispers of how she had been cast out for wreaking havoc among the court after King Judas died. The people still spoke of the Snow Princess and how she lived in the frost itself, always disappearing before anyone could find her.

Calista's smile vanished, her eyes full of fury. "Yes. The *exiled* princess. She continues to cause disturbances in the lower towns, rounding up human rebels for her cause. Riots, brawls, thievery… Her latest exploits left the village of Raya burned to the ground. But she's crafty and has managed to evade even my most skilled soldiers." She shot a glare toward the guards lining the wall, as if they were directly to blame for this.

"This has gone on long enough," she continued. "You must find and eliminate her before her crimes escalate and she starts a civil war among my people."

"Can you not command her with her blood?" I asked. As the queen's stepdaughter, surely the Snow Princess's blood would be among her stores, just like mine. That was how her magic worked—all she needed was a single drop to control someone.

Calista's nostrils flared. "She is too far for my magic to reach her."

My eyebrows lifted. *Clever princess.*

Calista leaned forward, bracing her arms on the gilded edges of her throne. "Do not fail me, Theron. I must have her heart. Agree to this bargain, and you will be permanently released from my service."

My mouth fell open in blatant surprise, my calm facade shattering. We had originally agreed on just the storm season. Holed up in the mountains, I would have been undisturbed in my cabin, as it was dangerous to travel during a snowstorm, and the queen would have been limited in her dealings as well.

But permanently? Could she truly continue without my services?

"You mean, I will be released from my contract?" I clarified. I needed her to say the exact words.

"Yes. You will no longer be in my employ. I trust the generous funds you have received from me over the years will be enough for you to live comfortably for quite a while." The knowing gleam in her eyes indicated she knew just how enticing this reward was for me. She knew how much I hated being her weapon.

And she was right. I did have enough funds saved to live comfortably for the rest of my life.

"I will not be labeled a traitor to the crown?" I asked, my eyes narrowing. It seemed like something she would do, to free me from my debts only to turn around and hunt me to the ends of the earth.

Calista laughed. "You *are* clever, my fearsome hunter. I

swear on my life and my crown that when you are released from my service, you will have no obligations to me or this court, and you will be labeled a free and respected citizen, provided you continue to abide by my laws."

"And my blood?"

The smile vanished from her face. "What about your blood?"

I knew she had a vial of it stored away for emergencies, in case I decided to betray her. This time, it was my turn to smirk at her. Did she really think I would agree to a bargain that only teased me with the illusion of freedom? No, if I was to be truly free of her, she could no longer hold on to my blood. "I'll be wanting that back."

Her nostrils flared. "Once blood goes into my vault, it does not come out."

"I will never be truly free as long as you have it," I countered. The pain of her magic would be more potent if the blood was fresh, but even a supply of my old blood would be powerful enough to cause severe damage.

I didn't know if my cabin in the mountains was far enough away to escape her reach. And I didn't want to test those limits.

Calista's eyes fluttered shut for a moment. "Very well. Upon your release, I will also relinquish all of your blood to you."

Shivering bones, she'd actually agreed to it. I didn't think she would. Her hold on me was iron-clad as long as she had that vial. This bargain told me just how much she needed this assignment done—and done quickly.

She was *desperate*. Desperate enough to let go of her most skilled assassin. My brain worked furiously to come up with some kind of loophole in her terms, but I couldn't find one. Still, I said nothing. This felt too easy.

Her eyebrows rose at my hesitation. Before she could revoke the terms of our bargain, I blurted, "I accept. I will bring you Princess Eira's heart in exchange for freedom from my duties to you and the crown, as well as any amount of my blood that you still possess."

"Very good." Calista waved an idle hand. "Now, be on your way. I'm certain you'll want to get started right away. After all, Princess Eira will be a difficult target to locate." Her mouth widened in a satisfied smile. "Probably your most challenging assignment yet."

I sketched a quick bow before departing the throne room. Each step sent a quiver of pain up my legs—an echo of the torture the queen had inflicted on me.

But it didn't matter. That would be the last time she would ever hurt me.

Because, challenging or not, I would kill the Snow Princess.

The Princess

I WRUNG MY HANDS TOGETHER, PACING THE LENGTH OF THE small sitting room in my cottage while I waited for the other human rebels to arrive.

"Stop fretting," Stella said from the armchair. She had one leg crossed over the other, her twitching foot the only sign of her unease.

She was nervous, too.

For the tenth time, my gaze strayed to the open window, where the wintry forest surrounded us.

When I'd been exiled, I'd sought refuge here in Knockspur, the last of the human lands. Calista didn't bother with villages like this one, which made it the perfect hiding spot for me to meet with my rebel friends. For years, we'd been gathering followers with the intent to take down Calista.

"What if it's not enough?" I asked Stella. My gaze darted to the piles of coins on the table. I had counted them twice. Five hundred sixty-two gold pieces.

It seemed like a lot to me. But I didn't know how expensive it would be to hire mercenaries and soldiers. Aside from me, the rebels were all human. It would be impossible for us to fight Calista's forces on our own.

Gareth, the human noble from the Shennith Province, would know the answer to that. Shennith housed the queen's armies, and Gareth, who was much older than the rest of us, had plenty of experience dealing with soldiers.

"If it's not enough, we will figure out a new plan," Stella said firmly. "You aren't alone in this, Eira. Even if it takes time to form a new strategy, we can do it."

I said nothing, crossing my arms and biting on the inside of my cheek.

That was just the thing. I *didn't* have time. In fact, I was running out of it. Each new day brought me closer and closer to my death.

"They're here," Stella said, rising to her feet and jolting me from my morose thoughts. I followed her to the window and scanned the frosty surroundings. Various fae creatures flitted about—including Frisk and Kendra. Rogun, a massive white dragon who resembled a snow beast more than anything, was curled up in the snow, snoozing contentedly.

Next to the large Crystal Icebolt, three horses appeared, each bearing a rider I recognized. Tansy was first, the human noble from the Vorreya Province. Her sandy hair was a frazzled mane around her face, but her chestnut eyes were bright as she dismounted.

Behind her was Denton from the Jarta Province. My heart did a backflip at the sight of his burly frame as he slid off his mount.

No, I chided myself. *That's over now. You're not allowed to look at him like that anymore.*

The third horse belonged to Gareth, and my heart seized for an entirely new reason. As soon as Gareth looked at the pile of coins, he would give me my answer.

Was my rebellion doomed? Would I die before I could dethrone Calista?

Our duty as royals is to defend this court against foes, my father had said. *To rid our kingdom of enemies who would harm our people.*

I hadn't known when he'd told me this that those enemies might come from *within* our very court.

But I would do my damnedest to eliminate Calista and uphold my father's legacy. He protected our people as best he could. With him gone, it was up to me now.

Stella threw open the door, and Tansy embraced her, shaking flecks of snow from her hair. Stella laughed, clutching her friend tightly. "Good to see you, Tan."

Denton came next, his dark eyes immediately finding mine. I went rigid, pressing my lips tightly together and offering the barest shake of my head.

No more.

Stella patted Denton's arm, and he gave her a forced smile before striding into the cottage. The sitting room felt so much smaller with his intimidating presence. I suddenly felt like I couldn't breathe, so I shifted my focus to Gareth instead. He scratched at his white beard, his black eyes lighting up when he saw me.

"Hi, Gareth," I said with a genuine smile, stepping forward to embrace him.

He squeezed me tightly. "Always a pleasure, darlin'. This cottage is a welcome respite from the shit going on out there." He jerked his thumb toward the door. "Huck and Lark are close behind. Huck had to circle back to lose the tails followin' him."

I blanched. "He's being followed?"

Gareth waved a hand. "It's nothin'. His uncle thinks he's cavorting with some lover." He wiggled his eyebrows.

I snorted. "If needed, I can write a scandalous letter for his uncle to uncover. Better for him to believe Huck is in love than that he's taking part in a rebellion."

Gareth's smile widened. "Please do, Snow. I'd love to read a saucy letter that will make the lad blush."

"Damn, Snow," came Tansy's voice from the sitting room. The clink of coins told me she was sifting through the stack. "You've nearly doubled our amount. I pity the lord you robbed."

"Don't," I said, plopping into an armchair and rubbing my arms. "He was an ass."

"Did he hurt you?" Denton asked sharply.

I cut him a glare. "No. I'm fine." I wanted to add, *And even if he did, that's not your concern anymore.* But I didn't want to draw too much attention. Already, Tansy was frowning and glancing between us.

Damn it, Denton, I thought, shaking my head and looking at Gareth. "Have you heard from Penelope?"

"No, but she's always rather quiet, isn't she?" Gareth eased himself onto the sofa, leaning forward and bracing his hands on his knees as he inspected the pile of coins. His eyes narrowed in concentration.

Was that disappointment on his face? Did we not have enough gold?

I would rob more nobles. Surely, we had to be close. Maybe a few more missions would get us what we needed.

"She's never missed a meeting," Stella said. "I'm sure she'll be here."

I nodded, thinking of the red-haired noble from the Cordenna Province. She was painfully shy, but when she spoke up, her ideas were often quite clever. It was why she was here in her uncle's stead, even though he had more authority in the province of Cordenna. That, and he was an old bat who would never in a million years ally himself with the vigilante princess of the Winter Court.

I moved to the seat next to Gareth, trying not to wring my hands together over and over. "What do you think?"

Gareth rubbed his chin again. "Hard to say."

"Hard to say because it's not enough, or because you aren't sure?"

His keen eyes appraised me. "Best to wait 'til the others get here."

My heart dropped like a stone. That couldn't be good news. If it was, why wouldn't he just say it?

There was no reason to wait unless we needed to regroup and come up with a new plan.

I sank back against the sofa cushion, my spirits deflating. Gareth stood and moved toward the door as pounding hoofbeats indicated the arrival of more rebels.

A warm hand came down on my shoulder. I looked up to find Stella's worried gaze peering into mine.

"I know," I said before she could reassure me.

She squeezed, and I leaned into her touch. Stella was always the one who understood me the most. She was like the sister I never had.

My attention returned to the door. Gareth had his arm around Penelope's narrow shoulders as the two strode inside. Her usually pale face had a soft blush creeping in. "Any trouble on the way, darlin'?"

Penelope shook her head, then glanced over her shoulder. "There's some commotion in the center of town." Her voice was thin and wispy, as if it might vanish in the wind.

I frowned. I hadn't noticed anything when I'd been in town earlier. "Soldiers?" My heart cinched with dread.

She shook her head again. "Not like that. Just more people at the pub than usual. More whispers. I couldn't make out what they were whispering about, though. Didn't want to draw too much attention to myself."

I nodded, making a note to do some investigating after our meeting. Whenever there was commotion, my first thought was that Calista had finally found me.

If I had to leave this wooded haven, it would break my heart. But I had been in Knockspur for years now. It was only a matter of time before my stepmother found me.

I swallowed hard, trying to push away my unease and focus on the task at hand. I patted the cushion next to me. "Come and sit, Penny."

She smiled at the nickname and sank next to me, unwrapping her scarf to let loose her wild red hair. Her green eyes widened at the sight of the gold on the table in front of us. "Shivering bones, that's a lot of gold."

Before I could answer, harsh voices echoed from the forest. Penelope tensed beside me, but I stood, recognizing the curt tone of Huck as he argued with Lark.

Those two never got along. But since they came from neighboring provinces, they often traveled together. I smirked. Perhaps we could spread rumors that *Lark* was Huck's secret lover.

Huck would be mortified. I almost laughed at the thought.

"Do you have to drink while we ride?" Huck griped as the two made their way into the cottage. "You absolutely reek. I'm not riding alongside that stench on the way home."

"How else do you think I can get through a three-hour

ride with your constant whining?" Lark said. His voice was smoother and slightly slurred, a sure sign that he was, in fact, drunk. He represented the tiny province of Quinton, and he didn't contribute much to our meetings. He was here because he was the only human from the area willing to join me. Even if he was sloshed more than half the time, he was loyal to a fault. That, and he was one of the best secret-keepers I'd ever met, even when he was drunk.

"You can continue your lovers' quarrel later." I tugged on Lark's arm to pull him into the sitting room. "We have work to do."

"*Lovers' quarrel?*" Huck sputtered, a blush creeping along his brown skin. "I don't—I wouldn't—"

Tansy burst out laughing, and Gareth covered his mouth to smother his chuckles. Meanwhile, Huck's face only grew redder.

"I wouldn't say no," Lark said with a shrug, his bloodshot eyes flicking over Huck's short, scrawny body with renewed interest.

A loud snort burst from me, and several others joined in with their laughter. Even Denton cracked a smile.

Once we were all inside, I glanced out the window to check that the animals were safe. Frisk was hovering near the porch—to eavesdrop, no doubt. He shot me a look of pure innocence through the window.

Ordinarily I let him come and go in the cottage, along with some of the smaller animals, like Kendra. But too many creatures would be a distraction.

And today, we needed to focus.

Just in case, I slid open the window. It kept me at ease, knowing I could hear them close by just in case trouble came calling, as it often did for me.

With a deep breath, I turned and faced my seven friends. Seven human nobles, one from each province. Even though they were technically nobility, their titles meant nothing. They were merely a charade, to keep up the appearance of peace. Decades ago, fae and humans were considered equals. But then the fae seized the lands from the humans, and we were left with nothing but anger, resentment, and fake titles. Even my title as princess meant nothing with my father dead and Calista hunting me.

But if my plan succeeded, we would overthrow Calista and give the land back to the humans.

My friends were seated around the table, eyeing the pile of gold. Gareth continued stroking his beard, but I recognized the bleak look in his eyes.

He heaved a sigh. "I'm sorry, darlin'. But it's not enough."

I'd been expecting this. But even so, I hadn't anticipated the crushing weight of disappointment. I felt myself deflating, and I couldn't even manage a halfheartedly chipper response.

My father's legacy. The rebellion. Our entire plan. It was as if it was all disintegrating before my eyes.

"We've been gathering coin for months," Stella objected, sitting forward and bracing her arms on her legs "How can it not be enough?"

"Mercenaries are expensive," said Gareth, his mouth puckered in a frown. "We knew going into this that it would be a long shot."

"Are we even close?" I asked, my voice tinged with desperation. If we were only off by a few coins, all I had to do was rob a few more carriages, and—

"No," said Huck in his clipped voice as he crossed his thin arms over his chest. "We aren't close. We would need to double this amount before we could hire any, and even then, it might not be enough to overthrow the queen."

I shot him an annoyed look. Huck was always the most pessimistic of us all, although he would argue he was *realistic*. "We can't just give up!" I protested. "We've come so far already."

"Eira," said Denton softly. "We need a new plan."

I forced myself to meet his gaze. It was still difficult to look him in the eye since we'd decided to end our complicated and undefinable romance.

For weeks, we'd met for secret trysts in the woods, the thrill of our undiscovered dalliances only fueling the fire between us. But we had both agreed it couldn't last, and after Huck had almost discovered us taking each other against an oak tree, we decided it was time to end it.

It was uncomfortable now. Mostly because I could tell he wanted more.

And I didn't.

But, of course, I had to pretend things were perfectly normal, because no one knew what transpired between us. I was the princess, and he was a noble of the Dahl Province. Our goal was to usurp my stepmother and establish myself as the rightful queen of the Winter Court. The last thing we needed was for word to spread of the Snow Princess and her secret human lover.

So I kept my gaze steady as I looked at him, my eyes roving over his tan skin, his milky brown eyes, and the light stubble on his chin that often tickled me when we kissed. "What do you suggest?" I asked him.

"Each of the provinces has a small band of followers," said Denton. "And we're human. We can lie, and we can avoid faerie bargains. Surely, that should amount to something.

Can't we try to sneak into the palace and start a riot from the inside?"

I spread my hands and scoffed. "How? The queen has tripled the guard since we started robbing her coffers. And *you* may be immune to faerie bargains, but I'm not." I self-consciously tucked my dark hair behind my rounded ears. Sometimes, I blended in with my human friends. Other times, I was reminded of how different we were. I was half fae, which meant that, biologically, I was bound by fae laws. Even if I looked like a human.

"But you have your magic," Stella pointed out, her eyebrows raised. Her pale eyes appraised me with part amusement, part awe.

"Yes, and as soon as *one* soldier discovers me, everyone will know what I can do," I said. "I can't risk it. It's the only thing I have over the queen."

"And what good is having an advantage over the queen if you never use it?" Denton said.

My nostrils flared in frustration. I opened my mouth to argue, but Tansy interjected. "Snow, aren't you friends with the King and Queen of the Shadow Court? Can't they help us?"

"Shadow Fae are scary," Lark said seriously.

"Definitely scary enough to chase the false queen away," Stella agreed.

But I shook my head. "Sybelle can't help. Their court is still at odds with the Earthen Court. If they send soldiers to us, it will leave them exposed, and the Earthen Court might attack."

No one spoke for a long moment. I glanced over the dejected expressions of my friends, feeling my hope dwindle.

Then, a soft voice to my right said, "I have an idea."

My gaze shifted to Penelope. Her cheeks immediately flushed when every eye turned to her.

"We utilize our connections," Penelope said simply.

Silence met her words. I cleared my throat. "What connections?"

"The creatures." Penelope gestured to the window, through which I could barely make out a trio of black-capped chickadees circling each other. Behind them, Mauro the great white stag pawed at the snow at his feet. Rogun still snoozed softly, with Kendra perched on his back. I knew Frisk was out there, too, though he was hidden by his snowy surroundings.

"I'm fairly certain sending a stampede of forest animals would draw a bit of attention," said Huck, his voice dripping with sarcasm.

"Shut it, Huck," Gareth said. "Let her speak. Go on, darlin'."

Penelope's face flushed a deeper scarlet, but she plowed on. "Our goal is to give the lands back to the humans. But humans aren't the only ones the queen has outcast. She also hates the unseelie." Once more, she pointed toward the window.

I flinched, then despised myself for it. Unseelie fae were known for being feral, unhinged, and often dangerous. But some of my best friends—these sentient creatures who lived in the forest with me—were technically unseelie. And I trusted them with my life.

Penelope had a point; Calista was determined to create the perfect empire of seelie fae. Which meant disposing of the humans and unseelie, who would taint the bloodlines.

The cruelest irony of all was that Calista was a Demon

Fae. Which meant *she* was tainting the bloodline with her black magic.

Unseelie fae were as gentle as lambs compared to the Demon Fae.

"We already have connections to the unseelie, thanks to Frisk and the others," Penelope continued. "I suggest we utilize those connections. Call in our allies, and reach out to others. Band together with those who have been shunned by Calista."

Tansy was nodding eagerly, and Stella had a spark in her eyes. I felt my own heart lifting at the thought of rallying more forces.

Allies can come to us in the most unlikely of places, my father had said.

But the hope within me faded at the same moment Gareth shook his head.

"In theory, it's a good idea. But forming an army takes time. Not to mention how dangerous some of the unseelie forces can be. They don't trust us. Many of them would kill us on sight."

"It would also be difficult to convince them to fight for us," I added. "If we don't have enough gold for seelie soldiers, we certainly don't have enough for the unseelie."

"Unseelie fae wouldn't want to get too close to the Winter Palace anyway," said Huck. "They are repelled by the queen's blood magic."

"For good reason," muttered Lark, rubbing his bloodshot eyes and taking another drink from his flask.

"The smaller creatures aren't as affected," Penelope said. "And they have the advantage of appearing like ordinary animals. As long as they don't talk, no one will suspect them.

Then they could slip into the palace undetected. Like Frisk. He's good at that."

"No way am I going in there."

We all jumped and turned to find Frisk coiled on the carpet by the front door. How he'd gotten inside, I had no idea, but the sight of him curled up on the floor like that brought a smile to my face.

He rose up on his legs and stretched with a long, lazy yawn. "Lark is right, there's a good reason we don't go near the castle. Her magic *reeks*. Even those of us who are small hate that smell."

"Frisk, what are you doing here?" I asked with a sigh. "As soon as the others find out you snuck in, they'll want to join, too. It'll be chaos."

"Oh, I just thought you would want to hear my brilliant plan. But, if you prefer, I can leave." He lifted his nose in the air.

I rolled my eyes. "What's your plan, then?"

His dark eyes surveyed me for a long moment before he said, "I propose we make a move on the queen's assassin."

A hushed whisper fell among those of us seated at the table.

Denton spoke first. "The hunter? That's the worst plan I've ever heard. He's unbeatable. How are we supposed to make a move on him?"

Frisk flashed his teeth, his eyes glinting. "You know what the villagers are buzzing about? They caught sight of the fearsome hunter not too far from here."

I held my breath. The assassin was *here*? In Knockspur? The fae never traveled this far into the human lands unless they had to.

Which could only mean one thing: the hunter was on assignment for the queen.

I exchanged a glance with Stella, who smirked knowingly at Tansy, who raised her eyebrows at Huck. Huck scoffed and crossed his arms again, clearly unconvinced, but Denton was nodding eagerly. Lark had fallen asleep, and Gareth gazed out the window as if no longer interested in our conversation.

No one was closer to the queen than her assassin. He knew her secrets, and he was powerful enough to give us an edge against her.

He could be our secret weapon.

Penelope shifted nervously in her seat. "How do we approach this without getting ourselves killed?"

"Well, there's eight of us," Stella said. "And only one of him."

"He's taken on fifteen opponents at a time and still won," I said as if reciting from a textbook. I'd never actually met the feared assassin—Calista always ensured I was far removed from her court dealings—but I knew enough about him to know he shouldn't be underestimated.

Yet Penelope's suggestion sparked a plan in my mind. Fae creatures disguising themselves as ordinary animals... I tapped my chin, a slow smile spreading across my face. "But you're right. As humans—or half human, in my case—we do have an advantage." I leaned forward, bracing my palms on the table. "All right, friends. I have an idea. And this one will work."

The Hunter

It didn't take me long to discover the princess was holed up in the small human village of Knockspur. All I had to do was travel to the various outlying provinces, those closest to the latest disturbances from the Snow Princess and her band of rebels, and make my presence known. It was strange to not use stealth as I traveled. I was so accustomed to maintaining a strong glamour, traveling only at night and avoiding the main roads.

It unsettled me, to be so out in the open like this.

But it was the only way to flush her out. I had spies and informants in all the provinces, and I paid them handsomely for their information. I lingered a few days in each area, then checked with my sources for any whispers among the humans.

It wasn't until I heard rumors of a robbed carriage and a flurry of speculation of Snow's human allies that I knew I'd found her.

Still, I was at a disadvantage. I didn't know what the princess looked like. But I knew she was half fae; if there was one thing I was good at, it was detecting fae creatures and their magic.

I would have to rely on that to complete my assignment.

Day after day, I ventured casually around the area, ignoring the hostile sneers and glares at my pointed fae ears. Let them talk. It was exactly what I wanted.

And yet, staying in an almost entirely human land was a new experience for me. Ordinarily, Calista would assign me to murder her foes and competition, perhaps a wealthy nobleman who was stirring up trouble in the court, or a high-ranking official from another kingdom.

She never sullied herself with the likes of humans. And for good reason. They were a feral, savage species who lived in the wild. They didn't belong with our kind. That much was evident in this small, filthy town. The humans didn't even clean up after themselves.

I resisted the urge to wrinkle my nose as I strode into the dank pub I had been frequenting over the past three days. As usual, I placed my coin on the bar and asked for a mug of ale. The owner obliged, his lip curling as he did so. But as much as he despised me, he still took my coin every day. He likely barely had enough funds to keep his business running.

Another reason to despise the humans. They had no concept of integrity or moral fiber. This man should have thrown me out on the spot because I was his enemy.

But no. He accepted my money out of greed, even though my presence made the other patrons uncomfortable. I didn't care if throwing me out on my ass would inconvenience my plans—at least I would respect him for it.

I sipped on the bland ale, brow furrowed as I wondered why Calista had waited this long to give me this assignment. If the princess had been wreaking havoc for five years, why hadn't the queen ordered me to kill her sooner?

"I haven't seen you here before, stranger," said a smooth, sultry voice.

I turned and found a woman leaning against the bar, her pale blue eyes appraising me with interest. Long, wavy black hair framed her heart-shaped face. She was quite attractive. For a human.

"Excellent observation." Dismissing her, I turned back to my mug of ale.

"What brings you to the human lands?" Undeterred by my flippant tone, she sidled closer to me, bringing a pleasant whiff of snow and pine. The scent reminded me of my cottage tucked away in the mountains.

"Business," I replied shortly, refusing to glance at her. My plan involved making my presence known, but I didn't have to be polite about it.

The woman crossed her arms and snorted. The sound was so unladylike that I swiveled to face her in surprise. She was watching me with a smirk curving along her full, red lips. "You're a charmer, aren't you? I'm sure all the ladies *swoon* over your gruff demeanor."

I blinked. Was she... teasing me?

"Yes, and that vacant expression? Enough to make me go weak in the knees." She pretended to fan herself. "Be still my beating heart."

My mouth opened and closed. No one had ever spoken to me like this. "Are you mocking me?"

The woman laughed, the sound vibrant and full. "Blood and ice, what's the matter with you? Have you never been around other people before?"

My jaw clenched. "My work generally keeps me isolated. So, no."

She leaned closer, her dark hair falling forward like a curtain. A faint, rosy musk mingled with the snow and pine scent. "Let me give you a clue. When someone teases you, the proper reaction is to either laugh or tease them back." She cocked her head. "So, which will it be, stranger?"

I scowled at her. "Teasing is for children. I would never bother with such improper behavior."

The woman immediately sobered, but her eyes still glinted with mischief. "Oh, of course, of course. Far too serious for that, aren't you?" She took a sip from her mug, her eyes flicking to the space between my legs. "It helps if your trousers are properly fastened, though."

I stiffened, then glanced down, only to find my trousers were just as they should be, concealing everything. When my scowl deepened, the woman only laughed again.

"Made you look." She took another sip of ale, her eyes sparkling.

I rolled my eyes. "What do you want, woman? If your goal is to bother me, you have indeed succeeded."

"I want to know what you're doing in my town," she said. "You haven't answered."

"Yes, I have. I'm here on business."

"And what business is that?" She leaned closer, and I shifted on my stool to put more space between us. Her eyes once again dropped to my trousers, and I felt my face go hot. I'd never had a woman act so forward with me before. It was unnerving.

She suddenly froze, her face going pale. "I—what is that?"

I followed her gaze and realized she'd discovered I was armed. Her frightened stare was fixed on the array of daggers along my belt.

"Weapons," I said shortly.

She swallowed hard, her throat bobbing. "Why do you need so many?"

"I'm a hunter." Not a lie. I just conveniently left out the bit about how I hunted people.

She shook her head as she slowly backed away from me, visibly trembling with terror. "No... No, please."

Alarmed, I stared at her. "Please what?"

"Please don't hurt me. Blood and ice, I swear, we don't want any trouble here." Her voice quivered.

In spite of how much she annoyed me, I couldn't stand her sniveling like this. Shivering bones, even her eyes were glistening with tears. Was she really *that* afraid of a few knives?

"Look, I'm not going to hurt you," I said.

"I don't believe you." She continued to back away from me. "Why would you be so heavily armed if you don't mean to hurt someone?"

"It's not you I'm after. I swear it. I won't do you any harm."

She narrowed her eyes at me. "You won't?"

"I won't," I repeated. My quarrel wasn't with the humans anyway—the Snow Princess was half fae, and this woman had rounded ears. "I promise."

The woman suddenly flashed a wide grin, her tears drying almost instantly. "Excellent. That's a binding bargain right there."

I went rigid in my seat. "What are you talking about?"

"You can't hurt me." She winked at me.

A chill skittered along my bones. Something wasn't right. "But you're human."

The woman snorted. "Many people make that mistake. I

am part human. But I am still bound by fae laws. Just like you." Her eyes took on that mischievous gleam again.

My chest seemed to be caving inward as the pieces slowly clicked into place. Fae bargains... Part human...

I was sitting next to the Snow Princess. And she had just tricked me into swearing not to harm her.

The Hunter

I WAS A BLOODY FOOL.

All I could do was stare, horrified, at the princess's smug expression as my brain struggled to make sense of it all.

The Snow Princess looked human. Why hadn't the queen warned me?

Shivering bones…

I remembered the keen look in Calista's eyes when she gave me my assignment. She omitted key information on purpose. She knew she couldn't afford to lose me.

This had all been a trap to ensure I would fail. She had no intention of letting me go.

"My, my, I've really broken you, haven't I?" The princess chuckled and waved a hand in front of my face. "Hello? Sir Hunter?"

I blinked and fixed a lethal stare on her, my nostrils flaring and my hands quivering with rage. Instinctively, I reached for one of my daggers, but a searing pain in my head had me hunching over the bar, groaning in agony.

Princess Eira barked out a laugh. "Blood and ice, that didn't take you long, did it? I must really get under your skin for you to want to murder me that quickly."

I dropped my hand, and the feeling dulled to an aching throb in my temples. Dazed, I blinked the fog from my eyes, once again cursing myself for my stupidity. It had been so long since I'd tried to break a bargain that I'd forgotten how excruciating the fae bond could be.

The last time I'd attempted such a thing was when Calista had given me my first assignment. When I'd seen the man I'd been tasked with killing—a fae lord of the Winter Court Calista no longer wanted on her council—he had been a charming fellow with a wife and four children. I had hesitated, not wanting to take his life. But when I'd tried turning away and leaving, the fae bond had taken hold of me. I had learned the hard way that I either needed to fulfill my bargain with the queen and kill him... or the magic of our agreement would kill me.

Movement snagged my attention. The princess sauntered toward the back door with a skip in her step. I nearly fell off the barstool in my haste to follow her.

She slid out the door, and I bounded after her, only to find a blade at my neck.

"One move, hunter, and I'll slit your throat."

I stilled, arms raised, as I scrutinized my attacker. He was a burly fellow, almost as tall as me, and twice as thick. A mop of light brown hair fell over his eyes, which bore into me with hateful rage.

"You really think your pitiful blade can stop me?" I asked.

The man grinned and pressed the cool metal tip to the flesh of my neck. I hissed as a trail of fire burned against my flesh.

Shit. The knife was made with iron. It *could*, in fact, kill me. I might be able to best him in a fight, but if that dagger cut me too deeply, it could be the death of me.

I glanced around, searching for a way out. But six other figures stood behind the man, all of them wielding weapons ranging from daggers to clubs to pitchforks. And lingering behind them all, that infuriatingly smug expression still on her face, was the Snow Princess. Her arms were crossed, her eyebrows raised in expectation.

"What do you want?" I growled.

"I want safe passage to the palace," said the princess.

I choked on a laugh. "No. Go ahead and slit my throat now because the queen will have my head if I sneak you in."

"Nothing would please me more," growled the man in front of me.

"Denton," the princess warned, her cheery demeanor faltering.

Denton sighed and fixed his murderous gaze on me once again. My eyes flicked over the crowd surrounding me. Some male, some female, but all of them were human.

So, the Snow Princess had allied herself with the humans. It wasn't surprising, since she was just as despised by the fae folk as they were.

"If you sneak me into the palace, my people will overthrow the queen," said the princess. "She won't have your head if she no longer holds the crown."

I snorted. "You think you and your small band of humans have any chance against her blood magic?"

"How about this?" The princess drifted closer, her pale eyes alight with energy. "We strike a bargain. You agree to bring me with you to the palace. And I'll agree to not only keep you safe from my stepmother's wrath, but also to release you from our previous bargain. Remember, in the tavern? When you foolishly said you wouldn't harm me?" Her mouth stretched into a wide grin.

I stared at her. "That means that, as soon as we set foot in the palace, I will be free to end your life."

The smile never wavered from her face. "That's right."

"Eira," Denton said slowly. "What are you doing?"

Eira ignored him. "Do we have a deal?"

"How, exactly, will you prevent the queen from killing me?"

"That's not your concern. But you know how fae magic works. If I swear it, it must come to pass. Otherwise, my life is forfeit."

Shivering bones, she was right. If she swore a faerie bargain that I would live, and Queen Calista still managed to execute me, then Princess Eira would die as well.

Was she insane? If the queen caught wind of this bargain, all she needed to do was end my life, and Eira would perish. She would get everything she wanted.

"You must be quite confident that you can overpower her," I said slowly, trying to buy myself more time before I responded. It would be idiotic to agree to such a bargain, but I had an iron blade at my throat. It wasn't as if I had much say in the matter.

"There's a lot you don't know about me, stranger," she said. "I have my methods, and I *am* confident I can best the queen."

"*Eira*," Denton hissed more urgently.

"Agree to my terms, or we'll end your life right here, right now," Eira went on, her voice resonating with authority. She lifted her chin, all humor vanishing from her face as her expression took on a deadly gleam. "It would be no great loss. Here in Knockspur, a member of the queen's fae court is bound to get himself into a bit of trouble. No one would bat an eye if they saw us cut you to pieces."

Once again, she was right. In fact, some of the humans in the area might join in and help them murder me.

Eira was now close enough to touch me, which I knew was exactly her intention. If she positioned herself in front of me and I tried to escape, I would be jeopardizing the bargain I made with her. If it came to a fight, I couldn't guarantee she wouldn't get hurt. All it would take was one flash of pain from the fae bond, and Denton would have the opportunity to cut open my throat.

"Tick tock, Sir Hunter." Eira cocked her head, her long hair draping over one shoulder. "What's your answer?"

I said nothing and offered my most fearsome glare. Somehow, this only seemed to amuse her, as her smile returned. "Let's give him a little incentive, shall we, Denton?"

The cold blade met my flesh once more, and a sizzling heat erupted along my skin. I gritted my teeth as the smell of scorched flesh met my nostrils. "All right. *All right*! I accept the terms of your bargain."

Denton immediately removed the knife. I massaged my neck, which still burned from the contact with the iron. "Swear it," I growled, still glaring at the princess.

She rolled her eyes. "Fine. I, Princess Eira of the Winter Court, swear to you..." She frowned. "What's your name?"

"Theron."

She wrinkled her nose. "What a droll name. All right, then, *Theron*, assassin and hunter and all-around brutal killer of the Winter Court, I swear to you that if you safely smuggle me into the palace, that I will release you from our previous bargain *and* ensure your survival should the queen seek your life." She spread her arms, eyebrows raised. "Good enough?"

I wracked my brain, sifting through her words before I muttered, "Use her name."

"Pardon?"

"Calista. Use her name."

The princess stilled, her expression frozen for one brief moment. And I knew I'd caught her. She'd only said *the queen*. If she managed to seize the throne before Calista hunted me down, then she could just let her stepmother end my life without a second thought.

Eira recovered quickly and hitched a smile back on her face. "Right. I swear to ensure your survival should *Calista* seek your life. Satisfied?"

Once more, I hesitated as I tried to find a loophole in her terms. When I was satisfied, I nodded once.

"Good. Now you swear it."

Damn. I was hoping that, since she was half human, she wouldn't require me to swear in my own words. If one party in a fae bargain didn't make a verbal vow, there were often loopholes to exploit.

With a sigh, I said, "I, Theron of the Winter Court, swear to smuggle Princess Eira safely into the Winter Palace, on the condition that she releases me from our previous bargain and guarantees my survival, should Queen Calista seek my life."

Eira offered a sickly-sweet smile. "Perfect. Our bargain is struck."

"Our bargain is struck," I echoed glumly. Power thrummed in my veins from the force of our bond.

"You're playing with fire, Eira," Denton said in a low, ominous voice. "We don't even know what his fae magic can do."

"I'm assuming it helps him kill people more efficiently," Eira quipped. "Otherwise my stepmother wouldn't have hired him."

I remained silent. I didn't want to give away anything. But if they were only speculating about my magic, I was at an advantage.

The only problem was, I had no special magic. Only basic fae glamour, which any ordinary fae could manage. For years, I'd practiced and searched within myself, but no power had manifested itself.

If Eira and her followers found out, then I'd be even worse off—if that was even possible.

"I'm coming with you," Denton said, standing a bit straighter so he appeared almost as tall as I was. There was a protective look in his eyes that made me wonder if he was more than just a friend to the princess.

"Like hell you are," Eira shot back. "You all have your duties to attend to. If you don't return, someone will notice. He agreed to the bargain, so your work here is done. I'll meet you at the full moon."

I frowned as I processed this information. Return where? Just where did these humans come from that was so important? I'd assumed they were local to Knockspur, but that clearly wasn't the case.

"Be careful, Snow," said one of the villagers, lowering his pickaxe. He was an older man with a white beard surrounding his pale face. "I don't trust the looks of this one."

"I don't either, which was why I got him to swear he wouldn't harm me." She cast me another smug look that made me want to strangle her.

With that thought came a searing heat straight through my brain. I clenched my teeth. Even *thinking* about hurting her triggered the magic of our fae bond. Curse this wicked woman.

Gradually, the humans bid farewell to the princess, some

clapping her on the shoulder and others embracing her tightly. They seemed quite fond of her—much fonder than mere allies.

At long last, only Denton and a short woman with blonde hair remained. The former kept shooting nasty looks my way. I watched him with mild curiosity.

"I don't like this, Eira," Denton whispered.

Eira shoved his shoulder. "Go, Denton. I'll be fine, I promise."

"You shouldn't—"

"Denton." Her tone sharpened. "*Leave.* Please." Her eyes widened with emphasis, and Denton's mouth snapped shut, his jaw going rigid.

Oh, yes. These two had definitely been lovers. Whether they still were, I couldn't tell. Tension rippled between them, but it could be because of my presence.

I could use this information to my advantage. A lover meant leverage. If I got my hands on Denton, it wouldn't be difficult to coerce Eira into undoing both our bargains.

At long last, Denton stomped off, his burly figure soon vanishing among the snowflakes.

I looked expectantly at the blonde woman, who had a small dagger clutched in her hand. Her eyes were fixed on the Snow Princess.

"You, too, Stella," Eira said softly.

The woman—Stella—only bared her teeth at me. I lifted my eyebrows, utterly unimpressed. The sight of this puny human wielding a butterknife did not faze me in the slightest.

"If you double-cross my friend, I'll chop off your balls and force them down your throat," she said. "Understood?"

I couldn't help but snort loudly. "Is that so?" I tugged on

my belt, exposing the array of long knives I had at my disposal, all of them longer and sharper than Stella's.

In a flash, Stella flicked her wrist, and her blade went flying. I dodged, but not quickly enough; the dagger grazed my wrist. Hissing, I cradled my hand, staring at the line of blood trailing down my skin. My flesh burned as if she had branded me with a hot iron.

Nostrils flaring, I shot a venomous look at Stella, who bowed. "I, too, have an arsenal of daggers. They may be small, but they are sharp. And made of iron, of course." Her lips curved upward in a cold smile.

Eira covered her mouth to stifle a laugh. "I'd listen to her if I were you."

Fury rippled through me, and I contemplated snapping the human's neck. I had no bargain with her, so it would not inconvenience me in the slightest.

But all Eira would need to do would be to step in between us, and it would be over. If I laid a hand on the Snow Princess, our bargain would punish me for it.

And, though I hated to admit it, Stella was quick and precise. If I hadn't moved, she would've sliced open my artery. For a human, her speed was impressive. I still doubted she could best me in combat, but right now, she had the advantage. I couldn't risk it.

"We'll be fine, Stella," Eira insisted, nodding at her friend.

Stella drew closer, her eyes as cold as steel as they drilled into me. For a petite creature, she had a rather fearsome gaze. Her jawline and nose were all sharp edges, and even her cold blue eyes seemed like chips of jagged ice. Everything about her was icy, unyielding rage.

I was certain she couldn't overpower me. But I still pitied the man who was on the other side of her blade.

At long last, Stella strode away, her lithe steps making me wonder if perhaps her line of work was similar to mine. She moved like an assassin.

Eira huffed a sigh and turned to face me with that same easy smile on her face. "Shall we set off for the palace then?"

I forced a yawn. "I don't think so. I'm awfully tired, and I've already booked a room here for the night." A slow grin spread on my face. "I'd like to linger in this town and see some of the sights first."

Her eyes narrowed. "I know what you're doing."

"Good. I certainly hope so. Because if you thought I'd make this journey easy for you, then you're a bigger fool than I am."

The Princess

My victory over the assassin was short-lived. True to his word, he proved exactly how much of a pain in the ass he could be.

We had only made it a few steps down the road when Theron suddenly shouted, "Ouch!"

I stopped short, staring at the hunter as he bent over, grabbing his knee with a pained expression on his face.

"What?" I snapped.

"It's my leg. I can't—" Theron broke off with an exaggerated groan, then sank to his ass right there in the middle of the road.

"What the hell are you talking about?" I demanded. "I didn't do anything to your leg."

"Perhaps it was the ride here," Theron said, massaging his knee with both hands. "But whatever it was, I'm not going anywhere tonight. I need to rest."

My nostrils flared. "There's nothing wrong with your damn leg."

"You don't know that."

"Fine. Tell me, point-blank, that your leg is wounded." I crossed my arms and waited.

Theron only continued to make anguished noises as he rubbed his knee.

I nudged him with my boot. "Nice try, hunter. Get up. This isn't going to work."

Theron wheezed a laugh. "Are you sure about that? I never said *when* I would smuggle you into the palace. As long as I do it—even if it's five years from now—I'm abiding by the terms of our bargain."

My heart stopped for a full beat as I processed his words. My blood ran cold, and my breath caught in my throat.

Shit, he was right.

"So, I suppose if you want me to move any faster, you'll have to forcibly drag me," he said.

My eyes narrowed as I considered doing just that. But Theron was tall and bulky. No matter how strong I was, I would buckle under his weight. There was no way I could carry him.

I rubbed my temples, struggling to rein in my temper. Blood and ice, this hunter would be the death of me. It was taking all of my restraint not to stab him right now.

But I needed him. And he knew it.

I don't have time for this, I thought angrily. The palace was in Taerin, the capital of our Winter Court. The large city was a five-day ride from Knockspur, if one traveled with minimal interruptions. With Calista hunting me, I often had to make detours or unexpected stops when I traveled.

The other rebels had agreed to meet me in Taerin at the full moon, along with any supporters and troops they could round up by then. That was two weeks away, and at this rate, I was concerned I wouldn't make it in time. Especially if Theron insisted on extending the journey as much as possible.

Not everything is given right away, my father had told me. *Sometimes, we must demonstrate patience. The patience to wait for better things.*

It was hard to be patient when I was so limited on time. The dark cloud of death hung over me, drawing closer every day.

But I couldn't exactly tell the hunter that.

I heaved a weary sigh of resignation, knowing that, at least for right now, I had no choice. "Fine. Let's get you to the inn."

Theron smirked and climbed to his feet effortlessly. It made me want to give him a *true* leg injury. I envisioned kicking him so hard that I shattered his kneecap.

The thought brought a smile to my face.

The hunter's leg seemed perfectly fine after that; he didn't bother putting on a show as we continued down the road, following the light of the setting sun as we made our way to the inn. The air chilled, and a brisk breeze whipped over us as we approached the threshold of the inn.

We stepped inside, and the crowd of patrons at the pub fell silent at the sight of the assassin. Several narrowed eyes fixed on him, then flitted over to me.

That was to be expected.

"Off to your room," I muttered, grabbing Theron's arm. I was anxious to be out of the public eye as quickly as possible.

He jerked out of my grasp. "I'm hungry."

"Shivering bones," I swore, glaring at the ceiling.

"The room came with supper," he said. "It's already paid for."

I waved a hand toward one of the tables, urging him to sit. He gave me a satisfied smile before sauntering over and sitting down. The couple from the next table over shot him a filthy glance, then stood and left.

Theron the dreaded assassin ordered the finest meal the pub served, followed by several helpings of dessert and ale to wash it all down. I had to sit there, watching him eat and drink, with flecks of food staining his golden brown beard, his charcoal eyes filled with mirth at the sight of my frustration.

After his seventh drink, his eyelids grew heavy. I knew he was hoping the nasty hangover the next morning would slow down our journey.

But he had no idea how relentless I could be.

While Theron continued with his gluttony, I ambled over to the bar, where the innkeeper was scrubbing a mug with a filthy rag. He scowled at me when I approached, his dark eyes flicking to the hunter still sitting at the table.

"He's disgusting," he spat, his thick gray eyebrows drawing together.

"I know," I said with a weary sigh. "I wish I could get him to leave, but…" I shrugged. "He refuses."

The innkeeper's eyes sharpened as he stared at me. "I thought you were with him."

I made a face. "I despise him as much as you. If it were up to me, I'd have slit his throat by now. But I don't want to bring the queen's wrath here."

The man's gaze darkened, and he nodded solemnly.

"But," I said slowly, drawing out the word, "I'll bet come morning, he won't be so quick on his feet."

The innkeeper's eyes narrowed. "What are you getting at, lass?"

"I can't overpower him on my own. I can be quite persuasive, but if my charm fails me, do you think you can gather some men to haul his ass out of here?"

He snorted. "Aye. It won't take much to convince my boys to give him a sound beating."

I smiled widely. "Perfect."

"Good morning, hunter!" I chirped, making my voice as shrill as possible. I shoved Theron hard in the shoulder.

He groaned, a crease forming between his eyebrows as he tried to roll over on his bed. I grabbed his arm and held it firmly in place. He stank of ale, and I was certain the drinks from the previous night were giving him a massive, throbbing headache right now.

That was my hope.

I leaned close to his face and shouted, "Are you awake yet?"

He swore, and his arm shot out—to strike me, no doubt. Before he could touch me, his body went rigid, the tendons on his neck going taut. His back arched. A grunt of agony escaped him, and his eyes flew open to glare at me.

I gave him my biggest smile. "That fae bargain is a bitch, isn't it?"

Last night, Theron had nearly drunk himself unconscious. The innkeeper's burly sons had hauled Theron rather ungracefully to his room. One of them had wanted to gut the hunter. Only after I'd paid him several gold coins had he agreed to leave Theron alive. I was fairly certain he had intentionally knocked the hunter's head on every corner along the way, but I was perfectly fine with that.

I'd remained in Theron's room for the night, sleeping on the floor with my head propped on the door. I trusted the alcohol to keep him asleep, but I didn't trust the other patrons not to come into his room and slit his throat in the night. Hell, I didn't even trust the innkeeper or his sons not to try anything.

As much as I despised the assassin, I still needed him to get me into the palace.

"I've taken the liberty of packing your things for you," I said to him brightly, grinning as I hovered over his bed. "As soon as you drag your lazy ass out of bed, we can leave."

Theron made a strangled sound, but I wasn't sure if it was a cough or a hoarse laugh. "I'm not going anywhere like this." His voice was gravelly and husky from sleep. "You'll have to—"

"Drag you out of the village, I know," I said in a bored voice. "The thing is… When the men downstairs had to haul your ass up the stairs and into your room, they seemed pretty incensed that you were still in Knockspur. In fact, I think I heard one of them say he would drag you out of town himself if you weren't gone by breakfast." My smile widened. "He was a huge fellow. Bigger than you, in fact. So I don't think it would be any trouble to elicit his help."

Theron's eyes narrowed. "You're lying."

"Can't lie, asshole. I have fae blood just like you."

His eyebrows flattened as if he didn't believe me. I wasn't surprised. The idiot didn't even know that half breeds like me had rounded ears. So he likely knew nothing about my fae blood.

He probably didn't think I had fae magic, either. This would work in my favor.

I clapped my hands loudly, and he flinched. "Come on," I said, striding for the door. "If you aren't downstairs in five minutes, I'll send someone up to fetch you. And he will be *far* less pleasant than me." With a wink, I left the room. I heard him swearing from the other side of the door, the sound like music to my ears.

I made my way downstairs and adjusted the satchel on my shoulder. Not for the first time, my fingers itched to dig through it and pull out my stepmother's mirror. To see the true nature of my condition. I had packed it, along with several extra daggers, right after my meeting with the rebels. I had wanted to be prepared before meeting the queen's dreaded assassin.

Not now, I told myself, though the urge to look into the mirror grew stronger every day.

I couldn't risk anyone seeing it. But I also couldn't leave it in Knockspur. It was too valuable. Too necessary. It was the only thing that could reveal the truth of Calista's nature.

If I wanted my people on my side, I needed to expose her as a Demon Fae. Otherwise, the kingdom would never follow me. They would always be loyal to her.

But first, I needed to get to her. And I couldn't do that without Theron's protection.

The innkeeper grumbled something about "unwanted visitors" when I turned in our key. I paid him a few extra coins and whispered conspiratorially, "For your trouble."

He shot me a dark look but took the coins. "That fellow is dangerous, lass. You shouldn't be around him."

"I know what I'm doing," I said, forcing a smile. "Besides, he can't hurt me."

"Not yet, at least," muttered a voice behind me.

I stifled a yelp, whirling to find Theron standing there with a scowl on his face. His dark eyes were clearer now, and he had his bag slung over his shoulder. I had expected his bumbling steps to echo around the inn, but he'd been stealthier than I'd expected, even hungover.

His bitter expression brought another smile to my face, and I hooked my elbow through his. His face pinched in disgust, but I tightened my grip on his arm, trying to ignore the massive size of his bicep. Shivering bones, he was strong. He could likely kill me with a single jab to my throat.

Bless you, fae bargain, I thought. "Thank you for the lovely room," I said to the innkeeper, guiding Theron forward.

In response, the innkeeper spat at Theron's feet.

Theron went rigid, his eyes burning as he glared at the man with all the intensity of a bloodthirsty killer. He was likely contemplating the many horrifying ways he could end this man's life.

I dug my fingernails into his arm and breathed, "Don't even think about it." If he dared to lay a hand on anyone in this village, I would make him pay for it.

For a long, tense moment, Theron and the innkeeper stared hatefully at one another. I impatiently tugged on Theron's arm. When he still didn't budge, I feared I *would*, in fact, have to make good on my threat to have him dragged from the inn.

How many men would Theron take down before they hauled him out of here? I didn't want to think about it. My free hand inched toward my dagger, recalling what Stella had taught me about the best places to cut. A few severed arteries would certainly slow him down. Perhaps I could stab him in the groin, too, for good measure…

Just when I thought Theron was about to unleash chaos, he turned away from the innkeeper and allowed me to steer him toward the door. I let out a breath of relief as we stepped outside. A fresh blanket of snow covered the ground, and the stillness of the wintry air was like a soothing balm. I inhaled deeply, relishing the feel of it. I loved winter mornings. They were so peaceful.

When I moved toward the woods, Theron stiffened, stopping us short. He jerked his arm out of my grip.

"The stables are this way." He gestured down the narrow road. "My horse is there."

I smirked. "We won't be riding a horse."

He merely blinked at me, and I relished the look of shock and confusion on his face.

"Come on, then." I turned toward the forest.

Theron didn't move. "I'm getting my damn horse, princess."

I snorted. "No, you aren't. You expect me to trust a beast that has been trained by *you*? Not a chance."

When Theron still didn't move, I said, "Don't make me go back there and get those men to drag you into the woods, because I will."

Theron's eyes darkened, his nostrils flaring. For a moment, I feared I *would* have to rely on the innkeeper's sons to get the hunter to come this way. But then he followed after me, his arms rigid at his sides.

I followed the worn path through the foliage, knowing my way despite the fresh powder of snow that masked the well-worn trail. To my surprise, the hunter followed with lithe grace, hardly making a sound. He was a predator when he moved. Not a twig snapped. The snow didn't even crunch with his steps.

Then, I remembered he was an assassin. A hunter. He was probably as comfortable in the woods as I was.

"Perhaps your fae magic is stealth," I said over my shoulder. I had never heard a person walk so quietly. The only reason my own steps didn't echo in the wood was because I knew exactly where to step. But it had taken me years of practice.

"Perhaps," he said vaguely. He was much closer than I'd thought, so I quickened my pace to put more distance between us.

It didn't take me long to reach the grove where Mauro liked to graze. Sure enough, I found him, poised and elegant, his magnificent antlers brushing snow off the branches as he turned his head to blink slowly at my approach.

"Hi there," I said with a wide smile. "Ready to go on a trip?"

Behind me, Theron stilled. "Are you talking to that stag?"

I almost snorted at the note of incredulity in his voice. It gave me an absurd amount of pleasure to cause him such bewilderment. Ignoring his question, I reached up and scratched Mauro underneath his chin. His eyes closed, and he rumbled a growl of approval.

"No," he grumbled.

A startled noise sounded from Theron, and I bit back another grin. I didn't often get to show off my relationship with faerie creatures, so I planned to savor it.

"I hate traveling," Mauro said.

I gave him my most innocent, doe-eyed look. "Come on, Mauro. You promised." My lower lip puckered in a frown that I knew would make him melt.

Mauro blinked once at me, then sighed heavily. "Fine. But only because you give the best neck rubs."

I smiled, then turned to Theron, who was watching Mauro with a vicious intensity.

"He's fae," the hunter murmured.

He didn't sound surprised; he sounded wary. His dark

eyes were shrewd and lethal as he appraised the stag, like one beast assessing another.

"No shit," I said in a flat voice.

Mauro lowered his head to glare at Theron. "Who is this? I don't like him. He smells like blood."

"This foul man is my companion," I replied, then frowned. "Sorry, I suppose I should say this foul *male* is my companion. Aren't you fae sensitive about that distinction?"

Theron's scowl deepened, his eyes still fixed on Mauro. "Some are. But the humans and fae of the Winter Court have mingled for so long that we've become desensitized to it." The disgust in his voice told me he was unhappy with this fact.

I rolled my eyes and said to Mauro, "Don't worry, he's not my traveling companion by choice. But he won't harm you. Right, Theron?"

Theron's body was rigid, as if prepared to do battle. "You trust this creature?"

I stiffened at the accusation in his tone. "Yes, I do. More than I trust you, as a matter of fact."

He scoffed. "Then you're a fool. Fae beasts are not to be trusted."

Mauro started pawing at the snow at his feet. "I really don't like this fellow."

"I don't, either," I muttered. "But we're stuck with him. If he causes you trouble, you have my permission to skewer him with your antlers." I shot Theron my widest smile, and his scowl deepened.

Mauro obediently sank to his knees while I climbed atop him. His fur was soft, and even without a saddle, his back provided a smooth ride. I had tried riding a wild stag once, and it wasn't the same. Very uncomfortable. Not to mention Mauro was so offended he wouldn't speak to me for a week.

"And I suppose I'm just meant to walk by your side, am I?" Theron said, spreading his arms.

"Don't be ridiculous. You'll ride behind me."

"I beg your pardon?" The words held the hint of a growl that put even Mauro's rumbling voice to shame.

"Mauro is the only one strong enough to carry us both." I settled into position on Mauro's back, my legs on either side of him.

"What about *my horse*?" Theron bit out. "Or *any* horse in the stables?"

"I can't risk leaving a trail for others to follow. Stable hands can be bribed for information." I tilted my head at him and narrowed my eyes. "Besides, I'd wager you spent all your coin on your generous helpings of ale last night."

Theron's gaze darkened, and, to my surprise, his cheeks flushed. I barked out a surprised laugh. I had indeed caught him. I was sure he was looking forward to providing yet another obstacle to our journey when he revealed his empty coin purse. He had probably expected the stable hand to call the authorities when Theron couldn't pay to have his horse cared for. A few nights in a jail cell would certainly have slowed our travels.

"So, it's your choice, Sir Hunter," I said. "You can try to keep up on foot, or you can climb up behind me."

"And if I refuse to leave until I find a proper mount?" Theron crossed his arms.

Mauro snorted in derision. "You won't find a mount with half my wit or speed."

"Mauro isn't the only fae beast here, you know," I said. "The forest is full of them, and they are *all* my friends. All willing to help me." I raised my eyebrows at Theron. "You can try to resist, hunter. But if you do, between me, the stag, the fox, and the dragons, I think we'll be able to force you on this mount."

Theron's face paled. *"Dragons?"*

I beamed. "Yes. Dragons." Never mind that Rogun was so big he could hardly move without falling asleep. Or that Kendra was so terrified of confrontation that she would bury herself in my cloak before approaching Theron.

The hunter didn't need to know that.

A muscle worked in Theron's jaw as he, too, glanced around the forest, no doubt searching for a way out of this predicament.

After a long, tense moment, he hissed a breath from his teeth. "Very well, princess," he spat. "You win this round."

A delighted chuckle escaped me as he stomped toward the stag, preparing to swing his leg over the side.

"Oh, no you don't," Mauro huffed. "Grab a log to use as a mounting block."

"You didn't demand a mounting block for *her*," Theron argued, and I had to laugh again at the lunacy of this deadly assassin arguing with a stag.

"I trust her," Mauro said. "And she's much smaller than you."

"Hey." I gently swatted one of his antlers.

"Just a fact, princess. You are quite petite."

I rolled my eyes. "Not as petite as Stella."

"Even the mice are not as petite as Stella."

To my annoyance, Theron was smirking. I snapped my fingers at him. "Mounting block. Now."

"I don't take orders from you, little princess."

I refused to rise to his baiting, turning my head away so I

didn't have to look at his smug face. A loud thump indicated he'd found a log. I scooted forward to make room for him as he used the log to hoist himself atop Mauro. To his credit, the great stag didn't even groan or shift from the additional weight on his back, though I knew he wasn't accustomed to carrying two travelers.

"You all right?" I asked, rubbing the side of his neck.

"Don't patronize me," he snapped.

I withdrew my hand as if he'd burned me, remembering that Mauro hated to be coddled. Theron adjusted his seating behind me, his chest flush against my back and his warmth surrounding me. I was irritated to discover he had a very pleasing scent of willow bark and something brisk and earthy that reminded me of the mountains.

"Don't fall off," I tossed over my shoulder before Mauro broke into a gallop.

Theron yelped, his arms tightening around my waist to keep himself secure on Mauro's back. I wanted to laugh, but the sudden closeness of his body was unnerving. I swallowed, choosing to ignore this opportunity to tease him, and instead focused on maintaining my own balance. I'd ridden Mauro plenty of times, but with Theron's added weight, it felt as bouncy and unstable as my first ride. I tucked my legs closer, my knees digging into Mauro's fur.

"Watch it," Mauro huffed.

"I don't want to fall!" I argued.

"I'm offended. You think I would let that happen?"

I relaxed my legs slightly, my heart softening at the indignation in the stag's voice. Mauro had never failed me before. I trusted him with my life.

"Are we truly to ride this creature the entire way to Taerin?" the assassin asked.

"Yes. He's rather good at navigating through the woods."

"We aren't taking roads?"

"Of course not. I thought you were supposed to be stealthy! What would people think if they saw me riding a stag?"

"That you're insane. And rightly so."

I jabbed my elbow into his gut, but my arm met hard muscle, and he didn't even flinch.

"Will you two be quiet?" Mauro barked. "You're distracting me."

I bit back a grin but fell silent. Generally, I didn't speak while riding—mostly because Mauro hated conversation. This would definitely be a trying journey for him.

For all three of us.

The Hunter

I DIDN'T KNOW HOW THE PRINCESS WAS ABLE TO GET UNDER MY skin. I could endure Queen Calista's taunting, but I couldn't handle the half-human Snow Princess? Absurd.

And yet, her presence, her teasing jibes, even the sound of her voice was so irritating it made my blood boil. How I would survive the entire journey to Taerin, I didn't know.

If it weren't for this damned fae bargain, I could have ended her life in seconds. Hell, the princess would probably have met her demise at the hands of the fae creatures she trusted so much. Her idiocy would do the job for me.

The thought brought a smile to my face, but a rough jostle from Mauro's hindquarters made my grin vanish. The beast was correct; he *was* fast. But my position gave me a bumpy ride, my frame lurching with each turn. I had to grip the princess's waist more times than I would have preferred. Each time I did, she stiffened ever so slightly. I wasn't even sure she noticed it, but I did. Part of my skill as an assassin was to take note of every move, every reaction of my enemy. And she visibly reacted to my touch. To my closeness.

Perhaps I could use that to my advantage.

After a few hours of hard riding, Mauro slowed to catch his breath, and I made my move. With a long sigh, I leaned forward, wrapping my arms tightly around the princess and nuzzling my face into her shoulder.

She jerked so violently I was nearly thrown clean off the stag. "What the hell are you doing?"

"What?" I asked innocently. "I'm tired and would like a rest."

"Not like that, you won't."

"Well, if it bothers you, you can continue on foot." I drew closer again, and she jabbed me with her elbow. Her pitiful blow only made me laugh. She couldn't hurt me.

"Keep your distance, hunter," she seethed.

I didn't move. "You're the one who insisted I ride the stag."

"You're doing this on purpose."

"And what if I am? What will you do about it?" My lips brushed her neck, and I felt her shudder slightly. My face flushed from the intimacy of the moment.

"Silence, both of you!" Mauro roared. His voice startled me so much that I withdrew from the princess, loosening my hold around her waist. "Blood and ice, you two are insufferable. Snow, this is the last time I do you any favors."

"You know you don't mean that, Mauro," she said, her tone immediately softening.

"Keep up this bickering, and perhaps I will. Don't test me."

The princess seemed unperturbed by the stag's threats. She shot a wary look over her shoulder, as if she expected me to wrap my arms around her again. When I did nothing, she reached into her satchel and withdrew a shiny red apple. At first, I thought she would feed it to Mauro as a peace offering. Then, she took a large bite, the crunch echoing in the snowy wood.

I wrinkled my nose. "So now you'll eat like the animals, too?"

"It's a sparkwood apple."

"So?"

She threw an incredulous glance at me over her shoulder. "You've never had one? You haven't lived until you've tasted a sparkwood apple."

"She's right," Mauro said.

"What's so special about these apples?" I arched an eyebrow as I scrutinized the apple in her hand. "Besides its blindingly bright color."

"The sparkwood trees are all over Knockspur," Eira said. "Their vibrant red leaves and apples were often mistaken for flames in the forest, hence the name of the tree. When you see it in full bloom, it looks like a great fire burning, even amidst the snow. It's quite a sight."

I frowned. I'd been all over the Winter Court and I'd never come across such a tree. "You're making this up."

"Can't lie, remember?" She took another bite. "The trees are rare in big cities. It's said that fae magic repels their growth." She shot a smirk at me. "A shame, really, that you fae folk have to miss out on such sweet juiciness."

"You're half fae," I said in a flat voice.

"Guess the sparkwood trees aren't bothered by that."

Mauro slowed to a halt, his breath coming in small puffs with each exhale.

"Why are we stopping?" I straightened, glancing around only to find we were still in the middle of a thick and unfamiliar wood, surrounded by snow-covered trees.

"I need to get my bearings." Mauro bent his head low so he could sniff the ground. One of his ears twitched. Only then did I notice the wood was completely silent. Aside from Mauro's panting, not a sound rang out. No twigs snapping. No snow crunching. No chittering birds or squirrels.

Not even a frosty breeze blew through the frozen forest. It was as if someone had stopped time.

Only once had I experienced such magic.

"Mauro," I said, my voice barely above a whisper. "When I say go, you must run. *Fast.*"

"What are you—" Eira began loudly, but I clamped a hand over her mouth to silence her, ignoring her indignant wriggling against my grip.

"You feel it, too?" Mauro murmured, his voice deep and low.

Now Eira was still, her body rigid with awareness. Slowly, I removed my hand from her mouth.

"Yes," I breathed. "We can't fight it. Our only hope is to outrun it."

"I can't outrun it while carrying you both," Mauro said solemnly. "It will catch us."

"What will?" Eira hissed in a trembling breath.

I gritted my teeth as the air grew chiller around us. "I don't suppose you have a powerful arsenal of fae magic at your disposal?"

Silence met my words.

"I didn't think so." With a grunt, I slid off Mauro's back.

"What are you doing?" Eira demanded.

"Mauro can outrun it and lead you to safety if I remain to fight it." I rolled my sleeves up to my elbows and drew a dagger in each hand. The princess slid off Mauro's back as well, and I glared at her.

"Princess," I growled.

"Hunter," she growled back, her pale eyes flashing. She drew her own knife, much smaller than mine but still deadly.

"Get back on the stag," I bit out.

"No. Without you, I have no chance of getting into the palace. *You* get on the stag."

"You don't even know what this creature is! It'll kill you in seconds."

She offered a wry smile. "Your faith in me is touching. Really."

"I'm not kidding, Eira. You have to get out of here."

"You two are both fools." Mauro pawed the ground nervously.

"Get to safety," Eira whispered, brushing her hand down the length of his nose. "I'll call for you when we're free."

Mauro snorted and ducked his head. "Don't die, Snow." With those parting words, he took off into the forest. Seconds later, an eerie black mist pooled into the wood, obscuring our surroundings. I knew only from her frightened, trembling breaths that the Snow Princess remained beside me.

"It's a Demon Fae, isn't it?" Her words were tinged with horror.

I frowned. Most fae believed the Demon Fae were a myth, something told to children in bedtime stories to frighten them into obedience. Just like fae beasts.

The genuine terror in her voice piqued my interest. Had she encountered a Demon Fae before? I made a mental note to interrogate her later.

I tightened my grip on my daggers as darkness flooded the forest. When it had once been bright as midday, now it was dark as midnight, with no moon to light our path. "The

Demon Fae often inhabit abandoned woods like these. I should have been more alert." If I hadn't been so distracted by efforts to torment the princess, I would have been able to sense it sooner.

Now, we would likely both die.

"How do we kill it?" she asked.

"I don't know. I've never done it before. Watch out for their claws; they are poisonous. They are weakest in the eyes."

"Does iron work on them?"

I turned to her, though I couldn't make out her expression. "Yes. But it works on us, too. If it takes your weapon from you, it can kill you with it."

I felt her shudder beside me as a low hiss erupted from within the darkness.

I crouched to one knee, pressing my hand against the snowy ground to anchor myself. Closing my eyes, I inhaled deeply, trusting my remaining senses. A foul stench filled my nostrils, growing stronger with every second.

"They can see in the dark," I warned the princess. "Our only hope is to distract it. Keep it confused."

"What if there's more than one?"

"They are nomadic and live in isolation. If there is another, they will fight each other before coming for us."

"Well, that's something."

How the hell could she be optimistic at a time like this? I was about to snap at her when a blast of a sharp, eye-watering aroma filled my nose, making me choke on my words.

"Down!" I roared.

The princess dropped to the ground beside me just as something lunged, a deep growl rumbling around us.

Keeping my eyes closed, I inhaled deeply, then slashed when the same pungent smell surrounded me. I barely nicked the creature, but it still hissed in fury. Hot breath blew against my face, and I jumped backward to avoid getting skewered by its claws.

The creature roared, incensed by my evasion tactics. Instinct had me opening my eyes, but darkness still surrounded me. I shut them again, but my hesitation cost me. Something huge barreled into me, slamming me backward until I collided with the trunk of a tree. I groaned as I crumpled in the snow, my ribs on fire.

I sensed the creature moving closer. I shoved myself backward, rolling in the snow, my shoulders bumping against roots and rocks. The Demon Fae crashed into the tree, and it snapped. Branches fell around me, and I scrambled to dodge the debris. Something small and hard knocked against my skull, and I staggered backward.

Eira screamed, and instinct had me lunging toward the sound, slamming into the large form of the beast. I tackled it to the ground, dragging it in what I hoped was the opposite direction of the princess.

The foul stench assaulted my nostrils as I blindly slashed with both daggers. The creature shrieked, the sound high and shrill. It burned against my ears, but I struck again. The beast's cry was a survival instinct meant to ward off attackers with the intensity of it.

But I was undeterred. I swung and sliced, choking on the putrid smell, ignoring my instincts to flee. The creature wailed as my blade met flesh. Hot liquid gushed along my arms.

Something sharp pierced my gut, and I roared, my senses overpowered by the pain. I fell backward, and the creature pawed at me again, its claws grazing my shoulder. The acid of its poison scorched my blood. I cried out again, the anguished sound ripping at my throat as I rolled onto my back, my body consumed by agony.

A turmoil of pain and fury burst within me, and something exploded from my chest. The ground seemed to rumble from the impact of my wound. I knew nothing but torment. My blood boiled, and fire raced along my veins, slicing me open from the inside out.

Never in my life had I known such pain.

Everything went still. At first, I thought I'd blacked out. But then, the creature released a hoarse wheeze, as if it were gasping for breath.

The princess let out a furious shout, and the Demon Fae released a high-pitched squeal. I heard the distinct sound of flesh tearing open. More liquid gushed, drenching me completely. The Demon Fae choked and gurgled, and I realized Eira must have sliced its neck open.

Something heavy collapsed beside me. Then, utter silence filled the forest. My blood still on fire, I blinked slowly as the darkness in the woods receded, allowing light to bleed through.

Clutching at the bleeding wound in my gut, I rolled over to inspect the dark creature that had attacked us. I had never seen one of the beasts before; my only encounter had been brief, and I'd fled the darkness before it could catch me. As I drew closer to the body, my breath stuttered in shock.

It was a man. He had pointed ears, light brown hair, and all-black eyes that stared up into nothingness. Long, black claws extended from his fingers, some of them coated with blood. *My* blood. Across his throat was a jagged bloody gash, no doubt where the princess had slit his throat.

Eira's eyes were wide, her face paler than death, as she stared at the dead creature in horror. Black blood stained her neck and the left side of her face.

"He... looks seelie." I swallowed down the bile that crept up my throat. "The Demon Fae look just like *us*."

The Princess

We decided to bury the Demon Fae. We didn't want anyone else stumbling upon it—or worse, another Demon Fae to appear, drawn by the smell of blood.

Unfortunately, there wasn't much to do about the bloodstains on our clothes. I used my waterskin to clean the black blood off my skin, but the hunter was covered in it. And it mingled with his own blood, which stained his clothes and hands crimson. He tried to stifle the bleeding, but he was losing too much.

I whistled for Mauro, and he arrived within seconds.

"Shivering bones, you survived," he breathed. His dark eyes fixed on Theron. "Oh no…"

"He's been poisoned," I said, wiping sweat from my brow. My hand came back slick with inky blood. "How far are we from the nearest village?"

"I'm fine," the hunter growled. "We need to find a river or stream to clean the rest of this blood. Otherwise we'll attract other fae beasts."

"He's right." Mauro pawed nervously at the ground. "If we head for town, we'll only draw the creatures there."

"But everything is frozen this time of year," I argued. "We won't find any bodies of water nearby."

"How did you kill it?" Theron's gaze was pinned on me, his coal-black eyes full of accusation.

I glared at him. "Can we discuss this later? You're dying."

"If you have magic that can help us—"

"I don't have any magic that can cure you! And that's our most pressing concern. So will you shut up and let me think?" The last thing I wanted to do was attract attention to my powers of invisibility. I dug through my pack and thrust a sparkwood apple toward the hunter. "Eat this."

He waved it away. "No."

"*Eat it*. You need your strength."

"I need a healer, not a damn apple!" he snapped.

Groaning, I shoved the apple back into my bag. *Stubborn ass.*

"The pixies," Theron said, his breath winded. "They have healing powers. There are colonies of them that live in the mountains."

"Pixies are unpredictable little bastards," Mauro grumbled. "They don't emerge unless they want to, and they rarely associate with the fae."

"Maybe not seelie fae, but they do associate with fae *creatures*," Theron said, raising his eyebrows.

Mauro snorted. "You want *me* to approach the pixies?"

"No. I want him to." Theron jerked his head to the side.

I followed the direction of his gesture and frowned. "You want… the trees to find the pixies?" Maybe the poison was messing with his head.

Theron rolled his eyes. "You can come out now."

"Damn." Frisk the arctic fox materialized, his snowy form

bobbing toward us. "I'd been so careful. How did you spot me?"

"*Frisk?*" I shrieked. "What the hell are you doing here?"

"What's it look like? I'm following to make sure you don't get yourselves killed."

"Oh, really?" I crossed my arms. "And where were you when the Demon Fae attacked?"

Frisk licked his paws idly. "Perhaps I was kicking snow in its face."

"You were not," I said with a laugh.

"All right, fine, I was hiding. But don't be mad at me. I'm not the only stowaway."

My stomach dropped. "Who—" I broke off, my heart skittering in my chest as I frantically looked around. "*Shit.* Kendra, where are you?"

For a moment, nothing happened. I felt Theron frowning inquisitively at me, but I was scanning our surroundings, my cloak, my pack—

Something clinked in my pack, and Kendra poked her white snout out of the satchel. Her wide blue eyes fixed innocently on me. "Don't be mad, Snow."

Theron made a choking sound, his eyes growing wide. "What... is that?"

Kendra released a puff of icy air before burrowing her way back into my bag.

"She was in your cloak for most of the trip," Frisk said. "When the Demon Fae appeared, she jumped into your pack and was with Mauro the whole time. Don't worry, she was safe."

"*Safe*," I scoffed, my heart still racing at the thought of tiny Kendra in close proximity to a *Demon Fae*.

Theron groaned and swayed slightly. His face was

growing paler by the second, his hand pressed to the bloody wound in his side.

Gritting my teeth, I said, "We'll discuss this later. Frisk, do you know where the pixies are?"

"Yes." Frisk lifted his head, his ears perking up. "The hunter is right. I *can* track them down. If anyone can do it, it's someone who can be invisible. Am I right?"

My lips thinned as I caught his meaning. He wanted me to go with him. "Right."

"We'll have to be careful," Theron said. "Pixies are ruthless and brutal. They value strength and trickery, and they consider themselves the strongest species. So it's best we don't appear threatening."

"And if we *do* appear threatening?" I challenged.

"Then you'd better hope you're the stronger opponent." Theron leveled a hard gaze at me. "Because if you fail, they'll devour you."

I held his stare, refusing to cower despite the way his words chilled me to the bone. I had once researched the pixies, thinking their magic could cure me and buy me more time. Unfortunately, it couldn't. My condition had festered for so long that it was incurable.

Besides, everything I'd read told me the pixies would kill me before I could utter a single word.

"We head for the mountains then," Theron grunted, moving toward Mauro.

"Don't you dare get blood on my fur," Mauro snapped.

"Mauro," I chided. "He's dying."

"Will you quit saying that?" Theron barked. "I'm fine."

Mauro huffed and knelt in the snow so Theron could climb on his back. "This is only because you fought to keep Snow alive."

"He just didn't want to break our bargain," I grumbled, but at the look of agony on Theron's face, something within me softened. Mauro was right—Theron *had* protected me. When I'd screamed as the creature drew closer, its rotten stench overwhelming me, Theron had assaulted it with a recklessness that had gotten him stabbed, skewered by the beast's claws.

If the Demon Fae hadn't been preoccupied with him, I wouldn't have been able to deal the killing blow. I wasn't sure what exactly he'd done to stun the creature like that—it had gone completely still, allowing me to make my move.

Whatever he'd done had saved my life.

And he had been prepared to face the creature alone while Mauro and I rode to safety.

Sure, the fae bargain might have claimed his life if he'd let me get hurt. But I wasn't so sure. Theron had a haunted look in his dark eyes, something that told me he'd seen enough death in his life.

Perhaps he didn't want to add mine to the list. At least not yet.

"Hop on, princess," Theron said in a bored voice.

I eyed Mauro's back uncertainly. I didn't like the idea of riding behind Theron, but it was safest if my arms were around him, keeping him astride Mauro in case the hunter passed out.

With a sigh, I swung my leg up and straddled the stag, tucking myself against Theron's back with my arms around him. He smelled of sweat mingled with Demon Fae blood, and that annoyingly charming scent of woodsy mountains.

"Don't try anything," Theron said over his shoulder.

I snorted. "Or what? You'll bleed on me?"

"Injured or not, I can still best you."

"We'll see."

"Oh shut up, both of you," Mauro said, rising to his feet. Theron grunted from the shift, and I tightened my grip around him to keep him steady. "I'm surprised you've kept quiet about their bickering, Frisk. Usually you love a good banter."

"Oh, I do love it, but I appreciate being a bystander," Frisk said, his voice full of amusement. "These two will rip each other's heads off before long. Can't find better entertainment than that."

I ignored them both. "Still with us, Kendra?"

The tiny dragon poked her snout out again. Her razor-sharp teeth were munching on something. "You're right, Snow. These apples are *delicious*."

"Don't eat all my damn apples," I snapped, but I couldn't hide the smile from my face as she disappeared in my pack, no doubt to continue eating.

I dug my heels into Mauro's fur. "As fast as you can, Mauro. I don't want to have to bury another body today."

"You won't," Theron growled.

I said nothing. Theron couldn't lie… but if he believed he would live, it wasn't a lie.

He could still die from this.

And then, my whole plan would be ruined.

Mauro set off at a brisk speed, and Frisk became a white blur beside us as we took off through the woods.

I tried to keep Theron conscious by teasing him. I poked his arm every few minutes, earning a grumble or two, and mocked him for losing a battle with a Demon Fae, leaving a fair princess to save his sorry ass. At first, he responded with his own barbed insults, but after a while, he slumped backward against me and fell silent. If he was still conscious, it was only just barely.

We were running out of time.

"Is it just me or is this hunter even heavier when he's passed out?" Mauro complained.

"Just focus on speed right now," I said quietly. I would never admit it, but I was genuinely concerned Theron would die before we made it to the mountains. "Frisk?" I couldn't see the fox, but I knew he was nearby.

"I'm here, Snow." His voice came from somewhere to my left.

"Why didn't you tell me about the Demon Fae?" My bones were still quivering from the incident, and I couldn't shake the empty look in those dead eyes or the foul stench of its magic.

It dredged up the horrifying memories of Calista that I thought I had buried deep. My hands wouldn't stop shaking.

"What do you mean?" Frisk asked, but there was an edge to his voice.

"You knew they were out here. And you didn't warn me." It wasn't a question. Frisk and Mauro were fae creatures; if anyone knew about the Demon Fae, it would be them.

I didn't know the Demon Fae lived in the woods, though. The only one I had ever encountered before was Calista. I assumed that all of them, like her, had been warped and twisted into monstrous creatures by dabbling in black magic.

I had no idea there were *feral* Demon Fae who actually lived out here, preying on travelers. Otherwise, I never would have settled in Knockspur. If there was even a *chance* of encountering another one, I never would have risked it.

Frisk was silent for several long moments. The subtle stiffness in Mauro's back told me the stag was listening carefully. Kendra poked her head out of my satchel, her wide blue eyes darting between the three of us with interest.

"We fae creatures don't like to associate ourselves with the Demon Fae," Frisk said at last. "They make us look bad."

"Us?" I repeated.

"The unseelie," Frisk said. "Demon Fae are unseelie, like us."

I knew my forest friends were unseelie. Any fae who could take the appearance of a non-human creature was technically part unseelie.

But that didn't explain why Frisk was comparing himself to a Demon Fae.

"What aren't you telling me?" I demanded.

"Just say it," Mauro mumbled, panting from the effort of sprinting for so long.

I swallowed hard around a lump in my throat, holding my breath as I waited for Frisk's response.

Frisk took a long breath before he said, "We fae creatures are... part Demon Fae. There is Demon Fae blood running through our veins."

My body jerked with surprise. He couldn't be serious. "You—*you*—are Demon Fae?" My voice came out as a high-pitched squeak. Every ounce of me was frozen with terror.

"Only partially," Mauro said defensively.

I shook my head, unable to process this. It was absurd. Based on the stories I'd heard, the Demon Fae were dark, terrible creatures—not at all like Frisk and Mauro.

"B-But you look *nothing* like them," I argued. "And the smell of their magic, it's... It's not possible!"

"We don't possess fae magic like they do," Frisk said. "And

our bloodline has been watered down by many other species over the generations. It's only a distant connection, really. It wasn't worth mentioning."

"Not worth *mentioning*?" I seethed. "Frisk—" I broke off with a frustrated sound, running my hands through my hair. Shivering bones, my head was spinning right now.

My gaze snagged on Kendra, who promptly ducked her head back inside my satchel.

"Hey!" I jabbed a finger at her. "Get back here. Did you know about this?" As a dragon, she wasn't part fae at all, but I suspected she knew more about fae bloodlines than she let on.

Slowly, Kendra poked her nose out of the bag. She sniffed once before replying. "I… suspected."

"Damn it, Kendra!" I wanted to scream into the sky. "Did *everyone* know except me?"

"Don't blame me, Snow," Kendra said, her voice quivering. "My dragon blood allows me to scent magic on other creatures. But it would have been rude for me to bring it up. It's… quite personal. And it wasn't really my place to share it with anyone."

I rubbed my forehead, trying to ward off the looming headache from absorbing such a shocking revelation. My entire world had been rattled. Everything I thought I had known for the past five years was a lie.

A hot lump formed in my throat, my eyes burning with unshed tears as I remembered the day I'd been told my father had fallen ill. How I'd suspected Calista at first.

But the physicians told me he'd been poisoned by a Demon Fae in the woods, and the creature had run off before the hunters could catch it.

Now that I'd seen what Calista was, I knew better. Calista had poisoned him.

And my closest friends shared the same blood as my father's killer.

"Now you understand why we don't like to announce it to the world," Frisk said bitterly. "People dislike fae creatures enough as it is. But to label us as Demon Fae? That's basically a death sentence for us."

"The hunter may be an ass, but he is right to be wary of fae creatures," Mauro said. "Not all are as friendly as we are."

"We never thought you'd encounter any of them, Snow," Frisk said apologetically. "The forest in Knockspur is only populated with civilized beasts like Mauro and me. But in the wilds, you'll encounter all sorts of monsters."

I was shaken. Frisk and Mauro—my friends—were *Demon Fae.* Deep down, I knew they were the same creatures I'd known all these years. And yet the truth of their bloodline rattled me.

My life in the palace had sheltered me from the existence of fae creatures. I knew they were out there somewhere, but they were so far from my reality that I never concerned myself with them until I was banished. And once I'd met Frisk, Mauro, and all the other sentient fae beasts that lived in the woods of Knockspur, I assumed they were just another species of fae. Like the unseelie.

Oh, how wrong I'd been.

"For what it's worth," Kendra chimed in, "the scent of Demon Fae I can smell on them is *quite* faint."

"Snow," Frisk said, "we are still your friends."

"I know," I said quickly. Too quickly. I *did* know that. And yet, they'd hidden their identity from me for years now. "But you deceived me. You kept this from me when I deserved to know."

Frisk and Mauro said nothing. I ground my teeth together, trying to subdue my anger. They might not have lied to me, but they'd hidden the truth. And it stung.

"We were just trying to protect ourselves," Frisk said at last. "You were the first seelie fae to truly befriend us, and we didn't want you to think of us any differently."

I had no response to that. Because if I *had* known they were Demon Fae, I would have fled from their presence. We never would have become friends.

"Besides, if you remained in Knockspur, you would never have encountered any other Demon Fae but us," Frisk went on. "There was no need to tell you. You would never be in any danger."

"But I would have left those woods eventually!" I argued. "It was always the plan for me to return to Taerin and take back the throne."

"Yes, but it didn't seem like..." Frisk trailed off uncertainly.

"Didn't seem like what?" I prompted. When the fox didn't say anything, I said, "Frisk!"

"It didn't seem like that was what you truly wanted," Frisk said, his tone chagrined.

His words stunned me. "What?"

"You seemed so content to live in the woods!" Frisk said hastily. "We thought—maybe even *hoped*—that you'd forget about this plan to take the throne and just live happily with us in the forest."

I hissed a breath through my teeth, prepared to throttle Frisk. "That crown is my birthright."

"We know. But, Snow, you belong in the forest. That is your true home."

"You know nothing about my true home. You lied to me for years, and now you claim to know what I want? What I need?" I huffed a hollow laugh and shook my head, too furious for words.

"We care about you, Snow," Mauro said, his deep voice gruff and strained. "And the queen is powerful. We didn't want to see you get killed."

"I'm so glad you two have such confidence in me," I snapped. "Do the others feel this way, too?"

"The humans?" Frisk asked. "No, they have complete faith in the success of this mission."

"But the creatures, yes," Mauro admitted. "They adore you, Snow."

"It's true," Kendra agreed. "We all do."

Something in my chest softened at those words. I knew Mauro included himself in that sentiment, though he would never say it aloud. How would I feel if one of them concocted a dangerous plan that would likely result in their deaths?

Besides, I'd been keeping secrets from them, too. I couldn't stay angry at them for this.

And in a way, they were right. A part of me *did* long to stay in the woods for the rest of my life, away from Calista and her poisonous clutches. The farther away I was from her, the safer I was. Perhaps I had put off this coup for so long because I was so content with my life in Knockspur.

But I couldn't ignore my people and their suffering at her hand. Regardless of my fears about my impending death, I had to save this kingdom from her.

Before it was too late.

Every creature, whether fae or human, deserves our respect, Father had said. *No one species is better than another.*

I had always interpreted that in favor of humans. But now I was thinking of my animal friends. Just because Calista was evil didn't mean that my friends were. I knew better than most how it felt to be judged by one's bloodline.

"Don't hide things from me again," I said to my friends. "Even the ugly truths you want to keep to yourselves."

"We won't," Frisk said at once.

"We're sorry, Snow," Mauro added.

"I know." I stared ahead at the blur of snowy trees, my jaw tight.

I could never tell them the truth—that the reason I was so afraid of the Demon Fae was because I'd encountered one before.

And it was the Queen of the Winter Court.

If all went according to plan, I would expose her to the entire realm. But if it didn't, I couldn't risk my friends knowing her secret.

Otherwise, she would hunt them down, too.

The remainder of our journey was stilted and strained. Mauro was panting from exertion, his flanks slick with sweat. I wasn't sure how much longer he would last. Frisk and I shared an uncomfortable silence. Though his white fur blended in with the snowy surroundings, I knew he was there. I often felt his gaze on me, but if he was looking for comfort or reassurance, I would give him none. I may have accepted their apology, but that didn't mean I was ready to talk just yet.

Not all monsters are the same, I had to remind myself.

And yet the terrifying appearance of Calista's Demon Fae form was hard to shake. What if Mauro and Frisk were hiding something equally terrifying?

An hour before sunset, we reached the base of the Athawood Peaks, the treacherous mountain range that lined the eastern border of the Winter Court. Just south of those mountains lay Taerin. Not many crossed the peaks because it was too dangerous.

But we needed to. It would cut our journey in half, and the hunter needed healing. Fast. He was fully slumped against me now, and it required immense effort for me to keep him upright. His skin was burning and covered in sweat, despite the flurries of snow swirling around us. The wind was sharper here by the mountains, the cold air stinging my cheeks. I had my scarf wrapped around my face, but the chill still bled through, undeterred.

"We need to go on foot from here," Frisk said. "It's too slippery for Mauro, and he needs rest."

"No complaints here," Mauro huffed, already sinking to his knees and resting his head against the snow.

I dismounted from the stag, then grabbed my pack and carefully extracted Kendra from inside. "Stay here with Mauro," I told her.

"But I want to see the pixies!" Kendra objected, raising her snout, her blue eyes full of indignation.

"If you join us, they are likely to make you their next meal," Frisk said flippantly, causing Kendra to curl herself into a ball in Mauro's fur.

"You two, make sure he stays alive." I jabbed a finger at the unconscious hunter's prone form still draped over Mauro's back.

"No promises," Mauro grunted, but he angled his head to fix one eye on Theron.

"I'm too scared to get too close to him," Kendra admitted. "But I'll blast Mauro if I notice any changes to his breathing."

Mauro merely snorted at this.

"Come on, Snow." Frisk set off along the narrow, winding path that led uphill. Wrapping my scarf tighter around my face, I hurried after him.

It was slow work. The ground was icy, and the wind threatened to knock me over. I had to pause frequently to adjust my footing. Though my boots were equipped for snow and ice, I'd never worn them in such hazardous conditions before.

When we reached a small plateau at the top of the first hill, I paused to catch my breath and snack on a sparkwood apple from my pack, squinting against the darkness descending around us. Frisk's eyesight was better than mine in the dark, so I had to trust he knew where he was going.

"Tell me something," Frisk said, his tail swishing as he paced in front of me.

"What?" I asked between bites, enjoying the way the sweet juice trickled down my throat. It distracted me from the bitter cold.

"You say it was always your plan to go back to Taerin and take back the crown," he said slowly, "so, why haven't you gone yet?"

I scowled. "You know why. We didn't have the funds for mercenaries. We still don't."

"You can turn invisible, Snow. And you know that castle better than anyone. Getting inside wouldn't have been an issue for you."

I clenched my teeth, prepared for the automatic response I usually gave people when they assumed my invisibility was foolproof. Before I could, Frisk jumped in.

"And don't bother telling me that a soldier would notice you. You're cleverer than that."

My nostrils flared, my anger rising. "What are you getting at, Frisk?"

"I just think Mauro and I aren't the only ones who feel like you belong in the forest."

"I want my father's crown," I said sharply. "This court isn't safe in Calista's hands."

"I know that. But I think if you really wanted this, you

would have found a way by now. It's been five years, Snow. And you haven't gone back once, not even to scope out the area."

I stilled, clenching my free hand into a tight fist and exhaling through my teeth. I knew Frisk's secret. Perhaps it was time I shared mine.

At least... part of it.

Stalling, I took another bite of my apple. When Frisk only stared at me expectantly, I heaved a sigh and said, "Just before I left Taerin, I encountered a Demon Fae. I barely escaped with my life. I'm worried it will hunt me if I return."

None of this was a lie. I just wasn't ready to tell him it was Calista I was afraid of. And that the farther away I was from her, the less power she had over my blood.

Frisk was silent for a long moment. "Ah," he finally said.

I waited for him to go on, but he didn't. "What?"

"That explains why you were so crazed when you found out about me and Mauro."

"I was not *crazed*."

"And it explains your reluctance to return. But, Snow, you *never* back down from a fight. What about this Demon Fae has you so spooked?"

"You know what they are!" I argued. "You know what they can do. I wouldn't have survived that attack without Theron there to distract it."

"No, you wouldn't have survived without your *invisibility*. That's what saved you. The Demon Fae can't see through your magic."

I shook my head, refusing to delve deeper into my confession. "I'm shaken from that experience, Frisk. I was young. And I know Demon Fae have an impeccable sense of smell. It'll scent me the second I return."

"Maybe." Frisk sounded doubtful.

"Weren't you just chiding me about diving into dangerous missions?" I snapped. "Where's that worry for my safety? Or are you no longer concerned?"

Frisk barked a laugh. "Don't try to turn this on me, Snow. I know there's more to your story, but if you aren't ready to share it, I'll respect that. I know what it's like to keep things to yourself—whether for your own protection or for others'."

His considerate response startled me. Normally, Frisk was relentless; if he wanted information, he would get it.

Perhaps this was a gesture of trust. One that I would need to return if I wanted to heal our friendship.

"Thank you," I said uncertainly. "I appreciate that."

"I hope that, one day, you'll trust me with the full truth," Frisk went on. "Even if it's painful."

I winced. Because yes, it *was* painful. Just skirting around the full truth had me quivering down to my bones. Those red eyes… the sharpened claws… the savage grin…

I shuddered and finished off my apple before tossing the core. I rubbed my arms. "How much farther?"

"Just one more peak to climb," Frisk said.

"You've been here before, haven't you?"

"What if I told you I simply have excellent tracking skills?"

I laughed. "I'd say that's bullshit and you know it."

He huffed another laugh. "This way, Snow."

We continued our climb, my eyes burning from the harsh wind, the billowing flurries intensifying the higher we went. I was grateful for the setting sun because it reduced the painful brightness of the snow, but it also lowered the temperature by several degrees. Despite wearing many layers, my insides rattled with my shivering.

"F-F-Frisk?" I mumbled, teeth chattering.

"Shh," Frisk said. I could no longer see him beside me.

I halted, my skin tingling with awareness. On instinct, I draped my invisibility over me like a cloak, raising one hand in front of me to ensure I was completely obscured. I saw nothing but the snowflakes.

With so much snow in the air, I couldn't see Frisk at all. But as I stood there, body quivering, I realized I didn't need to. A shimmering glow glinted in the distance, a mixture of pink and purple hues. I swallowed, my throat dry, as I made my way closer to the light. With each step, warmth crept through my layers of clothing, thawing my icy bones. I nearly sighed with relief, but I was too enamored with the brightening lights of the pixies' magic. Gold and crimson bursts joined the pink and purple, creating a kaleidoscope of colors.

It was absolutely breathtaking. Like the northern lights, but with more vibrant colors.

"Let me approach first," came Frisk's soft voice. I stilled again and waited, placing a hand on the snowy rock wall next to me for support.

After a moment, hushed murmurs met my ears. No doubt they'd sensed Frisk's presence. I held my breath. If they could spot Frisk in this blizzard, then I had no hope of blending in, even with my invisibility.

"I'm here to speak with Nyra," Frisk said, his voice loud and clear. I'd never heard him speak with such authority before. I was accustomed to his sarcastic drawl, but this voice spoke of power. It made me wonder what his life had been like before he'd come to Knockspur.

"Intruders are not welcome here," said a harsh male voice. "Be gone before we incinerate you with our magic."

"Don't make me speak her true name," Frisk warned. "Because I will. And she knows it."

A pixie's *true name*? Not many fae species possessed true names. That magic had died out long ago. This meant that Nyra had to be hundreds of years old—perhaps even a thousand.

The pixies' muttering intensified. I resisted the urge to fidget, my heart racing. Was Frisk in danger? Would the pixies harm him?

And how in the hell did he know a pixie's true name?

At long last, a light, female voice said, "I'm here."

"We request an audience with you, my queen."

I stiffened. *Queen*? Frisk didn't say anything about meeting a pixie queen.

"Since you've threatened me with my true name, I hardly have a choice, do I?"

"Give me your word you won't harm me or my companions, and I'll give you my word I will never utter your true name ever again."

The murmurs silenced completely, and my eyes widened. That was a hefty bargain. To know someone's true name was an enormous amount of power, and Frisk was offering to give that up.

"I give you my word," Nyra said at last.

"Then, our bargain is struck." Frisk's voice was loud as he called out, "You can join us, Snow!"

Steeling myself with a deep breath, I dropped my invisibility. I trudged through the snow, rounding a corner and squinting against the burning brightness of the pixies' magic. It glowed as brilliantly as the sun, illuminating the crowd of pixies clustered along the mountain ledge. A fire crackled in the center, but it wasn't amber—it sparked with dozens of different colors that shimmered in the air. And somehow, the pixies' magic repelled the blizzard, leaving a huge protective bubble around the encampment.

As my gaze took in each pixie standing around the fire, my heart lurched in my throat. I'd pictured tiny sprites with wings, but these creatures were quite different. Tall and elegant, the pixies resembled fae with great translucent wings stretched behind them like butterflies. Their skin glowed, ranging in color from bronze to violet to crimson. One pixie had fuchsia-colored skin, and another was forest green.

Every single one of them had all-black eyes that stared emptily at me. I suppressed a shudder at the endless depths of those animal eyes.

They reminded me of Calista.

As I moved forward, the wind instantly calmed as the safety of the pixies' magic surrounded me. I uttered a soft gasp. I hadn't realized how biting the wind had been until it vanished completely. I strode to the center where Frisk stood, and one pixie flashed a grin at me, revealing sharpened fangs.

"This is my companion, Snow," Frisk said, and I said a silent prayer of gratitude that he didn't give them my name. "One of our traveling companions is in urgent need of your medical assistance."

The pixie closest to us uttered a harsh laugh, and my eyes snapped to her. The pixie queen—Nyra—had rose-gold skin that glimmered like stardust and pearly white hair that flowed in long tresses down her back. A long, emerald dress covered the front of her body in two long swaths of fabric, but the entirety of her back side was left exposed.

"That would be *two* favors you've asked of me today,

Frisk," Nyra said, her sharpened teeth flashing. "And we do not share our magic with strangers."

"We are embarking on a mission that will forever change the future of this court," Frisk said. "If we succeed, it means a better life for everyone who is not a full-blooded seelie fae."

My mouth fell open in surprise as I gazed around the crowd of pixies with dawning realization. *Of course.* The pixies were fae—*unseelie* fae. They were likely part Demon Fae just like Frisk, and these were their bestial forms.

It would explain why they shared so many similarities to the Demon Fae.

It would also explain why they were bound to bargains, just like us.

The vastness of my ignorance brought a blush creeping up my cheeks. How much did I not know about my own kind? I had been so focused on defending humans that I had completely neglected the fae side of my lineage. The world was far bigger than the Demon Fae we had encountered in the forest. There were many different species of unseelie creatures, like Frisk and Mauro and these pixies.

How many more creatures lived out there, being painted as monsters by stories and folklore?

"Do not speak to me of fae bloodlines," Nyra growled, her face darkening with rage. "You do not know half of what my people have suffered for our heritage."

"We can change that," Frisk promised. "But if our companion dies, our mission is doomed to fail."

Nyra considered this, then angled her head toward me. "And what role do you play in all this, *Snow*?" She emphasized my name as if she knew full well I was hiding my true identity.

"She's not—" Frisk began.

"It's all right, Frisk," I said, relieved that my voice came out steady and even. "If we are asking them to share their magic with us, the least we can do is be up front with them."

"Snow," Frisk warned.

I lowered my hood and scarf. My heart drummed an erratic beat in my chest, but I forced myself to remain calm. This was a gamble… and I prayed it would pay off.

"My name is Eira. I am the rightful queen of this court."

The Hunter

It didn't take long for Mauro to slump into unconsciousness. Truth be told, I myself hadn't been able to remain fully awake for the entire journey like I'd hoped. I had been fading in and out of consciousness, so there were some gaps in my memory. But I'd heard enough.

So, the Snow Princess intended to take back the throne. And she was afraid of Demon Fae.

I could use this to my advantage.

I carefully eased myself off the stag's back, trying to suppress a groan of agony as icy wind howled around me. Despite the cold, it felt like my very blood was on fire. Every move prompted searing pain. I gritted my teeth so hard my head throbbed, trying to push past the agony.

Blood and ice, Demon Fae poison was a bitch.

Mauro didn't stir when I'd finally managed to slide off him. With a slow exhale, I rose to my feet, my head spinning.

"Where do you think you're going?" a small voice piped up.

I jumped, whirling around to find the source of the voice. Had a pixie snuck up on me? Perhaps it was another white fox, like Frisk?

Eyes narrowed, I scanned my surroundings, but the blizzard made it difficult to see. The wind stung my eyes, and the poison in my bloodstream was fogging my thoughts.

"Who—Who's there?" I asked, trying to sound fierce and intimidating.

Then, I noticed movement from the snow at Mauro's feet. A tiny white snout poked out from the flurries, sniffing the air. Gleaming blue eyes peered at me, full of suspicion and distrust. "Don't think you can just sneak away like that." Her voice quivered, but there was a stubborn edge to it that told me I didn't want to test her.

I frowned, crouching to my knees to get a better look at the creature. I had seen the tiny dragon emerge from the princess's pack after I'd been poisoned, but I had chalked it up to a hallucination. Her scales were so white that she blended in perfectly with the snow, save for her glowing blue eyes. They seemed almost more luminescent than the moon itself.

"What's your name?" I asked. I had heard of dragons who roamed the Winter Court, but I had never met one before. Understandably, they often stayed away from the palace and the crowds of courtiers. But sometimes, when I was tucked away in my cottage in the mountains, I could hear one of them roaring in the distance. I had always been curious as to what they looked like, but not curious enough to risk my life trying to track one down.

The small dragon huffed, and a puff of blue ice appeared in front of her snout. "Don't try to charm your way out of this, hunter. You aren't going anywhere."

I almost snorted at her insistence. In ordinary circumstances, it would be laughably easy to evade such a tiny creature.

But with the poison coursing through my veins, I was far too weak to do much at the moment.

From the edges of my hazy memory, I recalled a small voice expressing disappointment that she couldn't follow Eira and see the pixies for herself. Maybe I could convince this little creature to be on my side.

I heaved an exaggerated sigh, then lifted my palms as a sign of surrender. "All right. You caught me. I was merely curious about the pixies, that's all."

The dragon cocked her head at me, her eyes narrowing slightly. "Have you ever seen them before?"

"Once or twice," I said vaguely. "Their magic is astounding. Did you know it burns like fire? And it's multi-colored. It looks like an explosion of rainbow fireworks when it's on full display."

The dragon's mouth opened in awe, showing several of her minuscule, sharpened teeth. Like the fangs of a lovable kitten. "Really?"

I nodded. "But it's far too dangerous. It's probably better that you stay here and look after me."

The dragon's head drooped in disappointment. "Right." Her voice was full of resignation.

A moment passed. Then another. I tried to keep myself calm and still, but in truth, I itched to get moving. I was already on borrowed time.

But if the dragon flew ahead to warn Eira or the pixies of my movement, then there would be trouble. I needed her on my side.

"I'm Kendra," the dragon said in a small voice. "Snow doesn't take me on dangerous missions. Well, not very often. And when she does, I often hide."

I tilted my head at her, assessing. "Why? You're so small.

It would be easy for you to blend in." I gestured to the snow around us.

"True." Kendra's nose twitched. "But my eyes give me away. And poachers think they can harness magic from dragons. So if I get caught by the wrong people..." She shuddered, her scaly frame shivering. "It's too scary."

I rubbed my chin as if considering her predicament. "What if... you could see the pixies *and* stay hidden?"

Her head snapped toward me, her ears sticking up like an eager canine. "I'm listening."

"Come with me," I told her, leaning forward. "You can hide in my cloak. We'll sneak up on the princess and the pixies and watch from a distance. Completely safe."

She was standing up straight now, her tiny legs perched on the ground, her lizard-like tail swishing with excitement. "Are you sure?"

Fresh pain pulsed through me, and I pressed a hand to my wound. It was bleeding again. Damn. With a groan that wasn't at all forced, I said, "Yes. In my condition, it would be most unwise for me to draw the attention of the pixies. I just want to see what the princess is doing. And make sure she's safe."

Not completely a lie. I *did* want to see how Eira planned to keep herself alive amongst such bloodthirsty creatures.

Kendra's nose twitched again. Her gaze darted to the sleeping stag, then back to me. "I don't trust you."

"I would think you a fool if you did."

"Swear to me you won't hurt me."

I almost laughed. It seemed the dragon had learned a thing or two from the Snow Princess. "I swear on my fae blood that I will not hurt you or intentionally put you in harm's way." Technically I didn't need to mention my fae blood at all, but I thought it might mollify her.

Kendra blinked once, then nodded. "All right. But only for a few minutes. We should come back before Mauro wakes."

"Of course. Hop on." I leaned in closer, offering my shoulder to her. With a lithe jump, Kendra landed on my shoulder, then burrowed herself into my cloak. Her light talons made the tiniest of pinches along my arm and neck. They tickled, making me suppress a shudder.

"I should be able to track their footprints," I told her. "Ready?"

She let out a giggle of excitement. "Ready."

As it turned out, tracking the fox and the princess in the blizzard was trying enough even without the poison spreading through my body. But I had to grit my teeth and endure it. Those two would likely get themselves killed by negotiating with the pixies. I knew how to handle them, but I doubted the feisty princess would be able to behave herself. They'd likely already beheaded her.

Which, I realized, would be in my favor. Our bargain would be nullified with her death.

Even so, I had to know for sure. If the pixies *had* killed her, I would still need to carve out her heart and bring it to the queen.

As I moved forward, I kept having to pause to knit my magic over my wound. It wasn't much—just an intense burst of glamour to trigger my fae healing—but it allowed the blood to clot momentarily before the poison took over again.

Sooner or later, I would lose this game. Fae magic couldn't heal a poison like this.

"You're dying, aren't you?" came Kendra's soft voice. The

third time I had to use my magic, she poked her head out from the fabric of my cloak.

I sighed. There was no use trying to deceive her about this. "Yes. If the pixies don't heal me soon, I'll die."

"Then we should probably hurry up."

I nodded and pressed onward.

After what felt like an eternity, I found them. The pixie magic gave away their location, creating a kaleidoscope of brilliant colors against the night sky.

I wanted to remind Kendra to be silent, but she had buried herself in my cloak once more. She seemed to know that keeping herself invisible was the best strategy.

When I was a few paces away, I halted and withdrew my knives, laying them on the snow at my feet before I continued onward. To approach pixies with weapons was a criminal offense.

Another reason the princess would likely be killed. Such a shame.

But then I heard her as she declared with a loud voice, "My name is Eira. I am the rightful queen of this court."

I stilled at the power resonating from those words. Gone was the playful princess who tormented me night and day. Gone was the cheerful optimist whose grin made my blood boil.

These were the words of a queen.

Even the pixies were stunned into silence. Kendra had inched her head out to watch with wide, transfixed eyes.

But the princess wasn't finished.

"When I take back my throne, I intend to change Calista's unjust laws against those she calls *half breeds*." She spat the words. "I may not be unseelie, but I am half human. You aren't the only ones to have been mistreated because of your heritage. Humans are hunted and tortured for sport. We've been banished from our homes, forced to turn over our lands to the *superior species*." There was venom in her words that made me tremble.

How often had I thought those exact words? That the fae were superior to humans?

Kendra's head lifted, her eyes shining as she gazed at Eira. "She's incredible," she breathed.

"My father intended to change this court for the better," Eira continued. "He loved a human and saw her for the pure soul that she was. We are different, you and I. I may not have wings or pink skin or glowing magic. But I have a soul, just as you. We are more than just our appearances. We are more than our bloodlines. We are beings with desires and goals, feelings and ambitions, and a whole future of choices and decisions if we only have the freedom to make them. I vow that, as your queen, I will give you that freedom."

My mouth fell open. If the princess truly couldn't lie, then she had just made a hefty promise to some of the most savage creatures I'd ever met.

"How are we to believe your promises?" asked the white-haired pixie in front of Eira. "You are part human."

"I cannot lie," Eira said. "But, if you wish it, I will strike a bargain with you and seal it in blood."

Kendra sucked in a sharp breath, her small frame quivering on my shoulder. I couldn't blame her. The naïve princess was dooming herself. I knew for a fact that a blood bargain with a pixie was dangerous and volatile. Some fae were killed by the intensity of the pixie magic as the bargain was struck; they couldn't even survive long enough to fulfill their part of the deal.

As a half human, Eira didn't stand a chance.

"Snow!" Frisk objected.

The white-haired pixie threw her head back and laughed. "You are a fool, princess! You are issuing your own death sentence with this bargain."

"Then you will lose nothing," Eira said, her regal tone unwavering. "Strike this bargain with me. If I survive, you heal my friend. If I don't..." She shrugged one shoulder as if her own life mattered so little to her. "Then you owe me nothing."

I wanted to laugh along with the pixies. It would be far too easy for me to fulfill my bargain with the queen now. The force of the pixies' magic would kill the princess, and once the feral creatures were finished with her, I would carve out her heart and bring it to Calista.

Of course, I still needed to find a healer. A minor complication.

"All right then," said the white-haired pixie, her grin widening. "Let us strike this bargain. I hope you have made peace with your gods, princess, because you will meet them soon."

Eira flashed her own smile. "We'll see."

"Nyra, please—" Frisk began.

"Silence, fox," Nyra barked. "Your princess has made her decision. There is no turning away from this fate."

I inched closer so I could better see this pixie queen. She looked magnificent indeed with her long hair billowing in the wind, her inky black eyes wide with delight.

"Bring me the ceremonial dagger," Nyra commanded. A few pixies shuffled, and one broke through the crowd, reverently bowing as he placed a long, jagged dagger in the queen's hands.

Frisk was whispering something to the princess, but she

shook her head, her expression fierce with determination. She looked fairly confident for someone about to die. I squinted at her, trying to figure out what she was planning.

"Don't stand there and bleed on my doorstep," Nyra called out suddenly. "Come and join us, good sir. You can get a much better view from here."

Kendra let out a squeak and dived back into my cloak. All of the pixies turned their heads to fix their black eyes on me.

Well, shit.

The Princess

Of course Theron had been eavesdropping. I shouldn't have been surprised.

He didn't hear anything too damning, but when he witnessed the blood bargain, he would certainly have questions. He already noticed too much during the fight with the Demon Fae.

It was a risk I had to take. There was no other way to enlist the help of the pixies. I needed a show of strength right now.

And far more was at stake than just Theron's life. If the pixies assisted us, believing I would hold up my end of the bargain, then perhaps I would have allies in the war against Calista—more than just my band of human rebels.

Theron was wearing his signature scowl, his eyebrows lowered and his lips thin. His skin was ghostly pale, and he looked irritated that he'd been caught. He rubbed the back of his neck, the motion oddly stilted. My eyes narrowed as I scrutinized him further. Then I noticed a flash of brilliant blue, and my heart seized in my chest.

Kendra.

Theron's arm slid down to his side, then curled behind

his back. If I hadn't been watching for it, I wouldn't have noticed the small white shape darting out of his fingertips and vanishing into the snow.

Not only was Kendra with Theron, but the hunter was... helping her to escape? I wasn't sure if I was more touched or stunned by this show of affection for my scaly friend.

When Kendra had vanished from view, Theron hobbled forward. To his credit, he made it to the center of the crowd without falling over. Not only that, but he managed to climb up the mountain to get here. If it weren't for the shadows under his eyes and the pallor of his skin, I would question whether he'd been truly poisoned.

"A little worse for the wear, aren't you, darling?" Nyra crooned.

Theron only glared at her.

Nyra beckoned me closer with a look of glee on her face, and I approached, pulling up the sleeve of my shirt to expose my wrist. As I did so, I pressed my thumb hard into my flesh, infusing my invisibility into my blood. I didn't do it often because it hurt like hell. Fiery pain spread through my veins, and I bit down on my bottom lip so hard I broke skin, leaving a coppery taste in my mouth.

It's only for a few minutes, I told myself. *Just hold on to your magic for a few minutes. That's all.*

Black spots danced in my vision as the agony throbbed against my skull, pounding relentlessly. I could barely hear Nyra's voice as she uttered the terms of our bargain.

"I, Nyra, Queen of the Athawood pixies, swear with my blood that neither I nor my clan will hurt Princess Eira or her companions, and that we will heal her injured friend, provided that she swears to give my people freedom when she becomes Queen of the Winter Court."

Nyra looked at me expectantly, and I gritted my teeth, trying to think clearly through the blistering pain. My voice was stilted as I said, "I, Eira, Princess of the Winter Court, vow to give the pixies freedom when I become Queen of the Winter Court, in exchange for Queen Nyra's promise not to harm me or my companions, and to heal my friend."

Nyra sliced the dagger into her palm. Black blood oozed from her wound and dripped onto the snow. She brought the knife to my wrist with a hungry look in her gaze. I closed my eyes, focusing on channeling my magic further into my blood, praying this would work.

The sharp sting of the knife barely registered amidst the roaring pain in my body.

But I certainly noticed the stunned gasps around me.

Nyra cut into me again. More gasps.

"What sorcery is this?" she screeched.

I offered a weak chuckle. "Hmm, that *is* strange. It looks like I have no blood to offer you after all." I opened my eyes, taking in the wide gash on my wrist that exposed the pink underside of my flesh. But no blood.

Nyra stared at me with a mixture of rage and disbelief. "You tricked me! I'll have your head for this!"

"Ah, but you can't." I rolled back my sleeve, holding on to my invisibility for a moment longer. "The bargain prevents you from harming me if I survive the ritual."

"There *was* no ritual," Nyra seethed. "We did not complete the bargain!"

"Not true. I gave you my word, which is as true as any fae bargain. And you shed your own blood, which means *you* are bound."

I had to let her think I wasn't bound to the bargain. But

this wasn't true. My blood *had* been shed—it was just invisible.

I was still bound by the terms of the blood bargain. And infusing my magic into my blood lessened the force of the bond, keeping me alive. Otherwise, Nyra was right—the strength of her pixie magic likely would have killed me.

Nyra released a wild scream before lunging for me. I stood there, unflinching, as the fae bond stopped her in her tracks. She stiffened, her limbs going rigid and her hands clawing at her temples in agony. She roared in pain, falling to her knees in front of me.

I merely watched with a small smile on my face. My gaze flicked to Theron, who stared at me in utter shock. His eyes roved over me as if searching for some hidden weapon I was harboring.

Oh, yes, he knew there was something else at play here. I would need to be extra careful around him from now on.

"I didn't know you could do that," Frisk muttered, sounding impressed.

I shushed him, keeping my eyes pinned on the queen. When the pain of the fae bond subsided, she slowly rose to her feet, gasping for breath. A few pixies surged toward her, but she waved them away. She cocked her head, assessing me as if re-evaluating my strengths and weaknesses. I was certain she'd first seen me as a weak human. But now?

Now I was a worthy opponent.

Silence surrounded me, but I leveled an even stare at the queen, waiting for her response.

Her expression changed. A slow smile spread across her lips, and a deep, rich laugh resonated in her throat. Her laughter intensified until she threw her head back, her body quivering with her mirth. A few other pixies joined in, but most of them looked uncertain, as if they worried their queen had gone mad.

Nyra clapped her hands together with glee before fixing her eyes on me once more. "Oh, you surprise me, princess. Not many can do that." Her laughter subsided as she appraised me with warmth in her gaze. Or as much warmth as she could muster with her all-black eyes. "Come. Join us for a meal. I will heal your friend."

I lifted one finger. "By *join us for a meal*, do you mean…"

Nyra laughed again. "I mean we will feed you food that is safe to eat. Some pixie tribes feast on human flesh, but I assure you we do not."

Relief filled me as I drew closer to her. "Thank you for your hospitality, my queen." I felt my invisible blood trickling down my arm, so I tried to discreetly press my hand to it to stop the flow. Nyra might have warmed up to me, but that didn't mean I wanted to give away the fact that she had *actually* drawn blood.

"And thank you for the entertainment," said Nyra. "It is not often I witness trickery that rivals us pixies. Are you certain you have no pixie blood in you?"

I suppressed a shudder. "Quite certain."

"Brune, see to it that our guests are fed and have a place to rest for the night," Nyra said, turning to the orange-skinned pixie standing behind her.

"Oh no, we don't—" I started to object, but Nyra waved away my excuses.

"It's a blizzard tonight, princess. Do you intend to sleep on the ice?"

I fell silent at that. I thought again of my father's words: *Allies can come to us in the most unlikely of places.*

For good or ill, these pixies were now on my side,

provided I could deliver what I had promised. Perhaps it wouldn't hurt to stay and mingle with them. It might strengthen our connection and improve relations going forward.

Perhaps I could make my father proud.

Several pixies yelped, and I turned toward the commotion. Theron had collapsed, finally giving in to the weakness claiming his body. No doubt the strain of climbing the mountain had done him in.

"Ah," Nyra said idly. Her great lavender wings spread wide and she flitted in the air before zooming toward the wounded hunter with lightning speed. The rapid movement of her wings reminded me of a hummingbird—a blur of color that made me gasp with awe.

While everyone was distracted, I took a moment to tear a strip of fabric from my tunic and wrap it around the cut on my arm. When I was sure the wound was bound, I glanced up in time to see two brawny pixies hoist Theron up. His head lolled, and his damp brown hair flopped over his eyes. Blood and ice, he looked *terrible*. Seeing him like this made me realize just how much he had been holding back before. He must have pretended to be unconscious while astride Mauro.

That was one determined assassin.

Nyra lifted a hand and pressed it to Theron's chest. The hunter groaned, his body jerking violently. White light burst from the center of his chest, and he unleashed a horrible scream that made me jump, my skin and bones trembling in horror. I stepped forward, my hand outstretched, but I wasn't sure why. What could I do? But that scream... It was full of terror and anguish, a sound I never expected to come from a hardened warrior like Theron.

It shook me to my core. And as much as I hated him, I never wanted to hear that sound again.

The pixies seemed unaffected. They merely looked on with mild disinterest as if this were an everyday occurrence. I pressed a hand to my chest as the scream went on, shutting my eyes against the sound. But it burned in my ears, searing right through me.

The white light vanished. It was likely only a few seconds, but the duration of that cry made it feel like an eternity. When Theron went limp again, there was more color in his face. Only when silence fell among the pixies did I realize I was gasping for breath, my heart racing.

"Our magic isn't for the faint of heart," said the pixie next to me, a tall, wiry woman with bright pink hair and emerald skin. She winked at me conspiratorially as if we were sharing a joke.

"Your companion is healed!" Nyra announced, and the pixies all cheered.

"Is he all right?" I asked the emerald pixie beside me. Theron still looked limp and unconscious.

"Oh, he'll be fine." The pixie waved a hand. "He's healed, but he'll need to recover from the intensity of the spell."

I nodded numbly. As much as I didn't like the idea of spending the night with pixies, perhaps it was for the best if Theron was in too poor a shape to travel.

"I'll go check in with Mauro," Frisk said.

"Wait." I turned toward him.

He looked at me, his black eyes appraising me with curiosity. "What?"

"I—thank you. For bringing us here. For negotiating with the queen. I know that wasn't easy."

"Anything for you, Snow. Don't get into too much trouble while I'm gone. No more fae bargains, understand?"

I chuckled as he trotted away, his white tail bobbing until he disappeared in the crowd of pixies. Suddenly exhausted, I moved closer to the colorful fire and sank onto a log, my eyes pulled in by the explosion of colors.

"I'm here, Snow," whispered a voice in my ear. "Please don't be mad."

I closed my eyes, relief filling me as I turned to find Kendra tucked in my cloak, her tiny form balled up on my shoulder.

"I had to keep an eye on that hunter," she went on.

I smirked. *"Right."* With an exhale, I shook my head. "You need to be careful around him, Kendra. You can't trust him."

"He hid me from the pixies," she whispered in astonishment. "He ensured I wouldn't be seen."

My frown deepened. Yes, that didn't make sense to me. What had Theron been playing at? Was he trying to get Kendra on his side? Or did he have some other motive?

"Just stay out of sight," I muttered, as Brune, the orange-skinned pixie approached me. Obediently, Kendra burrowed herself deeper into my cloak.

"Refreshment for you." Brune shoved a platter into my hands. Startled, I accepted it, scrutinizing the sizzling meat alongside leafy vegetables and bright purple berries.

"Um," I said uneasily. "What kind of meat is this?"

Brune flashed his sharp teeth. "Best I not answer that, princess, since I cannot lie."

I shuddered as he bounded away, then steeled myself and inhaled deeply. Whatever meat it was, it smelled heavenly. I took a tentative bite, and an explosion of flavor caressed my tongue, the spices and seasonings making me groan with pleasure.

"Shivering bones, this is delicious," I said to no one in particular. I glanced around and found the emerald pixie smirking at me. "This isn't human flesh, is it?"

She laughed. "No. It's wyvern. Brune was just trying to scare you."

"Wyvern? Really?" I looked up as if expecting the dragon-like creature to screech and fly overhead. Kendra uttered a tiny gasp from my shoulder, and I felt her squirming. I couldn't tell if it was out of curiosity or fear. I wagered she had never met a wyvern before. I certainly hadn't.

"Oh, yes. They often dwell in mountains like these. The tenderest meat you can find. We wouldn't dare touch the fae breeds, but the feral ones aren't smart enough to dodge our traps."

"I see. And, uh, do you eat... dragon?" I tried to sound nonchalant. Kendra's trembling intensified.

"Certainly not," the pixie said haughtily. "Dragons are sentient, majestic creatures. We would never slaughter them for meat."

"Oh." I cleared my throat and sat up straighter. Kendra stopped shaking, clearly appeased by this response. "How long have you lived here?"

"A few hundred years," said the pixie.

I nodded, unperturbed. Though I was half human and wouldn't have as long a lifespan, I was accustomed to being around immortal creatures. "So do only *some* pixies eat humans, or what?" I took another bite of the wyvern meat and groaned again.

"Some do. But we do not associate with them. We believe

sentient species should be preserved." She flashed her teeth in a grin. "Even one as feeble as humans."

I shrugged one shoulder. "We are pretty feeble."

The pixie's eyes widened, and then she laughed before sinking to the log beside me. "I like you, princess. It's not often we meet humans who surprise us so."

"Well, I'm only half human, so that's probably it."

"Probably." The pixie crossed one leg over the other, her pale green wings quivering behind her. "My name is Sage."

"Eira."

"I know."

I shrugged again and took another bite.

"I knew your father."

The meat stuck in my throat, and I choked. After hacking and coughing, I finally spat the piece onto the ground and whirled to stare at Sage. "You *did*?" As far as I knew, pixies were a wild species who didn't mingle with the seelie or the humans.

Sage nodded, her smile vanishing. "He was a kind person. One of the few seelie who treated me with respect. We were discussing a negotiation between our kind, and I was to be ambassador for the pixies."

My heart lurched at this revelation. I'd had no idea.

Sage fixed her intense black eyes on me. "I think that's why my queen believed your claim. Not because of the blood bargain—but because you are your father's child. If anyone can unite the seelie with the unseelie, it's you."

My eyes burned with tears, and a hard lump formed in my throat. Blood and ice, I missed my father. He had done so much for our kingdom.

I shook my head faintly. "I don't know about that. Thousands of years of prejudice can't be erased overnight. But I'll certainly do my best."

"King Judas believed it could be done. And if it weren't for that wretched harpy he married, he might have accomplished it."

"My father was a well-respected full-blooded fae," I said. "Perhaps I could have earned the respect of the people for being his daughter, but once he died, Calista made it quite clear my human blood tarnished whatever claim I had to the throne."

Sage cocked her head at me. "You fear her."

I whipped my head toward her. "What?"

"The queen. You fear her, don't you?"

I swallowed, my appetite gone as I stared vacantly at the platter on my lap. "Of course I do," I whispered. "Who wouldn't fear a fae who has power over blood?"

"But you can do this trick again, can't you?" Sage gestured to where Nyra stood chatting with a few other pixies. "With your blood?"

I huffed a hollow laugh. "I'm afraid it's not that simple. This was more of a parlor trick. But the magic of the queen is quite literal. If she has my blood, nothing will stop her from wielding power over me."

Sage leaned forward, her black eyes glittering. "Then you must wield power over her first."

I would have laughed or rolled my eyes at the incredulity of that statement... if it weren't for the intensity in Sage's hardened gaze. Her expression was so full of fiery determination and harshness that all laughter died in my throat.

She was serious.

And perhaps she had a point.

I knew Calista better than anyone. She may have

distanced herself from me as soon as she'd assumed the throne. She may have despised and spit on me, but she'd still been my stepmother.

"If blood has power," Sage said slowly, "then you should seize it."

I blinked at her, my mouth falling open as realization clicked into place.

Calista's blood. If *she* could control a person with one drop of their blood... did that mean I could do the same with hers?

The Hunter

I felt as if I'd been trampled by a dozen stallions. It wasn't quite as painful as the slice of a Demon Fae's claws, but it was pretty damn close.

Groaning, I sat up, then winced from the sharp throbbing in my head. Shivering bones, this headache was worse than the hangovers I'd get from faerie wine, back when I spent every night drinking myself into a stupor. That had been just after—

I shut that thought down. *You aren't allowed to think about those years. Remember?*

I still drank human spirits, which weren't nearly as strong as faerie wine. But the wine of my folk could only be taken in small doses. Faerie wine didn't keep one's wits very well, and without my wits, I'd be dead.

I was in some sort of small circular cave filled with cots and several piles of blankets and quilts. A dozen lights shone from the ceiling, glistening in purples and blues and greens. It didn't take long for the memories to come flooding back.

The pixies. The princess. Her strange trickery with the blood bargain.

"Shit," I muttered, staggering to my feet and clutching at my head again. Blood and ice, that pixie magic was a *bitch*.

But I had to get up. If the princess had fled because I'd passed out, I would never forgive myself.

A quick glance over my body had me cursing again. I'd been so sloshed I hadn't even woken when someone had bathed me. I no longer reeked of Demon Fae blood, and I was wearing a fresh tan tunic and brown trousers. My daggers were resting on the ground by my cot. The pixies must have retrieved them from where I'd dropped them in the snow. Shaking off the disorientation, I clumsily strapped the knives to my belt and snatched the fur coat left for me next to my bed.

Head still spinning, I stumbled past the empty cots along the cave floor and made my way out into the snow. The bitter cold nipped at my skin, but it was far better than the blizzard from the night before. At least the wind was gone, and there were no flurries to blur my vision.

As soon as I stepped out of the cave, I sucked in a sharp breath. With the air clear, I could see *everything* from this high up. Several mountain peaks formed a ridge line that descended until it met the gleaming pearly spires of the Taerin palace. The surrounding villages were capped with snow, and in the distance, I could make out the Gray Lake, which was frozen solid. Its marble surface reflected the sun's light.

The Winter Court was breathtaking. I often forgot that.

"Ah, he lives," grunted a familiar voice.

Mauro the stag rose to his feet. He must have been resting just outside the cave.

My eyes narrowed. "Were you standing guard?" As if I were some sort of prisoner.

Mauro huffed. "We couldn't have you running away in the dead of night, now, could we?"

I rolled my eyes. "If I came all the way to Knockspur to find the princess, what makes you think I would just flee when she's still here?" I paused. "She *is* still here, isn't she?" I hated how vulnerable my voice sounded and wished I could take the words back.

Mauro snorted as if laughing at me. "Of course she's here. She's just down the slope with the pixies."

My mouth fell open. Eira was with the pixies? And Mauro was perfectly fine leaving her there with them? Nyra might have bargained to refrain from harming the princess, but pixies were tricksters. There were plenty of ways they could get around that.

Without another word, I descended the slope, pausing frequently to steady myself along the slippery ice. Faint music resonated from downhill, no doubt from the pixies' revelry. When I rounded the corner, I stopped.

A vibrant, jaunty tune was playing from some instruments I couldn't see, and the entire crowd of pixies was dancing around the colorful fire still blazing in the center of the plateau.

It didn't take me long to spot the princess. She stood almost a foot shorter than the pixies, and her pale skin was like a translucent beacon amidst the colorful shades of the pixies' flesh. She was near the fire, her body twisting and turning in rhythm to the music. Her arms lifted above her head, her wavy black hair tossed about with her movements. She had washed and changed out of her blood-stained clothes. Now she wore a light blue tunic with a leather corset cinched around the middle, her sleeves flowing and free.

Leather riding pants hugged her legs, accentuating her curves. Especially when she danced.

A wide smile lit her features, making her almost unrecognizable. I'd seen her smile, of course, but not like *this*. Not this expression of freedom and release, without a care in the world. The grins I'd elicited from her had been calculated and taunting, like a mask she wore to protect herself.

But *this* was the true Eira. The persona she didn't want me to see.

I stood there, momentarily caught off guard. I begrudgingly had to admit that this infuriating princess had surprised me. Not just in outwitting me, but in facing the Demon Fae head-on and risking her life in a bargain to save mine.

She was nothing like what I'd imagined. When Calista had described her wayward stepdaughter, I'd expected a spoiled, belligerent princess intent on dividing the court and wreaking havoc. But here she stood, dancing among the pixies as if they were her dearest friends. Somehow, despite marching into a tribe that would see her as an enemy, she had turned them into allies.

And damn, she looked beautiful.

"Like what you see, hunter?" drawled a voice.

I sighed and turned to find Frisk grinning slyly at me. Beside him, Kendra was gobbling up a handful of berries and paying us no attention.

My face flushed. "Why are you still here?" I asked the fox.

"I'll never leave Snow's side," he said, lifting his chin in determination.

"I mean why are you and the *princess* still here? Why haven't you left yet?"

"She has a bargain to fulfill." Frisk's whiskers twitched.

"Much as I hate that she is tethered to you, of all people, Snow never goes back on her word."

"If she's fae, it's because she has no choice," I muttered.

"You know it's more than that," Frisk snapped. "She didn't have to make a bargain to rescue your sorry ass, you know. That's twice now she's saved your life."

"Twice?" I laughed.

"Yes, twice. She killed the Demon Fae, didn't she?"

The smile slipped from my face, leaving a scowl in its place. I hated that Frisk was right. To be fair, she wouldn't have been able to kill the creature without my help. But saying that now would only sound childish.

"We'll need to get moving if we're to make it down the mountains before the next blizzard hits," I said.

Frisk chittered. "Good luck telling *her* that." He jerked his head toward Eira.

My brows knitted together in confusion. What was that supposed to mean? Shaking my head, I turned and made my way toward the crowd of pixies. A few parted to let me pass, but most of them were unperturbed by my presence. One tall, pink pixie even drew close enough to grind against my backside, her giggles echoing in my ears. It took all of my restraint not to bury my dagger in her thigh. I figured such an action wouldn't be well received.

I reached the princess just as she twirled into my arms. Instinctively, I caught her against my chest, and she laughed loudly, raising her face to meet mine. I waited for her expression to fall when she met my gaze, but instead, her eyes brightened, and she leaned into me. "Hunter! You're alive!" Her hips swayed, and she draped her arms over my shoulders, urging me to move with her.

I stared at her as if she'd grown three heads. What the hell was she doing? "Are you drunk?"

She laughed loudly. *Far* too loudly. A few pixies around her cheered in response. "Nonsense. I've only had one drink."

Warning bells clanged in my mind. My gaze snapped to an emerald-skinned pixie I recognized from last night. "What did you give her?"

The pixie flashed her teeth at me. "Only a bit of Winterwing Brew. It's our finest drink."

Shit. *Shit.* "She's part human," I growled.

The pixie laughed and twirled elegantly in time with the music. "I assure you, she is reacting quite normally to the brew." She began grinding against another pixie, who moaned with delight.

I swallowed hard, glancing over the crowd with fresh eyes. Every single pixie not only seemed enthralled by the music, bodies moving in perfect rhythm, but they also seemed... exceptionally aroused. A pair of females had their legs wrapped around each other, their wings keeping them afloat as they writhed together. Next to me, the emerald pixie began groping the one next to her, hands moving to the taut hardness between his legs.

My skin suddenly felt hot as Eira's hips met mine with more force. "*Dance,* hunter," she ordered.

I gripped her wrists and pulled them away from my shoulders. I was suddenly achingly aware of how heated her body felt against mine. "Eira, we don't have time for this."

Her lower lip puckered in a frown. "Of course we do. Don't be such a grump." She lifted our joined hands and twirled so her back was to my chest, then draped my arms around herself, tightening my grip on her. Shivering bones, the feel of her ass grinding against me...

I gritted my teeth, looking around the crowd to see if anyone was paying close attention to us. Every pixie seemed consumed by their own dancing, but I had a feeling if I lifted Eira into my arms and carried her off, it would cause a disturbance. Especially if she screamed. I definitely didn't want to anger these pixies, particularly if they were inebriated by... whatever was in their Winterwing Brew.

With a growl, I gripped Eira's arms tightly and whispered in her ear, "Would you come with me?"

She suppressed a shiver, leaning her head against me with a low moan. "Blood and ice, I love the sound of your voice."

I frowned. Even when drunk, fae still had to tell the truth. Did this still apply with the strange brew Eira had consumed?

"If you... come with me," I said hesitantly, feeling completely idiotic, "I can speak like this some more."

What the bloody hell was I doing?

To my surprise, Eira turned to face me, her eyes dark with desire. "Promise you'll growl in that low, *deep* voice of yours?"

My mouth twisted in disgust, but I tried to arrange my features into something neutral. "Um. Yes. I promise."

Surely, I could just growl a string of curses to fulfill this bargain later. But for now, I needed to extract her from this crowd as subtly as possible.

Eira squealed and clapped her hands together, then tugged on my arm to pull me away from the crowd.

Thank the gods.

I hurried by her side, trying to ignore the way her fingernails dug into my bicep, as if she was trying to feel her way around my muscle.

"So strong," she murmured, massaging my arm.

I recoiled but allowed her to keep hold of my arm, if only because it got us out of the crowd more quickly.

I found Frisk right where I'd left him. His lips spread, baring his teeth in what looked like a smug grin.

"How could you let her drink that brew?" I demanded.

Frisk barked a laugh. "How could I not? I certainly wouldn't be the one to get in the way of these pixies sharing their merriment with her."

"What did Snow drink?" Kendra asked, her white snout stained pink from the berries she'd eaten.

Ignoring her, I said to Frisk, "She's part human! You have no idea what it could do to her! She was sullying herself with that crowd of pixies."

Frisk's eyebrows lifted. "Sullying herself?" His dark gaze roved over Eira with interest. "Get ahold of yourself, hunter. She's still dressed, isn't she? She was only dancing."

Eira wriggled against me, pressing her chest to mine. I gave Frisk a pointed look. "I think there's a bit more than *dancing* on her mind."

Frisk chittered with delight.

"This isn't funny!" I snapped, trying to ignore the way Eira's breasts were pushing up against me. Gods, this was driving me *mad*.

"It's a bit funny," Frisk argued. At the sight of my glare, he rolled his eyes. "She'll be fine, hunter. It wears off eventually."

"Whisper some naughty things in my ear," Eira breathed, grinding against me.

I bit back a loud curse as Frisk laughed. Grabbing Eira's hand again, I steered her back toward the cave where I'd woken up.

Mauro was fast asleep right outside the entrance. "Useless fae beast," I muttered before practically shoving Eira inside.

She took one look around the messy cave, then proceeded to undo her corset strings.

"Shit!" I snatched her hands. My face was on fire. "What the hell are you doing?"

She blinked at me, her eyes wide and innocent. "Isn't this what you wanted? Why else would you want me alone?" She worked one hand free and slid it under my tunic, her fingertips exploring the planes of my chest. Her touch was featherlight, and a jolt of electricity shot through me.

I took a step back and groaned. "Eira. This isn't you. You need to wake up before you do something you'll regret." I could only imagine her horror and disgust. She would be *appalled* at what she was doing right now.

"Blood and ice, you're so *handsome* when you're angry." She was shifting her tunic down her shoulders. Her corset slid, revealing a generous amount of cleavage.

I fixed my gaze just above her hairline, determined not to stare. "Eira. You have a bargain to uphold, remember? We need to get to the Winter Palace."

"Surely we have a few minutes, don't we?" She was drawing closer to me. I tried pulling away from her, but a wall of hard rock met my back. "Look at me, Theron."

I wasn't sure if it was the command or the usage of my name, but I couldn't stop my eyes from meeting hers. My breath caught at the spark of energy dancing around her irises. She stood on her toes, pressing her breasts against me. Her full lips parted slightly.

"Tell me you don't want me," she murmured.

"I—" My mouth clamped shut, because damn, I *did* want her. She looked positively radiant right now, her hair wild, her tunic partially undone. She was gorgeous; I couldn't deny it.

But this was a mistake. Regardless of how attractive I found her, she was still loathsome.

"I don't want to do this," I said, my voice ragged. "Not right now. Not like this."

All truth. If, in some bizarre, parallel universe, Eira and I were ever to tangle romantically, I would want her to be completely lucid. Dallying with women who weren't of sound mind wasn't something that appealed to me.

"Eira..." I broke off with a sigh as she angled her face up to meet mine. Just one more inch, and I would be able to taste her soft lips. My eyes closed as I tried to focus on speaking, instead of the straining hardness in my trousers. Eira could feel it, too. She began rubbing herself against it, and I suppressed a moan.

"I want you to pin me against this cave wall," she whispered, her breath tickling my face. "I want you pounding into me so hard I forget my own name."

A strangled sound escaped me, and I had to close my eyes. "You don't want that," I said in a strained voice.

"Why not?" Eira asked, tilting her head at me in curiosity.

I put my hands on her bare shoulders and backed her up a step, my lungs straining to get enough air. "Because," I forced out, "if I were to take you against this cave wall, you wouldn't remember it at all."

Her brows knitted together in confusion.

"If we were to do this, I'd want to make sure you remember every blissful second of it," I said softly. "I'd want you to *remember* that it was the brutal assassin who made you cry out and beg for more. Not some stranger you happen to find attractive."

Eira's breath hitched, and her cheeks turned pink.

"There's that gloriously husky voice of yours again." She leaned in, and I turned my face away just before her lips made contact. She ended up kissing my cheek, but I was still utterly consumed by the gentle touch of that mouth on my skin.

Shivering bones, this woman would be the death of me.

"Promise me," she whispered against my cheek.

"Promise… what?" I grunted.

"Promise you'll kiss me at another time. A time when I'm myself again."

I blinked rapidly, unable to clear the foggy haze from my head. What was she asking? Shit. I couldn't do this…

"I—"

"Yes?" she prompted.

"I promise," I said through clenched teeth.

"Promise what? Say the words, Theron."

"I… will kiss you. At some point. In the future."

She withdrew slightly, a smile curving her lips. "Good. Now help me with this corset." She turned around, and I froze at the sight of her half-done strings.

"Um. What?"

"If we aren't doing this right now, I'd prefer to be fully clothed. It's quite chilly."

My eyes closed, and I practically slumped against the wall in relief. Thank the gods. She wanted me to *tie* them. Not undo them. My hands shook as I obliged, pulling on the strings.

"Harder," she ordered.

I went rigid at the command in her voice, unable to stop myself from imagining a very different scenario in which she would say that word. I bit down on the inside of my cheek, focusing on that point of pain, then tugged on the strings tighter. She grunted slightly as I continued to tighten them, then tied them off at the end.

"More," she muttered, her voice slightly slurred.

I frowned. "That's it. It's done."

She murmured a garbled strand of something unintelligible. Before I could ask what the hell she was talking about, she slumped backward against me. I caught her and rolled my eyes. "What now?"

Eira said nothing. Her body was completely limp.

Shit. "Eira? Eira!" I fumbled, turning her around to face me. Her expression was slack, her eyes half closed. I patted her cheek, and she blinked, her eyelids fluttering.

"Wine," she mumbled, her head lolling. "Sweet berries."

My brow furrowed. "What?"

She grumbled something else incoherent, her body tilting toward me. I caught her by the shoulders and shook her roughly. "Eira, *wake up!*"

She drew in a sharp gasp, eyes flaring wide. Squinting in confusion, she rubbed her temples. "*Blood and ice.* What the hell was in that drink?"

I stilled. "Eira?" I asked hesitantly.

She jumped, then turned her head to look at me with a befuddled expression. "*Theron?* What—where are we?" She jerked out of my grasp, staring around the cave in confusion. "What did you do to me?" Her eyes narrowed.

I almost laughed. Oddly enough, I preferred to be around the Eira who hated me instead of the Eira who wanted to pin me to the wall and kiss me. My face still heated from the thought.

"You drank some Winterwing Brew," I said, rubbing the back of my neck. "One of the pixies gave it to you."

Eira's eyes closed, and she rubbed her head again. "Gods, that hurts. How did I even get here?"

"I pulled you from the crowd. I was afraid you'd do something you would regret."

Eira squinted at me, her brow furrowing. "And... did I?"

I didn't answer.

Her eyes widened, and she placed a hand on her hip. "Theron, *did I?*"

I cleared my throat and dropped my gaze. "You... made advances. On me."

Eira's face slackened in shock. Then she covered her face with her hands. "Holy gods."

I chuckled. "It wasn't that bad. It was only for a few minutes."

To my surprise, she punched me in the arm. It wasn't very hard, but it was enough to make me stumble back in surprise.

"Bastard," she muttered.

"It wasn't my fault!"

"Right. And I'm sure it was *so* difficult for you to endure my flirting. You poor thing." She rolled her eyes, but she couldn't hide the blush creeping into her face.

I said nothing as she turned away from me with a noise of frustration. I couldn't exactly respond to her.

Not without telling her exactly *how* difficult it had actually been for me. Or how we had struck another bargain.

No, those words were better left unsaid.

The Princess

My head hurt like hell. I could only remember short snippets of the morning. Merriment, drinking, dancing... It was all a blur.

But one thing was certain: there was an aching, burning *need* throbbing between my legs that hadn't been there before.

And, regardless of how frustrated I was with him, the timbre of Theron's low growl only made that ache worsen.

After our awkward incident in the cave, Theron and I quickly packed our things to continue our journey through the mountains. We rejoined Frisk, Mauro, and Kendra and bade the pixies farewell. Theron begrudgingly thanked them for healing him, and I promised I would be in touch with Nyra regarding relations between our people.

Assuming I survived long enough to do so.

The weight of Calista's mirror hung heavily in my bag, and I was itching to pull it out and see the truth.

But I couldn't. Not with Theron watching my every move.

The steep, slippery slope was too treacherous for us to ride Mauro, so we continued on foot. Thankfully, we were so focused on trying not to slip and fall to our deaths that there was little time for chitchat. My face was still on fire from what had happened with Theron, and I felt his dark eyes drilling holes into me, despite how I avoided his gaze.

I was hopeful we would continue our journey in silence, but half an hour after we left the pixies, Theron disappointed me.

"I, uh, owe you thanks," he said gruffly. "For bargaining for me."

I blinked, frowning. I hadn't expected that. When I turned to glance at him, his eyes were fixed on the ice beneath him. A wrinkle formed between his brows.

Then, I understood. He was feeling awkward, too. Perhaps this was an olive branch, of sorts. An opportunity for conversation that *wasn't* awkward.

I could handle that.

"Yes, well, I can't fulfill my terms with you if you're dead, now, can I?" I asked, breathless from the climb.

"If I die, our bargain is nullified." There was a note of confusion in his voice.

"I still need you to get me into the palace."

"Ah, yes. This palace you grew up in and likely know all the passages leading into. And you need the help of *me*, the assassin everyone at the palace recognizes, to sneak you in without notice."

I shot him a glare. "What's your point?"

"I don't think you need me at all. I think you can get in yourself." He paused to take a breath as we maneuvered around a snowcapped boulder. "I think there's something else you need me for. Something you're not telling me."

I snorted, though my heart rate quickened at how much he had inferred. "Keep speculating, hunter. It doesn't matter why I need you. Just do your part so we can be finished with this."

Kendra shifted on my shoulder, her cold snout tickling my ear. "What do you think he means?" she whispered.

I gently flicked her. "Shh." I had no doubt Theron heard her question, which was more telling than she realized.

It meant I was keeping secrets from my friends. And judging by the spark in Theron's eye, he realized this, too.

"You all are so *slow*," Frisk grumbled. He lithely hopped from boulder to boulder without missing a beat.

"Not all of us have nimble paws," Mauro huffed. He was having the most difficult time, trailing behind me and Theron, his hooves sliding constantly over the slick ice. The poor stag didn't do too well on steep slopes. He was incredibly fast on flat land, but throw in a sharp incline and icy ground…

"Frisk, why don't you and Kendra scout ahead for us?" I asked, eager to distract them with a task.

Kendra huddled closer to my shoulder. "I don't want to."

"You're the only one who can fly," I argued.

"My wings are thin."

I sighed. "Fine. Stay curled up in my cloak and do nothing."

She exhaled, and a puff of icy air brushed against my cheek, making me shiver. After a moment, she eased out of my cloak and shook out her wings. They were thin and membranous—practically translucent. But I knew for a fact they could hold her weight in the air. She just didn't like flying.

"Ready, little one?" Frisk asked, his whiskers twitching.

"Don't call me that," Kendra said before taking off. She became a white blur in the air, and Frisk quickly vanished in the snow. I kept Kendra in my sights until she blended in with the white mountain, my heart lifting with relief.

"You worry about her," Theron observed.

My relief faded, and irritation rose up in its place. "Stop trying to figure me out, Theron. It's annoying."

"I think it annoys you more that you're giving yourself away so easily." Now he sounded amused.

I gritted my teeth and made no response. He couldn't argue with a silent opponent. Plus, with Frisk and Kendra scouting for us, hopefully the journey would be a bit more silent.

To my relief, Theron said nothing else. An hour passed as we climbed around icy rocks. My thighs burned from the constant strain of pivoting and trying to avoid slipping on ice. The wind picked up, stinging my nose and cheeks. I pulled my scarf tighter around myself, but the chilled air was relentless.

When Mauro's labored breathing turned into sharp wheezes, we stopped to rest. I pulled out a waterskin and poured some into Mauro's mouth. He greedily gulped it down, and I ensured he had a healthy amount before I drank from my own.

"How did you escape the blood bargain?" Theron asked suddenly. He had already drunk from his waterskin and was staring at me with accusation in his eyes.

I blinked innocently at him while leaning against a boulder to give my legs some relief. "I beg your pardon?"

"Don't play games with me, princess. How did you do it?"

I narrowed my eyes at him. *Play games with you? I saved your life, you ass. So stop interrogating me for answers you haven't earned."

He gaped at me, stunned. Good. He deserved to be

thrown off his high horse every now and then. I took another sip of water.

"If we are to travel together," he said, speaking slowly, "then I need to know how you are able to defend yourself."

"Do you?" I challenged. "Do you need to know? Because as far as I'm concerned, making your job difficult is far more appealing than disclosing all my secrets to you."

Fury burned in his gaze. "You can't—"

"I don't owe you anything, hunter," I spat, pushing off the boulder to stride toward him. I'd prepared for this interrogation and refused to let him win. "You came into a human village—*my* village—intent on killing me. The only reason I'm not dead is because I tricked you, so don't pretend like you're looking out for my safety out of the goodness of your heart."

"And who can blame me?" Theron spread his hands, his expression darkening. "You're exiled for a reason, princess. You're trying to cause a civil war. I heard you declare your intention to steal the throne from the queen. If I killed you, all this would stop. There would be peace in this court at last."

"Peace?" I cried out. "You talk to me of peace? The only ones at peace are those under Calista's thumb, the privileged fae she deems more elite than others. Fae like you. But what about everyone else? What about the half fae, like me? What about the humans? The unseelie? Like those pixies. They aren't savages. They deserve a free life, just like you. Would you take that away from them?"

Theron shook his head, baring his teeth in anger. "And you think throwing a fit will get you what you want? Riots and thievery aren't doing your court any good, either."

My head reared back. "Riots? What the hell are you talking about?"

"Don't play dumb. You've been wreaking havoc since you left Taerin, leaving carnage in your wake."

"I have *not*!" I was prepared to rip his throat out, then faltered. If he was saying these things, it meant he believed them to be true. He couldn't lie. My anger ebbed slightly. "What has Calista been saying about me?"

His mouth opened and closed. My abrupt shift had no doubt disoriented him. "What?"

"She told you all that, did she? Or rather, she implied it." I hissed out a breath and rubbed my forehead. Blood and ice, I should have guessed this would happen. Calista would never allow the court to think I was simply a poor, shunned princess. Of course not. She would vilify me, do all she could to paint a picture that I was the enemy she was protecting everyone from. "I've stolen, yes, but only from her coffers. Nowhere else. I…"

I deflated, my ire vanishing and leaving exhaustion and despair in its place. How was I supposed to win the court back when they believed I was a rogue, a criminal causing pain and suffering wherever I went?

"What did Calista say, exactly?" I asked in a tired voice.

"She said your latest exploits left the village of Raya burned to the ground."

My blood chilled. "She—She burned Raya to the ground?" My voice was a hushed whisper.

Theron stared at me, his brows furrowing. "Eira, what are you saying? Are you telling me you *didn't* do this?"

"Of course not!" Tears pricked my eyes, and I struggled to catch my next breath. "Raya… was where the human nobles and I last congregated. Calista's men found us, and we fought our way out. But I swear to the gods, when we left, the village was still intact. Calista—she must've... Blood and ice." A tear trickled down my cheek, and I impatiently wiped it away. A roar of rage built up in my throat, and I clenched my fingers into tight fists, my nails carving small crescents into my palms.

I needed to hit something or I would explode. I whirled on the hunter, who stared at me with a stricken expression.

He would make a nice target for my wrath.

"And who are you to fling accusations at me?" I snapped. "You're Calista's right-hand man! You do all her dirty work. Tell me, how many have you killed in her name? Does it bring you joy, to do such bloody work for a false queen?"

His fury returned, and he took a threatening step toward me. "You don't know anything."

"Neither do you, apparently, if you're swallowing the lies she's spewing about me."

"You aren't a fool, princess, so don't pretend to be. What is your dear stepmother's brand of magic?"

I scoffed and rolled my eyes. "What, are you quizzing me?"

"Answer the damn question."

"Blood magic," I growled.

"And how does she wield it?"

"All she needs is a person's blood and she can control them."

Theron lifted his eyebrows and fixed a flat stare at me.

Only then did the pieces click into place.

My heart dropped to my stomach. "She has your blood."

He huffed a dry laugh. "No shit, princess." He turned and draped his leather jacket over his arm. "Looks like we're both victims of Calista's scheming."

I didn't know what to say to that. It certainly didn't make Theron innocent; he was still a cold-blooded killer.

But he was under her control. Were his actions, his *words*, even his own? Was he reporting everything back to her?

My mind turned to the contents of my pack... and one item in particular that no one, not even my friends, knew about. What if Theron had seen it? What if he'd told Calista?

What if he found out about my condition? Did that mean Calista knew, too? Did she know I would die soon?

"Wipe that panicked look off your face," Theron grumbled. "I am perfectly lucid right now. She can only control me when she summons me."

"So, why hasn't she summoned you?" I asked, suddenly suspicious.

"She won't waste precious blood droplets unless she absolutely has to. It's the same reason she doesn't use my blood to *force* me to fulfill my assignments."

I scoffed at that. "No, you're just a killer by choice."

His lethal gaze shot to me, ire burning in his expression. "I didn't choose this, princess." And there was something so haunting about his voice that I had no reply to that. "At any rate, I'm still required to strike fae bargains with every assignment. It's how she keeps me in check. But she wouldn't dare use my blood to spy on me night and day. Of course, with every passing hour, she'll be wondering where I am, so there's no telling what she'll do."

I turned to glance at Mauro, who had been watching the exchange silently, his dark eyes alert. "We should keep moving," he said slowly. "Especially if the false queen is bound to call on you if you're delayed."

He was right, but I found I couldn't move. I felt like there was more to say to Theron, but I wasn't sure what. An apology? Condolences for his situation? How long had he been in Calista's employ? How long had he been forced to work for her with no way out?

"I don't want your pity," Theron snapped without looking at me.

My irritation returned. "It's not pity. Besides, I don't give a damn what *you* want, hunter."

"Obviously," he muttered.

His grumbling only incensed me further. "Gods, you are such a child."

He snorted. "*I'm* a child? You're like a toddler, with no reason or concept of danger. I've met goats with more sense than you."

In spite of the situation, I laughed. He whirled to look at me in incredulity. His expression was so bewildered that I only laughed harder. Something sparked in his eyes, an emotion I hadn't seen before, and it melted some of the tension between us.

"You're insane," he said slowly.

"I'm just picturing a goat... tricking you with... a fae bargain," I said between laughs, tears streaming from my eyes.

His brows knitted together, but that new emotion brightened his eyes. Something very close to amusement. "It would be far more preferable to our current arrangement."

"I doubt that. A goat can't possibly be as nice to look at as I am."

Theron rolled his eyes. "Far less of a torment, though."

"Ah, but tormenting you is such fun," I said brightly.

He groaned, but that same amusement lit up his face, making him almost unrecognizable. He looked so much... *younger*. Less burdened. His eyes seemed lighter instead of their usual coal-black. His brow was smooth and untroubled. "I've never encountered a target as thoroughly irritating as you, princess."

"I'll take that as a compliment."

"It's not."

"Have you two been like this the whole time?" asked a voice.

I glanced up to find Frisk standing in our path. Kendra was perched beside him, her gleaming blue eyes the only thing distinguishing her from the snow.

"Partially," Mauro grumbled in response.

"We have bad news," Kendra said, her wings twitching. "There's another blizzard approaching. A big one."

My heart sank. "Shit." I should have known from the way the wind intensified. The clouds were now a murky gray, darkening with each passing minute. I had been so distracted by my bickering with Theron that I hadn't noticed.

"How soon?" Theron's voice was sharp.

"Within the hour," said Frisk. "We need to find shelter. And fast."

The Hunter

The damn princess had distracted me. I was accustomed to traveling alone. If I were by myself, I never would have missed the signs of a blizzard.

It didn't help that the giant stag was slowing us down so much. On foot, I might have been able to make it back to the pixie caves before the blizzard hit. But with Eira and Mauro? Not a chance.

"Did you spot any caves nearby?" I asked Frisk, digging through my pack until I found my scarf. I wrapped it around my neck, ensuring it covered my face as much as possible.

"There's a small cavity about half a mile south," Frisk said. "It's not very wide, though, and it won't fit all of us."

"Don't worry about me," Mauro said. "My fur will protect me."

I cut a glance at the princess, who was shivering, her arms wrapped around herself. Her cloak wasn't doing very much to ward off the chilly wind.

She would die of frostbite before morning. Damn feeble humans.

I nodded at Frisk. "Show us the way."

The fox turned and hurried down the slope, his bushy

white tail bobbing behind him. I trailed after him, but Eira hesitated, her brows drawn in concern as she looked at Mauro.

"Go," he snapped. "I'll find my own shelter for the night and rendezvous with you after the storm."

"Mauro—" she said uncertainly.

I tugged on Eira's arm. "We have to go."

She jerked out of my grasp, shooting me a glare. "Don't touch me." With a huff, she strode past me, following after Frisk.

I bit back a curse, then gave Mauro one last parting glance. "Be safe."

He only grunted in response.

As much as I disliked my situation, I had no qualms with the stag. I didn't want him getting hurt.

I jogged to catch up with the Snow Princess. The white dragon was now perched on her shoulder, wings outstretched and trembling as if she might take off at any moment. Frisk's steps were quick and swift, and Eira kept cursing under her breath as she nearly slipped and fell at each turn. I kept grabbing her by the elbow to catch her before she fell on her ass.

After the third time, she seethed, "I said *don't touch me.*"

I released her arm, my brows raised at the note of hostility in her voice. "Fine."

A moment later, she slid. A yelp escaped her as her ass met the cold, hard ground. Just as I suspected.

I couldn't help but laugh. I offered a hand to help her up, but she smacked it away.

"Wipe that smirk off your face," she said as she clambered to her feet. "Stupid, smug assassin."

"Why are you so grouchy, anyway?" I asked, shoving my

hands deeper into my coat pockets. "Aren't you often annoyingly chipper?"

Her nostrils flared as she continued after Frisk, who lingered to allow us to catch up. "I don't like leaving Mauro behind," she muttered. "Besides, we might have outrun the storm if I—" Her mouth abruptly shut, and her face flushed.

"If you what?" I prompted.

Her eyes flashed, and she shot me a murderous look.

"If you… were faster?" I offered. "Taller? Less talkative? More nimble?"

She shoved my arm. "If I hadn't drunk the Winterwing Brew, asshole."

"Ah." I pressed my lips together, trying not to laugh at her again. Now that our roles were reversed, I could suddenly understand why my anger brought her so much pleasure. This was downright *delightful*. "Yes, I suppose flirting with me *would* seem like a poor use of your time when we have a storm to avoid."

This time, she struck me with a punch to the shoulder, but I barely felt it.

"It was quite entertaining, though," I went on, unable to hide my grin. "I wouldn't call it a waste of time on my end. I had never seen you *throw* yourself at someone like that."

She made a retching sound. "I would never. Not with the likes of you." Her lip curled as she gave me a look of utter disgust.

"Whatever you need to tell yourself, princess."

She turned to face me, eyes blazing. Before she could yell at me, Frisk announced, "It's right here."

I stopped short, my heart sinking. The cavity Frisk had led us to was indeed small. If anything, it was more of a small pocket of space underneath a particularly large boulder.

I worked my jaw in frustration as I considered our options. After a moment, I nodded to myself. "Let's get to work."

Eira glanced at me, then Frisk. "Who are you talking to?"

"Everyone." I unsheathed a knife from my belt and started hacking away at the ice near the boulder. "We need to build a barrier for the wind, and this pocket isn't big enough. Help me create a ridge surrounding this area, but don't dig too much underneath the boulder. We don't want to risk loosening it."

Frisk bounded forward, using his tiny paws to fling away chunks of ice and snow. Eira hesitated for a brief second before joining in, digging with her fingers. I showed them both how to pack the ice and ensure it provided a sturdy wall. When the cavity was wide enough for both me and Eira to crowd into, I scanned the skies. The wind had picked up, billowing around us. The sky was now a dark gray.

We were almost out of time.

A few leafless trees stood nearby. I reached up and grabbed two branches, then used twine from my pack to tie them together as a makeshift roof for our shelter.

"Will that hold?" Eira asked uncertainly, wiping sweat from her brow.

I shot a concerned look at her. "Take off your cloak."

Her mouth fell open. "Excuse me?"

"If you sweat in your cloak, you'll regret it when that blizzard hits. Trust me."

She huffed in exasperation but flung off her cloak.

I assessed our surroundings, chewing on the inside of my cheek. "All right. This will have to do. The shelter isn't big enough for a fire, unfortunately." I looked at Frisk, who was padding around the small crevice as if testing its boundaries. Kendra was nestled in Eira's cloak on the snowy ground.

"Will you two be all right during the storm?" I asked the animals.

"I'll be fine," Frisk said, lifting his head. "My fur is more than enough. I've weathered plenty of storms."

I nodded, then looked at Kendra. She huddled more tightly in Eira's cloak. "I don't feel the cold," she said in a small voice. "I'm a Crystal Icebolt."

I frowned. This didn't explain anything, as I was unfamiliar with dragon species. But, assuming she knew her own kind best, I nodded at this, too. "Good. You two stay close, but protect yourselves as best you can."

"Are we... not staying together?" Kendra's voice turned squeaky with apprehension.

"You're cold-blooded," I said. "If you curl up with Eira and me, you'll risk making us colder. And unfortunately, there's not a lot of room here." I gestured to the cavity.

"Surely, Kendra can stay," Eira argued. "She's quite small."

"No, it's fine." Kendra rose from Eira's cloak and spread her wings. "He's right. I don't want to make things more difficult for you. I'll stay with Frisk."

"I can keep her safe, Snow," Frisk promised. "I noticed a burrow nearby we can wriggle into if the storm gets too nasty."

Eira bit her lip, looking unconvinced.

"They are winter creatures," I told her. "Their bodies are built for survival."

She looked at me, eyes wide and full of fear. I expected her to glare or shoot a barbed insult my way. But right now, she was revealing her vulnerability.

She cared about these animals. Deeply.

The assassin in me should have perked up at this, immediately thinking of how I could use the fae creatures as leverage against her. How I should have tried that from the beginning.

But the cold heart within me throbbed with the realization that I didn't *want* to harm these creatures. They were innocent and clever.

And they weren't my target.

My hands were stained with the blood of so many. I didn't want to add any more lives than were necessary.

I drew closer to her, trying to convey the truth in my eyes. "I wouldn't say it if it weren't true, Eira. They will be all right."

She drew in a shaky breath, then nodded, swallowing hard. "Okay. Stay close, you two."

Kendra nodded, and Frisk chittered in response. In a flash, the two white creatures vanished in the snow.

Eira's breath hitched, and she quickly dashed a tear away from her cheek. Around us, the wind began to howl. Snow and ice stung my face.

"You'll need to undress," I told her curtly, already shedding my fur coat.

She went rigid. "What?"

"If we're going to survive this, you and I are going to have to be completely naked in that crevice." I jabbed a finger at the hole we'd created. "We're going to use our clothes as blankets to protect ourselves from the storm, and we're going to use our collective body heat to stay alive. This isn't a game. This isn't a night of passion. This is survival. Understand?"

Her lips grew thin, and her cheeks flushed a deeper shade of scarlet. Her eyes burned with indignation, and for a moment, I thought she would argue with me. I was fully prepared to shout at her until she complied, because we didn't have time for this.

But, to my surprise, she nodded stiffly and started taking off her clothes. I paid her no attention, focusing instead on undressing as quickly as possible. Each layer I removed left me colder than before, my body shivering and my bones rattling from the cold.

Just a few more moments, I told myself. *Just a few moments of discomfort, and it will be over.*

When I was fully naked, I hastily gathered up my clothing. I draped my fur coat on the snowy ground of the crevice, then lay on top of it.

I could hear Eira's teeth chattering. Her breath was labored with her movements. She was stepping out of her trousers, her pale skin slightly pink from the cold. I tore my gaze away from her naked form as she approached, her bundle of clothes tucked against her chest.

"As close as you can," I said without looking at her. When she made a noise of frustration, I said, "Survival, remember? The closer we are, the more heat our bodies will share."

"I'll bet you are just *loving* this right now," she seethed, climbing down to lay beside me. Her skin was icy, and she was still quivering from the cold.

I snorted. "Right. Because enduring a brutal storm with a woman I detest is *exactly* how I'd want to spend my night." I bit back a curse when Eira drew closer to me, the chill of her cold skin seeping into mine. Damn, she was frigid. I hadn't realized just how cold she really was.

When we were curled up as close as possible, I draped the remaining clothes over us, using our packs to tuck them in on all sides to block out the wind. I wrapped my arm around

Eira's shivering form and tugged her close so her back rested against my chest. Then, I pulled her cloak over our faces.

The wind was muffled, and underneath the layers of fabric, the outside world seemed far away. Out of reach. It was only our shallow breaths and the darkness of our makeshift cave.

For a long moment, we lay there quietly, the silence punctuated only by our breathing and the distant sounds of the storm.

"So, what would you have done if I wasn't here?" she whispered. "What if you had no one to curl up with during the storm?"

I hummed in contemplation as I considered this. "Ordinarily, I try to get underground. I've dug myself completely under the snow before. On my own, I can dig quite quickly." I paused before continuing, "But, truth be told, I'm usually a better planner than this. I try to stay ahead of the weather. This is… a unique circumstance."

"Because the Snow Princess got under your skin?" I could hear the smirk in her voice.

I exhaled a short laugh at that. "Indeed she did."

We were silent for a moment. The whistling wind sounded eerie, like the wailing souls of the damned.

"It didn't mean anything, you know," Eira said softly.

"What?"

"My flirting with you. It was just the brew."

I frowned. "I know that."

"And you were the only person of the same species as me. It was either throw myself at you, or throw myself at…"

"A pixie."

"Exactly."

She wriggled against me, and I was acutely aware of every

place her legs touched mine. Suddenly, my skin felt too warm. Too hot.

"So, whatever I did," she said, her voice getting softer. "Whatever I said... You just need to know. It wasn't really me."

"I know," I repeated. "Eira, I was only teasing you before because your reactions were amusing."

"Right. Of course."

We both fell silent again. I listened closely to the wind, trying to determine if it was getting stronger or fading out. I had no idea how long the storm would last. But so far, our clothes remained tucked around us. I felt the occasional bite of wind, but Eira's warmth was cocooned around me.

"So you weren't at all tempted?" she asked.

"What?"

"You weren't tempted to... *try* anything with me while I was drunk on that brew?"

I swallowed, my throat suddenly dry. *No, I wasn't,* I thought.

I wasn't tempted.

Not at all.

But the lie died on my lips. I could think it all I wanted, but it couldn't be spoken aloud.

I shifted slightly, then froze, painfully aware of how my arm rested against her bare breasts. Blood and ice, she was everywhere.

"I wasn't going to let anything happen," I said.

"Just tell me you weren't tempted, Theron," she said slyly. "Say the words."

I clenched my teeth so hard my head began to throb. "You were... very persuasive." I cleared my throat. "Perhaps, for a moment, I was tempted."

"Hmm." The amusement in her voice was clear. "Interesting."

"Is it?" I snapped. "I mean, it's as you said—it was either you, or those feral pixies. It's not outrageous that of every creature there, I found you the most attractive."

"Yes, well, *you* weren't drunk on Winterwing Brew. You had no reason for even *thinking* about physical attraction."

I fell silent at that, my nostrils flared and my blood roaring with indignation. *I did when you were pushed up against me in that cave,* I thought.

But saying those words would only make the situation worse.

"What do you think would have happened?" Eira breathed. "If you had drunk the brew, too?"

I stilled, my heart racing. If I *had* been stupid enough to drink that foul liquid—which was highly unlikely, as I swore to stay away from fae drinks—then...

I drew in a ragged breath as I let myself envision it for one dangerous moment. Eira and me, dancing in the crowd of pixies, our bodies entwined. Stumbling to the caves together, laughing as we shucked off our clothes. Pressing her against the cave wall, running my fingers along her soft skin. Kissing her. Tasting her. Thrusting into her so hard that I made her cry out my name, her fingernails digging into the bare skin of my back and shoulders...

Eira suddenly tensed beside me, and I snapped out of my delirious fantasy.

"Um, Theron?"

I didn't move an inch. In my chest, my heart raged a thunderous rhythm that would put the storm to shame.

"What?" My voice was husky.

"There's a—I think you—um…" Her leg shifted slightly, and then I knew *exactly* what she was referring to.

My hard cock was pressed fully against her leg. It would be impossible for her not to feel how erect it was.

"Shit."

She snorted. "Yeah."

My eyes closed as my face heated with embarrassment. "It's like you said, Eira. It means nothing. We're both naked together. My body reacts in a certain way around naked women. That's all."

"Sure." Her voice was full of amusement. I had the feeling she was trying very hard not to laugh.

Shivering bones, I wanted to disappear into the ground. No, I wanted the storm to blow away our coverings and dash me to pieces. I wanted the wind to carry me away into oblivion.

Eira giggled softly, then covered her mouth. "Okay," she said between chuckles. "I think we're even now."

I groaned, turning my head away from her. "Just… try to get some rest, princess. It'll be over soon."

"OH MY. HOW SCANDALOUS."

The soft voice jolted me from sleep. I blinked, bleary-eyed, squinting against the morning light that suddenly seemed far too bright. How had I slept through the rising sun?

I yawned, trying to stretch my arms in the bed... only to realize I wasn't in a bed at all.

Holy shit. In a rush, everything slammed into the forefront of my mind. The blizzard. The makeshift shelter. Cuddling *naked* with Theron.

Theron.

Blood and ice.

My body was draped completely over his. I had one leg wrapped around his waist and was half straddling him. He was still asleep, one muscled arm wrapped tightly around me with my face buried in his firm chest.

Completely naked. We were both *completely naked.*

And shivering bones, he was hard. *So* very hard. Just as hard as I'd felt him last night.

My face was on fire. I had to move. Had to get out before he woke up...

The voice from earlier snickered, and I glanced up, my heart racing.

Frisk and Kendra were peering at us through the shelter of branches Theron had made. Kendra looked shocked, but her wide blue eyes remained fixed on the pair of us tangled together as if she couldn't possibly look away.

Frisk looked smug. And I had a feeling he would be torturing me about this for years to come.

"Damn it all, Frisk, *look away!*" I hissed, flapping my free hand at him frantically. "I'm not even dressed, you disgusting thing!"

Frisk huffed, clearly offended by this. "What? It's not like *you* look away when I'm not wearing anything."

Theron grunted, his eyes flying open. His sleepy gaze shifted to me, and something warm stirred in the depths of his dark eyes.

Then, he uttered a strangled curse and wriggled away from me.

"Shit, shit, *shit.*"

Frisk snickered again. Kendra laughed so hard she wheezed a blast of icy air.

"Go find Mauro!" I barked at them. I just wanted my friends *away* from here. At least until I could get some clothes on. And put a healthy distance between myself and the hunter.

"He's here." Kendra tilted her wing to the left. "He didn't want to get too close."

"Well, at least *one* of you has some decency," I grumbled, shoving my way out of the warm crevice... and then immediately regretting it. The wintry air encircled my bare skin, making my flesh pebble and a shiver ripple over me.

Holy hell, it was *cold*. Teeth chattering, I fumbled for the first recognizable piece of clothing I could find. My arms were shaking. My whole body was numb with cold.

It took several minutes for me to dress, thanks to my numb fingers. It only made me feel a fraction of relief to know that Theron was also struggling. His cheeks and nose were red, and his hands shook even worse than mine.

Once I was clothed, I turned and found Kendra and Frisk grinning. All relief fled from me, and I scowled at them. "Hope you enjoyed the show."

"We did, thank you," Frisk said, unabashed.

"We just wanted to make sure you were still alive in there," Kendra said softly, half hiding her face under her wing.

I rubbed the back of my neck, face still hot as I recalled how *intertwined* my body had been with Theron's. Swallowing hard, I glanced at my friends. Kendra's eyes shone with genuine worry.

I sighed, my anger ebbing slightly. "I understand. Thanks for being concerned. Did you two make it through the storm all right?"

"Oh, yes," Frisk said. "*And* we didn't have to cuddle to do it."

"Shut it," I snapped, my stomach fluttering.

"I mean, we *were* rather close in that burrow," Kendra said slyly.

I chuckled, glad the dragon was on my side. "And Mauro?"

"I was able to bed down in a thicket," came Mauro's deep voice from a few feet away.

A wad of fabric hit my face. With a yelp, I reached up to remove it, realizing it was my cloak.

Theron had thrown it at me. His brow was furrowed, and

the usual frown was on his face. He wouldn't look me in the eye.

I couldn't necessarily blame him.

"I'll find us some breakfast," he said gruffly.

"Already done." Frisk tilted his head back. I followed his gaze and found two dead hares. One of them was frozen, frost coating its entire hide.

At my perplexed expression, Kendra said shyly, "I helped."

I gaped at her, then pointed to the frozen hare. "*You* did that? Damn, Kendra! That's a powerful blast."

She giggled, then buried her face behind her wing again.

"Fine," Theron said tersely, turning away from us. "I'll go look for firewood."

"What's wrong with him?" Mauro mumbled.

"He's annoyed by how attractive he finds me," I said loudly, enjoying the way Theron's shoulders tensed at my words. It helped to use humor to deflect my own embarrassment about the whole situation.

Frisk and Kendra laughed again.

The hunter stomped away from us, and I was all too eager to watch him leave. I couldn't keep my eyes from drifting to his backside.

No, Eira, stop it! I chided myself. Last night was a mistake that would not be repeated. And I wasn't allowed to look at him that way.

As the hunter disappeared, a new thought entered my mind. With him out of sight, perhaps I could finally delve into my pack and check Calista's mirror. It had been far too long since I'd looked.

I cleared my throat, glancing at Frisk, Mauro, and Kendra. "I'll... check for wood on the east side." I jerked my thumb in the direction opposite of where Theron had gone.

Thankfully, no one objected or asked any questions. I turned and headed toward the other side of the mountain, drumming my fingers along my leather trousers as I walked.

Just a few more steps.

I had to physically refrain from quickening my speed. I didn't want to arouse suspicion. And knowing Frisk, who could easily follow me without detection, he would want to know what I was hiding.

To keep up pretenses, I ducked under the branches of a tree, testing some of the fallen debris for anything dry. I would need firewood when I came back—to prove I hadn't been up to anything suspicious.

I counted to one hundred in my head, looking for wood all the while. I found a few good branches and cradled them in my arms before continuing my search.

After I counted to four hundred, I ducked behind a thick evergreen tree and dropped my branches, then hastily dug through the contents of my satchel. I cast aside a few sparkwood apples, spare clothes and daggers, and finally found the rolled-up towel. With shaking hands, I peeled the layers away to reveal my hidden treasures: the iron blade and the crystal hand mirror.

My breath caught in my throat at the sight of the mirror. It glinted innocently in the light of the rising sun, as if it were nothing more than an ornament. A piece of glass with an elegantly carved frame. An accessory for a princess.

But it was so much more than that.

Ensuring the iron blade didn't touch my skin, I eased the mirror off the towel and held it up to my face. All I saw was my own pale reflection staring back at me, my eyes wide with fear and my cheeks and nose pink from the chill. My wavy black hair was strewn messily about my face.

It was the reflection I knew well. But it was the magic lingering under the surface that I was most concerned with.

My breath shook as I whispered, *"Magic mirror, whose glass I see, reveal and reflect the truth unto me."*

The mirror quivered in my hand. Warmth spread from its handle, seeping into my palm and shooting up my arm. A white glow formed around the glass, shining so brightly I had to squint against it. My pulse raced as I waited.

The glow faded, and my reflection changed. Still the same woman, a scared and feral princess. But I had pointed fae ears. I now understood that this was how the mirror worked. It was revealing my true nature—as a half fae.

My skin was also no longer pale. It was covered in sickly green spots.

I swallowed down bile as I angled the mirror to inspect the rest of my body. Instead of showing my clothing, the mirror reflected the poison in my body.

It hadn't overtaken me completely yet. The juice from the sparkwood apples was keeping it at bay. There was truth in the myth that fae magic repelled the sparkwood trees. The opposite was also true: Sparkwood trees repelled fae magic.

Including the magic that had poisoned me when Calista had struck me with her claws.

One at a time, I lifted my hands to inspect them. One arm was covered in spots, but the other was not. And patches of my left cheek were still clear.

But that was it. The rest of me had been claimed by the poison.

I didn't have much time left. The apples weren't doing enough.

Tears pricked my eyes. If my father were alive, he would

be devastated. I thought of the pride in his eyes when he spoke about when I would become queen.

Now, that day might never come.

"Blood and ice," whispered a voice.

I yelped, jumping nearly a foot in the air and tucking the mirror behind my back. Frisk emerged from the brush, his dark eyes wide as he stared at me. "Snow, what happened to you?"

My heart still racing a mile a minute, I sighed in resignation. I should have known Frisk would follow me anyway. Even if I *hadn't* been hiding anything, he always liked to stay close.

"I'm dying," I whispered.

Frisk's head reared back. *"Dying?"*

"Shh!" I flapped my hand urgently, glancing around the wood to ensure the hunter wasn't lurking nearby. That was just what I needed, for the queen's assassin to learn all my secrets. "You were right, Frisk. There's a reason I haven't tried to get back to the castle. It's because even if I *can* seize the crown from Calista, I won't be able to rule for long."

Frisk sank back on his hind legs, his dark eyes pinned on the forest floor. For a moment, he had nothing to say, and I didn't want to fill the silence. There was too much to explain, and I couldn't do it here. Not with Theron close enough to eavesdrop.

It had been risky for me to pull out the mirror. But I had to know. If I was about to die tonight, I needed to prepare myself. By my calculations, I still had a week at least.

But not much longer.

"The apples," Frisk said suddenly, raising his gaze to meet mine. "That's why you eat them. To try to cure you."

"Yes. But it's not working."

"Why didn't you ask the pixies?"

I shook my head. "It's too far along. It's been infecting my body for years, Frisk. A simple healing won't work anymore. Nothing will stop it but my death or a reversal from the one who struck me."

"And who struck you?"

I laid the mirror on the towel and carefully wrapped it up alongside the iron dagger. "Who do you think?"

"Calista."

"Yes." I couldn't tell him the whole story—that she was Demon Fae, and her poisonous claws had infected me. Truth be told, it was a miracle I wasn't dead already. That was why I stayed in Knockspur for so long. The farther away from her poison I was, the longer I lived.

"I don't understand. If she poisoned you, and you're dying, why does she still want you killed? Why did she send Theron?"

I said nothing. It was too dangerous to say any more. I was grateful Frisk wasn't asking any questions about the mirror. Calista already wanted me dead for the secrets I knew. I couldn't implicate anyone else in her deception. I couldn't risk having her hunt my friends.

I straightened. "We need to get back before the hunter gets suspicious."

"Too late," said a voice.

My blood ran cold as a familiar figure stepped into view, arms crossed and expression lethal.

Theron.

Behind him was Mauro, his dark eyes curious as he appraised us. Kendra was perched on his antlers, her head cocked quizzically.

A satisfied smile spread across the hunter's face. "What is it you're hiding, princess?"

The Hunter

I hadn't seen much. The princess had been too careful, constantly checking over her shoulder, so I hadn't been able to track her as closely as I would have liked.

After Frisk and Kendra caught us cuddled together in the crevice, I'd felt... rattled. Waking up entwined with Eira had felt strangely comforting. As if to open my eyes and see her naked form next to me was completely normal. The most natural thing in the world.

When I'd snapped out of it, I hadn't felt like myself. I needed to be alone.

Only after I sensed Eira wandering off did I realize she had done the exact same thing. I needed to find out what she was hiding. I saw her pull something out of her pack, but I hadn't been able to identify what it was.

But in this moment, with her caught red-handed, she didn't need to know that.

I *had* heard them speaking of the queen. And Eira's condition.

She was dying.

The thought sent a confusing array of emotions spiraling within me. Relief, for then I would be free of my bargain with her. Bewilderment, because Frisk was right—why would the queen send me after a dying princess?

And, strangely... sorrow.

If I searched deep within myself, I was full of grief at the thought of Eira dying. And I had no idea why.

She was infuriating. My life would be much less difficult with her dead.

And, of course, I was bound by Calista to kill her myself.

But in spite of all that, I didn't truly want her dead. Not if I was given the choice.

Eira clenched a small bundle of fabric at her side, lifting her chin in defiance. "I don't owe you explanations, hunter."

"You've made that much clear." I drew closer, and her hold on the bundle tightened. "But if you think you can sneak away without anyone noticing, then you're more foolish than I thought."

Her nostrils flared, her eyes blazing with rage. But she said nothing. My gaze dropped to the wrapped object by her side. I could take it from her. It would be easy to wrestle it from her grasp, even if she put up a fight. Even with the fae bond punishing me for harming her. I had disarmed stronger foes before.

But there was something in the princess's eyes I hadn't seen before. And it stopped me, freezing me in place.

Fear.

I had never seen her afraid before. Not of *me*. She'd feared for the sake of her animal friends. She'd also been afraid of the Demon Fae, but fiercely so. Ready to fight. To survive at any cost.

But right now, for the first time, she was afraid of *me*. I had the upper hand, and she knew it. My entire livelihood relied on knowing my enemy and what they feared the most.

This woman feared me. She feared me exposing her secrets.

A hard lump formed in my throat, my next words dying on my lips. I didn't know what to say. When I had emerged from my hiding spot, I had known exactly what I would do: find the truth.

But right now, staring at this frightened princess and the defiance and ferocity still burning in her expression, I wasn't sure of anything anymore. This wasn't the vagabond princess the queen had painted a picture of. Eira had been raised to believe she would be queen someday. Instead, she'd been banished and hunted, barely surviving.

And I played a part in her suffering.

Something loosened in my chest, and I exhaled slowly. "Keep your secret, Eira." I turned away.

"What?" she blurted.

I glanced over my shoulder, amused by her bewilderment. "I said you can keep this secret. Our bargain requires me to bring you to the castle. I don't need anything else from you. So I'm letting you keep this one."

"Theron—" She took a step toward me, then faltered.

I turned to fully face her. She stared at me, lips parted and eyes wide, her face slack with shock.

"You aren't who I thought you were, Snow Princess," I murmured. "I'm a killer. A murderer. A blade the queen wields for her own will and pleasure. There is blood on my hands. I may be ordered to kill you. To end your life in the queen's name. But this much I can give you."

Something burned in her gaze, something new and unfamiliar, but I turned away before I scrutinized it. Before this princess unraveled me completely.

With the firewood Eira and I had gathered, we cooked the two hares and shared them between the four of us—Kendra refused, as she kept to a diet of worms, insects, and frogs, and she had recently eaten. I sensed Eira glancing at me repeatedly, but I ignored her gaze.

When we finished our meal, I put out the fire and packed our things, and we set off once more.

A strange new silence filled the air between us as we made our way through the woods, each step taking us farther and farther down the mountain. It wouldn't be long before we reached the base of the Athawood Peaks, and from there, the village of Tolston, which was on the outskirts of the Bloxham Province.

Home. Just a few more days, and I would be home.

Eira continued to stare at me, as if she didn't quite know what to make of me. As if she didn't recognize me anymore.

I wasn't sure I recognized myself.

For years, I had been forced to fulfill my contract with the queen. Nothing had stopped me. Nothing could deter me from being free of her, even for just a short season.

My skill in hunting came from my meticulous planning. But now, for the first time in my adult life, I had no plan. I had been determined to kill the Snow Princess and bring the queen her heart in order to buy my own freedom. But I realized that even if Eira and I succeeded in reaching the palace and nullifying our fae bargain, I wasn't sure if I could kill her.

I thrived on certainty. And right now, I was filled with doubt. I hadn't been this lost and confused since my father—

I shuddered, my steps faltering. My thoughts were so chaotic, spiraling into territories I'd forbidden myself from years ago.

Do not think of it. Never think of it.

"Theron?"

Jolted from my stupor, I stumbled over a tree root, cursing as I whirled to find Eira watching me, her pale eyes wide with concern. Mauro and Frisk were also watching. Even Kendra poked her head out from Eira's cloak to stare at me, unabashed.

"What?" I snapped, loathing the pity in Eira's expression. I would *not* be pitied.

"Do you need to rest?" she asked.

"No," I growled.

"Really? Because you seem... off."

"*I* seem off? What about you? Where are your quick barbs? Your relentless teasing?"

She smirked. "Are you saying you *miss* having me torment you?"

I rolled my eyes and turned away from her. I wasn't in the mood for this.

"Fine," she called after me. "But if you die of exhaustion before we reach the palace, don't blame me."

"I don't think it's exhaustion that's bothering him," Kendra mused.

"He probably needs food," Mauro said. "I'm always grumpy when I don't have food."

"You're grumpy all the time," Frisk said.

"Shut up," I barked. "All of you."

"He's not grumpy," Eira said. "He's downright *foul*."

"Definitely worse than Mauro," Kendra agreed.

I closed my eyes. The silence had been so much more

preferable, even if it was stilted. My mind refused to settle. If I didn't get control of this conversation, I would strangle someone.

I had to turn the tables on the princess. Agitating her seemed a lot more appealing than allowing this useless conversation to continue.

"What happened when you were banished from the palace?" I asked loudly.

Eira and the creatures' mutterings died in an instant. A cold, stunned emptiness filled the silence.

"What do you mean?" Eira finally asked, her tone wary.

"You expect me to believe Calista woke up one day suddenly hating you, then politely asked you to leave the palace, and you acquiesced? I think something happened. She was your stepmother for a while. Something had to have changed to make you leave. To make her hunt you."

More silence. Blissful, beautiful silence. Oh yes, I could do this all day. I mentally prepared more probing questions that would elicit awkward silences from the princess.

"You don't know anything," Eira hissed.

"You're right. That's why I'm asking."

"So I'm supposed to bare all my secrets to you just because you *asked*? Think again, hunter."

"How about this—a secret for a secret?" The words left my mouth before I could stop them.

Bad idea, Theron.

But it was too late. I couldn't take them back.

"Another bargain?" Eira asked warily. "Are you sure that's a good idea?"

"Don't you want to know something about me as well? I'll share one of my secrets if you share yours."

She hesitated. "Not just any secret. You have to answer one question fully. No omissions. No hedging."

One question. What were the odds she would ask the one thing I didn't want to answer?

The odds were high. Eira had a tendency to poke in the precise spots I wished she didn't.

But curiosity burned within me. I *did* want to know what had happened with Calista. Not just to understand Eira better, but to understand Calista. I hadn't particularly liked the queen, but I had always believed her to be the rightful ruler of the Winter Court. Now that my perspective was changing, I wanted to fill in the gaps. How far did Calista's deception go? What else had she been hiding?

"Fine," I said. "We have a deal."

"This is a bad idea," Frisk muttered.

Mauro snorted in agreement, but Kendra shushed them both, her blue eyes fixed on me and Eira. She seemed excited.

"Calista didn't banish me because of my human blood," Eira said, her voice firm. "She banished me because I stole something from her."

I frowned. That wasn't what I'd been expecting. "What did you steal?"

"A magical object that reveals truth. It's the only thing in the entire realm that can expose Calista's secrets."

"What kind of secrets?"

Eira laughed. "That's another question. Sorry, Theron, but that's the only secret I'll share today."

"No, you have to answer the question fully, princess. How did you escape? Why did you stay away? There's too much unanswered."

When she said nothing, I glanced over my shoulder at

her. She was chewing on her bottom lip, her eyes gleaming in a frustratingly familiar way.

She was scheming. Damn her.

"When I stole the object, Calista tried to stop me. Then she tried to kill me. I used fae magic to get away. And I've stayed away because I don't want to risk her taking the object back. It's the only leverage I have against her."

Shock rippled through me. Blood and ice, she was telling the truth. Leverage against Calista? That truly *could* turn the tides in favor of the Snow Princess.

Was this why Calista hunted her? Not to rid the court of her nuisance of a stepdaughter, but to silence her forever? To keep her secrets?

Now it made sense. This was why Calista hadn't ordered me to kill Eira until now. She hadn't wanted to risk me finding out what the princess knew.

"What is Calista hiding?" I asked.

Eira said nothing.

I tried again. "What fae magic did you use? And how?"

"That, dear hunter, is another secret you haven't earned."

I exhaled in frustration. "If you have leverage over the queen, why won't you use it? Keeping her secrets is only serving *her*. If you spread those secrets, then she won't be able to silence you."

"It's more complicated than that."

"How?"

"Well, for starters, who would believe me?" she snapped, her tone sharpening. "I'm half human. Most of the fae folk believe half breeds like me can lie. That I would say anything to win back my father's crown."

"So you're waiting for proof," I guessed.

"Proof. An army. A sure victory. Every piece needs to be aligned when I make my move, or it's all over."

She wanted a foolproof plan. I could respect that. Especially if she was dying. She wanted to make sure her one attempt was successful. Just in case she only had one shot.

"Your turn," she said, her tone cheerful once more.

Shit. Steeling myself, I said, "What's your question?"

"What were you thinking about when you stumbled just now?"

Damn. *Of course* she would ask that.

No omissions. No hedging. If I dodged the question, she would call me on it, and the fae bond would pull the truth from me by force.

I would tell her as much of the truth as I could muster. With the answers she'd given me, I owed her that much.

"I was thinking of my father," I said quietly.

The very air seemed to go still with my confession. I hadn't spoken of the man since he'd died so many years ago. Since I'd sworn never to think or speak of him again.

"What about him?" Eira asked.

"His death wrecked me in more ways than one," I said. "He was not a kind man." I paused. "It's because of him that I am contracted to the queen."

The bastard had been Calista's strongest supporter. He was her commander long before she'd married King Judas. His greatest ambition was to rid the court of all half breeds. He believed in a pure seelie fae bloodline.

"Why?" Eira asked. "What does he have to do with the queen?"

I paused. "That's another question."

"Bullshit. I answered more than that, and you know it. Tell me."

Fire burned in my blood, and I clenched my teeth against the pain of the fae bond. "Fine," I bit out. "He was in service to her, and he died before his contract was up. By law, I had to take his debt upon myself."

Eira was silent for a long moment. Then, she muttered, "Damn. That's harsh."

For some reason, hearing her so casually affirm the cruelty of the situation was more of a comfort than her suffocating pity from earlier. It made the situation light, which was what I needed right now.

"Yes," I agreed. "Fae law is a bitch."

She chuckled wryly. "So, why were you thinking of your father?"

I pressed my lips together. This was a truth I couldn't reveal because I didn't fully understand it myself. "Because my thoughts are a mess right now. And the last time my mind was this frazzled was just after his death when I had no purpose. No plan."

"Your mind is frazzled?" Eira asked. Something unreadable crept into her tone. Something I'd never heard in her voice before. "Why?"

I was torn between saying, *Because of you*, and *I don't know*. Both were the truth. I stopped walking and turned to look at her. Her ice-blue eyes were wide with curiosity, her expression open and earnest. No hint of scorn or taunting in her face. This, right now, was the true Eira.

Perhaps that was why I felt the need to be honest with her. I probably could have avoided the question, claiming I'd answered enough to fulfill our bargain. But something in her eyes drew the truth out of me.

"I already told you. You aren't what I expected, princess. And it's shaken what I thought I knew."

Her lips parted in surprise, and I held her gaze as understanding passed between us. No hatred, no animosity. No playful banter. Nothing but open acceptance. We still didn't know everything about each other. There were plenty of secrets we still kept.

But we weren't enemies in this moment. Perhaps we would be tomorrow. Or even an hour from now. But here in this space, we understood each other.

"I hate to break up this lovely chat, but I have bad news."

I blinked and turned to find Frisk approaching from the opposite direction. I wasn't sure when he had disappeared, but wherever he'd gone, he was now out of breath, his dark eyes full of apprehension.

"What is it?" Eira asked.

"I scouted ahead to the outskirts of Tolston," said the fox. "Ordinarily, it would be easy to sneak through undetected. But the area is crawling with the queen's soldiers. They caught wind that the Snow Princess was nearby. They know you're here, Eira."

THE HUNTER

I STEPPED FORWARD, ALARM PULSING THROUGH MY VEINS. "How? Why would soldiers be searching for her if the queen sent me to kill her?"

Eira and Frisk looked at me solemnly, and then I knew.

The queen thought I had failed.

Shit.

I ran a hand along my face, tugging at my beard in frustration. I had never failed an assignment before. Why was she so quick to assume I was unsuccessful?

Unless that had been her plan all along. I had speculated it before—that she had set me up to fail. Because who in their right mind would release a skilled assassin from their employ? Who would relinquish that kind of control?

Calista wouldn't. Oh, she would certainly pretend I had a fighting chance. But if she sent me on a doomed quest, then she would never have to release me or my blood.

I knew too many of her secrets. And she knew how much I despised my position. I'd become a liability to her. Just like Eira.

"Hunter," Frisk barked. "I can see that brain of yours

working, but right now, we need a plan to get through the village. Any ideas?"

I shook my head, struggling to rid myself of these incessant thoughts. They were getting me nowhere. Right now, it was safest to assume Calista wanted both Eira and me dead.

I turned to the princess. "Can you glamour?"

"Yes," she said at once.

"Good. We'll need a pretty convincing disguise. Frisk and Kendra, you stay with us. Mauro will have to wait on the outskirts of the village. He's too noticeable."

"Fine by me." Mauro pawed at the ground. "I'll meet you at our rendezvous point, Snow."

Eira dropped her gaze, her expression full of despair. Perhaps she doubted her chances of survival. I certainly did.

"You did well, old friend," Frisk said, nudging Mauro's leg with his tail. "You made it down the mountain."

"It wasn't that hard," Mauro said haughtily.

Eira was pulling her cloak on, adjusting the hood so it covered her face. I raised a hand. "Leave it down. The soldiers will be on the lookout for a masked or hooded figure. We'll have to be as open and unassuming as possible."

Eira's brows knitted together, but she lowered her hood, then smoothed her palms along her trousers. "Won't they recognize you?"

"Not with my glamour. Camouflage is my specialty." I arched an eyebrow and gave her a devilish grin. To my surprise, a small smile lit Eira's face. Her eyes gleamed, and uncertainty twisted in my chest. "What?"

"I've never seen you smile like that before," she said with a chuckle. "It's... quite disarming."

I leaned closer to her, my grin widening. "Do I unsettle you, princess?" My voice was low and rough.

She laughed loudly and swatted at my arm. "Stop that!"

"Shivering bones, you two are insufferable," Mauro grumbled.

"Indeed," said Frisk with a sniff.

"We aren't even arguing," Eira pointed out.

"The flirting is worse." Mauro shifted his dark eyes between me and Eira.

Warmth filled my throat, cutting off my reply. Eira's cheeks turned pink, and she coughed lightly.

"I love it," Kendra said from Eira's shoulder. "Keep going, you two."

My face heated, and I bit back a curse. This was ridiculous. We had more important things to discuss. I straightened, dropping my hands to my sides. "Let's see your glamour, princess. I need to know what we're working with."

Eira shifted her weight and exchanged an odd look with Frisk, for some reason. "It's solid," she said.

I rolled my eyes. "I can't just take your word for it, Eira. Show me."

"No."

My head reared back. "I beg your pardon?"

"Beg all you want, hunter. I'm not showing you my glamour."

Anger simmered in my blood. "We don't have time for this, princess. If you want to get through that village alive, you need to work with me on this."

"I swear on my fae blood that my disguise is flawless," Eira said firmly. "No one will be able to see or recognize me."

My nostrils flared. "Eira—" I growled.

"She's right," Frisk chimed in. "Her glamour is impeccable. Best I've ever seen."

"It's true," Kendra added.

"Agreed," Mauro chimed in.

I groaned and threw my hands in the air. "You and your *damn secrets*, princess! What do you think I'll do, run to the queen and share the secret to your fancy glamour? I'm on her list. She assumes I've failed, so I'm as good as dead. I am no longer an ally to the queen."

"That doesn't make you *my* ally," Eira snapped. "Besides, whatever happened to letting me keep my secrets?"

"I let you keep *one* secret," I said, my patience wearing thin. "Besides, keeping stolen treasures in your sack isn't the same thing as using magic that could kill or save us both. My life is on the line with this secret."

Eira shrugged, as if this didn't matter much to her. The indifference on her face made my rage boil over. With a roar, I balled my hand into a fist and struck the tree next to me. Pain bloomed along my knuckles, spearing through my body with a jolt. The tree shook, and a pile of snow plopped onto my head. Panting, I inspected my bleeding hand. The wound throbbed, breaking through my haze of fury.

"You finished?" Eira asked calmly.

"Careful, or I'll punch you next," I muttered. "Bargain be damned."

"Maybe I should ask to see *your* glamour." Eira crossed her arms. "Maybe it's not as good as you think."

Frustration prickled to life inside me, but the spark in her eyes told me she was doing this on purpose. She knew exactly how to irritate me. I heaved a deep breath, trying to clear my head.

This was why I worked alone.

"I have a contact in Tolston," Eira said. "If we can get to their dwelling, we can hide there until the area is clear."

I snorted. "Please tell me it's not the farm boy who's still in love with you."

Eira made a noise somewhere between a cough and a laugh. *"What?"*

"He means Denton," Mauro said.

Now her face was beet-red. "I know," she hissed. "I just—how did you—"

"How did I know?" Seeing her flustered only made me smirk at her. Finally, I had the upper hand. "His overprotective nature, the way he talked down at you like he owned you, his defensive stance when he stands alongside you... Shall I go on?"

"Please don't," Eira muttered, covering her face with her hands.

"He *is* overprotective," Kendra said.

Mauro grunted in agreement. Frisk snickered and ducked his head.

"You're not helping, Kendra," Eira snapped. She dropped her hands with an angry huff, but her face was still crimson. "It's not Denton. It's Stella."

I frowned. "Which one was Stella?" Then, just to irritate her further, I added, "It's hard to tell you humans apart."

"That is such a snobbishly fae thing to say. Besides, I'm only half human."

I shrugged as if this didn't matter, mimicking her motion from earlier.

Eira sighed. "Stella is the one who's good with knives. She threatened to chop off your balls."

"She has blonde hair," Frisk added. "Her eyes look just like Snow's. She's the human noble of the Bloxham Province."

The *human noble*? So, Eira wasn't just rallying ordinary

humans to her side, but human nobility. I had to admit, I was impressed.

"Frisk!" Eira chided, aiming a kick at the fox, who easily dodged it.

"What? Was that a secret?" Frisk chuckled again.

I vaguely remembered the petite human with the impeccably good aim back in Knockspur. "I don't think I'll be very well received by a human."

"For good reason," Eira said, shooting me a sharp look. "Just how many humans have you killed, anyway?"

"None," I said, lifting my chin. "We don't often trouble ourselves with the affairs of humans."

"By *we*, do you mean *Calista and I*?" Eira said, her voice full of venom.

My mouth opened, then shut again. *Damn, did I really say that?* I mentally ran through the words I'd just spoken. Shame trickled down my chest, making my heart sink like a stone.

Not only had I belittled humans, but I'd spoken as if the queen and I were affiliated. As if our decisions were collective.

The thought repulsed me.

"I'm sorry," I murmured. "I don't know why I said that."

It was, in fact, *snobbish* of me. Eira was right.

She glared at me, her jaw ticking back and forth. Clearly, my apology wasn't sufficient.

"Look." I spread my hands apologetically. "I was raised to believe humans were no better than slaves. In my youth, I knew that was wrong, but I didn't do anything about it. Then, with my position with the queen, I was too bitter about my own problems to bother with the humans." I paused, realizing I was rambling. But with my admission came a moment of clarity.

I was a hypocrite.

I'd spent my adult life resenting my father for enslaving himself to the queen, and, by association, enslaving me as well. But how many humans endured the same treatment? My father had believed in exterminating all creatures who weren't full-blooded seelie fae.

And I'd done nothing.

A hard lump formed in my throat, and I swallowed. I no longer saw the princess and the fae beasts before me. Instead, I saw generations of humans, tormented and enslaved, cast out of their homes, spit upon and persecuted all because of their bloodlines.

It had never bothered me before now. Why would I concern myself with the woes of humans?

But now, in my mind's eye, I saw Eira enslaved. Eira beaten. Eira imprisoned. That beautifully stubborn spark of light in her eyes completely snuffed out.

I couldn't stand it.

For so long, my life had never been my own. I never had the freedom to choose my own path. I was only a blade for the queen to wield.

But now that Calista was hunting me, I started to wonder —with the barest glimmer of hope—if there was another path for me. Another way out.

The tiniest thought appeared in my mind: *What if Eira's plan worked?*

What if Calista was de-throned? Imprisoned? What if she was prevented from ever controlling people again?

If I were truly free… what would I do with that freedom? As much as I wanted to disappear in my cottage in the mountains, I somehow knew I couldn't run away. Not when

I had seen just how cruel Calista could be. Not when I knew that humans and unseelie were suffering so much.

"I'm sorry," I said again, more solemnly this time. "You're right. I've been a complete ass. I will... try to be better. I promise."

Dangerous words to utter around Eira. But this time, I meant them. I wasn't making a bargain out of necessity or coercion.

I wanted to be different from Calista. Different from my father.

Eira nodded, her expression still tight. "Thank you. And... If we make it through this alive, I promise not to have you executed." She made a face, then added, "Well, at least not immediately."

I snorted. "Wow. What a generous gift."

"I know. I'll make such a magnanimous queen."

"Can you two please leave?" Mauro growled. He was reclined in the snow with his paws covering his snout. "I'm not sure I can endure another second of this."

Before Mauro could make another comment about flirting, I nodded and jerked my head toward the woods. "Let's go. We'll assemble our glamour on the way." I cocked an eyebrow. "Unless you still don't trust me."

She eyed me up and down with pursed lips. "We'll see."

With that, she strode past me with a jaunty lilt to her step, Frisk trotting beside her. My eyes were drawn to the sway of her hips, and something hot burned in my chest. Had her curves *always* looked that appealing? And had she always walked like that?

Realizing I was staring, I averted my gaze and hurried after her and Frisk.

Frisk kept watch ahead of our steps and warned us when we got close, but it was unnecessary. Even from a distance, we could make out the hurried footsteps and cacophony of voices that echoed through the trees. I knew the village of Tolston well; I had often traveled through it on my journeys. Ordinarily, it was a humble, quiet hamlet.

But as Eira and I approached the edge of the wood, the village was almost unrecognizable. The buildings and cobblestone roads were the same, but the area was filled with soldiers in full armor, swords and metal clinking as they walked, barking orders at the townsfolk. Villagers bustled about, hurrying out of the way of the militia men. Soldiers burst into homes without warning, tossing belongings about as if searching for something.

I exchanged an alarmed look with Eira. *She banished me because I stole something from her.* Was that what the soldiers were looking for?

More importantly, why did they think the stolen object was *here*? Had word spread that Eira was making her way to the palace? If so, wouldn't the soldiers have tried to intercept us on the mountain?

Something wasn't right.

"Glamour," I muttered to Eira.

She nodded and withdrew behind me, most likely to hide her secretive magic. But it was just as well; I would prefer her to remain behind me anyway.

I searched within myself for my magic, which had grown sleepy and dormant from disuse during our days of traveling through mountains and forests. A low hum emitted from within my chest, and I focused on it, drawing it out. My skin prickled as I donned my most comfortable glamour—that of a tall, stocky farmer with sandy hair and tan, calloused skin. This was the glamour I often wore when traversing through Tolston. In fact, some of the villagers would likely recognize me.

That could work in our favor, if I was a trusted townsperson.

I glanced behind me, but the princess was nowhere to be found. Eyes wide, I scanned the trees behind me. She and the fox had completely disappeared.

What the hell?

"I'm here, hunter." Something sharp flicked my nose, and I winced.

"Damn you," I grumbled, and her chuckle echoed in my ears. I wanted to stay and scrutinize her glamour—blood and ice, how did she do that?—but we needed to move quickly. "How far away is your contact?"

"Stella lives on the other side of the village," Eira whispered.

Well, shit. "Is she expecting us?"

"Yes. But we have a contingency plan in place for situations like this, when things get dicey."

"What's the contingency plan?"

"She gets out. We rendezvous at the castle at the full moon with everyone else."

I swore under my breath. "You are impossible, Eira," I growled. "That might have been nice to know earlier."

"We can still use her home as a hideout even if she's not there," Eira said. "That doesn't change our plans."

I rolled my eyes. "All right, stay close to me. As effective as your glamour is, I doubt it would stop someone from running right into you."

"That's happened before," she said.

"Why am I not surprised?" I muttered before moving forward, my steps shifting from snow-covered brush to ice-slick cobblestone. A carriage wheeled past me, occupied by at least half a dozen soldiers.

It looked like Calista was preparing for a siege. Was there an outside threat I didn't know about?

"This is weird," Eira whispered in my ear, no doubt noticing the same thing.

"Agreed. Keep a sharp eye. And try not to talk." I hissed the words out of the corner of my mouth, hoping no one noticed I was speaking to myself.

We idled down the road, my insides quivering with nerves. Every instinct told me I should run and flee from the presence of so many soldiers. But nothing was more suspicious than someone running away. Instead, I forced my steps to be slow and casual, meeting the gaze of each person I passed by and dipping my head politely in greeting. Harlan, my villager persona, was a kind fellow, the type of person who helped a stranger in need and smiled at children.

He was the exact opposite of myself. Which made him the perfect disguise.

"Should we get a horse?" Eira whispered.

"No," I said under my breath. "It will take us longer, but horses and carriages are more likely to be stopped and searched. And *stop talking.*"

She huffed angrily but said nothing else. Mercifully.

Our leisurely pace down the road was excruciating. Every soldier who hurried past flicked their eyes over me briefly before moving on to the task at hand.

I was no threat. Just a farmer making his way to the tavern after a long day of work in the field.

"Do you even know where you're going?" Eira asked.

"*Yes*," I ground out. "Follow my lead and *be quiet*."

"So demanding."

"You there!" bellowed a voice.

Shit. I stilled and turned to the speaker. A trio of swordsmen approached, the metal of their armor clinking with their hurried steps. The one in front lifted his visor, eyes narrowed as he looked me up and down. "What's your business here?"

I raised my eyebrows and pressed a hand to my chest before glancing behind me as if expecting the soldier to be addressing someone else. "Don't mind me, good sir. Nothing but a local farmer." Being unable to lie meant I had to speak in fragmented sentences. But it worked for my persona.

"Where?" barked the soldier.

I pointed down the road in the direction we'd come from. "Down that way. I'm tired and could use a drink."

"The tavern's closed," the soldier said. "You should make your way home immediately. There's a curfew in place, and anyone outside after dusk will be arrested."

Curfew? What the hell? I didn't have to force the look of alarm on my face as I asked, "What's going on? Is the village in danger?"

"Queen's orders," he said curtly. "Now, if you wouldn't mind..." He gestured in the opposite direction, waiting for me to walk that way.

Damn it all.

"I—I have someone expecting me," I said.

"I don't care," the soldier snapped. "We're telling *everyone* to go back to their homes, even your friend."

"But—please. It's extremely important."

The soldier dropped his arm, his dark eyes blazing as he drew closer to me. I had to squash the instinct to straighten my shoulders and look him in the eye. Instead, I pretended to cower under his scrutiny.

"I said *leave*. If you don't follow orders, I'll be forced to arrest you. Is that what you want?"

Several soldiers across the street were watching curiously. A few were making their way toward us. Not good.

I lifted my palms in surrender. "All right. Apologies, good sir. I know you're just doing your duty to the crown. I'll—I'll do as you say."

I turned on my heel, then froze as a voice boomed, "Theron! Is that you?"

The Princess

During Theron's exchange with the soldier, I'd slowly backed my way into an alley. The hunter was right; being invisible didn't stop me from running into solid things. And he was attracting a lot of attention.

But when a militia man addressed him by his name, my blood ran cold. I instinctively ducked further into the shadows, even knowing no one could see me.

A thick, meaty fellow with gleaming gold eyes and pointed fae ears approached. He wore a belt full of knives and a bow and arrow strapped to his back. His wolfish grin made my skin crawl.

Theron stiffened, his nostrils flaring and his eyes sparking with recognition. The quivering muscle in his jaw told me all I needed to know.

This soldier was an enemy.

"Vikros," Theron said tersely. "You're a bit far from home, aren't you?"

Vikros drew closer until he stood directly in front of Theron. Theron was taller, but Vikros was twice as thick.

"The queen enlisted my services," Vikros said.

"What for?" Theron bit out. "I wasn't aware of any threats to the city."

"Ah, but how would you know? You've been missing for days."

Shit.

Theron's eyes narrowed. "Missing? She sent me on an assignment a week ago. I'm simply making my way back to her."

Vikros's gaze raked over Theron's body with a smirk. "In disguise?"

"It's a habit," Theron snapped. "Part of my job requires subtlety. Something you could take note of."

Vikros barked out a laugh. "Ah, I do miss your scathing barbs, Theron. Always such a delight." He jerked his head toward Theron, and several soldiers surrounded him, swords drawn.

I lurched forward, though I wasn't sure what I could do. My pulse roared in my ears. The smart thing would be to leave, to find Stella and hide until the chaos settled down.

But I couldn't. I couldn't just leave Theron to Calista's wrath. He was nothing more than a slave, forced to do her bidding.

I refused to let her destroy him like she had my father.

I drew closer, my steps slow and careful.

To my horror, Vikros's eyes shifted to me, spearing right through my glamour. I froze, waiting for his gaze to glance over me and move on.

It didn't.

A slow smile spread on his face. "Who's your lovely friend?"

A chill skittered down my spine. *No, no, no.*

I tried to retreat back into the alley, but Vikros stepped

forward, blocking my path. He eyed me up and down, his smile widening. "Clever glamour. Unfortunately, I'm immune to it. It's why the queen hired me."

"Vikros!" Theron roared. He moved, but a dozen swords closed in on him, stopping him. Fury burned in his dark eyes as he looked over the weapons pointed at his chest, no doubt calculating how he could fight them all off.

The odds weren't good.

Vikros grabbed me by the collar and dragged me forward, but I wasn't about to come quietly. With a shout, I stomped on his toes, then jabbed my elbow into his gut. He grunted, clearly unharmed by my feeble attack, but he was surprised enough to release me. I ducked down low, drawing my daggers and slicing into his shins. He growled, his large arms swiping for me, but I rolled away, keeping low and using my petite stature to my advantage.

"Get out of here, girl!" Theron bellowed. *"Run!"*

Girl. He intentionally hadn't used my name.

He was protecting me.

But judging by the way Vikros had looked at me, he knew exactly who I was.

I draped my magic over me, going invisible once again as I sprinted away. Even if Vikros could see through it, the other soldiers couldn't.

"Stop her!" Vikros yelled.

The soldiers scrambled forward, then faltered, obviously bewildered by Vikros's orders to seize an invisible girl.

I had almost rounded the corner and vanished from sight when I heard it.

A child's scream.

"Do it!" Vikros shouted.

I stilled, whirling to find a soldier dragging a child by the arm, forcing the boy to kneel in the middle of the street.

Rage and fear shuddered through my bones. *No...*

"*Run!*" Theron urged me. "Don't stop!"

But I couldn't. Every fiber of my being had me frozen in place, staring in horror as more soldiers appeared, each of them dragging a human child no older than ten years old. The youngest looked to be about three and had tears streaming down her face.

The guardsmen in front of the row of children all drew their swords.

My feet were moving before I could stop myself.

"Eira, *no!*" Theron cried.

I hadn't realized my invisibility was gone until a swordsman grabbed for me. I dodged him just in time, running straight for the line of soldiers. The children's cries intensified.

I wasn't sure what I could do, but I had to do *something*.

Before I reached the children, Vikros stepped in front of me, eyes gleaming. "I thought that might draw you in. The queen did say you had a soft spot for humans. There aren't many in this village, but I was able to round up a few before you showed up."

"Those are *children!*" I shrieked, lunging forward, trying to fight my way around him. "It's *me* you want. Don't hurt them!"

Vikros's massive arms wrapped around me, pinning my limbs in place with ease. No matter how determined I was, I couldn't get past his bulky frame.

"Vikros, this is too far!" Theron bellowed. "These are innocent children of the Winter Court!"

"There are always casualties in war," Vikros said idly.

"Besides, this is under the queen's orders. There is no love lost in a human death."

I felt the blood drain from my face as I stared at the line of children in horror. All of them were weeping openly now, cringing from the blades directed at them.

"You have me!" I argued. "Let them go. Please!"

"As much as I love to see a woman beg," Vikros said with a savage grin, "we can't leave any witnesses to this incident."

I struggled against him with a scream. Fury, pure and volatile, coursed through my veins, igniting a fire within me. My horror and shock melted away, making way for the red creeping into my vision.

Vikros turned to the soldier closest to him and gave a quick nod.

The men in front of the children raised their swords.

Theron screamed something unintelligible. I channeled all of my focus on those innocent children who shared blood with me, who did not belong in this battle...

I bit down hard on Vikros's arm. He yelped and staggered back, loosening his grip on me. With my free hand, I dragged my dagger along his stomach, digging deep. Blood gushed, running freely from his wound. He roared in agony, but I was already sprinting away, diving in front of the closest swordsman before he could strike the doe-eyed girl before him.

"*Eira!*" Theron shouted.

The blade struck me, slicing through flesh and bone, cutting a path of fire through my chest. White light consumed my vision as I collapsed, feeling nothing but the burn of sharp steel. Hot liquid ran down my body, drenching everything.

And then, all at once, the pain vanished. I gasped as my

vision cleared, and the blood stopped flowing. Stunned, I looked around. Was I... dead?

The soldiers all stared at me in shock and confusion. One of them turned to Vikros, who was clutching his own wound, though it was not nearly as fatal as mine had been.

"Sir?" said a guardsman uncertainly.

"Eira, move," whispered a familiar voice.

I didn't have to look to know it was Frisk. In a flash of white fur, he dived for the nearest soldier, connecting with his face and clawing at the man's flesh. Shrieks filled the air, followed by the clopping of hooves. The children dropped to the ground, arms covering their heads.

I sat up in alarm to see a horde of animals emerge from the forest. Mauro arrived, followed by several other creatures: deer, squirrels, rabbits, birds, and some I had never seen before. Even Kendra was among them, white wings flapping and blue eyes blazing.

Kendra, who always hid from a fight. Kendra, who was too frightened to show her face to strangers.

She was here now, undeterred and unafraid.

All the animals charged forward with snarls and chitters and chirps, heading straight for the soldiers.

"Blood and ice," I whispered. My eyes flew to the human children, worried they would be trampled. But the animals seemed to be targeting only the soldiers. The creatures easily weaved around the children. A few of the little ones peeked around their arms, one eye open as they watched the fray in awe.

In a flash, Theron was by my side. The creatures must have attacked the men who held him. Panic creased his features as he looked me over. "Eira. You—are you—"

"I'm fine." I patted my chest in bewilderment. Though my

clothes were still soaked in blood, the pain had completely vanished. I tugged down my collar and gasped.

A large gash was carved into my flesh, but... it wasn't bleeding. Not a single drop oozed from it. It was like it was suspended in time, frozen solid. I wasn't healed, but I wasn't dying, either.

"How?" I asked weakly.

Then, my eyes fell to Theron's hands. They glowed ice-blue, his fingers flexed as if poised to strike.

Something in my chest hummed in recognition. I stared at him. "What did you do?" I couldn't keep the awe out of my voice.

"I—I don't know." His hands started to shake as his gaze dropped to the glow. I recognized the chaos in his eyes; it was similar to when he'd told me his mind was frazzled.

He was about to lose it. And we couldn't have that.

"Help me up," I ordered.

"Your wound..."

"Do it, hunter. We don't have time. We have to get the children out of here."

The little ones seemed to realize their lives were not in imminent danger. Several of them were openly gaping, wide-eyed, as the animals attacked the soldiers.

Theron nodded and reached for me. Ignoring the strange blue glow, I took his hand, expecting his magic to burn me. Instead, it felt pleasantly cool, like pressing ice to a scorching burn. He hoisted me up just as a soldier raced toward us, sword drawn.

I raised my dagger, but Theron was quicker. He ducked to avoid the man's strike, then punched him in the nose. Theron hooked his foot under the soldier's leg, bringing the man crashing to his knees. In seconds, Theron had the guard's blade in hand and had plunged it into the man's neck. Then he turned back to face me as if this kill had been as ordinary as breathing.

And in that moment, I reminded myself he was a killer. But right now, he was on my side.

Bile crept up my throat, but I swallowed it down, knowing the dying man had been about to impale a child with that very sword. I nodded at Theron, and together, we hurried toward the line of children, who were still watching the battle in shock and amazement.

"Come on!" I cried, urging the children forward. "Come with me!"

The doe-eyed girl I'd taken the hit for scrambled forward, hanging on to my arm as if I were a lifeline. The other children followed suit, rushing to our sides.

"This way," Theron urged, his tone surprisingly gentle as he guided them down the street. I had to trust he knew a safe place to take them. I threw a glance over my shoulder to ensure we weren't being followed. Vikros's wound was still bleeding, but he was able to aim a kick at Frisk. The fox easily dodged it with a snicker. Mauro slammed his hooves into the chest of a soldier. Kendra shot a burst of ice at another. Several birds flitted around the soldiers' faces, taunting them.

It would have been hilarious if I hadn't been worried for the animals' safety. But I didn't have time; the human children needed to get out before they were killed in the crossfire.

I hurried after Theron—who had two children in tow—our footsteps light and quick. With each movement, something tugged at the wound in my chest, like stitches pulling free. Was Theron's magic wearing off? How long did I have before I started to bleed out again?

"In here," Theron said, throwing open the door to a four-story building. The children rushed inside without argument, but I hesitated, shooting him a curious look.

"What is this place? Is it safe?"

He nodded. "It's an inn. I'm well acquainted with the owner. He'll keep the children safe."

When I narrowed my eyes at him, he groaned. "Come on, princess. You have to trust me on this."

"I don't have to do anything," I said with a sniff, shoving past him and into the building.

"You are infuriating," Theron muttered as he slammed the door shut, then called out, "Derek!"

A bald, portly fae man with a huge black mustache appeared, then faltered as he took in me, Theron, and the ten children we'd brought with us. He scratched at his shiny scalp. "Ah... Harlan. What is this?"

"The queen's soldiers were causing trouble," Theron said shortly. "These little ones are in danger. Can you look after them?"

Derek straightened, his eyes darkening with a lethal gleam that almost matched Theron's. "Of course." He turned to the children. "Come with me, little ones. I have a nice, comfortable room you lot can have. It's got extra locks for your security. I'll close up shop and wait with you in there myself."

A few children nodded eagerly. One ran up to Derek and wrapped her arms around his legs, sobbing into his trousers. Derek patted her head awkwardly and led the children up the stairs. I watched them go, then turned to Theron.

"How did you know he would help? He's fae."

"Not all fae despise humans," Theron said softly, his voice low. Fire still burned in his gaze, but his tone was gentle.

Only then did I realize we stood alone in the lobby of the inn. I drew closer to him, thinking of how he had risked *everything* to save me, to save those children.

"Theron," I whispered, gazing up at him as my confused thoughts whirled with awe and gratitude. "You could have just let me die." I swallowed hard. "My death would have nullified our bargains."

A pained expression crossed his face. "No," he said softly, raising a hand to run his knuckle along my cheek. "I couldn't let you die, Eira."

I stared at him, suppressing a shiver of delight at the gentleness of his touch. Though I'd seen him kill a man, and I knew he'd done far worse, I delighted in his skin against mine. A rush of warmth coiled low in my belly, igniting something new and frightening.

I wanted him to touch *more* of me.

I leaned forward, but something ripped violently within my body, and blood seeped out from my wound. A bout of dizziness washed over me, and I swayed into Theron's arms. He caught me against his chest, his warm body a comforting support as I struggled to regain my balance.

"Eira?" His panicked voice was the last thing I heard before darkness took me.

THE HUNTER

After ensuring Derek had the children securely hidden, I lifted Eira into my arms. I didn't know how the strange enchantment around her injury had broken, but if I didn't do something quickly, she would die.

I couldn't let that happen.

All I could think of was how the princess had sprinted into the path of that sword to save a child she didn't even know.

She will not die. I won't allow it. My bargain with Calista be damned.

I had to find a healer.

There was one place I could take her, but it was risky. The healer who usually tended to my injuries lived in the village, and she was much more discreet than the healers at the palace. However, she was still very loyal to the queen. If Calista had gotten to her first, or if the healer recognized Eira, we were doomed.

But I had no other choice.

Shouts echoed in the street as I crept out the back door, using alleys I knew well to avoid the main road. Either the forest animals had retreated, or the soldiers had killed them. I hoped

Mauro and Frisk and the others had gotten away. What they'd done was a great risk, but it had saved us. We wouldn't have been able to escape or get the children to safety without them.

"Hang in there, princess," I whispered, trying to keep her awake. Her pallor had taken on a grayish hue, and her eyes rolled back. Each inhale was ragged, but at least she was still breathing.

Taking the back roads meant more twists and turns, more jostling that elicited whimpers of pain from Eira. But I could move more quickly. Fewer people traversed these roads, and those who did tended to mind their own business.

Eira was strong. She would make it. She had to.

At long last, I arrived at the healer's doorstep and pounded relentlessly on the door. Dusk had fallen, and most of the village was silent because of the curfew. My frantic knocking echoed along the street, but I kept it up until the door finally swung open.

A white-haired fae stood in the doorway, her sleepy dark eyes narrowed at my haggard appearance. She glanced up and down the street in curiosity. "What the hell are you doing here, Harlan? Don't you know the place is swarming with soldiers?"

"Heal her," I ordered through clenched teeth. "Please."

Only then did she seem to notice the woman draped in my arms. Her eyes widened, and she stood back to let me in. I hurried inside without another word.

The healer, Lavinia, closed the door behind her and crossed her arms. "What is this, Harlan? I won't harbor any fugitives."

"Just heal her and we'll be on our way. I beg of you." My voice broke on the last word.

She dropped her arms, her jaw slack with surprise as she took in my drooping form and broken expression. "Blood and ice, I've never seen you like this before. Who is this girl?" She squinted, scrutinizing the princess.

"She's my—my—" I fumbled for the words before I finally said, "We are bound. Her life is tethered to mine. I have to save her. Please."

Lavinia sighed and nodded. "Bring her to the table." She strode toward the back of the house, and I followed. With quick work, she cleared the kitchen table, and I laid Eira's prone form atop it. When Lavinia peeled open the blood-soaked tunic to inspect the gash, she hissed out a long breath. Then, she mumbled something unintelligible and ran her fingertip along the jagged edge of the wound. Slowly, she looked up at me, her eyes full of accusation.

"What happened to her?"

"A soldier struck her," I said.

"That's not all. This mark is infused with fae magic. *What happened?*"

I said nothing because I wasn't even sure myself. What *had* happened? I'd seen Eira get stabbed, and something in me had exploded. I'd felt my fae magic roar to life and spear forward, desperate to save her. But I couldn't explain what it was or how it had happened.

I had willed her to stay alive… and she had.

"I can't heal it if I don't know the extent of the injury," Lavinia went on, her tone sharpening. "Tell me, Harlan."

"I—I don't know what happened. I used my magic, but I've never done anything like that before." Quickly, I explained to her as best I could how I'd thrust my power toward Eira in order to save her.

Lavinia rubbed her chin in contemplation, then dropped her gaze to my hands. "What color was the magic?"

"Blue. Light blue."

Her eyebrows shot up, and she hurried over to the kitchen cabinets, digging through drawers until she withdrew a long chain with a pale blue crystal dangling on the end. "Like this?"

I frowned. The gem was the exact shade my hands had been. "Yes. What is that?"

"Larimar. It's used for necromancy."

I blanched. *"What?* You've been practicing necromancy?"

"Oh, hush. I only use it to enhance my powers, particularly when a patient teeters between life and death." She gave me a long, knowing look. "You, my friend, are a life weaver."

"A what?" I shook my head. She had to be mistaken. "No. I don't *have* fae magic. All I can do is glamour."

"Well, that's not true at all, based on what you told me." Lavinia grabbed a cloth from the counter and began pressing it to Eira's wound to staunch the bleeding. "Your magic is necromancy."

"I did not perform necromancy," I growled. "I didn't raise anyone from the dead. She was still alive!"

Lavinia shook her head with a sly smile on her face as she continued to apply pressure to the wound.

My anger and impatience took over, and I gestured wildly to Eira, still lying prone on the table. "Can you heal her, please? She doesn't have much time left."

"Well, you could easily just bring her back to life, with magic like that." But Lavinia obliged, raising her bloodstained hands in the air. Purple magic ignited on her fingertips as she pressed them against Eira's wound. The princess jerked violently, her face crumpling in pain, but I took that as a good sign—it meant she wasn't as close to death's door as I'd feared.

I drew closer, but Lavinia snapped, "Back up, boy. I need space to work."

I grumbled a curse before turning away to let her work her spells. Hovering wouldn't help, and watching Eira twitch and cringe as Lavinia worked on her would do me no favors, either. Reluctantly, I withdrew from the room, forcing myself to inspect the strange specimens floating in jars on the shelves in the sitting room. I tried to ignore the moans and cries coming from the kitchen. I knew firsthand that Lavinia's particular brand of magic hurt like hell, but it was the most effective healing I'd ever endured. Except for maybe that of the pixies.

After what felt like an eternity, Lavinia emerged from the kitchen, wiping her bloody hands on a rag. "It's done. She'll live."

Relief filled my chest, and I sagged against the wall. I hadn't realized until that moment how exhausted I was.

"That Demon Fae did a number on her," she went on with a weary groan. "It made the spell much more difficult for me."

I blinked at her. "Demon Fae?"

"Yes. I could sense its poison in her. I was too preoccupied with sealing her wound, so I didn't have time to inspect it further."

I stared at her in confusion. The Demon Fae had poisoned *me*, not Eira. Then again, I had been bleeding profusely while riding Mauro alongside her. The scent of my poisoned blood likely still lingered on the princess.

"Rest." Lavinia pointed to the small sofa behind me.

I shook my head. "No, you need to tell me more about this necromantic magic you mentioned."

Lavinia smirked. "Ah, yes. You necromancers must be careful with the power you wield. You seem rather fond of this girl, hmm?" She gestured to the kitchen behind her. "Be careful not to kiss her, boy. It is said necromancers possess the kiss of death."

I gaped at her, horrified.

She laughed and waved a hand. "Oh, calm down. I'm only kidding. Unless you channel your power into the kiss, it's harmless."

"How can you be so sure my magic is necromancy at all? And why hasn't this magic shown itself before now?"

"My guess is you weren't under enough duress for it to come to life. Necromancy is powerful, but it's bloody difficult to awaken. Many necromancers spend their entire lives trying to activate their magic with no success. Some could only activate their powers if they bound their magic to an enchanted object."

I frowned. "An enchanted object?"

"Yes. With the right spell, anyone can link their magical essence to an object imbued with power. It enhances an ability, but it's risky; once cast, the spell empowers this object, creating a sort of conduit for your magic. If anyone were to acquire this conduit, they could destroy it and potentially disrupt the connection to your magic completely." She paused, then eyed me shrewdly. "But I have a feeling you won't need to resort to such methods." Her gaze dipped to my belt of knives, which I usually glamoured. But my magic was depleted, and my mind was only on Eira. At the moment, I was too tired to care.

"You're a hunter," she said.

"Yes."

"It's easy for you to take a life, yes?"

I hesitated. "I'm very good at what I do."

She snorted. "I'm sure you are." She rubbed her chin again. "Now that is interesting."

"What?"

"Perhaps your necromancy has already manifested itself. In your *work*." She said the word with a knowing smirk, as if she knew exactly the kind of work I did.

I stared at her. "Necromancy has nothing to do with my work."

"It has everything to do with it, you foolish boy. Necromancy isn't just the art of raising the dead. It is the art of a life weaver. A necromancer holds the threads of life in their hands, whether it's to preserve a life or to end it."

I shook my head. "My hands have never glowed like that before."

"The glow is only an indication of a powerful manifestation of the ability. It can still be demonstrated in other ways, though. Tell me, when you have the intent to kill, do you ever fail?"

I swallowed, not wanting to answer. My anonymity was a precious thing, especially right now when the queen wanted my head.

Lavinia's eyes glinted. "Well, if you *were* a hunter who never missed their mark, I would speculate the magic is assisting you."

I opened my mouth, prepared to argue that perhaps I was just a skilled hunter, when I faltered. In all my years of training in weapons and combat, my aim had always struck true. Even in my early years when I was a beginner, I had thrived, attributing it to my natural knack for hunting.

But perhaps there was another power at play, one I had never realized was there before.

A cold, sickening dread filled my chest as the pieces finally connected in my mind.

"This new power could change the future of our court," Lavinia said with a hungry gleam in her eyes. "The queen could do great wonders with a gift like yours."

The sickening feeling only intensified until I had to brace my hand on the wall to keep from fainting. "She already knows."

Lavinia's eyebrows rose. "How? You only just found out yourself."

My eyes closed against the dizziness that threatened to consume me. It all made sense now. Why else would Calista elevate my father, a man with no rank or status, to the position of commander? Why else was she so determined to keep me in her service?

And why, when I was intent on leaving her employ, did she give me an impossible task, knowing I would fail? In five years, neither Calista nor her trusted soldiers had been able to apprehend the Snow Princess. She assumed I would also be unsuccessful.

She knew about my magic. My father must have had the same power, and she sought it in me as well. And she couldn't bear the thought of me using my powers elsewhere. So instead of releasing me from my contract, she doomed me with one final assignment. One that would either get me killed or mark me as an enemy to the crown.

Because if *she* couldn't utilize my powers... then she would ensure no one else could.

I awoke to a crackling fire and the smell of smoked meat.

With a jolt, I sat up, then patted my tunic in search of the bloody wound that should have killed me.

How was I alive? And where was I?

My gaze flitted about the room. I was lying on a table in a cozy dining room. The opposite end of the room led to a small kitchen where a short, white-haired woman was humming to herself as she cooked meat atop a wood-burning stove.

I swallowed, my mouth dry, as I tried to take stock of the situation. I was in a stranger's home and somehow miraculously healed. Where was Theron? And Frisk, Mauro, and Kendra? Had the animals survived?

As gingerly as possible, I slid off the table, checking my garments once more for bloodstains. But it seemed this strange woman had dressed me in fresh clothes. I was wearing a blue tunic that was a bit too loose on me, along with baggy trousers.

"Don't try to sneak away," the woman called without turning from her cooking. "I already know you're awake."

I froze, my eyes wide. For half a second, I considered going invisible and just disappearing. But she already knew I was here, and if I used my magic to get away, it would only make her *more* suspicious.

Besides, I had to find Theron.

Clearing my throat, I asked, "Who are you?"

"My name is Lavinia. You must mean a lot to Harlan for him to come begging me to heal you." She shot a curious look over her shoulder, and I caught a glimpse of pointed fae ears under her white hair.

Harlan. Right. Theron's alias.

I ignored Lavinia's pointed remark because I couldn't really explain it myself—Theron had *begged* her to heal me? Instead, I asked, "Where is he?"

"He's resting."

"I'm right here."

I whirled and found Theron standing in the doorway of the dining room, arms crossed and expression darkened with rage. He, too, had changed. He now wore a leather tunic with holsters for his daggers, along with black trousers that hugged his legs in ways that made my toes curl.

But all heat left my body when I saw the lethal look in his eyes—directed at me.

"We need to leave. Now." Without another word, he turned and stalked from the room.

Lavinia huffed in exasperation and smoothed her hands along her apron before marching after him. "Before supper? I'm almost finished with the meat."

I followed both of them into the small sitting room that boasted a long, squashy sofa that Theron no doubt had been resting on.

"We've already overstayed our welcome," Theron said

tersely, donning a cloak I hadn't seen him with before. Without looking at me, he tossed an identical one my way. I caught it and stared at it, fingering the soft fabric uncertainly.

"Where did you get these clothes?" I asked.

Theron didn't answer. Lavinia turned to me and said, "He keeps a stash of clothes here for when he needs it."

"That's enough," Theron barked. His steely gaze shifted to me. "We're leaving."

"And what about the handsome payment you promised me?" Lavinia placed her hands on her hips.

Theron, halfway to the door, paused, his shoulders tightening and his stance rigid. "I left it on your counter."

Lavinia's face lit up with glee, and she rubbed her hands together. "Excellent."

Theron swung open the door, and I hurried after him. Just before we left, Lavinia shouted, "I'll catch you next time you're in a dire emergency, foolish boy!"

The door slammed shut as I struggled to match Theron's brisk pace. When I caught up, I grabbed his shoulder and spun him to face me. His brows pulled together, and he gave me his fiercest scowl.

"Theron," I said breathlessly. "What happened? How did we end up here?" I glanced around. As far as I could tell, we hadn't left Tolston. The street and buildings looked the same.

"You were dying. Lavinia healed you. I paid her." His words were clipped.

"What did you pay her?"

"Ninety gold pieces."

My jaw dropped. "Theron—"

"We don't have time to argue about this. We need to move if we're to make it to the palace before dawn."

"Before dawn? Why? The queen wants us both dead! We need to re-think our plan."

"There is no plan," Theron snapped. "I'll deliver you to the palace, as promised, and our bargains will be fulfilled. We can be rid of each other at last."

I tried to ignore how much his words cut. "What are you talking about? Why are you acting like this?"

He met my gaze, his mouth curling into a snarl. "How could you have been so reckless? So *stupid?*"

My chest tightened, and my face heated. "Theron, what's—"

"We could have escaped, Eira," he seethed. "Now she knows you're here—and with me! We are *both* targets now. Sneaking you into the palace is impossible thanks to your recklessness. But I'm bound by this damn bargain, so I have to get you there somehow. We don't have any other choice."

My heart sank like a stone, but indignation rose up inside me. "I get it," I snapped. "You're right. This is my fault. But I don't regret it. Vikros would have killed those children. That blood would have been on my hands."

"If anyone knows what it's like to have hands stained with blood, it's me," he growled. "Unless you wield the blade, your hands are clean."

"That's not how I see it!" I shouted. "You and I are not the same, Theron. We play by different rules. This is a line I *will not cross.*"

"And Calista knows that. That's how she'll trap you, Eira."

"I am different from her," I said firmly. "I will not stand by while innocent people are slaughtered, even if they are humans. And I will stand in the path of that blade every time, even if it kills me."

Sorrow flared in his eyes, and his expression shifted, his

ire melting into a look of pure devastation. "That's what I'm afraid of, Eira. I'm afraid it *will* kill you."

"Is that so bad? It's what you've wanted this whole time."

He huffed a dry laugh and shook his head, running a hand through his hair. "If you think I still want you dead, then you haven't been paying attention."

I took in the exhaustion etched into his face, the weary despair and anxiety. The panic he'd endured... because of me. How he'd begged Lavinia to heal me and paid her handsomely for it.

I thought of his tender words as he'd touched my cheek after we'd gotten the children to safety. *I couldn't let you die, Eira.*

My heart softened as I realized his words were true. He wasn't the cold-blooded assassin I'd first met. The man who only looked out for himself. The hunter who followed orders.

He had saved my life and the lives of those children. He had defied the queen in front of dozens of witnesses.

He had stood by me. My actions had angered him, but he'd still stood by me.

"I'm sorry," I said quietly. "I'm sorry for what my choices have done to you. You... deserve to be free, Theron."

He closed his eyes with a long sigh. "No, I don't. I've been a fool. I deserve whatever the queen has in store for me."

"You don't mean that."

"Yes, I do. Do you know what my magic did?" He gestured to my chest where my wound had been.

I shook my head, my heart racing in anticipation.

"I'm a necromancer, Eira. A life weaver. I hold the threads of life and death in my hands." He raised his palms and glared at them as if they were directly responsible for our predicament. "These hands that have only known death... have had the power to preserve lives this entire time. And I only used them to kill."

A necromancer? My mouth opened, then closed as something clicked into place. "The Demon Fae."

He frowned. "What?"

"*You* killed the Demon Fae."

"Eira, what the hell are you—"

"I slit its throat, but something strange happened just before I struck. You shouted, and the creature just... froze. It started making this odd choking sound, like it was suffocating. At the time, I didn't think. I just acted while it was distracted. But I think *you* took its life before I did."

He said nothing. His dark eyes grew distant as he considered my words. After a long, tense moment, he shook his head and looked at me with interest. "I don't want to talk about my magic. I want to talk about *your* magic. How did you vanish like that?"

Panic shot through me, and I backed up a step.

"No, no, you don't get to withdraw from me like that." He drew closer, practically pinning me against the brick wall of the house next to us. "I told you about my powers. Now you tell me about yours. How did you do that? Is that how you fought the Demon Fae? By vanishing like that?"

I struggled to breathe evenly. I couldn't reveal this about myself. Every instinct in me screamed to ignore him, to avoid answering the question.

But he had saved my life. He had risked everything.

I owed him this.

Slowly, I nodded. "That's my fae magic. Yours is necromancy. Mine is... invisibility."

His eyes grew wide, and he sucked in a breath. For several

heartbeats, we only stared at each other, processing this new information. Then, his voice a soft murmur, he said, "The princess became the very snow on the ground."

"What?"

"There are whispers about you, Eira. Rumors that you can disappear and *become* the snow. That's why you're called the Snow Princess. That's why no one can find you."

I chuckled. "Is that what they say? Well, I'm flattered."

"Is that how you escaped the queen?"

My smile fell. "Yes."

His jaw ticked back and forth, and he nodded. "It's starting to make sense now. But why hasn't Calista told everyone about your gift?"

"I only used it once. My guess is she didn't know for sure what I'd done. Perhaps she thought it was just an effective glamour, or a trick of the light."

Theron frowned in contemplation. "True. There are all sorts of fae gifts out there. But what I still don't understand is what *this* has to do with anything." From his satchel, he withdrew Calista's enchanted hand mirror.

My heart lurched in my throat, and I reached for it before I could stop myself. Theron held it high above his head, his eyebrows lifting expectantly. "It's important, isn't it?"

"Give that back!" I hissed, jumping to try to snatch it. I knew I looked ridiculous, but I didn't care. I had to get it back.

Theron only smirked. "I'm not giving this back until you answer my question. Why is it important?"

"Theron, I'm warning you!"

"What are you warning me of, princess?"

With an angry growl, I drew my dagger and aimed it at his throat. "Give. It. Back."

His smirk only widened. Still holding the mirror above his head, he wrapped his free arm around me, twisting me so my back was against his chest. Somehow, he yanked the dagger from my grasp, letting it clatter to the ground. Gasping for breath, I shoved against him, but his grip was solid as steel. He wasn't yielding.

"You were saying?" His breath was warm against my ear, and despite my predicament, I found my insides churning from the sound of his voice, low and rumbling. I could feel it resonating from his chest against my back.

Blood and ice, it was the most delicious sound.

"Theron, you don't know what you're dealing with," I whispered.

"Then *tell me*." His voice was a caress against my ear.

My mouth went dry. My invisibility was one thing, but this mirror? No one knew about it, not even Stella. How could I share that secret with him?

"I—I stole it from Calista," I said.

"Hmm, I figured as much. Why? What's so special about it?"

"It's enchanted."

Theron waited. When I said nothing, he chuckled, his chest humming from the sound. "You're going to have to do better than that, princess."

My eyes shut against the warning pulsing through me. *Don't do it. Don't do it.*

But I had to. Theron would keep me in this alley all night if I didn't talk.

Shivering bones, I couldn't believe I was about to tell him this.

"Do you remember me telling you about stealing a magical object that reveals truth? It's this mirror. This is what I stole. Calista didn't banish me because of my human bloodline. She banished me because of the mirror. It's the only thing in the entire realm that will reveal who she really is."

"And who is she really?"

I forced myself to take a slow, steadying breath before I said. "She's a Demon Fae."

Theron went rigid behind me. I yearned to turn and look at him, to gauge his reaction, but he still had my back pressed to his chest. I felt his heartbeat quicken from my words.

"That can't be true," he breathed.

"It is. I can't lie. I saw it with my own eyes. She transformed in front of me."

His pulse fluttered, and I felt him swallow. "You must have been mistaken."

I gritted my teeth. "Don't patronize me, Theron. This is the *truth*."

He released me, and I whirled to face him, eyes wide. My chest twisted with anxiety, and I realized with a jolt of awareness just how desperately I needed him to believe me.

I needed him on my side.

Please believe me, Theron.

His dark eyes were narrowed, his brows knitted together. A muscle worked in his jaw, and his nostrils flared.

Slowly, he shook his head, and my heart dropped down to my stomach.

He doesn't believe me.

The wave of disappointment that crashed over me was enough to douse any heat I'd felt from earlier. I felt myself drawing a step away from him.

He opened his mouth to speak, but a shout from down the alley drew our attention.

"There they are!" A guardsman pointed to us, and three other soldiers appeared behind him. They each drew their swords and stormed toward us. "Stop where you are, in the name of the queen!"

The Hunter

I didn't have time to address Eira's claim. Though my head was reeling, the sight of the guards racing toward us snapped me into action.

I grabbed Eira's arm while simultaneously shoving the gilded hand mirror into my pack. She managed to swipe her dagger from the ground before we bolted down the alley.

Eira lagged behind, struggling to keep up with my loping strides, but my grip on her arm kept her close. I urged her left, then right, the narrow pathways familiar to me from my travels through the town over the years.

After several minutes of sprinting, her sharp gasps turned into pained wheezes. "I can't," she rasped. "I can't—"

I cursed and slowed my pace, glancing over my shoulder. I could no longer see the guards, but their echoing shouts still sounded close by. My gaze roved up and down the alley, trying to get my bearings and figure out the best path to take. If I were on my own, I could easily outrun the guards until I reached my destination.

But Eira wasn't as fast as I was. And if the guards caught her...

No. I couldn't let myself think about that.

I needed a new plan. I worked my jaw back and forth, scrutinizing the mud-stained buildings. The one directly across from me had a sign that read, *The Wild Stag*.

I immediately thought of Mauro and how offended he would be at the thought of a run-down building like this named after his kind.

From the other side of the grimy window, a moan of pleasure rang out.

Well, Mauro would be even *more* affronted to learn that a place called The Wild Stag was a house of pleasure.

I stilled, an idea occurring to me. Taking Eira's hand, I led her a few paces down the alley until we reached a crossroads between buildings. Several brothels lined the winding path, and more carnal sounds filled the air. From outside the buildings, various couples were pressed against the brick wall, groping one another.

"Theron," Eira hissed in warning, but I didn't listen. I tugged her forward until we reached a gap between the buildings. I gathered our packs, weapons, and cloaks and shoved them on the ground so they were hidden behind our legs. Then, I leaned in, crowding her against the wall.

Her mouth fell open, her cheeks flushing as she glanced around us in alarm. "What are you doing?"

"We need to blend in," I murmured, my heart racing at the thought of what I planned to do. "Do you trust me?"

Her mouth opened, then closed. For a moment, I thought she might say *no*. She had every reason to. Hell, *I* probably would, if our roles were reversed.

But before long, she was nodding, her eyes shining with an earnestness that made my chest constrict. Swallowing hard, I leaned closer, hovering over her, my chest flush with hers.

Blood and ice, I hoped this worked. If it didn't, we would be caught, and it would all be over.

I can fight the soldiers, I thought. *Eira can use her invisibility to get out, and I can fight them off.*

But even as I thought the words, doubt crowded my mind. That plan hadn't gone too well last time. And if Vikros was nearby, he would spot Eira in seconds.

My mouth went dry as I lowered my head, trying not to lose myself in the piercing ice-blue gaze Eira had pinned on me. She was staring, wide-eyed and lips parted, as I angled my face to meet hers.

And she wasn't pulling away.

Just do it, Theron, I thought, frustrated that I was putting this off. *This is for your survival. It doesn't mean anything.*

It would also resolve one of our previous bargains. Which meant I wouldn't have to deal with kissing her ever again.

Just this once, I told myself.

A shout split the air, and several people cried out in alarm. My heart jolted, and I knew we were out of time.

Before I could react, Eira seized my collar and dragged my mouth to hers.

At first, I was so shocked that I held perfectly still. Her soft lips pressed to mine, and she arched against me. As the commotion drew nearer, I snapped out of my stupor and put my hands on her waist, pulling her closer. Her mouth moved fervently over mine, coaxing more kisses from me. Her tongue flicked along my lip, and I met it with my own. Heat burned between us, scorching and all-consuming.

Heavy footfalls approached. I drew back a fraction, panting against Eira's lips, and whispered, "Do I have permission to touch you?"

"You already are," she breathed.

"I mean… elsewhere?"

"Yes." Her eyes were full of heat and longing, stoking something low in my belly.

I pressed into her fully, pinning her to the brick wall, then hitched up one of her legs until it was wrapped around my middle. Then, I ground against her, drawing a gasp from her lips. I bent down and kissed her neck, dragging my lips up and down the column of her throat. Her fingernails dug into the back of my neck, her hips writhing underneath me. I kept one hand under her thigh, holding her leg up. My fingers inched higher and higher until she shuddered and let out a soft whimper.

"Louder," I ordered.

A ragged moan poured from her mouth, and shivering bones, it did sinful things to me. My cock hardened, straining against my trousers, and she rubbed against it mercilessly. The friction of the fabric between us was both maddening and intoxicating.

I pulled the collar of her shirt, dragging it down to expose one of her pale shoulders. I brought my mouth to it, my tongue gliding over her soft skin. Eira's hand ran through my hair, tugging on it to bring me closer.

A soldier ran past us. Then another.

"You need to make noises, too," Eira hissed as more guards approached.

I made a low growling sound, and Eira's leg tightened around me, almost imperceptibly. I wasn't even sure if she realized she'd done it.

In the pixie caves, I recalled her saying she loved my low, gravelly voice. A smile quirked along my lips. In a rough tone, I said loudly, "That's it, love. Harder."

Her breath hitched, and she uttered a soft gasp. "Oh,

damn." She wrapped her other leg around me. I brought my hips closer to hold her upright against the wall. She drew back to stare at me with half-lidded eyes, her lips slightly swollen from our kisses.

"You aren't playing fair, hunter," she panted.

I only arched an eyebrow at her in response.

To my surprise, she grinned, her expression feral. "I can play, too." She lifted her hips and wriggled directly on my arousal. Then, she slid a hand between her legs, easing it under the waistband of my trousers until her fingers gripped my cock.

I went rigid, then slammed against her with a bit too much force, pressing her back harder into the wall. Molten desire flooded my veins.

This was pure torture. I was torn between wanting this to be over and wanting to rip off Eira's clothes and take her against this wall, witnesses be damned.

More soldiers darted past us. Eira's grip on me tightened. My eyes shut against the onslaught of heat cutting through me.

"How does that feel?" she breathed in my ear.

A strangled sound escaped me, and I didn't have to exaggerate it. This devious princess would be the death of me. My hand rested on her waist, and I inched it upward, tracing fingers along her ribs until I reached the bottom of her breasts.

She stilled as I pressed a thumb against her nipple. Even through the fabric of her tunic, she quivered under my touch. I pressed harder, kneading her breast between my fingers. Her head rolled back, and she cried out.

"This way!" shouted a guard.

Two more men shot past us, and I distinctly heard one of

them say *healer*.

I froze, my heart lurching with recognition. My senses homed in on the men pounding through the alley, trying to catch snippets of their conversation. Eira's moans faded, her eyes sparking with clarity as she, too, listened.

"The old healer tipped us off," one of the men was saying. "The assassin is here, as is the Snow Princess."

Shit. Lavinia had called the guards, the conniving bitch.

If the queen knew for certain Eira was in the village, she would tear apart every building until she found us.

Eira's eyes widened as she processed the words. Our faces were only a breath apart; to a bystander, it would look like we were still kissing.

"What do we do?" she whispered.

There were still too many guards in the alley for us to slip away unnoticed. But if we waited too long, the area would be swarming with them.

"We need a diversion," I breathed.

Her eyes suddenly lit up. She brought two fingers to her mouth and let out a faint, high-pitched whistle.

I stiffened before clapping a hand over her mouth. The sound hadn't been too loud, but a few people nearby were looking around in confusion.

"What the hell are you doing?" I growled.

Her gaze was full of amusement. Slowly, I lowered my hand enough for her to respond.

"Summoning reinforcements," she said with a grin.

I frowned, not understanding.

A small white shape landed on her shoulder, and my head reared back in shock. Kendra's brilliant blue eyes darted from Eira to me and back again.

"Why are your lips so red?" she asked.

Eira's cheeks flushed. She hastily removed her hand from my trousers, then dropped her legs so they were no longer wrapped around me.

I hated how much my body yearned for her warmth.

Eira cleared her throat. "Are Mauro and Frisk safe?"

"Yes. They are a few streets over. We're following the commotion. I assume that's why you two are cuddled up in this alley?"

"It is. Can you distract the guards so we can slip away?"

Kendra ducked her head under a wing. "I don't know, Snow."

"Please? We could really use your help."

Kendra flared her wing so it nearly covered her entire head. She let out a small squeak of fear.

"Kendra," I said, and she lifted her wing, her eyes snapping to me. "You can do this. You were incredible against the soldiers earlier. I watched you fight them off when they threatened those children. It was... Well, it was quite admirable."

Kendra's head rose, her eyes brightening. "Really?"

"Really. I was very impressed. And I don't say that lightly."

"It's true," Eira added. "He hates saying kind things."

I shoved her arm, and she elbowed me in response.

"It's just for a few seconds," Eira went on. "You don't even have to get that close to them. Just fly nearby, draw their attention, and let us slip away. Shoot some ice blasts at them from a distance."

Kendra tilted her head, considering this. "I think I can do that."

"You definitely can," I said encouragingly.

Kendra glanced between us, then scrutinized Eira. "Why is your sleeve pulled down?"

Eira made an exasperated sound, her cheeks reddening further as she adjusted her tunic. A few more soldiers moved past us, their pace slower than the others'. I worried they would look at us too closely and recognize us. I pressed closer to Eira, trying to block her and Kendra from their view. I considered asking the princess to turn invisible but realized it would look even weirder if I were pressed up against the wall by myself.

"All right," Kendra said, stretching out her wings. "When you hear my call, it's time to move."

Eira nodded. "We'll meet you at Stella's house." She beamed with pride as Kendra leapt off her shoulder and took off into the sky. The dragon's tiny form vanished, and I resisted the urge to turn and watch her fly away. I needed to look like a brothel patron, not someone acquainted with a dragon.

I kept my face close to Eira's, our cheeks touching. Her erratic breathing matched mine. I could feel her thundering heartbeat even through her tunic.

From behind us, a scream rang out. Then another. I made to move, but Eira pinched my arm.

"Not yet," she hissed.

I held perfectly still, waiting. I itched to turn and look at the cause of the commotion, but I needed to keep Eira hidden.

Then, a shrill *caw* sounded, like the amplified crow of a raven.

This time, it was Eira's turn to grab my arm. Together, we bolted, taking off down the alley. I shot a quick glance over my shoulder, barely containing a snort of laughter.

Kendra, the fierce but tiny dragon, was flying around the guards. She leapt from shoulder to shoulder, shooting bursts of ice directly into each soldier's ear while they fruitlessly swung their swords at her. I heard the familiar low bellow of Mauro and caught sight of a flash of his antlers as he joined the fray.

Though I longed to linger and watch the show, Eira pulled me forward. We rounded the corner, and the soldiers and animals faded from view.

The Princess

My body was still buzzing from adrenaline and the feel of Theron's hands. Not to mention how that deep, gravelly voice of his made my stomach flutter...

I shoved the thought from my mind as we raced between alleys, my shorter legs struggling to keep up with Theron's longer ones. I trusted him to navigate through this network of backroads; it had been far too long since I'd been to Tolston, and even then, I certainly hadn't taken a route like this before. A stitch formed in my side, and each gulp of air sent a stab through my lungs.

"How far is Stella's home?" Theron asked, barely even winded.

I shot a quick glance at the unfamiliar and grimy buildings that surrounded us, unsure of how to answer. After a moment, I wheezed, "Half a mile... south of... Miller's Forge."

Theron's steps faltered, his brow furrowing. A keen, calculating look crossed his face, and then he nodded before leading me to the left. "This way."

The dusty path took us downhill, and we took another left. The buildings thinned out, becoming sparser the farther we ran. When Theron tugged my arm, guiding me to the right, we emerged on an empty cobbled road. My mouth fell open as I recognized the town square with the church bells in the center. A statue of my father rested in the center, covered with a light dusting of snow. The sight of it made my throat tighten. There were stables to the left, and I heard the soft nicker of a horse.

Somehow, the backroads had led us straight to the heart of the village. Ordinarily, this place was bustling, but now, in the dead of night, it was eerily silent—the curfew, no doubt.

"We can't linger here," Theron muttered, his gaze roving over the empty square before he urged me forward.

I knew he was right. Already, the heavy footfalls of soldiers nearby made me want to bolt. I was tempted to shroud myself in invisibility, but I knew it would do no good. I couldn't extend my magic to Theron. Besides, with Vikros after me, it would be useless anyway.

As we crossed the courtyard and ducked into another alley, several shouts rang out. Theron shot a concerned look over his shoulder.

"Will your animal friends be all right?" he asked.

I bit back a smile at the note of worry in his voice. "They'll be fine. They know where Stella's home is."

Theron nodded, but a wrinkle remained between his brows. My chest warmed as I realized how fond he'd grown of Mauro, Kendra, and Frisk.

The cold assassin had a soft heart after all.

The alley we squeezed ourselves into was so narrow that we couldn't walk side by side. In some places, I had to turn myself to the side and inch forward, the brick buildings brushing my chest and backside.

"We'll have to slow our pace from here," Theron said,

grunting as he sucked in his stomach and wriggled past a particularly small gap.

"No shit," I said with a snort, but I was grateful for the reprieve from all the running. I still had a cramp in my side.

For a moment, our trek was silent save for the occasional grunting and scuffling as we shifted around. After a while, I cleared my throat, my heart hammering madly in my chest.

"You didn't say anything," I said hesitantly, "about Calista being Demon Fae."

Theron's shoulders went rigid, but he did not reply.

I swallowed, a lump forming in my throat. "You don't believe me, do you?"

"I never said that."

"You didn't have to."

He cut me an exasperated glance. "What do you want me to say, Eira? I can't lie. I've worked with Calista for years. I think I would know if she were Demon Fae."

"I saw her demon form," I insisted. "The mirror only reveals truth. She has a powerful glamour; it's how she hides her true nature. But with the mirror, I can expose her for what she is."

Theron was shaking his head, and anger bubbled up inside me.

"How can you dismiss this so easily?" I argued. "Think about it. She controls people with their blood. What kind of fae magic does that?"

"Stop." Theron shifted, only able to angle his body halfway to face me. His expression was dark with fury. "Do you even hear yourself? You don't have to convince me she's evil. I get it. You hate her. I do, too. That doesn't mean she's a Demon Fae. I've fought them, Eira. I know what they look like. What they smell like. What their magic is like. I'm not a fool."

"It's not just *you* she's been fooling," I insisted. "It's everyone! Even my own father. Her disguise is flawless. It's why she has to be stopped."

Theron ran a hand down his face as if I were some wearisome child he was forced to deal with. "This is ridiculous. Just stop, Eira. We have enough problems on our hands without these delusions."

My blood chilled to ice in my veins. Despair crashed through me, followed swiftly by rage.

Damn this hunter. Damn his stubbornness and his stupidity. If he didn't want to see the truth, then fine.

He wasn't on my side. He never would be. And it would be best if I accepted that now.

I huffed a dry laugh and forced a cold smile on my face. "All right, Theron. I trusted you with this secret, and you treat me like shit for it. You want to be an asshole for the rest of your life? Go right ahead. I'm done. You said it before: Let's just get this over with so we can be rid of each other once and for all."

Regret crossed his features, and he grimaced. "Eira—"

"Don't talk to me," I snapped, my tone icy. "Just keep moving."

A muscle feathered in his jaw, and he nodded once before turning and continuing down the alley. All the while, I tried to ignore the aching pit in my stomach.

Despite my doubts, a part of me had thought he would believe me. That he would be my ally in this.

But in the end, he only belonged to her—Calista.

And perhaps he always would.

The air grew warmer the closer we got to the forge. The

narrow alley deposited us directly in front of Miller's smithy, the air sweltering and the street echoing with the sounds of clanging metal.

Theron made to step forward, then suddenly stiffened, his arms going rigid at his sides.

"What is it?" I glanced up and down the street, expecting to find soldiers. But it was empty.

When I looked at Theron, his head was thrown back, the tendons along his neck standing out. With a loud shudder, he fell backward into me. I barely caught him, resting against the brick wall for support.

"Theron?" I grunted from his weight, then eased him to the ground so I could get a better look at him.

I crouched in front of him, and my heart dropped like a stone.

His eyes were all black. His mouth opened wide as he inhaled a rattling gasp. I had seen this before.

He was being summoned by Calista.

I shook his shoulders. "Snap out of it, hunter. Stay with me."

He made a choking sound, like he couldn't get enough air.

I slapped him hard across the face and shook him again. "*Wake up*! You have to fight it, Theron!"

In a flash, his arm shot out, his hand aiming for my throat. Just before he touched me, he cried out in pain, his back arching as he twisted violently away from me. His head hit the brick wall behind him, and he let out a pained groan.

"Shivering bones," I muttered, drawing closer to him. His eyes were closed, his brows creased in anguish. I put my hands on his cheeks, then lifted one of his eyelids.

His eyes were back to normal. He jerked away from my

grasp, blinking rapidly, his breaths sharp and ragged. "Eira. What... What..." He winced, bringing a hand to his head.

"It was Calista," I said grimly. "She's using your blood to call on you."

Theron stared at me, his face draining of color. "Shit. *Shit.* Eira, she'll order me to kill you. And—"

"And if you try, the fae bargain will take your life," I said quietly.

Theron shook his head, scrambling to his feet. He stumbled, leaning against the wall with another groan. "I... I have to get out of here. I have to get away from you."

I grabbed his shoulders before he could stagger off somewhere. "What are you doing?"

"Eira, you aren't safe!"

I snorted. "When am I ever?"

"If she commands me to do something to you, I *have* to do it." His voice was tortured, and the haunted look in his eyes told me he'd done unspeakable things under Calista's influence. "I don't know which one is stronger, her blood magic or our fae bargain. But I don't want to find out. You have to let me go."

I took a shaky breath and squeezed his shoulders. "There might be another way."

His brow furrowed. "What do you mean?"

"I watched Calista for years. Sometimes she didn't even know I was there. And there is one thing that makes her hold on someone a bit less potent."

His gaze turned wary. "And what is that?"

"Loss of blood."

THE HUNTER

My eyes narrowed at the princess, every alarm bell ringing through my body. "How much blood loss?"

Her face twisted in an apologetic grimace, and that was all I needed to know.

I sighed, running a hand down my face. "How do you know this? Tell me specifics."

"I was watching from the hall when Calista was raging to our captain of the guards that a commander wasn't answering her summons," Eira said, wringing her hands together. "She ordered the guards to find him at any cost. Turned out, he was in the infirmary. He had been attacked by a gang of bandits, and they'd cut off his arm. He died later that day."

Perfect. So the only successful instance of resisting Calista's power had been enough blood loss to kill a man. I swallowed hard, my mind straining to find a solution to this that didn't involve me dying.

A necromancer holds the threads of life in their hands, whether it's to preserve a life or to end it.

Lavinia's words rang in my head. Though I loathed the healer for her betrayal, I knew she'd spoken the truth.

I had the power of life and death in my hands.

But my magic was still new to me. I couldn't even wield it properly when I was at full strength, let alone suffering from blood loss. How could I be certain I could survive?

Eira crossed her arms over her chest. "I see that calculating mind of yours working hard. What are you thinking right now?"

I huffed a dry laugh. "I'm thinking I'm either going to die from blood loss or from the fae bargain claiming me. The odds are pretty bleak."

Eira placed a hand on my arm, her blue eyes earnest. "I'll keep you alive as best I can. We can take this slow. A little blood at a time. I'm sure that every drop you lose weakens her power bit by bit."

My nostrils flared, agitation rising up inside me. I was so damn *helpless*. I was a liability, and I would be slowing Eira down. She had plans to put in motion, and now I was standing in the way. My chest tightened with apprehension. "Eira, if I'm injured, I can't protect you."

She blinked, her expression startled. "You don't need to. Our bargain only stated *you* couldn't harm me."

I made a noise of frustration and placed my hands on her waist, pulling her closer. Her eyes widened slightly. "I don't think you understand," I said in a low voice. "I don't care what Calista has ordered me to do. I can't see you hurt. It would be far worse for me to have to watch *you* suffer than to endure whatever horrors Calista has in store for me."

Eira's breath hitched, and she moistened her lips. My gaze darted down to her mouth—a mouth I knew tasted as soft and smooth as rose petals. "I—I don't think you mean that."

My brows knitted together. "Why not?"

She gave a short exhale, her expression full of incredulity. She let a hand fall on her thigh. "Are you serious? You called me *delusional* earlier. Forgive me for not believing that you care about me all that much."

My eyes closed as shame crept into my chest. She was right. She had every reason to despise me. Hell, I even despised myself. A lump formed in my throat, and I found it difficult to swallow. "I... regret the words I said to you earlier," I said in a strained voice. "I'm sorry."

"Does that mean you believe me now?"

A dull throb began to pound through my skull, making it hard to concentrate. Blood and ice, I couldn't *think* right now. I couldn't find the right words to say. Anytime I spoke, I only made things worse.

All I did was hurt her over and over again. It was all I was capable of doing.

Pain. My job, my *life*, was only meant to inflict pain.

I inhaled deeply, my insides quivering from the intensity of my thoughts. I had to make her understand that I *was* on her side... but I was also conflicted. About my life. My purpose. *Everything.*

Slowly, my eyes opened to find hers full of hope and vulnerability. She was worried I would dismiss her claims again and call her insane.

Delusional. I'd actually said that.

I was such an asshole.

"I don't know," I said at last. When her expression fell, I slid my knuckle under her chin, forcing her to meet my eyes. "Please let me finish."

She took a shuddering breath and nodded, urging me to continue.

"You have to understand that I've been working for

Calista for over a decade. That's more than ten years of my life I've devoted to killing in her name. For the good of our court. For the good of my people. Or... so I thought." My hands began to shake, so I dropped my arms to my sides, clutching my fingers into tight fists. "If what you say is true, then that means that everything I've done, all the lives I've taken... the blood that's on my hands, it... it..." I broke off with an anguished groan, running my hands through my hair. My head was *spinning*. My thoughts were flitting about so quickly I couldn't make sense of them.

Calista, a Demon Fae.

Could Eira's claim be true? If it was... Gods, it would change everything.

Every contract. Every mission. Every bargain.

A lie. A deception.

All those people I killed. All those lives I ruined.

It was all for nothing. A waste. An abomination.

I was a cold-blooded killer. Not for the good of my court, but for a pretender who didn't belong on the throne. For someone who used me as her puppet to eliminate threats to her rule. I had always disliked the way Calista had ruled, but I had never considered it my place to question it. I had somehow convinced myself that it was for the best.

I sagged backward against the brick wall, my chest wound up so tightly that I couldn't breathe. Eira's warm hands pressed against my cheeks. I stared down at her, struggling to see straight, to think clearly...

Then, those ice-blue eyes were holding mine. Grounding me. Anchoring me. Keeping me still. I gazed into them, drowning in them, and my heart rate slowed. The raging inferno of my thoughts quieted. There was only her and those frosty eyes. Eyes I would gladly fall into and never come out of.

My breathing reached a steady, even pace. Her gaze continued to pin me in place.

When all was quiet within me, I said softly, "It is easier for me to dismiss your claim because then it won't completely unravel my life and my past sins. Even if, deep down, I know what you say is the truth, right now... I can't accept it. Not yet. Not until my mind—my *heart*—can fully process the crimes I have committed on behalf of an imposter." My voice broke on the last sentence, and the lump in my throat tightened. My eyes stung, and my chest constricted again.

But I forced myself to look into the icy depths of those eyes, to let her soothe the heat roiling in my gut. I didn't deserve it. But I was still grateful for it.

I hadn't realized a tear had streaked down my cheek until Eira caught it with her thumb and smoothed it away. Her own eyes were moist as she said to me, "I understand. But you aren't a monster, Theron. I never thought you were. And even if you do accept my truth, it doesn't make you evil for what you did. You were only trying to free yourself."

I shook my head and sniffed, dropping my gaze. "It's not good enough."

For years, I had only thought of myself and *my* freedom. Meanwhile, humans like Eira, along with the unseelie, were being persecuted and hunted on Calista's orders.

I had known about their suffering. And I'd done *nothing*.

I might not have had a choice in my assignments. But I was still afforded freedoms. As a member of the court, there were ways I could have helped. I could have quietly defied Calista, finding ways around our bargains.

I could have done so much more.

A sudden, searing pain shot through my head, setting me ablaze. Fire burned in my veins. I crumpled, and Eira and the alley disappeared from view. Blackness swallowed me whole as Calista's face appeared in my mind.

Kill her, she commanded. *You must kill the princess.*

"Eira," I groaned, my voice sounding far away. I was fading. Soon, Calista would claim me. But I had one ounce of clarity left. I had to make it count. "Eira, *cut me.*"

THE PRINCESS

THERON'S EYES WERE ALL BLACK AGAIN. I BACKED AWAY FROM him, my heart stuttering in my chest.

Not again. Not now.

His cheek was still moist from his tears. I thought of his broken expression, the tormented look in his eyes. He was so burdened by his sins. By his self-loathing.

And now, Calista had hold of him once more.

Fresh rage burned within me at the thought of my horrid stepmother and what she was doing to Theron. She was torturing him. Taking away his free will.

Caging him.

"You can't have him, you bitch," I growled, gritting my teeth as I drew closer to Theron. He groaned in pain, sagging backward and blinking rapidly.

He was fighting. Pride swelled in my heart.

Taking advantage of his inner struggle, I drew another one of his knives. I angled it above his wrist, then hesitated. I cast a quick glance around the darkened alley.

No one was around. It was still nighttime, and with the curfew, very few civilians were wandering about.

I brought the blade closer, then hissed in a sharp breath. Damn. I really didn't want to hurt him.

A growl escaped him, and he lunged for me. I yelped, slicing into his wrist. Crimson blood spurted, dripping onto the ground.

I gasped, letting the knife fall as I staggered backward. I hadn't meant to cut him so abruptly. I had acted on instinct.

Theron hissed sharply, pressing a hand to his wrist to stem the flow. He grunted, then let out a choking sound. His head rolled back as he fell against the brick wall behind him. White crept into his eyes once more. He blinked, and they were all black again.

I reached for him, pressing his shaking hand between mine. "You can do this, Theron. Come back to me." My eyes darted to the steady flow of blood gushing from his wrist. Shivering bones, he was losing so much. I needed to bind the wound quickly.

But his eyes... Calista still hadn't released him.

Shit. What if this didn't work? What if I inadvertently killed him?

A low, keening moan poured from his lips, followed by a strangled sob. He lifted his uninjured arm to his head, clutching at his temple in agony. "Eira," he choked out. "*Eira.*"

"I'm here," I whispered, my eyes burning with tears. I took his face in my hands and pulled him closer. "Look at me, Theron. *Look at me.*"

His eyelids fluttered, then slid open. Relief soared within me at the sight of his normal onyx eyes, though slightly bloodshot.

"That's it," I murmured, holding his gaze. "Stay with me, hunter."

His face was looking paler, and he began to sway.

"I have to bind your wound," I said quickly. "Are you still with me?"

Slowly, he nodded. He didn't look fully lucid yet, but I couldn't tell if that was because of Calista's influence or the blood loss.

I would have to risk it.

I hastily ripped a strip of fabric from the bottom of my tunic and began wrapping his wrist tightly. The first layer of fabric was completely soaked through with blood, so I wrapped it a second time, and then a third for good measure. My ragged tunic now barely hung below my belly, and the sleeves were a bit high. If I moved or stretched too far, I would reveal my abdomen and possibly my shoulders, too. It would be quite scandalous to a bystander. But it would have to do.

I turned Theron's hand around, stroking my finger down the length of the bandage to ensure it was still dry. When I looked up, I found him staring at me, his breathing ragged and his eyes slightly dazed. His face was still pale.

"Better?" I peered hesitantly into his eyes, waiting for them to turn all black again.

He licked his lips and nodded again.

"Are you sure?" I asked, my voice firm.

"My head is clear, if that's what you're asking. I can't hear her voice anymore." His voice was rough and strained.

I exhaled, letting my frame sag. "Good." At least that was settled. For now.

If Calista kept calling him, I wasn't sure how much I could hurt him. I was really hoping she didn't have much of his blood left in stock.

The odds were slim, considering he'd been in her employment for over a decade.

A loud metallic clanging sound rang out from the forge in front of us, making us both jump. We both glanced nervously toward the commotion. So far, no one had emerged from the smithy yet, but it was still the quiet hours of early morning. Most people were asleep, save for the blacksmiths who liked to get an early start.

We were running out of time. The sky was turning pink with the early signs of dawn. Soon, the streets would be swarming with civilians and soldiers.

"Can you move?" I asked Theron.

"Yes," he said gruffly. "We've lingered here too long."

I rolled my eyes. He said that as if we'd gotten lazy and taken a nap instead of having to fight off the influence of a power-hungry Demon Fae queen.

"Ready?" he asked.

I nodded, and the two of us crept forward. Theron was crouched low to the ground, so I followed suit. Before long, my legs were throbbing from maintaining a squatting position. I bit down on my lip, determined not to complain. If Theron could manage it, despite the strain of battling Calista's blood magic, then I sure as hell could do it.

We edged around the building, Theron pausing occasionally when he noticed movement. When we neared the front, he peered around the corner, then swore under his breath.

My eyes widened in alarm, my pulse quickening. "What is it?" I mouthed.

"Soldiers," he whispered. "Stationed around the smithy."

My heart lodged itself in my throat as I gave him a panicked look. What were we supposed to do? We couldn't get to Stella's house without passing the forge.

Theron jerked his head toward the other side of the building, and I nodded. We turned back the way we came, coming toward the back door of the smithy. Just before we reached it, the door swung open. I scrambled backward, nearly falling on top of Theron. He dragged me out of the way just before a blacksmith strode out of the building, wiping his face with a rag.

"We need to go into the forge," Theron whispered. His voice was right at my ear, and I realized his hands were wrapped around me, pressing my back to his chest.

I swallowed hard, my face suddenly hot as I scooted away from him. "How will that help? There are still soldiers stationed outside."

"It's not unusual for blacksmiths to wear cloth masks to protect their faces," he said. "You can use your invisibility, and I'll dress myself as a blacksmith. If I walk out of a smithy, my face covered and ash staining my clothes, the soldiers will think I'm just an ordinary blacksmith."

I arched an eyebrow at him. "Are you sure about that?"

"My livelihood depends on my blending in," Theron said, giving me a flat look. "Yes, I'm sure."

"And what if Vikros is there?"

"Then you'll cover your face, too, and blend in along with me. Just follow my lead."

I resisted the urge to snort at that, refraining from pointing out that *following his lead* might be difficult if my deranged stepmother happened to summon him again.

We crept closer to the back door. The sounds of a hammer striking metal rang out, blaring against my ears. The air swarmed with heat, making me feel sleepy.

Theron carefully eased the door open and peered inside, holding up a hand to indicate I wait. My heart raged inside my chest as I waited for someone to notice him and cry out in alarm.

But nothing happened.

After a moment, Theron slid inside. I summoned my magic, draping my invisibility around myself, before I followed him.

As soon as I entered the smithy, an inferno surrounded me, making the air stifling. I struggled to breathe around the ash and scorching heat. A massive kiln was built into the center of the smithy, and several men in aprons surrounded it. Some hammered away at their metal, while others plunged tongs into the hot coals.

A few people turned to glance at us as we entered. I stiffened, but Theron said smoothly, "Morning. Is Miller around?" His arm came around his back, and, without looking, he snatched a bundle of black fabric from the shelf behind him and tossed it to me. Even though I was invisible, I was already tying it around my face. I choked on a gag when the smell of sweat filled my nostrils. But it helped block out the heat, so that was something.

I inched closer to Theron, who was wearing his glamour from earlier, now donning his *Harlan* persona.

"He went to get more scrap metal," muttered a blacksmith as he wiped sweat from his brow. His eyes narrowed, and he pointed his hammer at Theron. "Haven't seen you round here before, lad." His tone was laced with suspicion.

"I come and go," Theron said, grabbing a rake from the wall as he approached the kiln. "Clean up here and there. Tell Miller that Harlan says hello."

"Aye, Harlan!" called a voice from across the forge. A burly fellow with curly red hair was grinning from underneath his cloth mask. "It's been an age. Where you comin' from?"

"Athawood Peaks," Theron supplied. "Good to see you

again, Bran." He grunted as he started scraping out loose bits of scrap metal and coals from the kiln. His movements were steady and precise, as if he knew exactly what he was doing. When the area was clear, he pulled the bellows off the wall and stoked the flames.

I was gaping at him, unable to process this. He actually *looked* like a blacksmith right now. If I had stumbled into this forge, even knowing what Theron looked like, I wouldn't have been able to notice it was him. Between his glamour, the face covering, and his confident movements, he truly did blend in.

I'll be damned, I thought, knowing he would brag about this later. I had clearly underestimated him. My eyes snagged on the ash coating his fingers, and I barely caught a glimpse of him wiping the soot on his face in between his movements.

Smart. I inched toward the forge and did the same, rubbing ash over my face and clothes to make me as unrecognizable as possible.

Bran, the red-haired blacksmith, huffed a low chuckle. "Those mountains, boy... You're lucky the storms didn't blow you away."

"They almost did," Theron said with a laugh.

Shivering bones, he was *laughing*. The sound was so foreign to my ears.

I shifted so I was closer to Theron, the heat of the kiln making me sweat. "We need to move," I whispered.

His brows drew together for a brief second before his face smoothed over.

"Those soldiers still out there?" he asked.

Bran grunted. "Won't leave us alone, those bastards."

Theron was shaking his head. "Bloody shame. I'll bet work has slowed."

"Damn right," said the first blacksmith.

Theron rubbed the back of his neck and sighed. "Better find Miller, then. I might be able to help."

Bran jerked his head toward the door. "He hasn't been gone long. You should catch up with him quick."

Theron patted the man on the shoulder in thanks.

"Come back and tell us some stories from those haunted mountains, will ye?" Bran let out a hearty guffaw.

To my shock, Theron joined in, the sound jovial and so full of life that he seemed like a completely different person. I never thought a grouchy man like him could utter such a noise.

"The things I've seen..." Theron jabbed a finger at Bran. "It'd make you shit yourself, old man."

Bran howled with laughter, and the other blacksmith joined in, too. Even I cracked a smile, unable to help myself. Theron was moving toward the door, and I hastened to follow, worried the door would close on my face.

I didn't notice the hammer on the floor until I tripped over it and crashed into a table of swords. They clanged together loudly, the weapons sliding over one another.

Theron was several steps away from the table. Both blacksmiths froze, their eyes shifting to where I stood. I knew they couldn't see me, but my face still drained of color.

Shit, shit, shit.

The Princess

"The hell was that?" The first blacksmith shoved his tongs onto the shelf and stomped toward me.

"You got a critter in here?" Theron asked.

Sweat dripped down my neck as I carefully inched away from the table and toward Theron. I narrowly avoided colliding with the huge blacksmith who had come to investigate. He ducked his head under the table and looked around.

"Sounded bigger than a rodent," Bran mused. "Maybe you brought some spirits from the mountain with ye, Harlan!" He chuckled again, but his eyes darted around nervously.

"Best be off then," Theron said. "Don't want to bring more trouble to this place."

"Where did you say you were from?" asked the first blacksmith, straightening to glare at Theron with suspicion.

"Athawood Peaks," Theron supplied.

"Come off it, Jed," Bran chided, but Jed held up a hand to silence him as he looked Theron over.

"I mean, where are you *from*?" Jed persisted. "You born on that mountain?"

Theron forced a laugh. "'Course not. I'm from here. Travel often for my trade, is all."

"Which trade would that be?" Jed crossed his arms over his massive chest.

Damn it. We were in trouble. Even Bran was squinting at Theron as if just realizing how little he knew about the man. Theron couldn't lie, so there was little he could say to get out of the situation.

Making a calculated decision, I grabbed a chisel from the ground and hurled it toward the back door. It slammed against the wall, falling to the ground with a loud *clang*.

All three men jumped, and Theron shot an exasperated look my way.

"Shivering bones!" Bran hissed, jabbing a finger toward where I'd thrown the tool. "Somethin' be there, brother. Best go look."

"I'm not lookin'!" Jed argued, then pointed at Theron. "*He* must have done it."

"It wasn't me," Theron objected. "I didn't move a muscle."

Jed's brows knitted together.

"You think a soldier got in?" Theron asked, cocking his head in curiosity. "Maybe they be spying on you."

Jed straightened, his eyes growing wide. With a low curse, he stomped toward the back door in several angry strides. "You bastards don't want to mess with this forge no more!"

Bran was following him, wielding his hammer in the air.

"Move," Theron hissed at me, and I obeyed. We hurried to the front door, and Theron threw it open. Just before we strode out into the cold air, I heard Bran shout, "I think I saw something move!"

I had my fingers wrapped around Theron's arm as the icy air whipped around us. I breathed in, grateful for the relief from that sweltering heat.

But the relief died as soon as I saw the line of soldiers

positioned outside the forge. And standing in front of them was Vikros. He wore a fresh tunic and seemed unharmed, which meant he had gotten his wound healed.

Perhaps the traitorous Lavinia had fixed him up.

I went rigid, but Theron squeezed my arm, reminding me we were trying to blend in. He had a pair of tongs in his hand and moved with firm, purposeful strides as if he had somewhere important to be.

A few soldiers glanced our way. Vikros's eyes skated over me for a brief second. My heart jolted, my pulse roaring in my ears.

But his eyes traveled over me, returning to the soldier next to him as he murmured something I couldn't hear.

I exhaled, but Theron tightened his grip on me. We weren't safe just yet. My legs strained to keep up with his pace as we made our way down the road. In the distance, the sun was rising, bathing the town in a soft golden glow.

If we continued down this road, we would reach Stella's home. But it also meant we were out in the open.

My head was swimming, the heat from the forge still lingering with me. I shook my head vigorously, trying to clear it.

"There's a small wooded area around the corner," Theron whispered to me. "If we can make it there, we'll be safe."

I nodded, but fog crept into my mind, clouding my thoughts. My feet shuffled to a stop, as I feared I would fall over. I swayed, suddenly dizzy. I crammed my eyes shut and took a deep breath.

"Eira?" Theron's voice sounded far away.

Heat swelled in my veins, making me feel uncomfortably warm. I swallowed, my throat dry. "Blood and ice," I muttered, my tongue tasting like sandpaper. "I really don't feel well."

Large hands came down on my shoulders, and I was grateful for the weight there to ground me. "Eira." Theron's voice was laced with urgency. "You have to keep walking. Just a little further."

"Mmm." I tried to move my feet, but they wouldn't budge. How far were we from the soldiers? Were they watching us?

Move, Eira! I thought to myself. *Move now!*

I was struggling to draw breath. My vision blurred, and I swayed again.

Blood and ice, I was about to faint. And then the soldiers would come investigate. Vikros would recognize us.

Theron's arm came around my waist, bringing my hip to his. With a grunt, he lifted me and continued shuffling forward with me at his side. I tried not to lean into his weight, but my head was so fuzzy.

I curled my hand into a fist, pressing my fingernail into my palm. The pressure point sent a bolt of clarity through my mind.

I eased my weight on my feet and off of Theron, hobbling forward as best as I could.

A few more steps.

I applied more pressure from my fingernail, digging into my skin.

Step. Step. Step.

The fog drew closer, threatening to suffocate me. I swallowed hard, trying not to vomit.

I dug my nail in hard enough to draw blood. But still, my clouded mind darkened.

"Almost there," Theron muttered. He sounded a mile away. I had to strain to hear him.

The air shifted. Leaves crunched under my feet. Then, I was suddenly weightless. Theron's wintry smell enveloped me as he carried me in his arms. I pressed my face to his chest, breathing in his comforting scent.

"We're in the woods," he murmured. "You're safe, Eira."

I tugged the black cloth free from my mouth, sucking in sharp gulps of air. It tasted cold and biting and *fresh*. For a moment, I thought I could think clearly again, the icy air soothing to my ash-filled lungs.

But then the heat overcame me, and I slumped against Theron's chest. "I—I don't know what's wrong with me."

"Eira. Does Calista have your blood?"

I stilled, my eyelids fluttering open. "Y-Yes," I whispered.

Theron's face paled. "*Shit.*"

"But… she's never been able… to call me before." I was strangely winded, as if I'd run a mile.

"You were likely too far away when you were in Knockspur," Theron said grimly. "She knows you're close by, so she probably figured this was the perfect time to summon you."

I shook my head as a strange taste filled my mouth. "This—This is different. *Feels* different. Look at my eyes. Are they black?" I tried blinking up at him, but my eyelids were suddenly so heavy.

Theron frowned, staring hard at me. After a moment, he said, "No. They're still blue. But your cheeks look very red." He pressed a hand to my forehead. "Damn, Eira. You're burning up."

"I don't understand this," I said numbly. "I—I don't feel right. What's happening to me?"

"When was the last time you ate?"

Shivering bones, I could barely remember my own name, let alone what I last ate. "Can't… think."

But Theron was staring at my upper arm, his eyes wide. My ripped tunic had slid upward when he'd lifted me. As I followed his gaze, I realized what was so shocking. A patch of sickly green spots marred the skin just below my shoulder. It seemed to surround the faint pink scar from—

My heart jolted in my chest.

The scar from when Calista poisoned me. It was the exact place where her claws had struck me. I'd done my best to hide the scar up until this point because I wanted to avoid any questions about it.

But now, the same spots that I saw in Calista's hand mirror were visible to me, to Theron... to *everyone*.

"Eira," Theron said, his breath shaky. "What is that?"

I vaguely recalled how Theron had burned up with a fever when the Demon Fae had poisoned him.

"This is where Calista cut me," I whispered, my head spinning. "This is how she poisoned me."

Theron was shaking his head now. "That's impossible. Eira, if she cut you years ago, you would already be dead."

My brow furrowed, and I closed my eyes. But it didn't help. I still felt dizzy, as if I were on a rickety boat in the middle of a massive storm. "Distance," I finally managed to say. "A-And apples. I need... an apple." I couldn't form the words. Somehow, I couldn't bring myself to explain to him that the more I distanced myself from Calista, the less her poison affected me.

That, and the sparkwood apples helped keep the poison at bay. It had been a while since I'd eaten one.

"My bag," I said tightly. "Please."

"You don't need a damn apple," Theron snapped. "You need a healer."

"I'm serious, Theron. The apples help."

I felt him stiffen. "Wait. Are you serious?"

I uttered an impatient groan. Theron clutched me tighter with one hand, using his other to shuffle through my pack.

"Here." He placed a cool apple in my palm. I immediately lifted it to my mouth and bit into it. It was ripe and delicious. The juice trickled down my throat, bringing a burst of flavor to the hazy dryness still lingering in my mouth.

"Mmm," I hummed with satisfaction, letting my eyes close again. The fog in my head abated slightly. I took another small bite, savoring the sweetness of it.

"That's why you urged me to eat an apple when I was injured," Theron murmured, his voice sounding so close. As if his lips were right at my ear. I suppressed a shiver as that deep, rumbling timbre seemed to ripple right through me.

"Yes, you idiot," I said. My head fell against his chest, but I didn't care. "I was trying to help."

Theron snorted. "You can't blame me for thinking otherwise."

I sighed sleepily. "You're right. I can't."

We held still for another moment. I focused on my breathing as, bit by bit, clarity crept into my mind. The feverish heat of my body gradually faded, and I no longer felt like the world was spinning. I let myself rest against Theron's chest while he held me. I didn't care that we were covered in soot and sweat. I didn't care that he was touching me, my skin now warm for a different reason. I didn't care that I probably needed to pull away before one of us did something we regretted.

At long last, I lifted my head to find him watching me, his eyes full of intensity and longing. The corners of his eyebrows were pinched in concern, as if he still worried I might faint.

I swallowed hard, trying not to feel awkward. "I…" I cleared my throat. "Um. Thanks. For helping me through that. You can put me down now."

"Right." Theron carefully set me on the ground, his hands remaining on my waist in case I fell. I blinked a few times, testing my weight with one step. Then another.

No dizziness. No fog.

Theron's hands fell from my waist, and I instantly yearned for his heat once more. His touch gave me strength. It had been so comforting. Empowering, even. Like with him holding me, I could overcome any obstacle.

I took a moment to take in my surroundings. We stood in a tiny copse of trees with a blanket of snow and leaves at our feet. Through the thin, leafless branches, I could make out the main road that led to Stella's house. That meant we were near the outskirts of Tolston.

"Between your sickness and my blood, it will be a miracle if we make it to the palace," Theron said, his voice full of dry humor.

I shrugged one shoulder. "It's okay. I can just stab you again."

He snorted. "Bet you enjoyed that, didn't you?"

I couldn't lie, so I only grinned at him.

His expression sobered, and he lifted a hand to the patch of green spots just below my shoulder. His thumb grazed the faint pink scar, his touch feather-light. I closed my eyes, my skin pebbling with awareness from his gentle touch.

"I never got spots like this," he said thoughtfully.

I opened my eyes to look at him. His jaw was tight, his lips thin. His brows drew together as a conflicted expression crossed his features.

"I don't think the poison was in your system for long enough," I said softly. "I did my research. Extensive doses of Demon Fae poison cause spots like this to appear all over one's body." My voice caught in my throat, and I took a shaky breath. "No one who had the spots ended up surviving."

A muscle feathered in his jaw, and his nostrils flared. "You can't give up, Eira. If you've survived this long, then maybe there's still hope."

I didn't want to answer, because I was fairly certain there *was* no hope. I just had to survive long enough to see my plan through. If I could de-throne Calista and get my seven human nobles on the court, then I knew the kingdom would be in safe hands.

I forced a chuckle. "Careful, hunter. You're starting to sound like you actually care."

He offered me a wry smile. "Imagine that." He pulled a handkerchief from his pack and handed it to me. When I frowned at him, he gestured to his own ash-stained cheek. "For the soot."

I chuckled and wiped my face, then handed it to him. He did the same. When he lowered the cloth, I smirked at the smear of ash still staining his forehead. "Here."

I drew closer, taking the cloth from his grip, and slowly dragged it over his forehead. I tried to ignore the heated lock in his eyes, but my gaze was pulled to those onyx irises. They burned me. Inflamed me. Consumed me.

I kept my hand against his face for a moment longer than was necessary, unable to resist the pull of those eyes. My fingertips trailed over his brow. His jaw. I wanted to lean into him. To touch *more* of him.

My heart quivered, my throat knotting. With a shuddering breath, I stepped back and said in a strained voice, "Stella's house isn't far now."

Theron nodded and cleared his throat. "Yes. We should keep moving."

I offered a nervous smile and handed the cloth back to him. We set off through the woods, and I tried fruitlessly to steer my thoughts away from the strange, tender moment we'd just shared.

THE HUNTER

Eira and I didn't speak another word until we reached her friend Stella's house. My mind was a conflicted mess, tumbling between the fear of being summoned by Calista again and the confusion of whatever I was feeling for Eira.

She had been ill. Feverish. Incoherent. And in that moment, I had been utterly terrified of losing her.

Now that she was well again, I had these tangled thoughts to sort through. I already knew I couldn't kill her when the time came to settle our bargains. But I was beginning to suspect—and fear—that what I felt for her was something deeper. More intense.

Something I couldn't hide from for much longer.

Stella's home was a log cabin at the end of the road, lined by the forest through which Eira and I passed. As we approached, I was surprised to find Frisk trotting out to greet us. His thick white coat of fur was shining and spotless, as if he hadn't been part of a gruesome battle just yesterday.

Eira rushed over to him, and he hopped into her arms, nuzzling against her chest as if he were a kitten. She pressed a kiss to the top of his head, and he leapt from her arms, landing on his feet.

"You tell Mauro about that and I'll claw your eyes out," Frisk said, sitting on his hind legs as if the show of affection hadn't happened.

"Mauro? Is he all right?" Eira asked.

"He's in the back. We figured he'd be a bit too conspicuous hanging around the front door."

Eira chuckled. "I agree. And Kendra?"

"She's napping by the fireplace. Apparently, you assigned her an arduous task." Frisk's keen eyes sharpened, and I tensed, wondering how much the dragon had told him. Did he know what Eira and I had done to escape the soldiers' notice? Kendra had been oblivious, but if she had told Frisk what she'd seen, he would have been clever enough to put the pieces together.

"What about the other creatures?" Eira asked. I could have sworn her cheeks had turned pink, as if her thoughts mirrored my own. "The ones who helped us fight off the soldiers. Are they all right?"

"We lost a few rabbits," said Frisk. "All the fae beasts survived, though."

My eyes widened in shock as I processed this. "There were *mortal* creatures fighting with us?"

Frisk fixed his dark eyes on me. "You really need to get this into your thick skull, hunter. Species isn't everything. Unseelie, seelie, fae, or human... Get those damn divisions out of your head or it'll be the death of you."

I could only blink at him as he led Eira into the house. For a moment, I lingered in the front yard, my head reeling with the notion that this infuriating princess and her animal friends had turned my entire way of thinking upside down.

I wasn't even sure who I was anymore. A week ago, I would have said I was a full-blooded seelie fae, an assassin for the Queen of the Winter Court, only one assignment away from a blissful retirement.

Now, I was a wanted fugitive who had turned against the queen and fought her soldiers, aiding and abetting the vigilante princess who sought to start a civil war in the court.

The fact that I was a full-blooded fae meant nothing now.

But perhaps that was how it *should* be. Why should my bloodline give me any amount of privilege? Why did that matter to me at all?

My jaw went rigid, my teeth grinding together as I was forcibly reminded of my father. *Humans are worthless,* he'd said. *They were put here by the gods to test us. To make us stronger. We must use that strength to wipe them out and prove we are the more dominant species.*

Never in my life had I agreed with my father's practices and beliefs. And yet, somehow, the idea that the seelie fae were the more dominant species *had* been ingrained so deeply in my brain that I didn't even notice the belief was there.

Damn you, old man, I thought, cursing my father. Even after he'd been taken from this world, his ideals still haunted me, dragging me down like a weight I hadn't realized I'd been carrying.

And it was exactly why it had been so difficult for me to believe the queen was a Demon Fae. Because she had risen to power, claiming the throne of the Winter Court. So *of course* she had to be full-blooded seelie; it was the only thing that made sense. Why else would my father have served her?

And yet, thinking of Eira and everything she had gone through... I knew she had more sense than I gave her credit for. How could I have accused her of making this up? Of being delusional?

Guilt and shame and regret warred within me, making it hard to breathe. I couldn't focus on this now. There were more important tasks at hand.

Voices echoed from the open window of the house, startling me from my thoughts. There would be a time for introspection later—assuming we survived this at all.

The odds were slim.

With a deep breath, I entered the house, following the sounds of excited whispers and murmurs. When I reached the living room, I found Eira embracing a woman with pale blonde hair I'd seen once before—in Knockspur, when the humans had ganged up on me. She had been the one with the stellar knife skills.

Stella withdrew from the embrace and fixed a cold stare on me, her chin lifting in defiance. "So, the fearsome assassin is still with you, is he?"

I wasn't sure how to respond to that. But she didn't draw a weapon on me, so I saw that as an improvement.

"Stella, you shouldn't even be here," Eira chided, ignoring my presence completely.

Stella gripped Eira's hands in both of hers. "I heard whispers that the Snow Princess had been captured. I had to come and see for myself. I knew you wouldn't have been caught so easily."

Eira's shoulders deflated, the motion so subtle I almost missed it. "I *was* caught. Stabbed, actually."

Stella's pale eyes grew wide. "Blood and ice, Snow! What happened?" She scanned Eira's body as if searching for a wound.

Finally, Eira turned to face me, though she wouldn't look me directly in the eye, for some reason. "Theron brought me to a healer. He saved my life."

My heart tumbled from the fervor of her words. I swallowed hard, wanting to deflect her praise because it hadn't been courageous at all. It had been the cowardice of a desperate man.

And in the end, the healer I'd trusted to save Eira had betrayed us. So perhaps it hadn't been a wise choice after all.

Stella blinked and glanced between us in confusion. "The... assassin? Saved you?"

"Yes." Eira still refused to look directly at me. Was she angry with me? "I wouldn't be here if it wasn't for him."

"Eira saved me, too," I chimed in, feeling completely awkward throughout this whole exchange. "She had plenty of opportunities to let me die. But she fought to keep me alive."

Stella sniffed. "Well. That's more than I would have done."

Eira elbowed her friend. "If you thought I was captured, you should have left. That was the plan."

"To hell with the plan," said a gruff voice.

A blade was in my hand as I whirled at the newcomer. From the next room emerged another human, this one also familiar—the burly fellow who'd held an iron blade to my throat in Knockspur.

Denton. The farm boy clearly still enamored with Eira. His dark, intense gaze was fixed on her as if he owned her. Anger simmered in my veins.

Eira straightened. "Denton? Shivering bones!" She raced toward him, throwing herself into his chest. His arms wrapped around her in a tight embrace.

The anger within me boiled over, my teeth clenched so hard my head was throbbing.

"Who else is here?" Eira asked, eagerly looking around as if expecting more of her friends to appear.

But Stella shook her head. "It's just us. The others are rallying forces and will meet us at the palace."

"We figured if the two of us died here, the others could still continue with the plan," Denton explained.

"Didn't you just say *to hell with the plan?*" I asked, my voice dripping with sarcasm.

Denton's gaze shifted to me, and his stance went rigid. "I see you haven't rid yourself of this nuisance yet."

"You were there when we struck the bargain," Eira said. "I had no choice."

"That's not true. You could have refused to bargain with him *at all.*"

"Denton—"

"Come on, Snow, you don't need him. We can do this without his pretentious fae ass."

"Actually, you can't," I said loudly.

The three of them turned to look at me.

"Eira needs me to get into the palace," I went on, fixing a hard stare at her. "Isn't that right?"

Eira offered a nervous chuckle. "Theron, we no longer have the element of surprise. The queen and all of her soldiers are searching for us."

"If I can distract the queen by giving myself up, then *you* can sneak in on your own. I'll still be fulfilling my bargain with you."

Eira's face paled. "Theron—"

Denton huffed a dry laugh. "Turn yourself in? I don't believe it for a second."

"He can't lie," Eira snapped.

"He said *if*. It doesn't mean he'll do it." Denton drew closer to me, a challenge lighting up his gaze. "Tell us this is your intention, hunter. Prove me wrong."

I met his gaze, unwavering. His intimidation tactics wouldn't work on me. Because for the first time in days, clarity burned through my thoughts.

This was what I needed to do. My own life be damned; I'd spent too long allowing my father and Calista's crusade against humans to escalate. Eira could make more of a difference in this court than I ever could. It was more important for her to survive than for me.

This was my penance.

With a firm, steady voice, I said, "It is my intention to turn myself in so Eira can sneak into the palace undetected."

The truth in my words rang out in the small room, and Eira's eyes went wide. She was right. I couldn't lie. And that meant I had just vowed to face certain death to give her a chance at accomplishing her goal.

THE PRINCESS

I HAD TRIED MY DAMNEDEST TO DEFLECT MY HEATED thoughts about Theron, to ignore the way his piercing gaze seemed to melt my bones.

But when he made that bold declaration in front of Denton and Stella, I almost lost it.

He couldn't be serious.

Was he honestly considering offering himself up as bait—a sacrifice—for me? He was supposed to want me dead. He was supposed to be Calista's pet.

My muddled brain couldn't process this at all.

A shocked silence filled the room. Even Denton had nothing to say to Theron's bold admission.

"Get your things together," I told Denton and Stella. "We'll leave within the hour." I strode toward Theron and grasped his elbow firmly. "Come with me."

He didn't object and allowed me to lead him out of the room and into Stella's tiny, cramped kitchen. I shoved him against the wall, and the cabinets rattled from the impact.

"What the hell's the matter with you?" I hissed.

His brows drew together, anger sparking in his eyes. "What are you talking about?"

I shoved him again, so frustrated I couldn't even think straight. "Why? Why are you doing this? After everything I did to keep you alive, you're just going to throw it away?"

"I'm not *throwing it away*—"

"I will not let you do this," I growled.

"Careful, princess. You're starting to sound like you actually care."

My eyes narrowed. "You don't get to throw those words back at me."

"Why not? Don't pretend like you'd be upset if I died. I've been awful to you. I was sent to kill you. This would provide a diversion for you *and* get rid of the pesky assassin who's been a thorn in your side from the beginning. There is no downside to this scenario."

My eyes felt hot as I stared at him, taking in his calm expression. He uttered the words without an ounce of regret or sadness. He seemed perfectly content to accept his fate.

"Theron," I said in a choked whisper, dropping my gaze. A lump lodged itself in my throat, cutting off my words.

"Don't argue," Theron said, his voice surprisingly gentle. "I know you still hate me. You haven't been able to look at me once in the last hour."

My eyes flew up to meet his in shock and indignation. "That is *not* true. I—I'm looking at you right now!"

He held my stare, unflinching. "Yes. But for how long?"

I blinked at him. He gazed right back at me. Testing me. My heart raced, then seized in my chest as the depths of those dark eyes drew me in.

He was looking at me like I was the only person in the world. A precious treasure he didn't want to lose. Someone worth dying for.

I *wished* he wouldn't look at me like that.

And at the same time, I wished he would never stop.

My stomach fluttered. My toes curled. And damn it, I had to look away. I gasped for breath, struggling to calm my racing pulse as I closed my eyes.

"I knew it." He sounded dejected.

I made a frustrated sound and fisted his tunic with both my hands, pulling him closer to me until our noses brushed. "Don't presume to know me or my feelings," I said through clenched teeth. "I do *not* hate you."

Theron's face slackened in surprise, and damn if that didn't send a bolt of satisfaction through my chest.

"You... *confuse* me," I confessed. "And I don't understand you. Sometimes you seem loyal to Calista without even realizing it. Other times, it seems like you're on *my* side and despise her as much as I do. You still can't accept that she's a Demon Fae. You risk your life to save mine, but you don't believe I belong on the throne."

"I never said—"

"You didn't have to," I said softly. "I can feel it, Theron. I feel your disdain for me and my kind. You don't believe humans belong in the Winter Court. You never did."

He sighed, his frame sagging with defeat. His brows creased as a pained expression crossed his face.

"You're right."

My mouth fell open. I had expected him to argue or defend himself. I hadn't expected him to agree with me. "What?"

"You're right," he repeated, and this time it was despair burning in his eyes. He sighed and ran a hand through his hair. In the next room, Stella and Denton were speaking in hushed tones, no doubt gossiping about our private conversation.

"Do you know why my father's death affected me so much?" Theron asked.

I shook my head, confused about this subject change but intrigued enough to urge him to continue.

"For most of my life, my father saw humans as pests that needed to be stamped out of existence. He made it his life's goal to obliterate them, starting with our court." His nostrils flared, his gaze full of fire and anger.

"I grew up resenting humans. Not because my father taught me to hate them, but because they claimed his attention more than I did." He sighed and looked away, and when his gaze met mine again, I couldn't mistake the sadness I saw there, nor the hint of hurt and bitterness that were layered underneath it all. "He was so obsessed with his hatred for humans that he didn't have time for me at all. And when he was killed, I was so incensed, so full of wrath because... I *missed* him. Because in spite of how he ignored me completely, I still loved him, and the emptiness he left in my heart made me angry at the injustice of it all."

My heart twisted at his words. His relationship with his father was so different from my relationship with mine. While my father had been kind and nurturing, always supportive of me and never once causing me to doubt myself or my heritage... Theron's father had been distant and unkind.

I swallowed the lump in my throat and stared at Theron as he continued, "Then, I was left with his contract to the queen. The debt he had incurred because of his war against humans. So, in truth, I was raised to hate humans. But not in the way you think. In my mind, humans took my father away from me. And so, I wanted nothing to do with them."

He offered a wry laugh, his face twisting into a disgusted

grimace. "I tried so hard *not* to become my father, lost in the bloodthirsty quest to destroy all humans, that I didn't realize it still happened anyway. I may not have actively fought against the species, but my indifference was just as harmful."

"Theron," I whispered weakly.

"I didn't realize," he said in a strained voice. "Didn't realize what I'd become... until I met you."

I could only gape at him, stunned by his confession.

"There is a division in this court that only you can heal, Eira. I believe that now. I spent so long ignoring the problems, looking out only for myself, that I never saw just how broken this court really is."

Tears burned in my eyes, and I wet my lips, my throat suddenly dry. "Why are you saying all this?"

He took both my hands in his, his calluses gently scraping against my fingers. I felt a shiver of pleasure from the lightness of his touch, the warmth of his skin against mine.

"I'm sorry," he murmured. "I'm sorry for my abhorrent behavior. And I'm sorry I dismissed your claim about Calista. I didn't believe you before. But I do now."

My heart leapt. "You believe she's a Demon Fae?"

He nodded, his mouth quirking into a devastating half smile that made my stomach flip. "Frisk was right. I was so caught up in the notion that fae were superior that I didn't see what was right in front of me." He sighed, ducking his head. "You're right; her magic is disturbing. Monstrous, even. I've thought it myself dozens of times. But if she *is* a Demon Fae, then whatever magic she's using to fuel her glamour must be powerful. She's been fooling the entire court for years."

"Which is why you *can't* turn yourself in to her." I released his hands only so I could bring mine to his face, framing his cheeks with my fingers. The tickle of his beard against my palms was intoxicating, and I brought his face closer to mine. "You *can't*, Theron."

Sorrow burned in his gaze. "I'm doomed anyway, Eira. As soon as I return to the castle and report that I failed my mission, I'm dead. I'm only delaying the inevitable."

I shook my head, refusing to believe it. "Theron—"

"The only reason she needs me is because she wants access to my magic. I don't know why she never tried to use my blood to activate my necromancy. But now that I've awakened it on my own, I—"

"She can't," I blurted.

He froze. "What?"

"She can't use a person's blood to wield their magic. She can only use it to control their body."

He blinked, his brows knitting together. "I don't understand."

"I told you before, I often spied on her. Her magic is limited. She doesn't have unfettered access to another fae's magical abilities. I know because she was desperate to use Lord Kensington's storm magic, but she never could, even when she had access to his blood."

Theron's gaze turned distant, his eyes growing wide. "I remember him. She was frustrated he wouldn't do as she asked."

"Right. Because she was commanding him to summon a storm, and he wouldn't do it. His magic wasn't hers to command." I clutched his face more firmly in my hands. "She *can't* force you to use your magic, Theron. No matter what she does to you, you can't forget that."

He pressed his lips together, his gaze contemplative.

"When she finds out I've activated my necromancy..." He broke off, his eyes closing in anguish. "Eira. I *have* to do this."

Panic twisted in my chest as I processed his words. "Theron, please."

"Once we get back to the palace, I'm no longer bound to our bargain. She can force me to hurt you. But I can't—I can't bear to put you in harm's way. I can't..." He broke off, his head dropping in misery.

He was so consumed with sorrow that I couldn't handle it. Without thinking, I brought his face to mine and kissed him hard.

I didn't care that Stella and Denton were in the next room.

I didn't care that we had a mission and were running out of time.

All I knew was Theron was in pain, and I had to do something about it.

His lips were smooth, the beard on his chin tickling my face.

I'd intended for the kiss to be brief, something to snap him out of his despair. But a deep, startled noise escaped him, the sound vibrating through me, and before I knew what I was doing, my hands were gripping the fabric of his shirt, dragging him closer. He angled his head to deepen the kiss, his tongue sweeping along my lip, and then I came undone. He tasted far more alluring than he smelled, and I wanted to feast on *all* of him. To memorize the sensation and carry it with me. My lips parted further for him, my tongue meeting his, and he groaned into my mouth.

That sound made my insides quiver with need.

His hands slid to my waist, drawing me to him until my

body was aligned with his. My arms wound around his neck, my fingers threading through his wavy hair. Fire burned in my veins, scorching through every inch of me. Every spot where he touched me ignited until my entire body felt like it had molten lava coursing through it.

I kissed him over and over, my lips hungry for more. My body was flush against his. My hips ground into him as I pinned him against the cabinets. I needed more of him. *More.*

"Eira," he murmured against my mouth, the sound a prayer and a plea. I caught his lower lip between my teeth, and he let out a strangled groan.

I pulled away to gasp for breath, unable to see straight, to *think* straight. All I knew was the blissful haze of losing myself in him, of the painful desire churning inside me.

I wanted him. I didn't care that he was a killer. I didn't care that he worked for Calista.

Every fiber of my being *ached* for this man.

"I thought I irritated you," I said breathlessly. "Now, here you are, willing to sacrifice yourself for me."

He gave a wry chuckle, his eyes dark and heady in a way that made my knees go weak. "No one has gotten under my skin like you have, princess."

"Tormenting you is my absolute pleasure."

"Not a torment at all." His voice was low and husky in that perfect way that raised the hair on my arms. His hand lifted, and he trailed the tips of his fingers along my jawline. "In fact, you've dug your way into my heart, peeling back layers I didn't know were there. You've stripped me bare, princess."

His gaze burned with a heat that melted my insides. His fingertips left a trail of fire along my skin. "Have I, now? I'd like to see what that looks like, hunter." My eyes flicked over his body from top to bottom, and my legs felt wobbly just imagining him without clothes. I hadn't gotten a good look at him when he'd undressed during the blizzard, but I could envision it now. That toned, muscular chest. Those powerful legs tangled up with mine. "I have a feeling I'll like what I see."

Desire sparked in his eyes, and he leaned closer, that wintry scent enveloping me. Blood and ice, I wanted to *bathe* in that scent.

"Snow," barked a voice.

I jolted and stepped backward, my face burning as I found a scowling Denton standing in the hall, a bag slung over his shoulder. His face darkened with fury as he glanced between me and Theron.

Shit.

"We're ready." Denton's voice was stiff. Without waiting for a response, he turned and strode toward the door.

I rubbed the back of my neck, feeling foolish and disappointed all at once. What had I done? Had I really just *kissed* the assassin?

And... had he kissed me back?

We had kissed in the alley before, but that had just been for show to avoid getting caught by the soldiers.

Here and now—this felt real. *Was* it real?

No, that wasn't important. What *was* important was getting into the palace. This dangerous game the hunter and I played—it wouldn't end well for either of us.

"Eira," Theron said softly.

I couldn't look him in the eye, but I also knew I couldn't let him go through with his plan. I clutched his wrist. "Please don't get yourself killed, Theron. There's another way; I'm sure of it."

He said nothing, but I heard his breath hitch and felt his hot stare burning into me.

Before his hungry look unraveled me completely, I stepped away and strode to the front door, trying—and failing—to focus on the task at hand.

Theron scouted ahead to ensure the road was free of soldiers before we set off. Not wanting to draw too much attention to us, Mauro, Frisk, and Kendra took a different route to rendezvous with the rebel soldiers. Denton, Theron, Stella, and I made our way toward the palace. We planned to weave through alleys when we got to the town square, just as Theron and I had done earlier. I was tempted to use my invisibility, but the other three would still be visible either way. Besides, I'd recently eaten a sparkwood apple. The apples had a tendency to stifle my invisibility, since they repelled fae magic. I could still use it, but it wasn't as effective.

I glanced at the small patch of green spots on my arm, an aching dread eating away at my stomach. It was probably better to keep eating the apples. Even if it hindered my fae magic, my invisibility was no good to me if I was dead.

With a sigh, I dug through my pack to ensure I still had a few more apples left. My fingers brushed over the bundle of fabric that held the mirror.

Or... *used* to hold the mirror. It was significantly lighter. Then, I remembered Theron still had it.

Somehow, the thought didn't bother me. In fact, part of me felt it was safer with him than with me.

He and Stella were walking a few paces ahead of me. I stared at the back of his head, wondering how we had gotten here—to the point where I trusted him.

A small smile tugged at my lips.

"Are you out of your mind, Snow?" Denton hissed at my side.

I took a moment before responding. "What do you mean?"

"You and the assassin. You can't be serious."

I turned and fixed a steely stare on him. "You don't know anything, Denton."

"The hell I don't. I saw you two earlier. You're telling me that was nothing?"

"It was—" I broke off, my words faltering because I couldn't lie. "None of your business," I finally finished.

Denton swore and grabbed my arm, stopping me in my tracks. "You're playing with *fire*, Eira. You aren't thinking straight."

I jerked my arm free of his grasp, my rage mounting. "Don't tell me what I'm thinking. You don't own me, Denton. And you never have."

"I care about you! I don't want to see you hurt. Or killed." He stepped forward, this time grabbing both my arms and pinning me in place.

"Denton—"

Denton was suddenly shoved off me, his hands releasing my arms. He fell forward, barely catching himself before his face hit the snow. With a grunt, he climbed to his feet, seething.

Theron stood before me, his expression dark with fury, his arms rigid at his sides.

In a flash, Denton was on his feet, teeth bared. "Want to try that again, hunter? You might not be so lucky." He drew a blade I recognized—an iron dagger.

"Denton." Stella stepped in front of him, palms raised. "Don't be an idiot."

But Denton was glaring at Theron. "What did you do to her, huh? Did you cast a spell on her?"

Theron said nothing. A muscle flickered in his jaw, and his nostrils flared. He looked like a predator about to strike.

Denton raised the blade.

"Denton!" I shouted, trying to insert myself between them, but Denton shoved me out of the way. I stumbled, righting myself just in time to see Theron swing his fist.

The blow sent Denton staggering. When Denton raised the blade again, Theron snatched his free arm and twisted, pulling the same maneuver he'd done to me when I'd threatened him. In seconds, the iron dagger clattered to the ground, and Denton's back was against Theron's chest. The assassin's arm was around his throat.

"You won't touch her again," Theron said, his voice dangerously soft. "Unless she asks you to. Understand?"

Denton made a choking sound, but Theron maintained his grip. "She. Is. Not. Yours." Theron enunciated each word with a low growl.

Something hot stirred in my chest, and a strange, wild part of me wanted Theron to say, *She's mine.*

I shook the thought from my head and said loudly, "Theron! Let him go." Denton's face was turning purple.

Theron released his hold, and Denton doubled over, wheezing. For a long, tense moment, the three of us stood there stiffly, watching Denton catch his breath. Gradually, his face returned to its normal tan color, and he straightened, his expression contorted with anger. He wiped a trickle of blood from his nose and spat on the ground at Theron's feet.

"She's not yours, either, hunter," he said.

I rolled my eyes. "I'm not anyone's, all right? Both of you, get a grip. We have a battle to fight, remember? And if you two don't stop acting like children, we're going to get caught before we even get to the palace."

Denton muttered something unintelligible before swiping his dagger from the snow and sheathing it. Without another word, he marched forward, making his way down the street.

"He sometimes forgets that you're half fae," Stella said in a soft voice. She was watching me with a concerned look. At my furrowed brow, she offered a small smile.

"It's easy for him—for all of us—to forget that you aren't a full-blooded human like we are. That half of your heritage is..." She paused, waving a hand at Theron, who eyed her warily, not saying anything. "Dangerous," she finally finished.

Even *I* didn't know what to say to that.

"I'll talk to Denton," Stella promised, her gaze flitting to Theron, then back to me. "And I trust you to take care of yourself. Just... remember to be careful, Snow."

I opened my mouth to reply, but before I could, Stella turned and hurried after Denton, no doubt looking to smooth things over with him. She had always been the calm to my storm, and only now did I realize she played that role with Denton, too. As I watched her fall into step alongside him, his shoulders lowered just a fraction at her presence.

My heart lifted, and for the first time, I wondered if that was what Denton needed: a calmness to his storm. A safe harbor for rest. Not someone like me, who only stoked the fire even more. But someone like her, who balanced him out.

I felt Theron's gaze on me, and I looked at him. Darkness still swirled in his eyes, though his fury had softened slightly. Right now, he looked like the fearsome hunter. The skilled assassin who never missed his mark.

And yet, I wasn't afraid.

I drew closer to him. "You can't do things like that."

His brows knitted together. "He grabbed you."

"I know. He's an ass for doing that. But he's my ally." I paused. "*Our* ally."

"Our?" he repeated, his eyebrows lifting.

I raised my chin to look him in the eye. "You're with me, right?"

A flare ignited within his eyes, scorching me from the inside out. "Always," he murmured.

"Good." My voice came out a bit strained, and I stepped back, worried Denton would see us and throw another fit.

I strode forward, trailing after Stella and Denton. Theron fell into step beside me, his presence silent but comforting.

We still had no plan. I suspected Theron would ignore my pleas and try to give himself up as a diversion.

But perhaps I could use my invisibility to sneak in, and he wouldn't have to. I refused to lose him. I wouldn't lose *anything* else to Calista.

I pulled out an apple from my pack to munch on, but it was more out of nerves than anything else. I needed something to do with my hands, something to chew on besides the inside of my cheek, or I would go mad.

"You and those damn apples," Theron muttered.

I grinned and held it out to him. "See for yourself. It'll amaze you. You'll be dumbfounded by how delicious it is."

"I highly doubt that."

"What, are you afraid?"

He snorted, then swiped the apple from my grasp and bit into it. He thrust it back into my hands, but not before I caught the slight widening of his eyes, or the way his tongue darted from his lips to catch the juice trickling down his chin.

The motion of that tongue sent a coil of heat through my belly.

I forced the image from my mind and smirked at him. "I knew it."

"Knew what?"

"It's delicious, isn't it?"

He huffed a laugh but said nothing, which only confirmed my suspicions. I elbowed him with a chuckle. "Theron, the dreaded assassin, brought to his knees by a delicious apple."

"I was not *brought to my knees*."

"I don't know, I saw the look on your face. This apple changed your life, didn't it?"

"No." A slow grin spread on his face.

I poked his arm. "It did. You love sparkwood apples, just like everyone else. Admit it!"

"I'll do no such thing." But his smile only grew, and more of that delicious heat flared in my core.

I wanted to keep teasing him, if only to make him smile and laugh, but Denton was shooting us a nasty glare over his shoulder, so I fell silent.

The four of us made our way slowly and quietly down the street. Just to be safe, I gave Denton a wide berth. Stella remained by his side, for which I was grateful. As we walked, something gnawed at my insides. After a while, I realized what it was: the area was too quiet. My instincts screamed that something was wrong.

It's just the curfew, I told myself. *That's all. It's quiet because everyone is shut in their homes right now.*

Even so... with a curfew in effect, where were the soldiers patrolling the streets?

A sinking feeling settled low in my gut. Something was wrong.

I gripped Theron's arm tightly, stopping him. His arm was already stiff, all corded muscle, taut with awareness.

We shared a somber look. He, too, knew something was off.

His dark eyes suddenly went wide. Then, he tackled me to the ground. I grunted as my head collided with something hard and lumpy.

Three arrows whizzed past us, embedding into the snow a few feet behind us. Right where I'd been standing moments before.

"Take cover!" Theron bellowed.

Stella and Denton glanced around in alarm before darting out of the street. I didn't see where they fled to, but I assumed they were using the buildings as cover.

Theron and I, however, remained in a tangle of limbs in the middle of the street. A clear shot for anyone who wanted to harm us.

On instinct, I draped my invisibility around myself like a cloak, even knowing it wouldn't conceal me very well with the apple still in my system.

Then, a loud and familiar chuckle sounded nearby, and I knew my invisibility wouldn't do any good.

Vikros.

The Hunter

Vikros and a crowd of armed soldiers emerged from their hiding spots, surrounding me and Eira on the cobbled road. I looked around to find that Eira had vanished… or rather, partially vanished. I could still make out a faint outline of her body next to me, though from a distance, she would have seemed fully invisible. I extended a hand and felt her fingers take mine. Electricity ignited between us, and though I couldn't see her clearly, that simple bit of contact was a solid reassurance.

She could still flee, I told myself. Even with Vikros able to see through her magic, he was just one man. She could outrun him.

But she didn't move. And something told me she wouldn't run even if I asked her to.

The stubborn, beautiful woman.

"Smart move, lingering in the village," Vikros said, a smug smile on his face as he approached. "We thought you would have left immediately, so we had all the main roads under close watch." He cocked his head at me, his dark eyes glittering with malice. "Or perhaps it was a foolish decision, remaining here." He spread his arms wide, gesturing to the soldiers closing in on us.

I knew Vikros. He had a tendency to be overconfident, especially when he had the upper hand. Perhaps I could use his hubris to my advantage.

"You can't stop me, Vikros," I said loudly.

He barked out a laugh. "You may have bested me in hand-to-hand combat before, old friend, but even *you* can't stop a dozen soldiers coming at you at once."

A dozen soldiers. Possibly more lurking in the shadows. Stella and Denton were nowhere to be seen, but that was a good thing. If Vikros had captured Eira's friends, he would boast about it. Perhaps use them as leverage like he'd done with the human children.

The reminder of Vikros's savage methods sent rage boiling through me. My fingers flexed at my sides, itching to strangle the man. Magic burned beneath my skin, eager and at the ready. Out of habit, I pushed it away, then froze.

A necromancer holds the threads of life in their hands, whether it's to preserve a life or to end it.

I had the power to end Vikros's life right here and now. All I had to do was find his life thread.

But how did I *do* that? Each time I'd used my necromancy had been a complete accident. I hadn't seen any threads at all.

Think, I urged myself.

But I also had to keep Vikros talking.

"How much is she paying you?" I blurted.

Vikros's eyes narrowed. "Who?"

"The queen. I'll bet she's holding back. You could milk her for more, if you had the balls."

Vikros's face contorted with rage.

"What are you doing?" Eira hissed, her breath close to my ear.

"Follow my lead," I muttered back. I needed to buy more time. If Lavinia was right and I'd been using necromancy while hunting, then perhaps it would be easy to tap into that killer's instinct. I just had to trigger the same responses within myself.

Adrenaline.

Intense focus.

In both instances—the fight with the Demon Fae and Eira's injury—rage and blinding pain had preceded the necromancy. Something had exploded within me. Desperation mingled with fear and fury, pain and panic, urgency and a raw, feral thirst for blood.

Vikros was speaking, but I didn't hear him. Blood pounded in my ears, drowning everything out.

Then, Eira spoke, and my focus homed in on her words.

"I don't know, Theron, I'll bet he's too *small* to ask Calista for anything, let alone more gold."

Vikros snarled something unintelligible and drew his sword, pointing it at Eira.

I didn't need to conjure that desperation and fear. It surged through me of its own accord, every fiber within me roaring at the sight of a blade aimed at the princess.

"You will address the queen as *her majesty*," Vikros spat.

I felt Eira stiffen next to me. "She is a false queen, and I will address her as such."

Vikros drew closer. Though I couldn't see Eira, I knew the point of his blade was within inches of her face.

No! something within me screamed. *Do not touch her!*

I clung to that wild panic and expanded it, like adding

fuel to a raging fire. It burned up everything inside me, leaving a path of violent agony in its wake.

The sensation ignited the magic within me, and it was as if a lever had been pulled, triggering my necromancy.

Suddenly, I could see threads *everywhere.*

The air went still, as if time had stopped. Vikros stood unmoving before me, his arm poised to strike Eira. The soldiers surrounded us, weapons raised.

But between each figure was a long, gleaming blue thread. They crisscrossed and overlapped like the strands of a spiderweb. Each one glowed with an ethereal power, the same exact shade of blue that had resonated from my palms. The same color as Lavinia's gemstone.

Life threads. I was looking at each individual's life thread.

All I had to do was pull one.

But I had to pull the *right* one.

Struggling to maintain my focus and hold the magic in place, I glanced over each thread, tracing the strands to the individuals around us. The soldiers' overlapped with each other, but I found one thread that stood out, wrapped tightly around Vikros like a cocoon. Two other threads were twined around him. I followed their path and found them attached to Eira and myself.

For one, horrifying moment, I stared at my own thread.

I had the power to end my own life… or preserve it.

A life weaver.

It was almost too much. My brain was on fire as I balanced the chaos of the magic raging inside me. It festered like an open wound. Necromancy thrived on pain; I understood that now. But I had to be enduring the pain the entire time in order to trigger it.

I had to act quickly or the agony would consume me. I couldn't save Eira if I was unconscious.

Very carefully, I spread my awareness forward, focusing on Vikros's thread. It glowed brighter as my magic drew closer. I pictured invisible hands grasping the line, felt the way it stretched taut under pressure. I closed my eyes, and envisioned myself snapping the strand in half.

A loud *crack* echoed in the street. In a flash, all the visible threads I'd seen vanished, and reality slammed back into me, pressing on my chest so heavily I couldn't breathe. The air was squeezed out of me, and I choked, my lungs screaming.

Shouts echoed around me. Black spots danced in my vision, and I knew I would pass out. I would die. Couldn't breathe, couldn't think, couldn't *live*...

Sharp fingernails dug into my cheeks, and there was Eira, her eyes wild with panic as she stared at me. Slowly, her muffled voice became clearer as my senses returned. "Pull yourself together, hunter!" she was saying. "We need to move, *now*!"

I blinked, and the scene came into focus. Vikros had collapsed, and a few soldiers hurried to examine him. But I already knew he was dead.

The others kept their weapons pointed at us, but they were distracted, their eyes on their fallen commander. A few shifted their feet, and I knew this was our opportunity.

Vikros was their commander. What would they do now? They answered to the queen, but she wasn't here.

A soldier without orders was like a fish without water. They wouldn't know what to do.

Chaos was our ally.

I sucked in several deep gulps of air, struggling to loosen

the tight ball of nerves in my chest. With a swift nod, I took Eira's hand and squeezed. "Invisibility," I whispered.

Half her mouth lifted in a knowing smile, and she vanished again. Even though I could no longer see her, I still felt the warmth of her hand in my grasp.

More soldiers were shouting. Their swords faltered, as they no doubt scrambled to find out where Eira had gone.

I allowed myself three more breaths before I sprang into action. My movements were more sluggish than normal, but the swordsmen had no chance. Even on my worst day, I was a better fighter, and right now, they were confused and disoriented.

Easy prey.

I ducked to avoid a blow, then struck the man in the throat. With a twist of his arm, the sword was free, and I had a weapon. Two more men rushed me, and I swung the sword, slicing a deep wound in the neck, then severing the man's head completely. My sword clanged as the second soldier attacked. We sparred, and I saw an opening. A swift jab to the exposed part of his underarm and he was dead.

I removed his head as well, for good measure.

The remaining soldiers continued to advance toward me, but fear was etched into their faces.

I might have shown them mercy. But each and every one of these men had threatened Eira. They had seen her face. Her magic.

My magic.

They couldn't be left alive.

It took me less than a minute to end their lives. I didn't need their threads to do it, and the motions were as simple, as effortless, to me as breathing. The swing of a blade. Duck, parry, a slash to the throat. My sword clashed with one soldier while I drove my fist into the stomach of the one creeping up behind me. They were armored and outnumbered me.

But I was faster.

Soon, there were only five left. Then three. Another thrust of my sword, and the last soldier's head went rolling.

Panting and covered in blood that wasn't mine, I surveyed the carnage that stained the street.

Thirteen men, including Vikros, lay dead before me. The street was completely empty, though it should have been bustling at this time of the morning. I caught a glimpse of a few terrified faces peering at me from windows across the street.

Witnesses. Plenty of villagers had seen me kill the queen's men.

If I wasn't already marked for death, I certainly would be now.

"Eira?" I asked quietly.

No answer.

Had she, too, fled for her life? Had she seen me slaughtering soldiers and left, horrified by the sight of me?

I was evil. A monster.

My throat tightened at the thought of her disgusted and frightened expression. How could she think otherwise?

"Eira?" I called out again.

"I'm here." Her voice was far away, and clarity speared through my frenzied thoughts. *Of course* she would have taken cover. I could have accidentally taken her head off.

She dropped her invisibility, and there she was, lingering by a shop across the street. She approached me with a level stare, her face betraying nothing.

"Stella and Denton left," she said, as if answering an unspoken question.

Good, I thought. If they had lingered, they would have either been caught or killed in the chaos. "But you didn't." My gaze never wavered from Eira's.

"No. I didn't." Her eyes held mine, and I couldn't look away even if I wanted to.

"You're not afraid?" I asked.

Eira gazed around, her eyes taking in the slaughtered soldiers, the victims of my wrath. Her face remained impassive as she said, "You are frightening, Theron. A killer. Brutal and lethal. I can't deny that." She looked at me once more. "But I am not afraid."

Several heartbeats passed, and I felt Eira scrutinizing me, as if peering into the deepest and darkest parts of my soul. But instead of fleeing from the monster she saw within, she drew closer to me. Her steps were careful and steady as she navigated around the bodies strewn about the street.

After what felt like an eternity, she stood before me. Slowly, as if afraid she would startle me away, she lifted her hand and pressed it against my cheek. And when she spoke, her words speared straight through me.

"Because I know you are so much *more* than just a killer, Theron."

I opened my mouth, but no words came out. Her declaration rendered me speechless. I was going to say, *I know*, but I couldn't. That would have been a lie.

Was I more than just a killer? I had been the queen's assassin for so long, working in the trade I knew best because it came easily to me, that I wasn't sure I knew *who* I was anymore.

"Who am I, princess?" I whispered.

She brought her other palm to my cheek so her hands framed my face. For a moment, we stood there sharing breath until our heartbeats were synchronized.

At long last, she murmured, "You are mine." Her lips met mine in the tenderest of kisses, as if I hadn't just committed vicious, violent acts in front of her eyes. She kissed me as if I were something fragile, something in need of protecting. As if she wanted to shield me.

I was the protector. *I* was the fighter. But Eira touched me, kissed me, like I was the most precious thing in the world. I had just exposed the vilest parts of myself to her, leaving me bare and vulnerable.

And right here and now—despite the bodies strewn around us, the blood soaking my clothes and the snow at our feet—Eira was accepting me. *All* of me.

Tears burned behind my eyes as my mouth roved over hers, claiming her just as she had claimed me.

You are mine.
You are mine.
You are mine.

The Princess

I should have been afraid. The sight of Thercn decapitating soldiers—*my* soldiers—should have horrified me. It should have sent me fleeing from his presence, not kissing him or making wild declarations like, *You are mine.*

What the hell did that even mean?

He was my hunter? My protector? Something... more?

I didn't know what we were to each other. We were physically attracted to one another. We had built trust between us by saving each other's lives.

But... what did all that *mean*?

I was dying. There was no cure. And if I failed in my mission, Calista would kill him for not fulfilling his assignment.

Whatever existed between us was already doomed.

So, why did I say it? Why did I say he was *mine*?

I couldn't form a coherent thought. Every time I tried, my throat closed up and my head spun so chaotically I couldn't see straight.

So I discarded those thoughts, vowing to sift through them another time.

If I survived long enough.

After our kiss, we hastily made our way down the road, knowing Calista would soon send more guards to investigate. And we didn't want to be anywhere nearby when they arrived.

Though he was covered in blood and grime, I remained close by Theron's side, grateful Denton and Stella had gotten away. I hoped they were moving forward with the plan instead of waiting for me.

Besides, I didn't fancy another lecture from Denton about how dangerous Theron was. No doubt this provided plenty of ammunition for him to use against me.

But I trusted Theron with my life. I had no hesitation about it. I knew he would keep me safe. He would die to protect me.

It wasn't because of our bargain; it hadn't been for a long time. He had risked his life to save mine more than once. And now, the thought of losing him, of parting from him, made my chest cave inward on itself, crumbling until there was nothing left.

I struggled to keep up with Theron's brisk pace, squinting against the morning sun peeking through the trees. Ordinarily, the streets would be crowded with people, but I had a feeling Vikros had enforced another curfew to keep the area clear so his men could ambush us.

It didn't matter, though. We were now so close to the palace that the spires loomed ahead of us, casting shadows along the road. Once we crossed the bridge that led to the portcullis, we would officially be in the city of Taerin, where the nobles and royals lived.

By the time the villagers emerged from their homes, we would either be inside the palace... or captured.

Just before we reached the bridge, I veered to the right, traipsing through a grove of trees that lined the palace walls.

"Where are you going?" Theron asked, though he followed me without hesitation.

"I used to sneak around the palace as a child," I explained. "This is the most discreet way in and out." A small smile spread across my lips. "I thought by now I would have forgotten, but it's come back to me so easily." I didn't even have to glance down to know where to step. My shoes had worn a path through these woods over the years, and now, after all this time, it was like I was home again. My feet found the familiar rhythm, falling into step as if I could slide easily back into the role of the invisible princess.

But everything was so different now. This was no longer my home.

It hadn't been since my father had died.

"Our best bet is to get in through the servants' quarters," I continued. "Once we reach the outer wall, there's a small entrance we can use."

"There are likely guards swarming the palace, though," Theron said, his tone full of doubt. "It might still be difficult for us to get in." His gaze shifted to me, and I knew what he was implying.

"I refuse to let you surrender yourself," I said flatly. "That's not an option, Theron."

He grimaced. "Eira…"

I stopped and turned to face him, giving him my most withering glare. "I cannot do this without you. Swear to me you'll stay by my side."

He said nothing. His eyes burned with a desperate intensity that made my knees go weak.

"Theron, *please*," I said in a strained voice.

"I swear I will... try."

I placed both my hands to his cheeks, grasping his face to force him to meet my gaze. "I. Need. You. Don't you dare think you are dispensable."

"Aren't I?" Darkness and misery clouded his eyes. "This kingdom needs you, Eira. But it doesn't need me. I've done nothing but destroy lives. Perhaps it's time for me to atone for that. If my sacrifice helps you get your throne back, it will be worth it."

"Don't say that! You are not defined by the role that was forced on you, Theron. Once Calista is defeated, you will have the freedom to choose the life you want. You will have the chance to be different. To do better."

"I don't deserve that freedom!" he argued.

I lifted my chin. "Well, *I* say you do. And I'm the rightful queen of this realm, so my word is law."

He didn't smile at that. Not even a glimmer of amusement shone in his eyes.

"Theron," I tried again. "If it weren't for you, I would be dead ten times over. You may be a hunter, but for the past two days, you have used those skills to *protect me*. You aren't a killer; you're my defender."

He only blinked at me, his eyes dark and fathomless. He was drowning in his self-loathing, and nothing I said would reach him.

I would need to try something else.

My hands fisted his shirt, and I pressed my mouth to his, fierce and desperate and bruising. His lips parted for me instantly, as if he'd been waiting for this. *Yearning* for this. My tongue met his, the two colliding with desperate urgency. He sucked on my lower lip, then nibbled it. I let out a strangled noise as my blood turned molten.

And in that moment, I decided I was done fighting whatever this was between us. I didn't care that I was human, that he was an assassin, that our bargain might doom us both. I didn't care that I was dying or that we had a mission to fulfill or that Calista would likely kill us.

There was only him. And me. Alone in this forest.

His chest was now flush against mine, but he stepped forward, backing me against the trunk of a tree. I gasped as every hardened plane of his body angled perfectly with mine, our hips meeting as he pinned me to the tree.

"Theron," I breathed, grinding my hips against him, urging him closer, though there was no space left between us.

He lowered his hands, teasing the waistband of my trousers. I gasped as his cool fingers met my bare flesh. The icy air nipped at my skin, but blood and ice, I was on fire. Even if I was naked in this snowy forest, I still wouldn't have felt the chill.

With his other hand, he slid his fingers under my tunic and roamed along my stomach and abdomen. I hissed in a sharp breath, breaking our kiss to tilt my head back, reveling in his touch. He brought his mouth to my neck, his tongue gliding up and down the column of my throat. A moan poured from my lips.

I gripped his belt, cupping him through his trousers. A low, feral sound rumbled in his chest.

"Tell me you want me," I whispered.

"I want you," he rasped against my neck, his hand lifting higher until he grazed the underside of my breast.

My fingers slipped into his trousers, stroking his length. Gods, he was so hard. Just envisioning his fullness inside me made my mouth go dry.

"Tell me you'll *live* for me," I commanded, running my fingers up and down his length.

He groaned, the sound ragged, as his teeth clamped down on my throat, firm but not hard enough to break skin.

"Tell me, Theron."

He withdrew from my neck, breathing heavily. "Shivering bones, Eira, what are you doing? Would you let me take you right here against this tree just to get me to promise not to get myself killed?"

I lifted my chin to meet his gaze, my nostrils flaring. "Yes, I would. Not just to get that promise from you, but to show you how much I need you. I would have you take me *anywhere*, Theron. Here in this forest, or in the middle of the street in front of dozens of witnesses. Even covered in blood and grime, I do not care. I need you. I need your touch. *Now.*"

My hips rolled again in silent demand. I forced my eyes to hold his, daring him to continue. Would he stop now? Or would he meet my demands?

He held my gaze, desire bleeding through the gloom that had lingered in his dark eyes for too long. Then, his hand under my tunic lifted, cupping my breast completely, his thumb pressing against my hardened nipple.

Oh, *gods...*

My eyes closed as flames roiled within me. He caught my nipple between his fingers and pinched it. Moisture pooled between my legs, my breaths coming in sharp pants.

With his other hand, he slid lower, beneath my trousers and undergarments until he found my slick center. I bucked against him, and he grazed his fingers along the moisture gathered there.

A noise escaped me, a cross between a sigh and a moan.

"Like that?" he murmured.

"Yes," I gasped.

He slid a finger inside me, and I cried out.

"Careful, princess. Others will hear us."

"I told you—I don't care," I breathed. And I didn't. In this moment, nothing else existed except us. The logical side of me knew we needed to move, to get to the palace, to hurry before anyone saw us.

But my body was *on fire*. And every facet of my mind homed in on his fingers inside me.

Nothing else mattered.

He pressed me more fully against the tree, his fingers working and pulsing within me. I writhed against him, driving his hands deeper, riding his fingers as they curled inside me and brushed against my inner walls. Tension built in my body, rising higher and higher, bringing me closer to that edge. I closed my eyes as our bodies found a rhythm together. He pushed and stroked, one hand thrusting into me while the other continued to massage my breast.

He brought his mouth to mine again, capturing my feral sounds, his teeth dragging along my lower lip. A growl of pleasure rose up in his throat, and then, I fractured. Release sent waves of pleasure rolling off my body. I trembled as his fingers continued moving, continued exploring. My climax shuddered through me, leaving me limp and gasping in his arms.

He removed his hands, backing away from me, and I immediately yearned for his warmth.

And he knew it. The smirk on his face told me as much. He'd satisfied me while leaving me wanting more.

It was torture.

"Shivering bones, you're such an ass," I said, my voice slightly hoarse.

He laughed. My eyes dipped to the bulge in his trousers, and I lifted my eyebrows expectantly.

But he only gave me an amused look. "Let's get a move on. Don't you have a throne to take back?"

I shoved his arm. "I'll get you for that."

"Oh, I hope you do," he murmured, his voice low and sultry.

Heat pooled in my core once more, but I forced my feet forward, adjusting my trousers and tunic as I tried to recover from how thoroughly he had unraveled me.

I didn't care that he'd brought me over the edge, only to withdraw before he found his own release. I didn't care if he bested me, winning this battle of wills between us.

He was laughing again. He was teasing me. Perhaps he hadn't promised not to sacrifice himself. But this was a start, and that was enough for now.

A smile spread across my lips as I considered this a small victory. But my smile fell when my stomach suddenly started churning. A strange heat crept up my body, making my cheeks and neck feel flushed. My head spun. I stopped moving as the world around me tilted, threatening to bring me down.

"Eira?" Theron's voice sounded so far away.

Shit. I swayed slightly, and then Theron was there, his hands on my waist, securing me in place.

"The poison?" he asked urgently.

Bile crept up my throat, and I feared if I spoke, I would vomit. So instead, I just nodded once.

Theron gently eased up my shirt sleeve and hissed out a low breath. Blinking through the dizziness, I followed his gaze.

The green spots had spread. They now covered almost my entire arm, ending at my wrist.

"Apples," Theron muttered, grabbing my pack from me and digging through it. I closed my eyes, trying to focus on remaining upright.

A little longer. I just need a bit more time. Please, I can't die yet. Not yet.

There was still so much I had to do. I had to expose Calista. I had to get my human friends established in the court.

I still had to save my kingdom.

"Here." Theron thrust an apple in my hands. I immediately took a bite, and the cool juice trickled down my throat. I uttered a soft sigh as I took another, the fog in my mind receding and the hazy fever fading. My breathing slowed, and my heart rate was steady once more.

When I finished the apple, Theron gave me a grim look. "That's the last one."

I held his gaze, my expression solemn.

All it would take was one more fever, one more bout of dizziness, and the poison would claim me.

After this, it would be over.

THE HUNTER

A SENSE OF FOREBODING HUNG OVER US LIKE A DARK CLOUD AS Eira led me deeper into the forest. Using the trees for cover, we skirted around the palace, winding toward the back. The grove opened up to the rear side of the towering wall. On the other side were the gleaming walls of the castle.

"Are you planning on climbing the wall?" I asked incredulously.

Eira smirked. "You'll see."

"You do love to torment me."

"After what you did to me back there? You deserve it."

"Fair point."

She chuckled, and for a moment, everything seemed normal. But then her expression fell and her eyes dimmed. The harsh truth of her reality set in.

She was dying.

She probably only had one day left, at the most.

In one day, this beautiful woman will be dead.

No. I couldn't accept it. I *would not* accept it.

I would kill Calista myself if I had to. Perhaps slaying the Demon Fae who poisoned Eira would reverse the curse. But even as I thought it, I knew it wasn't true; killing the Demon Fae who had poisoned *me* hadn't solved the problem.

My chest constricted so tightly that I couldn't breathe. The thought of losing Eira, of watching the life leave her... it twisted in my gut like a dagger.

As I watched Eira approach the wall, which stood several feet above her, I vowed to change her fate. Regardless of what happened to me, I *would* find a way to save her.

Eira's hands ran along the length of concrete as if searching for something. Before I could ask what she was doing, she made a noise of triumph and inserted her hand into a small groove etched into the wall.

I tilted my head, brow furrowed, as Eira inched her hands upward, finding several more identical grooves.

She rolled up her sleeves and backed up several steps. Without warning, she broke into a run before leaping onto the wall. Her fingers scrambled for purchase until she grabbed hold of one of the grooves. She clung to it, hoisting herself up with a strained grunt. Her breathing came in sharp puffs, but she was grinning.

"Blood and ice, Eira!" I hissed, my heart pounding. "You could have warned me. I would have given you a boost."

"Where's the fun in that?" she asked as her left foot found another crevice to balance on. "I'm sorry to say you might be a bit too burly for this task, hunter. Perhaps you should wait in the woods while I take my kingdom back." She gave me a mischievous grin over her shoulder.

I rolled my eyes and strolled forward. "I'm more nimble than you think."

"Oh, I'm intimately aware of how *nimble* you can be." She winked at me, her cheeks slightly pink.

Heat coiled low in my belly, and I tried not to think about

the desperate sounds she'd made earlier or how my fingers still smelled like her arousal. Clearing my throat, I tried to focus on the wall before me, scrutinizing it.

When I stood within a few inches of it, I crouched down low, then leapt. My hands caught hold of the grooves with ease.

"Now you're just showing off," Eira muttered.

I chuckled. "So were you. Don't deny it."

"What, you weren't impressed even a *little* bit?"

I looked at her, this stunning rebel princess who had risen above every challenge she ever faced. "Everything about you impresses me, Eira."

She ducked her head, but not before I noticed the smile curving along her lips or the reddening of her cheeks. "Be careful. I was young when I carved these holes; they were meant to hold much smaller feet."

"*You* carved these?" I asked in surprise. The wall was made of hard concrete; it would've taken a great amount of strength to dig into it.

"It took me months. And I had some help."

"You are certainly full of surprises, princess."

"I have to keep you on your toes. Literally, in this case."

I laughed at that.

We were silent as we climbed. My muscles still ached from the intensity of using my necromancy, but I was able to lift myself up without too much difficulty. Eira's breaths turned ragged, and her face shone with sweat. I paused often, letting her set the pace. She likely hadn't made this climb in a long time.

When Eira reached the top, her fingers curled around the edge of the wall, and she slowly raised herself up. I shot a quick glance below to ensure no soldiers had discovered us climbing the wall. Thankfully, the area was clear.

Eira settled in a sitting position on top of the wall, hunched over and panting. I pulled myself up beside her, and we sat there, gazing at the trees as we caught our breath. I glanced behind us at the castle that rested a few yards away from the wall. We were so close to getting inside. To facing Calista and fulfilling Eira's plan.

And yet, I wanted to put it off as long as possible.

"Why did you feel the need to escape as a child?" I asked. "Calista only became queen a few years before you were exiled. That means you must have done this before your father remarried."

She nodded, her gaze turning distant. "My whole life, I've had a difficult time feeling content with where I am. It was something I didn't realize until Frisk pointed it out. I'm always making plans for another place, another home..." She shook her head, then turned to look at me. "But this is the last time. The last plan. This will either work... or it won't."

Her expression turned grim, and my stomach sank. I knew we were thinking the same thing.

Even if the plan worked, we were both still doomed.

"Theron, I want you to live," she said softly, her voice tight with emotion. "I want you to survive this."

I sighed, looking at her with a tenderness I didn't know I could feel. "I want you to live, too, Eira."

Her eyes darkened, as if she could read the hidden meaning in my words.

I want you to live. But you won't. And maybe I won't, either.

The hard truth of it all was, no matter how much I begged for her to live, the poison was still spreading through her body.

And I was still bound to Calista.

Neither of us could change our circumstances.

We didn't rest for long before we climbed down the other side of the wall, the descent much easier on my strained muscles. When we were a few feet from the ground, I jumped, and Eira followed suit. My arms caught her, wrapping firmly around her. The delicious smell of her sweat mingled with that familiar snow and pine scent. My hands tightened around her waist, drawing her back to my chest.

"Careful, princess," I murmured in her ear. "Wouldn't want you to fall."

She shivered slightly and leaned into my touch, her head resting against my shoulder. I had the insane urge to touch her again, to elicit more sounds of pleasure—to finish what we started in the woods.

Blood and ice, this was foolishness. We had already wasted enough time.

And yet, I couldn't pull away from her.

In the end, Eira was the one to withdraw, stepping forward and refusing to meet my gaze.

Something shifted in the air, and every one of my senses went on high alert.

Someone was here.

In a flash, I grabbed her and clamped my hand over her mouth, tucking her against my chest once more. I quickly tugged us both into the shade of a tree and out of sight. A tall, thin man with dark skin came into view. He scanned the forest as if searching for something.

Us, perhaps?

He wore a servant's livery with the Winter Court crest stitched into the fabric. But if he was a servant, why was he searching the woods outside the palace?

Eira elbowed me in the gut, and I released my hold on her.

"It's just Huck," she whispered. "Thank the gods! I wasn't sure if he'd make it."

Huck finally spotted us, and his eyes widened. He waved us over, then turned and darted into the bushes.

Eira strode toward him, but I grabbed her wrist.

"Can we trust him?"

"Yes," she said at once. "He's part of the rebels looking to overthrow Calista. If I can't trust him, I can't trust *anyone*."

I nodded, remembering how loyal her human friends had been back in Knockspur. We rushed forward, following after Huck, and found him crouched in the bushes, his eyes fixed on the servants' entrance at the back end of the palace. Four guards stood sentry by the door, blocking our way in.

"How did you get out?" Eira whispered.

Huck gestured to the uniform he was wearing. Only then did I notice his hair was flattened to cover the roundness of his ears. His disguise was just as convincing as a glamour. No one would look twice at him.

But me and Eira? She was the shunned Snow Princess, and I was a wanted fugitive. We hadn't exactly been quiet during our altercations in Tolston. The witnesses may have already reported what they'd seen to Calista.

That, and I was covered in blood and dirt. The evidence was damning.

"I have a room and supplies ready for you," Huck said under his breath. "We just have to get past them without drawing attention." He looked at Eira and raised his eyebrows. "Any ideas?"

"I can use my magic," she said. "But it won't help him." She jerked her head toward me.

Huck flicked his gaze over me once, a look of disdain crossing his features. But, to his credit, he didn't question Eira's apparent trust in me, nor did he make any objections to my being here.

"Huck, you go in with Eira," I said, staring at the guards as a plan began to form. "I'll be right behind you."

Eira grasped my arm, her eyes filled with panic. "You can't attract any attention."

"I won't."

"And you can't give yourself up."

"I won't."

Her eyebrows lifted as if she hadn't expected me to say it. I couldn't blame her; the thought to turn myself in *had* crossed my mind.

Eira bit back a smile, her eyes swimming with relief. "All right. It's only fair you keep me in suspense, since I do that to you all the time."

I grinned at her, and her breath hitched.

Huck turned to Eira. "You ready?"

In a flash, Eira turned invisible, blending in with the foliage. Like before, I could still make out a faint outline of her body. But it would be enough to deceive the guards, especially with Huck to distract them. "Ready," she said.

Huck climbed out of the bushes. The rustling of leaves indicated Eira followed after, leaving me alone.

Ordinarily, getting past four guards would be easy. But incapacitating them before they could shout for assistance? Not so much.

Still, my plan was solid. I knew it would work. I watched from the bushes as Huck—with Eira invisible beside him—approached the door. Huck's shoulders were rigid, his steps stiff. He was certainly no actor, but luckily, the guards weren't equipped to detect suspicious behavior, especially not in servants. The men barely acknowledged Huck as he strode through the door, throwing it open widely so the unseen Eira could trail after him.

Now, it was my turn.

I couldn't rush the men; I was too far away. The moment I emerged from the bushes, they could shout for more soldiers, and it would be over before I even reached them.

But there *was* something I could do from here.

I closed my eyes, taking a deep breath as I tried to conjure the panicked desperation I'd felt when Vikros had threatened Eira.

When she'd been stabbed.

When she'd almost died.

My chest tightened, and I couldn't breathe. My hands curled into fists, my fingernails digging into my palms and bringing a fresh burst of pain.

Yes, *pain*. There it was. I clung to it, digging deeper, fists shaking... My fingernails broke skin, and blood trickled down my hand.

The air went still. I wasn't sure how I could tell with my eyes closed, but something otherworldly *shifted* as my magic slid into place. My eyes slowly opened, and the world seemed darker. Colder. The sun had dimmed, leaving me in a shadowed wood.

And four blue strands glowed before me.

My mouth went dry as I stared at them, wide-eyed. Could I pull all four?

No. It had nearly killed me when I'd pulled Vikros's thread. I didn't think I was strong enough to use my magic on four people.

Besides, if I failed and left one of them alive, it would ruin my plan.

I swallowed hard, hands still shaking as I tried to maintain control of my power. Tracing my finger in the air, I followed the path of the middle line of thread—this belonged to the tallest, burliest soldier of the four of them. My fingers curled around it, and I gave it a single sharp *tug*.

The man grunted and fell to one knee, clutching at his heart. His eyes bulged, his back arched, and he let out a strangled, choking sound. His face turned purple.

The other men held him upright so he wouldn't fall, asking panicked questions to one another.

"What happened?"

"Can you hear me?"

"Something's wrong with him!"

I smoothed out the man's thread, watching with bated breath to see if my plan worked. I had never done this before. If I failed...

The injured man let out a rattling gasp, color returning to his cheeks.

"My chest," he sputtered. "My *heart*."

"He needs a healer," said another guard.

They all glanced at the one on the far left. Judging by his graying beard, he was the most superior of the four.

"All right," he said. "You two, take him to the healer. I'll stand guard until your replacements show up."

The two healthy soldiers nodded in agreement before hoisting the burly fellow upward, draping his arms over their shoulders. After a moment, the three of them shuffled off, and I smiled in triumph. With an exhale, I let go of the power within me, slumping forward with a gasp.

After several deep breaths, I unsheathed a knife at my

side and flung it toward the last remaining guard. It struck him in the throat, and I knew he was dead before he hit the ground.

It was a shame to have to kill him; the man had only been doing his duty. But, like the soldiers under Vikros's command, he had to die.

If I had to choose between protecting Eira and protecting this stranger, I knew who I would pick.

I darted out of the bushes and eased open the door. With a grunt, I dragged the soldier's body inside. When I reached the dark hall, I let the door swing shut. A quick glance told me the hall was deserted, thank the gods. I lingered there in the darkness for a brief second, waiting for shouts or approaching footsteps—some indication that someone had seen me kill the man.

But there was nothing but silence.

Then—

"Ouch!" I hissed as something sharp pinched my arm.

"You seriously couldn't do one simple task without killing someone?" breathed a voice in my ear.

I exhaled, the sound somewhere between a sigh and a laugh. Relief mingled with amusement in my chest, and I felt as if I could breathe freely for the first time in an hour. "It's what I'm good at. Come on, help me hide the body."

"This one's unoccupied." A door to my left magically swung open. I pulled the soldier's body inside. Eira's grunt told me she was helping. Together, we managed to stuff him into the closet and close the door before returning to the hall.

"You had me worried for a moment there, hunter," Eira said softly. "I thought you might have gone and done something stupid."

I grinned, wiping sweat from my brow. "Didn't mean to cause you such distress, princess."

She huffed in exasperation. "Come on, then. Huck has created a diversion so you can get to the infirmary without being spotted."

"Infirmary?" I asked incredulously. "Won't someone see us?"

"Not since Calista declared that a *human* infirmary was a wasted wing in the castle," Eira said, her voice dripping with venom.

"Ah." Yes, I did recall her shutting down that area. Now she referred the sick or injured to the palace healer or Lavinia.

"We need to get you cleaned up," Eira muttered. "Shivering bones, how did you get so *filthy*?"

Murdering people tended to be fairly messy. I shrugged and said, "I have my ways."

"Yes, but as elusive as your assassin ways are, we don't want to make some poor servant faint at the sight of you. That would be the *opposite* of stealth."

I grinned, shaking my head as Eira tugged on my arm, guiding me toward a shadowy staircase. From down the hall, echoes of the bustling servants bounced off the walls. The cook was shouting orders. Maids were scurrying about. I was about to ask what Huck's diversion was, when I heard a distinctly loud *crash* echoing from the kitchens. Screams rang out, and a cacophony of voices drifted farther away from us as everyone ran to go investigate.

Still clutching Eira's arm, I followed her up the staircase, my head spinning as the taxing ordeal of using necromancy twice finally caught up to me.

When we reached the top, Eira whispered, "Wait here."

The door creaked open just a fraction. After a moment, she said, "All right, let's go."

I frowned as we emerged in a barely-lit hall. Old, dusty paintings lined the walls, and the blue carpets were frayed along the edges. It looked like no one had been in this hall in years.

"Father wanted to dedicate this entire hall to humans," Eira said, her voice bitter. "In honor of my mother. Obviously, when Calista entered the picture, that plan went to shit."

I swallowed hard, unable to stifle the thought that I had contributed to such a hateful divide in our kingdom. "When you're queen, you can bring his plans to life."

She didn't say anything, but she didn't have to. I knew she was thinking she wouldn't be alive for long enough.

I had to believe she was wrong. There was a way for her to live. There *had* to be. And with my necromancy... perhaps *I* could save her. I had done it once before. Maybe, with the right amount of focus and strength, I could do it again.

We made it to the double doors at the end of the hall. Eira pushed them open, and I strode into the massive space, eyes wide. Floor-to-ceiling windows illuminated the room, highlighting the dust particles in the air and coating the floor. Several rows of cots lined the floor, spaced evenly to allow patients enough room to climb on and off. On the far end of the room was a set of shelves with shattered jars and tubes. A washbasin rested on the table underneath, along with a pile of clean rags, which Huck must have prepared for us.

Eira shut and bolted the doors before dropping her invisibility.

"Where's Huck?" I asked her, noticing we were alone in the infirmary.

"He went to rendezvous with Stella and Denton. Frisk, Mauro, and Kendra are rounding up the other fae beasts. They're all waiting for my signal. Our safest bet is to make our move when the guard shift changes in one hour. That'll be the best opportunity to slip past."

I arched an eyebrow. "What's the signal?"

She smiled slyly. "You'll see." She strode across the room to the washbasin, dipped a clean rag in the water, and wrung it out. "Now, let's get you cleaned up, you foul man."

"Foul?" I drew closer to her, a smirk playing on my lips. She staggered backward, but I continued my approach until I had her practically pinned against the wall.

Her eyes grew wide, and something heated sparked in her gaze.

"Does my scent bother you?" I asked. I'd meant for the words to sound playful, but my voice was husky.

She raised her eyes to meet mine. "No." She spoke in a gentle murmur, like a whispering wind brushing against my face. Slowly, she lifted the wet rag and brushed it along my cheek. "Your scent reminds me of a snowy forest in the mountains."

Stunned, I could only stare at her as she wiped away the grime, her movements cautious. The moisture was cool against my skin.

"My cottage," I whispered.

"What cottage?"

"I have a cottage in the mountains. It's a... refuge for me. My goal was to fulfill my contract with the queen and retire to live out there on my own. Undisturbed."

Half her mouth curled in a smile. "That sounds quite nice. Too bad I completely ruined those plans."

I stilled her hand, forcing her gaze to meet mine. "You didn't."

She wet her lips, drawing my eyes to the flick of her tongue. She dragged the edge of the rag against my lower lip, tugging it downward. A groan built in my throat from the slow, seductive movement.

Eira's eyes burned into mine, but she continued her meticulous work, rubbing the cloth into my beard, sweeping away coats of dirt and blood that had been caked in. With her free hand, she traced a faint scar that ran from my temple to my cheek, then another just above my eyebrow.

"I never noticed these before," she said. "How did you get them?"

"The small one was from a soldier in the Sea Court," I said. "I was young and cocky, and he almost got the better of me. The longer scar is from the first Demon Fae I fought."

Her eyes lifted to mine once more, worry and admiration glowing in her gaze. "You live a dangerous life, hunter."

"Yes, I do."

She returned to her cleaning, the rag running down my neck and dipping under my collar. Water trickled down my chest, and I shivered.

"There is... a lot more of you I still need to clean." Eira dropped her gaze as she plunged the rag into the bowl to wring it out once more. The clear water was now stained with flecks of brown and red.

Need pulsed within me from her words, and I remembered how close we'd come to taking each other in the woods earlier.

Did she really mean it? Before, I hadn't been certain if she truly wanted me, or just wanted me to *feel* something, to keep me from making a stupid choice like getting myself killed.

But now?

Eira withdrew the rag from the bowl and slowly began to lift my shirt. When I tensed, she raised her eyes to mine again. Her eyebrows lifted expectantly. "What, you're too bashful to let me clean you?"

A heady laugh burned against my throat, but it sounded hoarse and strained. She eased up the edge of my shirt, then slid the rag underneath to wipe across my chest.

"Blood and ice," I whispered, closing my eyes to relish the feel of the cloth gliding along my skin.

"This will be easier if you remove your clothes," Eira said. "Unless you want me to do it."

A hot lump formed in my throat, and I couldn't breathe for a moment.

Eira was tugging at the bottom of my shirt, and I let her lift it over my head. She surveyed me with heated desire brimming in her eyes. She pressed her lips together before continuing to scrub at the dirt and blood on my chest.

My skin was on fire everywhere she touched me. As the wet rag glided along my skin, all I thought of was how much I yearned to grab her waist and pull her against me.

Eira hissed suddenly. "Damn, Theron."

I followed her gaze, noting a gash along my ribs that was trickling fresh blood. The wound must have reopened when I'd dragged the soldier's body into the closet.

"Here." She moved to the table and tore several long strips of fabric before wrapping them around my chest, securing the cloth over the wound. I could only stare at her and the determined, focused glint in her eyes as she worked. She might have been teasing me before, but now she was committed to the task at hand. I was breathless at the sight of this fierce, unstoppable woman.

No one had ever cared for me when I was wounded before, except perhaps my mother when I was a child. For most of my life, I'd had to take care of myself. Survive on my own. Tend to my wounds in solitude.

The sight of Eira so devoted to cleaning me and wrapping my injury—it made my throat go hot with unexpected emotion.

No one cared... except for her.

When she tied off the cloth, she rested her palm against my chest, as if to feel my heartbeat. She went perfectly still, her breath quivering. "Better?" she whispered. She gazed up at me, those infinite blue eyes pulling me in.

My hand clasped hers, pressing it closer to my heart.

"Eira," I said quietly.

"Theron."

Our gazes held for a few heartbeats before I found my voice again. "What did you mean back in Tolston... when you said I was yours?"

Her lips parted in surprise, and she said nothing at first. Her eyes dropped, then lifted again as if she had to force herself to meet my gaze. "I—I meant that you... you..." She licked her lips and tried again. "I want you to be mine. I want you to belong to me. To stay by my side. To fight with me."

"As your soldier? Your protector?"

"As my lover. My partner. My equal."

My breath hitched. The blush in her cheeks deepened, but her pale eyes held mine.

Lover.

Gods, this woman would be the death of me. She tormented me, taunted me, frustrated me... And yet, everything inside me sang with conviction from her words. Because I wanted her by my side, too. As my partner. My equal. My lover.

I didn't even care that I had failed. Years of killing and hunting, and this was the first time I had failed. Instead of taking her heart, she had claimed mine.

It felt like a victory instead of a defeat.

I leaned in until my nose brushed against hers. She sucked in a breath, her eyelids fluttering.

Just before my mouth met hers, I murmured, "I *am* yours, Eira."

THE PRINCESS

I am yours, Eira.

The words rang in my mind again and again like the chiming of a bell, the echo endless and eternal.

I am yours. I am yours. I am yours.

With desire thrumming through my body, I wrapped my arms around his neck and brought his mouth fully against mine. Together, we staggered backward until we hit the wall, making the nearest sconce rattle.

His lips were moist and deliciously warm as they moved over mine, claiming me, devouring me, tasting me thoroughly. His tongue slid between my lips, and I responded with my own, ravishing him fully.

My hands slid along his chest, roaming the firm expanse of his broad shoulders. Gods, he was a masterpiece. His tan, sculpted muscles rippled with each movement. My fingers ran along the ridges of his abdomen. He groaned from my light touches, and satisfaction bloomed inside of me.

Yes, I certainly did love to torment him.

"Eira." The sound of Theron murmuring my name, his voice hoarse and ragged, nearly undid me.

His mouth was on mine again, his kisses more urgent and

desperate, as if he couldn't hold back any longer. His hips pressed against me, pinning me fully to the wall. With a moan, I raised my legs, wrapping them around him and bracing my back against the wall. Heat and longing throbbed in my core. Yearning for more, I ground myself against him. The friction of our clothes and bodies elicited a gasp from me.

More. I needed more.

"Take me to one of those cots," I ordered.

His mouth was on my neck, and I threw my head back, offering more skin for his lips to explore. When he responded, his breath tickled my throat, making me clench my legs tighter around him.

"Those tiny cots," he whispered, panting against my neck, "will not suffice. There is not enough space… for the things I want to do to you, princess."

Flames of desire and need coursed through me mercilessly. Shivering bones, this man drew out the most intense arousal I had ever experienced in my life. Nothing—*nothing*—had ever felt this potent, this violent. I was torn between shoving him onto a cot myself and begging for him to take me right here against this wall.

All I could manage was a small whimper, and I hated myself for it. It gave him power over me.

He chuckled, and his teeth scraped against my throat.

Oh, yes, I was done for. There was no point in fighting it.

My fingernails dug into his back, and he rolled his hips with a low growl. Encouraged by this, I raked my nails along his shoulder blades, rubbing my core against him. He moaned, the sound strangled, and I knew I was driving him mad, too.

We would undo each other completely. A frenzied collision that ensured mutual destruction.

Nothing sounded more appealing to me.

"Take it off," I gasped, my hands tangling in his hair as he ran his tongue along my neck. "Please."

"What? Your clothes? Or mine?"

"Yes. Both. Everything." I couldn't think straight. All I knew was his hot tongue was gliding up and down my throat, and *good gods*, it was the most intoxicating experience, to have him taste me so completely.

His mouth remained on my skin while his hands dipped just beneath my rear. He shifted slightly, and then his trousers fell to the floor.

And, blood and ice, he was there. Every glorious inch of his length was taut and pressed fully against me.

But he wasn't finished. His hands were on my waist now, his fingers sliding beneath my trousers. He curled one finger down low, just above my center.

I gave a sharp gasp. He was so close, yet still so far from where I needed him to be. "Gods, Theron," I moaned.

"You aren't the only one who knows how to torment, princess," he breathed. "Tell me what it is you want."

"I want…" Shivering bones, I couldn't think. Stars burst in my vision as his finger trailed lower. I bucked against him, my hips grinding. "*Theron—*" His name was a weak sigh on my lips.

"Mmm." His mouth was on my throat again. "Yes, my queen?"

He had never called me that before, and I liked it a little too much. The desire to taunt him bled through the heated chaos of my thoughts, and I teased, "I *command you* to service your queen."

"I believe that's what I'm doing."

I tugged on a fistful of his hair, jerking his head backward to look into his eyes. They scorched into mine, burning with intensity.

"Touch me," I said. "I want you to do despicable things to me, hunter."

A sly grin spread across his face. If one look could melt me, this was it. The way his lips curled upward, the glint in his eyes, the pink swollenness of his mouth from kissing me... All of it was enough to set me on fire.

"As you wish."

He tugged on my trousers until they fell to the floor, leaving me half naked. His grip tightened around my thighs as he pinned me against the wall, then shifted me upward until my legs rested on his shoulders.

And then, he brought his mouth to my center.

I stiffened, the back of my head hitting the wall with a loud *thud*.

He pulled back and laughed. "Careful, my queen, or you'll attract some unwanted attention."

I was burning, burning, burning. I couldn't even form a clever response.

He brought his mouth to my core again and flicked his tongue between my legs. Oh gods, I would die right here. My thighs tightened around him, bringing his face closer. His tongue slid deeper into me. My hips rolled as I moaned. If not for his body pressing me to the wall, I would have collapsed. My fingers worked their way through his hair, scratching his scalp.

"I can't—I *can't*—" I didn't even know what I was trying to say.

"Can't what?" he murmured against me.

"Can't... breathe. Can't..." I broke off with a curse, my eyes closing as he dragged his tongue up and down ever so slowly.

When his teeth nipped at me, a scream built up in my throat. Hastily, I shoved my knuckles in my mouth to block out the sound.

Theron laughed. He was *enjoying* this.

"I've never felt more satisfied to weaken my prey," he said, his tone smug.

"I swear to the gods, if you don't take me *right now*, Theron," I said, my voice ragged, "I will torment you for all eternity."

"Hmm, I might still enjoy that."

"Damn you."

"Tell me you're mine, Eira."

I had to pause to take a breath. Stars ignited in my vision, and I feared I might pass out. "I—"

"Yes?"

Gods, his arrogance was infuriating. There was no way I would let him win this. "I'll say it if you take off my shirt."

He chuckled. "So demanding."

"Well, I *am* your queen."

"Yes, you are."

Slowly, he slid me back down until my legs were around his waist once more. His hands tugged at the laces of my corset until the loose fabric fell down my shoulders. I shrugged out of the corset and tunic, and he discarded both onto the floor. His hands went to my shoulders, then traveled down to my breasts. His thumbs circled my nipples, and a riot of pleasure coursed through me. My heels dug into his back. Moisture pooled between my legs, and I rubbed more persistently against him.

"Cot," I moaned. "Now."

"No, I like you right here, princess."

"It's *queen*." I shoved against the wall until he stumbled backward, his hands on my ass. Together we staggered, and with a loud *thump*, we sank to the floor. He laughed as his head fell backward, his arms still around me, keeping me from sliding off him.

Now straddling him and fully in control, I wriggled my hips, feeling his arousal nudging closer to my core. His eyelids fluttered, and a low, husky sound emitted from his throat.

"What was that?" I teased, dragging my center against the length of him.

His moans grew louder, his head thrown back, his back arching. The muscles and veins stood out against his neck and shoulders. "Eira," he panted.

"Hmm, I like the sound of that." A smirk played on my lips. "It sounds like you want something from me."

He laughed, but the sound was more of a wheeze. "Well played, princess."

"*Queen*." My hand gripped his cock firmly, and he cursed.

"Queen," he said in a rasp.

"That's better."

"Eira—*Eira*—" His words broke off with a strangled groan as I squeezed. "*Shit*, Eira."

"Consider this retribution for the torture you put me through."

I ran my fingers up and down his length, stroking and teasing.

"Please," he begged. "Blood and ice, *please*…"

The sound of desperation in his voice made me ache. I was torturing myself as well as him by prolonging this.

No more. I couldn't take it.

In one swift movement, I sank onto him, allowing him to fill me completely. I gasped as heat filled my core. His flesh was hot against mine, throbbing and pulsing within me. I closed my eyes, biting my lip to keep from crying out.

"Oh," he panted. "*Oh.*" His hands tightened on my thighs, and I rocked against him, driving him deeper. He lifted his hips, and I couldn't stifle the moan that burst from my mouth.

"That's it," he breathed. "Harder, Eira."

My hips rolled, my legs spreading wider. Pleasure, intense and volatile, consumed me until I couldn't see. All I *felt* was him, slamming into me, deeper, deeper, deeper...

"Theron," I gasped, leaning forward, bracing my hands along his chest. He grunted, thrusting harder, faster.

Together, our bodies found a rhythm. The floor shook beneath us. My sweat mingled with his, making our skin slick. His hands pressed into the small of my back, grounding me. The friction of him burrowing into me was too much. *Too much.*

I threw my head back, uttering several breathy sighs of satisfaction, the only sounds I could manage with the sensations firing through my body. I couldn't even feel my own skin; my bones had melted from the sheer intensity of it. He had pierced through me, shattering me into pieces. Mind-numbing release enveloped me, dissolving me until there was nothing left.

This man, this hunter, had completely destroyed me.

I was his. Now and forever.

No force in the world could rip me away from him.

I pressed my hands to his chest as his hips jerked, and he

shuddered, meeting his own release. He let out a loud, slow groan, his eyes closed and his eyebrows lifting. He drove into me one final time before he collapsed underneath me, panting and slick with sweat.

I smiled contentedly and lay my head against his chest, enjoying the rapid thudding of his heartbeat.

I wasn't sure how long we lay there. I could have stayed like that for hours. Days, even. Theron's hand stroked small circles along my bare back, the soothing rhythm almost putting me to sleep.

"I made a bargain with you, you know," he murmured, his voice a soft rumble.

"Hmm?" I asked sleepily.

"In the mountains. When you were drunk on the Winterwing Brew that the pixies gave you."

I frowned and lifted my head to look at him. His eyes were closed, but a lazy smile was on his face. He looked so relaxed. So at ease. "What are you talking about?" My memories of that day were hazy, thanks to the brew.

"You were quite persistent in your advances. You wanted me to kiss you and... do other things to you."

My face heated, but I found myself chuckling. "Did I, now?"

His smile widened. "You did. And... the only way I could get you to stop was if I swore to kiss you at some point in the future."

I covered my mouth, my eyes growing wide. "Theron, you *didn't*."

He laughed. "Truth be told, I knew if I didn't make that bargain with you, you would break down my defenses. I might have relented. I might have given in and kissed you.

Perhaps taken you against the cave wall like you were begging me to."

I let my head fall against his chest again, my face on fire. "I can't believe this." I whacked him lightly on the arm. "And I can't believe you didn't *tell* me!"

"I wasn't planning to. After that moment in the alley when we were hiding from the soldiers, my bargain was fulfilled. I didn't need to bring it up again. But... After kissing you once... I knew it wouldn't be enough. I would want more. I will *always* want more of you, Eira."

I leaned in and pressed a soft kiss to his lips. His mouth captured mine once, fervent and tender, before I curled up against his chest again.

"I would make a thousand more bargains just to kiss you, Eira," he whispered as his hand resumed its circular motions along my bare back. I grinned into his chest, drinking in his scent and relishing this feeling. Just us, two lovers lying together, reminiscing of fond memories we had shared together.

For one beautiful moment, we were merely two people in love. Nothing more. No threat of death or war hanging over our heads. No bargains to fulfill. No bloodthirsty queen seeking our deaths.

Eventually, Theron's hand dropped, and I felt his breathing slow as he dozed off. His eyes were closed, his arms around me now limp.

I watched him with a smile, pleased with how peaceful he looked. His eyebrows were raised, his expression relaxed. I was so accustomed to seeing him scowl, his brow furrowed, the weight of the world darkening his face, that for just one second, I allowed myself to enjoy this carefree Theron.

I knew there was so much we had to do still. But for a few minutes, I could give him this respite from the world.

I only wished I could join him. Though he'd effectively exhausted me, I couldn't sleep.

There was too much on my mind.

My gaze snagged on my bare arm. The green spots had now spread to my hand, the small specks dotting each of my fingers. My entire left arm was covered in the poison.

Carefully, I eased off Theron, keeping my hands against his chest to hold him steady. When I was certain he wouldn't wake, I quietly tugged my clothes back on. Then, I crept back over to the table with the basin of water. Our bags lay on the floor, and I dug through them until I found what I was looking for.

The mirror.

With everything going on, I'd almost forgotten about it. But the poison spreading through my body was constantly on my mind, reminding me I was on borrowed time.

I was almost certain that when I uttered the words, the mirror would show me the poison had spread everywhere and I only had a few minutes left before my heart gave out.

But still... I *had* to know.

If these were my last moments alive, I could certainly have done worse. Making love to Theron was a delight I never could have predicted.

I only wished I could have taken Calista down before my death. I wished I could have carried on my father's legacy.

Just as I raised the mirror to my face, I heard her voice.

I see you, Snow Princess.

My blood ran cold. For one horrible moment, I thought she'd found her way into the infirmary.

But no. Through the reflection of the mirror, I saw her smirking at me, her eyes full of triumph.

Calista. My stepmother.

She'd found me.

The poison in my body burned hot. Fire scorched my veins. Darkness clouded my mind, and I was powerless to fight it.

Come to me, Calista commanded. *Bring me the mirror.*

THE PRINCESS

A HAZE OF FEVERISH FOG CLOUDED MY MIND. MY MOUTH tasted like sandpaper. I could see nothing but vague, blurry shapes around me. Gold lights. Cream-colored walls. A door slammed shut in the distance, the sound echoing against the vast walls.

Panic spurred me forward, and I collided with a wall. I groaned, and black spots appeared in my vision. Blinking blearily, I tried to clear my head. I leaned against the wall I'd run into, the cool marble strangely soothing to my flushed and overheated skin. Like a soothing balm to the sweltering heat I couldn't escape.

My breathing was wet and ragged. I couldn't get enough air in my lungs. I allowed myself to stand there, propped up by the wall while I tried to breathe.

I didn't know where I was or how I'd gotten here. I had no idea where Theron was, either. I tried to speak his name, but only a hoarse gurgle came out. Shivering bones, my head wouldn't stop spinning.

I lifted one of my arms, squinting through the murky delirium of my fever. I could vaguely make out the blurry green splotches of the poison that had completely taken over my arm. When I lifted the other, my heart jolted.

It, too, was covered in green spots.

A sick feeling rose up my throat. I was dying. This was it.

Then... how had I made it *here*? And where *was* here?

I pushed up from the wall, straining with every ounce of strength I possessed. My limbs shook, making me feel frailer than an old crone. I took several shallow breaths, trying to remain upright without falling.

"Theron," I rasped, but my voice was nothing more than a wisp in the air.

I needed a sparkwood apple.

I needed time.

I needed a *cure*.

No... I just needed Theron. He was all I needed.

"Theron," I tried again, louder this time. The sound of my voice resonating in my chest sent a modicum of clarity to my senses. Shapes came into view, and I caught a glimpse of a sparkling gold chandelier as my vision adjusted.

The sight made my breath catch in my throat. I was in the grand hall. Gleaming marble walls and pillars surrounded me. An ornate crimson rug lined the floor. Everything was so familiar, and yet it felt like a shadow of another life. A life that was no longer mine. A flood of memories assaulted me, rushing through my mind like the rapids of a river.

My father, a warm, gentle smile on his face. Calista, with her arm in his, her cold smile telling me what my father was too blind to see: she was cruel and unkind. Even from the first moment I saw her, I knew she would never love me as her own daughter. I wasn't even sure if she loved my father.

And yet, he'd been enamored with her. Completely besotted. When I'd expressed my concerns, he'd tucked me into a tight embrace and kissed my head, murmuring reassurances that with time, Calista would come to love me as he did.

And then he had died. Poisoned by the wife he adored so much.

Footsteps echoed nearby, jolting me from my thoughts. I stumbled forward, ducking behind a pillar. My pulse raced as the footsteps drew nearer. They were heavy and purposeful. Certainly not the light footsteps of a maid or a servant.

I peered carefully around the pillar, my vision still not as crisp as it normally was. My brow furrowed as I made out a vaguely familiar bulky figure. I sighed with relief.

It was Theron.

"What are you doing?" I hissed at him.

He turned, his dark eyes sharpening as he looked me over. "Are you hurt?" He strode toward me and grasped my shoulders, looking me over as if to assess for injuries.

I clutched him in a tight embrace, my face crumpling in part despair, part gratitude. All I'd wanted was *him*. I was dying, but he was here. That was all that mattered.

He grunted in surprise, his arms circling around me. "What's this for?" he murmured. Then, he withdrew slightly, a frown on his face. He pressed a hand to my forehead. "You're burning up."

"I—I can't fight it anymore, Theron," I said weakly, my hands trembling as I clung to him. "I'm sorry. I'm just... glad you're here with me now."

"It's all right, Eira. I have something that might help." He dug through his satchel until he withdrew a familiar shiny red apple.

I choked on a laugh, covering my mouth to stifle the sound. "A sparkwood apple? How the hell did you find one?"

He grinned and handed the apple to me. "I have my ways. I figured you'd be hungry for one right about now."

The sight of that beautiful red apple brought tears to my eyes. *Time.* This bought me more time. Time to defeat Calista. Time to help my rebel friends.

Time to be with Theron.

Without hesitating, I swiped the apple from Theron's grasp and bit into it. A strange, satisfied smile spread on his face. It wasn't the gentle, affectionate smile I'd been expecting. No, this expression was... triumphant.

My chewing slowed as I narrowed my eyes at him. "What..."

"How could I forget the filthy little rodent you were, always climbing those trees to snack on apples?" Theron sneered, his face twisting until he became something unrecognizable. "Like the wild creature you are."

I opened my mouth to speak, but no words came out. My tongue was completely numb. Aching shivers wracked my body, and I slumped against the wall, suddenly dizzy again. The usual clarity I'd associated with sparkwood apples was gone. Instead, the fever only intensified, making me feel hot and cold all at once.

"And when I cut them down because they interfered with my magic, you *cried*," Theron spat, his face continuing to shift. His tan skin paled until it was bone-white. His eyes brightened to a light brown.

"You—You—" My tongue was so heavy. Why couldn't I speak?

My eyes fell to the apple in my hand. It was oozing a bright green liquid. With a yelp, I dropped it, but it was too late. The damage had been done.

When I looked at Theron again, it wasn't Theron at all.

It was Calista, still wearing that triumphant smile.

"I only had a few drops of your blood," she continued, her voice oozing with glee. "I had to save it for the perfect moment. Your human blood weakens my control over you, unfortunately. My powers are most effective with full-blooded fae. But once you were in Tolston, I could sense you. And I could sense *this*."

She lifted the hand mirror. She must have pulled it from my bag. I tried to reach for it, but my arms wouldn't move.

"I commanded you to bring me the mirror, and this was as far as you got before the fever claimed you." She clicked her tongue as if chiding me. "Pathetic. My poison from years ago must have been stronger than I thought. I almost didn't need to fill you with more of it. But I didn't want to take any chances."

Fire consumed my veins as the poison destroyed my body from the inside out. I had been fighting one dose of her poison already—and I'd been losing.

She had now filled me with another dose. It was over.

"Goodbye, Snow Princess," said Calista.

She had won. She had poisoned me—again.

And this time, there was no escape. I couldn't turn invisible and flee like before; I was far too weak.

I'm sorry, Father, I thought in despair. *I failed you.*

The fire was spreading much more quickly now. Perhaps it was the poison already lingering in my blood. Or perhaps Calista had somehow given me a stronger dose of it.

But I only had moments left. My consciousness was fading fast.

Scream, I told myself. *You have to scream. Now!*

I drew in a long breath, but darkness pressed in on me, threatening to consume me.

Scream, Eira!

The voice in my head sounded like Theron. If he were here with me, he would shout at me to hold on. To withstand the poison coursing through my veins.

Scream!

I opened my mouth wide and unleashed a piercing shriek that bounced off the walls, resonating in the castle like a shrill siren.

Calista smacked me across the face, silencing me. The pain of her strike sent me over the edge, and I blacked out.

The Hunter

Sleep, Theron, a soothing voice crooned.

So, I slept. A small, nagging part of my mind asked, *Why?*

But the command resonated so firmly within my body that I had no choice but to obey. I was so very, very tired.

Why was I tired? Warmth and heat flooded my body as the memory of what I had been doing a few moments ago came closer to the surface. But the deep slumber claimed me before I could identify it.

No matter. I needed the rest.

Strange, chaotic images flooded my mind as my dreams spiraled. I saw Eira, bleeding out on the floor. Her scream echoed in my ears, burning through my skin and melting my bones. I saw Calista with blood dripping down her chin. I saw my father, pointing a menacing finger at me, his spit flying as he scolded me for falling in love with a filthy half breed.

And through it all, Eira's scream continued to plague my mind.

A bolt of clarity speared me, and my eyes flew open.

"Eira." My voice was sluggish and incoherent.

As my dreams faded, her scream lingered, floating down the hall and surrounding me like a fog.

"*Eira!*" I jumped to my feet, swaying from the sleepiness that still clung to me.

Sleep, Theron.

Blinking rapidly, my brow furrowed as I identified the voice.

Calista. She was using my blood to command me to sleep.

That could only mean one thing: she had Eira, and she didn't want me interfering.

I fumbled with my clothing, tugging on my shirt and trousers as I fought to stay lucid. Then I staggered to the door, still fighting Calista's influence, my eyelids heavy... so heavy...

"*Hunter!*" barked a familiar voice.

I jumped, peeling my face off the wall. I must have leaned against it and fallen asleep once more. Swearing, I righted myself and found Frisk the fox standing at the open door.

"You've got some spittle on your chin, lazy-ass," he snapped.

"It's not *me*," I protested. "It's the queen—the false queen. She—She—" My head drooped once more.

"Snap out of it!" Frisk swiped his paw at my shin. His claws ripped at the fabric of my trousers—not enough to draw blood, but enough to jolt me from my haze.

I stared down at the fox as he cocked his head at me.

"You called her the *false* queen."

"Yes. Eira is the true queen. *My* queen."

Frisk's whiskers twitched as if he were trying to smile. "Took you long enough. Come on, we've got to move. Snow gave the signal. The castle is under attack."

"What was the signal?"

"Her scream."

I froze as the horror of Eira's scream washed over me once more. Shaking off the feeling, I hurried after Frisk down the hallway, staying on his tail as he wound through the halls and padded up the stairs. Frantic servants jostled past, some shrieking and others barking orders. I made out words like *under attack* and *the princess*.

I strained to hear just *what* exactly had happened to the princess, but I couldn't make out any details. Cursing under my breath, I quickened my pace.

A resounding roar from outside rang out, making the walls and floor tremble. I froze, heart pounding as I looked around in alarm.

"What the hell was that?"

"It's just Rogun," said Frisk, sounding bored.

"Who's Rogun?"

"He's a huge dragon from Knockspur. He's come to help us."

My eyes rounded. A massive *dragon* was fighting with the rebels? Kendra was one thing—she was incredible, but far too small to make much of an impact when facing Calista's armies.

But something much bigger? That could turn the tides of the battle in our favor.

"Don't get too excited," Frisk chided. "He's a sleepy fellow. Has to nap every hour or so to keep up his strength."

My spirits deflated, but Frisk was chuckling.

"The false queen doesn't know that, though," Frisk said slyly. "Come on, we need to keep moving."

We reached the top of the stairs and burst through the door. When we entered the echoing entrance chamber above, I froze as something shimmery caught my eye.

A glowing blue thread.

I stopped, my heart hammering in my chest as I drew closer to it. It extended all the way down the hall, nearly translucent. If not for the glow of the sun streaming through the stained-glass windows, I might not have seen it.

"Eira," I whispered.

Frisk faltered at that, whirling to face me. "What?"

"I can see her thread."

"What does that mean?"

I didn't have time to tell him about my discovery of magic. Instead, I channeled my power and stretched my mental awareness toward the thin string. It was already fragile, as if only the finest strand was holding it together.

She was dying.

But I was a life weaver.

My pulse racing, I pressed my magic into the strand, envisioning layer after layer wrapping around it, thickening it, strengthening it...

"Hunter," Frisk hissed.

I ignored him, my eyes closed and sweat beading along my brow. I couldn't afford any distractions.

One wrong move, and I would accidentally kill Eira instead of save her.

Live, I willed the thread. *I command you to live.*

Light shone against my eyelids, and Frisk gasped. I didn't dare open my eyes, though. I kept my mind focused on my task. On Eira.

Magic seeped out of me, draining me. I hunched over as the sensation of a heavy weight on my back dragged me lower and lower.

At long last, I felt the power within me fade. As I reached out again, Eira's thread was sturdier.

She was still alive. For now.

Panting, I opened my eyes to find Frisk gaping at me.

"She's dying," I said, gasping for breath as if I'd sprinted a mile. "My magic is keeping her alive, but it won't last forever. Come on, I can follow her thread to find her."

To his credit, Frisk didn't ask any questions. He merely trotted after me, his paws clacking on the marble floor.

The thread weaved down the massive hall, and we rushed past several elegant paintings of snowy landscapes, and one regal portrait of the late king. I stopped as Eira's life thread slid through the double doors that led to the throne room.

She was in there. And Calista was likely with her.

I couldn't avoid this forever.

Turning to Frisk, I said, "Stay out of sight. Calista doesn't know about you, and I'd like to keep it that way. Just in case she has something sinister waiting for us."

"If Snow is in there, I'm coming," Frisk insisted.

"Calista can use you as leverage against her," I argued. "And me."

Frisk's ears drooped. After a moment of silence, he said, "I didn't realize you cared, hunter."

"Yes, well, you and Eira are a lot alike. You work your way into someone's skin, and by the time you realize you care, it's too late to change your mind." My voice was gruff, but Frisk's nose twitched, his eyes shining as if he saw right through my grumbling.

"I'll rally reinforcements," Frisk said. "Just remember, you aren't alone. Neither of you are."

I nodded as he darted away, grateful the small creature wouldn't be put in harm's way. At least not right now.

With a deep breath, I pushed open the doors and strode into the throne room.

Sure enough, Calista was waiting for me, sitting atop her throne with her glistening silver crown resting on her bronze hair. Her eyes gleamed with triumph as she surveyed me.

How had I ever believed this woman was seelie? Everything about her marked her as a demon, from her skeletal features to her blood-red lips.

I knew now that not all unseelie fae were monstrous. But this woman was.

I approached her slowly, my body on high alert, tense as I awaited whatever ambush she had planned.

Then, I noticed Eira's prone figure lying at Calista's feet, her long curls sprawled around her. Her eyes were closed, and her skin was paler than death. The patches of green spots were visible on her skin—her arms, neck, face... Everywhere. It was no longer just condensed to one arm.

The poison had spread.

Anger and panic spiraled in my chest, and it took every ounce of my restraint to keep from rushing to her side.

She's alive, I reminded myself. *Her thread is still intact. She's alive.*

"Well, dear hunter," Calista crooned, crossing one leg over the other, her expression almost lazy. "It hasn't been that long since we last saw each other, but things have certainly changed, haven't they?"

I lifted my chin, refusing to rise to her taunting. "Yes. They have."

Calista waved an idle hand toward Eira. "Her life is mine. I suggest you say your goodbyes while she still breathes."

"What have you done to her?" Despite my best efforts, I couldn't keep the growl out of my voice.

Her thin lips spread into a satisfied smile, as if she'd caught me. "I have poisoned her."

I shook my head. "Demon Fae poison doesn't work that fast."

Calista's smug expression slipped for the briefest of seconds, and I stifled a chuckle. She didn't realize I knew her secret.

Perhaps she thought the truth would die with Eira.

Oh, how wrong she was.

"This isn't the first time she was poisoned, you know," Calista said, clicking her tongue in dismay. "It happened years ago. It's uncanny how she seems to attract the worst sorts of creatures, don't you think?"

A bitter taste filled my mouth as I recalled the green splotches on Eira's arm. The poison had been slowly working through her body for years. And now, with more of the queen's poison working through her system, she likely only had moments left.

"Apparently, the Demon Fae cursed her with their poison, enacting a spell that would prevent her from healing," Calista went on. "Somehow, she's kept the poison at bay this whole time. But with another dose of it, it's spreading even faster. It won't be long now. Soon, my court will be rid of the rogue princess for good."

"No." My heart was seizing in my chest. It couldn't just be *over*.

Eira couldn't die. Not like this. Not now.

"This *is* a delightful sight," Calista said with another laugh. "I don't often shock you, Theron, but when I do, it is a real treat." She clapped her hands together as if she were watching a performance instead of gloating over poisoning her stepdaughter.

Bile crept up my throat. I couldn't breathe. Oh gods. Oh *gods*...

What was I supposed to do? I couldn't let Eira die.

But I couldn't heal her poison. I could only keep her thread intact for a short span of time. Just like her stab wound, I hadn't been able to fix the injury. I'd needed a healer.

She was dying. She *would* die.

"You two have grown... quite close recently, haven't you?" Calista said, arching a single eyebrow. "It seems she's worked her charms on you, if she managed to convince you to break our bargain."

"I—I—" Shivering bones, I couldn't speak.

"You know what this means, don't you?" Calista's voice turned icy. "You—and your blood—belong to me."

Pull yourself together, Theron! I ordered myself. I couldn't break down now.

Calista believed she had me. But Frisk was out there, rallying reinforcements. The soldiers were under attack. Did Calista know this?

Did she know I'd awakened my necromancy? Had Lavinia told her yet?

"No," I blurted.

Calista's brows furrowed. "No what?"

"No, I didn't break our bargain."

She chuckled. "Don't try to talk your way out of this, Theron."

"I promised I'd bring you her heart." I gestured to Eira's prone form. "And I have."

"You promised you would kill her," Calista seethed.

"No, I didn't." I remembered that moment clearly—the moment I was certain I'd agreed to my freedom. "I promised you her heart in exchange for a release from my duties and the return of my blood. Never once did I vow to kill her, nor did I specify what condition her heart would be in when I delivered it to you."

Calista's mouth opened and closed, her eyes widening a fraction. "But I…" She trailed off, her face paling.

In spite of the situation, I found myself smirking. "It is a real treat to shock you, Your Majesty."

Her lips thinned, and fury brimmed in her eyes. She opened her mouth to speak, but before she could, I said, "You are right, though. The princess is dying. I can see that now. Can I bid her farewell? I did grow… quite fond of her."

Calista's eyes narrowed as she looked me up and down, as if searching for a hidden weapon. At long last, she waved her hand. "Yes. Say your goodbyes. There is nothing you can do for her."

I had to let her believe that. With a nod, I drew closer to the princess.

"Bargain or not," Calista said suddenly, "you will not leave this palace alive, Theron. I trust you know that."

I met her gaze. "I do." Then, I crouched to the ground, kneeling next to Eira's motionless form.

Still alive, I had to remind myself. Because she did look well and truly dead. Her lips were gray. Her chest wasn't moving.

The thin thread of life surrounding her was no longer a strengthened cord. My magic had faded, and the poison would claim her soon.

But I had one last idea. I didn't even know if it would work, but I had to try.

I leaned closer to Eira, digging down deep into my well of power, summoning everything I had left. I focused on the pain of this moment; it wasn't hard to conjure it. The sight of Eira lying before me felt like cleaving my chest into two pieces. I clung to that feeling, allowing the anguish of this moment to spread through my body and soul.

What was it Lavinia had told me? *It is said necromancers possess the kiss of death. Unless you channel your power into the kiss, it's harmless.*

If necromancers possessed the kiss of death... perhaps we also possessed the kiss of life.

I focused all my power into a single breath. Energy sparked behind my lips. They tingled and burned from the force of my magic.

A faint light caught my eye. My lips were glowing.

Calista noticed it, too. She abruptly stood and said, "Wait!"

Ignoring her, I pressed a kiss to Eira's cold lips, pushing my magic into her as I exhaled what I hoped was the breath of life into her mouth. I poured it into her, every ounce of myself, every drop of power and energy. I gave it all to her.

My frame sagged as my life force bled out of me and funneled into Eira's mouth. Darkness clouded my vision, and a harsh ringing sound blared in my ears, drowning out Calista's scream.

The last thing I heard before I lost consciousness was the sound of Eira's loud, rattling gasp of air.

The Princess

Sudden clarity pierced through the dark haze of my mind, and an intense array of sensations assaulted me all at once. My skin felt hot and cold, the light shining through the windows was far too bright, and an animalistic screech of fury made my ears throb.

Slowly, my eyes opened. An invisible force seemed to tug directly from the center of my chest, like I was a marionette on strings. I jerked upright violently. Some innate instinct had me on my feet, my skin prickling with awareness. Adrenaline flooded my body, fear and energy bursting within me, alerting me that something was wrong, that I needed to *move*.

Another roar of rage split the air. Claws swiped for me, and I ducked and rolled away, righting myself with my dagger in hand.

I faced Calista, whose long, red claws extended from each hand, fury boiling in her eyes.

"How?" she roared, advancing toward me.

I backed up a step, heart pounding. A flood of confusing and disorienting emotions swelled inside me, overwhelming my senses. The room smelled of the sharp, cool cleanliness I associated with the palace I grew up in.

It smelled like despair.

Calista advanced, and my spine stiffened. I was the prey, and she was very much a predator homing in on its target.

"How *what?*" I asked, panting.

"How did he heal you?"

I faltered, unsure of what she was talking about. But she gestured to the throne room floor, and my heart stuttered in my chest.

Theron lay dead at my feet.

No. *No.*

"He... what?" Theron was no healer; he was a necromancer.

In a flash, the memory came back to me: Calista, glamoured as Theron, giving me a sparkwood apple that was infused with her poison. Darkness overcame me, and I was certain I had died.

Theron had power over life and death. But he couldn't heal a fatal wound. He'd only stopped my wound from bleeding out in Tolston, and it had merely been temporary.

Something shimmered in the sunlight, and I gasped. A glowing blue thread was suspended between Theron and myself, as translucent as a spider's web.

It was the same shade of blue as Theron's magic.

Blood and ice.

Theron had *given* me his necromancy. But how?

Warmth tingled on my lips, an echo of what I'd felt just before waking up. I brushed my fingertips along my mouth, my hand shaking. Theron had kissed me. But it had been more than just an ordinary kiss...

Calista lunged for me, and on instinct, I draped my invisibility over myself, narrowly dodging her attack.

"That trick worked once on me, foul brat," she spat. "But it won't work again."

I danced out of her reach, my footsteps feather-light. She snarled, her nostrils flaring as she sniffed me out. She was right; I couldn't avoid her strikes forever. As an unseelie fae, her senses were heightened.

And with the juices from a sparkwood apple still in my system, my invisibility wouldn't last long. It certainly wasn't as effective. If she looked closely enough, she would be able to see me.

How long had I been unconscious? I remembered screaming, signaling to my allies to move forward with the plan. But if I was unconscious for the next phase, the plan couldn't continue.

I was so disoriented by my thought process that I didn't see Calista moving toward me again. Something heavy slammed into me, and I crashed to the floor, tumbling across the marble, my limbs throbbing. Pain speared through me, and I sensed my invisibility fading.

Shit.

With a groan, I rolled out of the way just in time, narrowly avoiding another strike of Calista's claws. Gasping, I climbed to my feet, hastily checking my body for open wounds. All it took was one drop of blood, and she would have me.

"Go ahead," I rasped, glaring at Calista. "Use your Demon Fae magic, Calista. Show me who you really are."

Her eyes narrowed into tiny slits. "I can kill you easily, girl. With or without my powers."

I spread my arms. "Then go ahead."

She smirked, triumph gleaming in her eyes. "I don't have to. I have plenty who will do the deed for me." Her hand went to the small glass vial attached to the necklace at her throat. She poured a drop of blood from it onto her finger and sucked on it. Her eyes closed, and power thrummed around her as she no doubt tried to summon soldiers using her blood magic.

I waited, still trying to catch my breath, my eyes fixed on the throne room doors, which remained closed. *Come on*, I thought. *Tell me I'm not too late.*

If all went according to plan, Stella, Denton, Huck, and the others would have rendezvoused with our rebel allies, and the troops would have stormed the castle by now.

Calista's smile vanished, her eyes flying open, shock etched into her face. Either her soldiers were busy fighting for their lives, or they were dead and couldn't respond to her command. "What—" She, too, glanced toward the doors, then back at me, accusation burning in her eyes. "What did you do?"

"I did whatever it took to claim my birthright," I said. "That throne is mine, Calista."

Fangs flashed as she bared her teeth at me. "You think that can stop me? Those pathetic soldiers aren't the only tools I have at my disposal." She withdrew a vial of blood from her skirts, and my own blood ran cold. With a savage grin, she uncorked it, pouring a droplet of blood on her finger and bringing it to her mouth. Her eyes closed, her expression smoothing.

I tensed, my arms rigid at my sides as I waited to see who she would call to her aid. A commander? A powerful fae warrior?

My heart jolted in my chest when Theron shifted on the ground, his body sliding eerily along the cold marble floor.

A sickening feeling rushed up my stomach, churning violently. I was going to be ill. I was *losing* my mind...

Theron's body was distorted, limbs bending at awkward angles as he rose from the floor. His eyes remained closed, his face deathly pale. He looked like a rag doll being tossed around.

And that was exactly what he was.

He was not himself.

He was not in control.

He was *hers*.

Tears stung my eyes. I watched in horror as he stood before me, each movement jerky and unnatural, like he was a demon possessing a human body for the first time.

Step. Step. Step. He inched toward me, feet shuffling awkwardly on the floor. He lacked the powerful prowess, the firm strides, of the hunter I was so accustomed to.

This man was a complete stranger.

"*Kill her,*" Calista hissed, her voice resonating and bouncing off the walls of the throne room.

"No," I moaned, shaking my head as I backed away from Theron.

I couldn't fight him like this. The alleys in Tolston were one thing; that was when he was actively resisting her influence.

But this? Was he even still alive? Was his consciousness in there at all?

Or was Calista controlling his corpse?

My vision swam as tears filled my eyes. "Theron, please," I whispered.

He continued trudging forward, his body lopsided, his

stance crooked. From his belt, he drew a dagger and angled it toward me.

A hot lump formed in my throat. I shook my head, my back meeting the wall. I had nowhere left to retreat. My hand shook as I brandished my dagger.

He attacked, blade swinging. I blocked his strike, then jabbed my dagger toward his arm. I just had to cut him. Just one cut…

His blade met mine, the sound of clashing steel ringing through the throne room. With a swift movement, he twisted my wrist, and the dagger fell from my grip. He kicked it away, and I watched as it skittered along the floor, too far for me to reach.

Theron raised his dagger again.

"Theron!" I cried, lifting my hands as if I could stop him. As if I could do anything.

Theron thrust his dagger forward. I dived underneath him, dodging the swipe of his blade. He struck again, and I ducked. Back and forth we fought, him slashing and me dancing away from his advances. Sweat poured down my neck, drenching my tunic. My breathing quickened, my pulse racing. A flush crept into my face, making the room feel too hot.

Swipe. Dodge. Parry. Thrust.

This couldn't go on forever. I couldn't win by avoiding him.

I had to disarm him. I had to get the knife out of his grasp.

Blood and ice, what if I accidentally killed him? What if he was still alive in there, but I wounded him so badly that he would never wake up again?

With his next strike, I aimed a jab to his abdomen. He let

out a keening groan and hunched over, arms wrapped around his stomach.

"No!" I shrieked, covering my mouth with my hand. "Theron, I'm sorry—"

He lashed out, his knife meeting my forearm. I screamed, jerking backward as hot blood gushed down my arm, dripping onto the floor. From behind Theron, Calista licked her lips, eyeing the pool of blood hungrily.

Shit.

Theron's dagger was wet with my blood. He brandished it toward me, eyes still closed, face still cold and impassive.

"Theron," I said again, my voice raspy. Blood continued dripping from my arm. "Theron, *stay with me*. You can fight this. You have to fight this!"

"He cannot hear you," Calista hissed, inching toward me. Her nostrils flared, her eyes fixed on my blood on the floor.

All she needed was one drop. One drop, and I would be at her command.

She could order me to hold still while Theron slit my throat.

She could order me to cut out my own heart.

My stepmother would *win*.

"*Theron!*" I sobbed, trying to snap him out of this. But he didn't flinch. He didn't even crack open his eyes.

My perfect, rugged hunter was gone.

I sank to my knees. Theron stood over me, looming like a specter about to shepherd me to my death.

My face was moist with tears, my arm soaked in blood. I stared up at Theron, my heart shattering into pieces at the sight of his body being used like this.

He would hate this. With every fiber of his being, it would destroy him if he knew he was doing this.

"I love you, Theron," I whispered.

He aimed the dagger for my throat.

Just before he slit it, a gleam of pale blue ignited in the air. Without thinking, I grabbed it.

And the entire world froze. Theron stopped moving. Calista was still as a statue, eyes gleaming as she eagerly watched me. Between my fingers was the delicate blue thread of Theron's life.

His life.

Shivering bones... *He was still alive.*

"Theron," I breathed. With slow, careful movements, I released the thread one finger at a time, worried if I jerked too hard, I would accidentally snap it in two.

Still alive. Still alive. The words resonated in my head like they had their own pulse.

When I let go of the thread, the air shifted once more, and Theron moved. His body jolted, and he let out a strangled choking sound. His chest seized, and the knife hovered midair.

For a brief moment, his eyes flew open, and that familiar onyx gaze fixed on me.

In a flash, it was gone, his face going slack again. But that was all I needed.

He was still in there. He was still fighting.

The thought lifted my heart, giving me the energy and motivation I needed.

He wasn't dead. I could still save him.

With his next strike, I grabbed his wrist, then rammed my knee between his legs.

Theron moaned, and I ignored how the sound broke me as I swiped the dagger from his loosened grip. I stepped toward him and dragged the blade gently along his palm. He hissed in pain, jerking away from me. His eyes fluttered open again, regarding me with confusion and horror.

"Eira," he groaned.

A relieved smile split across my face.

But it was short-lived.

The moment he said my name, he collapsed, crumpling into a heap on the ground.

"No!" I screamed, racing toward him. I touched his face, his shoulders, his hair, trying to rouse him. "Theron. *Theron*! Wake up!" I shook him, but his head only lolled onto my lap.

With a screech, Calista hurled the glass vial onto the floor. "Useless idiot!" she roared, her expression venomous. "I need more blood!" Her eyes darted to the crimson liquid still dripping from my arm.

A wild, animalistic sound burst from her. Her lips pulled back from her teeth with a feral snarl, and she pounced. I dived to the floor, covering the puddle of blood with my body. Calista slammed into me, and we crashed in a pile of limbs. Her claws tore at my clothes. I shoved her face away from my throat before she could rip it out with her fangs. My foot connected with her stomach. Hissing and spitting like an enraged animal, Calista roared, the sound making my ears throb.

I managed to kick her hard in the temple, and she fell backward, toppling to the floor. After ensuring I had mopped up every drop of my blood with my clothes, I scrambled to my feet, angling myself away from her.

I didn't know if she could somehow siphon the blood staining my clothes and use it to control me. But I didn't want her getting close enough to find out.

Her eyes were redder than death as she stood, back

arched and claws extended. We faced each other, bodies poised for battle as we circled one another like vultures.

"You were always going to lose," Calista seethed. "You never had what it takes to rule this court. Your weak bloodline *failed* this kingdom." She waved a hand toward me, her face twisting in disgust. "You may appear a queen, but your beauty is only skin-deep. In truth, you are nothing more than a cold statue, carved in ice and glass. Beautiful on the outside, but void of anything substantial on the inside. I alone am strong enough to protect the realm."

"With what?" I snarled. "Your Demon Fae gifts? You've been lying to your people for years! Hunting those of us who aren't full-blooded seelie fae, as if we're *less* than you. If the court knew that you were the very thing they were hunting, this entire kingdom would collapse!"

"If they knew what I was, they would still follow me over you!"

"Are you sure about that?" I reached into the folds of my tunic, intending to withdraw the hand mirror… and froze. My blood ran cold. With wide eyes, I stared at Calista in horror.

A slow smirk spread across her face as she lifted the mirror. "Is this what you're looking for?"

Shit. I had forgotten she'd taken it when she poisoned me. "I'll get it back from you. I stole it once, and I can steal it again."

Her sneer returned. "Stupid, foolish girl. I *always* know where the mirror is. If you take it, I will find it again."

I thought of the soldiers pillaging Tolston, searching every home. "You were looking for it. You knew it was in Tolston."

"Of course I did. You have *no* idea the magic that mirror contains."

"It contains the truth," I said. "I can expose you, Calista. Once my allies arrive, we will take the mirror from you and summon the nobles of the court. I'll use the mirror to show them who you really are."

She barked out a harsh, grating laugh. "You truly are clueless, aren't you? This is so much more than just an enchanted mirror. It is bound to my very essence. I can sense when it is near. Its magic *calls* to me. But go on, take it. Try to use it and see what happens."

She shoved the mirror into my hands, her eyes gleaming. I clutched it tightly, my skin prickling with unease. This felt like a trap. The gleeful look on her face told me she *wanted* me to try it.

Calista's smile only grew. Even with her mirror in my hand, she knew I was doubting everything about my plan. She knew I couldn't win if I didn't know for sure the mirror would work.

The throne room doors crashed open. My heart lurched as seven familiar faces appeared: Denton, Stella, Gareth, Huck, Tansy, Penelope, and Lark—the human nobles. My closest friends stood in the open doorway, flanked by soldiers wearing red bandanas and brass breast plates.

The rebels. *My* rebels. They were war-torn and bloody, but they were alive.

A smile broke across my face. They'd done it. They were *here*.

Calista's head whipped toward the newcomers, her face twisting with rage. "Guards!" she shrieked.

"No one is coming, *false queen*," Denton said, his voice

booming. "The castle is ours. All that stands between our true queen and her crown... is you."

As one, the soldiers and my human friends raised their swords. Pride swelled in my chest, and tears burned in my eyes. Until this moment, I hadn't truly realized the loyalty these people had to me.

I was their queen. Their leader. And they were prepared to die for that truth.

I lifted the mirror. "Step down, Calista," I commanded, my voice ringing with authority, "or I will show the world who you really are."

Calista's nostrils flared, her eyes wide as she looked around the room as if searching for allies. She would find none.

We had won.

A low, manic snarl built up in her throat. Spit flew from her lips as her features twisted. Huge, leathery wings sprang from her shoulders, and her pale skin darkened until it was an ashy gray. Darkness spilled from her feet, spreading across the floor like ink.

"You want to expose my true nature?" Calista hissed. "Go ahead. I'll kill all of you before you utter a single word."

Before I could object, Calista's darkness swallowed me whole.

And then, the throne room erupted in screams.

THE HUNTER

MY EARS WERE RINGING. PAIN AND CHILLS AND A STRANGE sense of frailty gripped my limbs, freezing me in place. I wanted to vomit and scream all at once, but I couldn't move.

It felt as if a very piece of my soul was missing. As if I was on death's door, my limbs as weak and feeble as an old man.

I'd given my magic to Eira. My magic was my very life force.

I was truly dying.

And yet I was still here. I had awakened briefly, catching sight of Eira's tear-stained face as she looked up at me in desperation and relief. I could *hear* her screaming my name.

Darkness took me. As much as I wanted to be with her, that abyss pulled me under. Fading in and out, I caught echoes of Eira's conversation with Calista. The false queen had said the mirror was bound to her very essence.

The words struck something familiar within me, something important… but I couldn't grasp what it was.

The darkness claimed me again. For a moment, I thought I'd finally succumbed to death. But the rotting stench that stung my nostrils was horribly familiar. It brought me back to the surface again, my senses awakening. Dread coiled in my chest.

Demon Fae.

Calista had dropped her glamour.

Which meant Eira was fighting her. Alone.

Eira. *Eira*. She would die. Calista would kill her.

I had to move. *Now*.

Gritting my teeth, I shoved every ounce of strength into lifting my arm. Slowly, my body shifted, and a burst of pain shot through me, powerful enough to make me slump backward in defeat.

I couldn't. I *couldn't*.

Then, I heard her scream again. The sound pierced me, boiling my blood, setting my insides on fire. The agony of hearing her suffer was far worse than the agony of my failing body.

"Eira!" I bellowed.

And my arms moved. Then my legs. White-hot flames burned inside me, and I roared, raging against it, fighting my own body as I climbed to my feet. My very skin was melting off my bones. I was dying, dying, dying... Needles in my flesh, tearing and slicing. I could feel nothing and everything at once.

Eira cried out again, and a bolt of clarity entered my mind. I clung to it, and my feet shuffled forward. Through the haze of pain, I heard her voice.

"Theron!"

I was coming. She had to know I was coming for her.

With each step I took, sounds became clearer. Shouts. Screams. Some familiar, some not. I recognized Denton's voice, and Stella's. Which meant Eira's friends were here.

I was torn between relief that she wasn't alone, and dread that her allies would be slaughtered.

Move, I told myself. *Just keep moving.*

"No!" Eira shouted. Her voice was closer now.

I needed to *see*. How could I protect her if I couldn't see?

Focus, I thought. *Use your other senses. You're a hunter. You can do this.*

I closed my eyes, though it didn't matter because it was pitch black. Still, the motion helped me activate my other senses, relying fully on them. Calista's foul odor burned in my nose, but it was farther away now. I sensed Eira's familiar frosty pine scent and focused on it, drawing closer to her.

A horrifying scream echoed in the room. This wasn't like the other shouts and cries; this was the sound of someone dying.

A sickening crunch followed, then a loud, wet *thud*.

I flinched. And Eira's voice broke on a sob.

Calista had just killed one of her friends.

Panic pulsed through me. I knew Eira was about to do something reckless. Something she would regret later.

On instinct, my arm shot out and clasped hers. She jumped, pounding a fist against my chest, and then froze.

"Theron?" she whispered.

"I'm here."

She collapsed against my chest, clinging to my tunic and weeping openly. "I can't—I can't—she's *killing* them, Theron."

"Her thread," I murmured. "Can you see Calista's thread?"

"What? No! I can't see anything!"

Shit. I wasn't sure if the necromancy would work in the darkness.

Then, something else sparked in my mind. Something I'd forgotten.

"Where's the mirror?"

"I have it," Eira said. "It's right here."

"Give it to me, Eira."

She stiffened. "What?"

"You have to trust me."

"I trusted you before. But you turned out to be *her*. How do I know you aren't Calista?"

My fingers worked their way up her shoulder until they caught a strand of her hair. Slowly, I cupped her face and brought her mouth to mine, pressing the barest of kisses against her lips. "I'm yours, Eira," I breathed.

She trembled in my grasp, her breaths coming in sharp pants. "Blood and ice, you're *alive*! How? Calista—she was controlling your body. You were *dead*!"

Shivering bones. Calista had controlled me while I was unconscious? I hadn't even known that was possible. "I don't know how," I said, "and I'm so sorry. But I need the mirror *now*, Eira."

Something cool and metal brushed against my fingers, and I clasped the handle of the mirror firmly. Without hesitation, I hurled it to the ground, and the glass shattered, the sound ringing in the vast room.

"What have you done?" Eira cried.

"Trust me!" I said again.

A deep, menacing roar exploded from the other side of the room. The ground shook, and energy swirled around me like a funnel cloud, stinging my eyes and tousling my hair. Eira shrieked in alarm. I held her against my chest again, shielding her. The wind intensified, whipping mercilessly at me until I was certain it would carry me away.

Light bled through the darkness, slowly at first. Shadows and shapes took form. Some lay motionless on the floor. And in the center of the carnage was Calista, her skin tough and leathery, with great black wings stretched behind her back. Fangs extended from her lips, covered in blood. Her bright red eyes widened as the darkness of her magic faded. Bit by bit, the black mist receded as if being washed away by an invisible rag. In moments, the throne room was in full view once more, and I sucked in a sharp breath at the crimson blood that stained the floors.

Several bodies were strewn about, some missing limbs. Most of them were soldiers wearing the rebels' red bandana.

But one of them I recognized. A woman with white-blonde hair.

Her head was completely severed from her body.

Stella.

Eira sank to her knees, erupting in sobs. I clutched her shoulders, my eyes fixing on Calista to see what she would do next. She whirled, her red eyes frantic as she looked around the room.

"Where is it?" she hissed. *"Where is it?"*

"You mean the source of your magic?" I asked. With my foot, I nudged the broken glass on the floor. "It's gone, Calista."

Lavinia had told me of a spell that could bind fae magic, enhancing someone's power. *If anyone were to acquire this conduit, they could destroy it and potentially disrupt the connection to your magic completely.*

That was how Calista had maintained a flawless glamour all these years. She had bound her magic to the enchanted mirror. It empowered her.

But without that mirror intact, the source of her strength was gone.

Now, she was stuck in her Demon Fae form. And she wasn't powerful enough to conjure her darkness anymore.

A noise of rage burst from Calista's lips, her face twisting into another snarl. "Foolish boy! I don't need *magic* to slaughter everyone in this room!"

I pulled a dagger from my belt and flung it toward Calista. At the same time, she lunged. The blade barely nicked her shoulder. She screeched as she careened toward me.

But I was ready. The moment before we collided, I ducked, slamming into her abdomen. She roared as we toppled over. My fingers caught the corner of her wing and tugged. Flesh tore, and black blood oozed. Calista screamed as I pulled another dagger and rammed it into her side.

Something heavy rammed into the back of my skull—Calista's wing perhaps? I groaned, my mind spinning as I slumped over. Calista shoved me off her, and I fell backward, my head hitting the hard floor. Stars burst in front of my eyes.

Calista's crimson gaze appeared above me, her mouth spread wide in a smile. She raised a clawed hand.

My foot connected with her shin. She twisted, arms flailing before she fell. I leapt for her, prepared to bury my dagger in her throat, but her uninjured wing flared out and knocked me in the face. I toppled again, rolling on the cold floor as blood ran down my temple.

I turned just as Calista dove for me, claws out, a look of lethal delight on her face.

A burst of ice exploded in front of her face, covering her nose and cheeks with bits of snow.

I froze, eyes wide. A tiny white figure hovered in front of Calista, wings flapping with furious intensity.

Another icy blast hit Calista directly in the eye. She howled in agony, covering her eye with her hand.

Kendra flitted around Calista and shot more ice into her ear. Calista shrieked, trying to swat at the tiny dragon. But Kendra was determined, easily dodging strikes here and there. The dragon's blue eyes took on a glint I had never seen before. She grabbed at Calista's hair with her talons, then sprayed ice into her shoulder.

I wanted to whoop with triumph, my heart soaring as this tiny, beautiful creature took on the Queen of the Winter Court.

But my joy was short-lived. With a roar of fury, Calista's wings stretched open wide, and she swung both arms wildly.

Her claws struck Kendra in the wing, making the small creature crumple and fall to the ground. Calista's eyes narrowed on the dragon, as if just realizing how small she was.

A savage smile spread across her lips. She drew closer to Kendra, who was too weak to move out of the way.

"No!" I bellowed, racing forward.

But Eira was faster.

With a shout, the princess dived, coming between Calista and Kendra. Cold horror numbed my veins as Eira tackled Calista to the ground.

No. *No...*

Together, they grappled. Calista's claws swiped. Eira shrieked, but their shapes were such a blur that I couldn't see if Calista had drawn blood.

A high-pitched squeal of pain, shrill and piercing, rang in the room. It was a sound I'd never heard before.

Panting, Eira climbed to her feet, squeezing two fingers together, her pale eyes burning with fury.

Calista writhed on the ground, her wings folded inward, her body twisted in agony. "Stop!" she moaned. "*Stop!*"

Eira bared her teeth as she pressed her fingers tighter together. Calista's screams intensified.

My mouth fell open. What was Eira doing? And how?

"Blood has power, doesn't it, Calista? And *your* blood is no exception."

Realization struck me. I squinted and caught sight of a faint black stain on Eira's fingers.

Demon Fae blood.

She was using Calista's own blood against her.

"I can snap your life thread right now, Stepmother," Eira said softly. "It would be easy. Without your darkness, I can see it clearly."

"Then, do it!" Calista roared, her body still contorting on the floor.

"You deserve to suffer first." Tears glistened in Eira's eyes, but her face was filled with rage.

Frantic footsteps echoed in the hall, and a dozen figures filled the open doorway.

"What is this?" bellowed a voice.

I straightened as I recognized the man in front. Lord Rand Alistair, a high lord of the Winter Court. Next to him was Idell Newsome, a high lady. My eyes scanned the others in the crowd, recognizing them all from court.

Standing in front of them, his tail swishing with smugness, was Frisk.

I huffed a laugh. He certainly *had* gathered reinforcements.

Horror struck the faces of each noble as they took in the sight before them—the dismembered soldiers. The Demon Fae, unable to hide or glamour herself. And Eira, standing like the queen that she was, commanding Calista like a puppet.

"The throne is mine," Eira announced. Tears, dirt, and blood mingled on her face, but she looked as regal as ever, her chin lifted in defiance. Grief and anguish still raged in her eyes, but she held it together for this moment she had worked so hard for. "Your queen is an imposter. She has been deceiving you for *years*. I am here to expose her true nature and claim my birthright. You can either join me or be arrested for treason. The choice is yours." She squeezed her fingers together, and Calista unleashed a fresh scream of pain.

Several nobles flinched, including Lord Rand. "What—What are you doing to her?"

"With her blood, she can be controlled," Eira said. "I am only inflicting on her the same thing she has inflicted on her subjects."

"You are human," said Lady Idell. "We cannot follow a human queen."

"I am *half* human," Eira barked. "My father was a full-blooded seelie fae. There is more seelie blood in me than there is in this false queen lying at your feet. I will only ask one more time: Will you join me?"

Rand's chest puffed as he threw his shoulders back, his brown mustache quivering as he spat, "We will *never* follow you, human scum."

Fury burned within me, and I took a step toward him. Eira stopped me with her free hand, grasping my shoulder.

"Take them away," she said.

I frowned and followed her gaze. A loud, familiar snort echoed in the chamber.

Rand jumped, and the nobles all turned to find a row of

large animals crowding them, with Mauro in the lead. Stags, foxes, birds, sheep, rabbits, and other creatures I had never seen before loomed closer to the nobles until the lords and ladies were surrounded. And behind them, just visible in the hall, I made out the vibrant skin and hair of the pixies. Nyra had sent them to our aid as well.

I couldn't help it; I laughed. The sight was so ridiculous. These men and women with their haughty principles and misguided loyalty were *cowering* before an army of creatures.

It was ridiculous, and yet, it was beautiful. Because Eira had rallied together everyone Calista had been hunting. Now, all the victims of the false queen's hatred were turning on her—both the unseelie and the humans.

Mauro bowed his head, using his huge antlers to poke at the nobles. Rand swatted at him, but it was no use. To avoid being skewered, Rand darted out of Mauro's path, but the stag pushed onward, herding the nobles into a line that led out of the throne room.

"Ah—wait—*princess*!" Rand objected.

But Mauro didn't stop. He jerked his head forward, and Rand yelped as the antlers pierced his flesh.

"Move," Mauro growled. "You had your chance."

"*You can't do this!*" Idell shrieked. Her voice bounced off the walls, even long after the nobles had been escorted out of the throne room.

"They were never going to pledge loyalty to me," Eira said softly. "I knew they wouldn't."

"Then, why give them the chance?" I asked.

"I wanted to be fair. And I needed them to witness this." Eira gestured to Calista, who still lay sprawled on the marble floor. "Once the nobles go to trial, their words will be a testimony against Calista." A small smile lit her face, but it didn't mask the sorrow in her eyes. "They'll be forced to tell the truth."

I nodded, my eyebrows raised. I was impressed. "Looks like you have a few vacancies to fill, Your Majesty."

"No." She waved a hand at her friends still standing in the middle of the room. "My court is right here. All except for one." Her somber gaze shifted to Stella's body. Her lower lip trembled, and another tear streaked down her face. "I—I can see her thread, Theron," she whispered.

My blood chilled. "Don't. Don't do it, Eira."

"It's broken. But… it calls to me. I can mend it. I know I can."

"Eira—"

"She can't." Her voice was suddenly fierce and full of that fire I knew so well. "She can't take anything else from me, Theron. I can't let her. She's already taken too much. This—This is *too much*."

She spread her hands, and before I could stop her, her fingers were moving, twisting and turning as she gathered threads.

"Eira, *no!*"

But it was too late.

Eira's body went stiff, jerking wildly. She threw her head back and screamed.

The Princess

Calista's thread remained intact.

But Stella's was broken.

It was such an easy fix. A life for a life. The simplicity of it called to me, beckoning my magic forward. I couldn't refuse, not when the answer was so plain.

It was an exchange. That was all.

I pulled Calista's thread, then tugged on the broken remains of Stella's. My hands knew what to do even if my mind didn't. This magic was still so new to me, but my fingers seemed to move of their own accord, as if they *knew* this power. They knew what to do with it.

And so, I wove the strands together, substituting Calista's for Stella's. The nobles had seen Calista's true form. My stepmother had served her purpose.

A torrent of pain shot through me, stifling my movements. My back arched, and I threw my head back with an anguished scream as fire burned my blood, scorching me from the inside out. Gods, the pain was *too much*.

And yet, I'd never felt more alive. The sharpness, the sting of it, brought clarity to my mind, which had been bogged down by sorrow and trauma. I could see clearly. The scream continued to pour from my lips, but I kept my hands suspended in the air, still holding on to those pieces of thread, those strands of life.

I had to continue weaving. I had to finish this.

Gasping, each breath wet and ragged, I kept moving my fingers, determined to complete the exchange. This magic could kill me if it wanted to. But I refused to lose another person I loved.

Warm hands pressed against me, drawing me close. I sank into Theron's embrace, using his solid form to support me, to keep me upright. His woodsy mountain scent surrounded me, enveloping me in something so comforting and familiar that it felt like home. I leaned into it, relying on his presence, his strength.

He was here, even though he should have died. Somehow, he was here.

With him by my side, I could do this.

My fingers continued working despite the pain. The glowing pieces of thread shifted and moved at my command, and as I continued, the fire in my blood subsided. My breathing calmed, my pulse slowing. With one last firm tug, my work was complete.

Calista slumped over, her form limp and unmoving. And Stella's body knitted itself back together, bit by bit, her head and limbs moving together as if an invisible hand were stitching her up.

With a loud gasp, Stella jerked upright, her eyes wide as she ran her hands up and down her body in shock. Her throat and torso were drenched in blood.

"Shivering bones, Eira," she said hoarsely. "What did you do?"

I laughed, overwhelmed with relief and sudden exhaustion. And then, my strength left me. I fell against Theron's firm chest and succumbed to the darkness.

My head was spinning. My mouth tasted like sand. With a hoarse cough, I opened my eyes, my vision blurry. Where was I?

A chair creaked nearby, and a familiar voice said, "Eira?"

I tried to speak, but it was like gargling pebbles. I swallowed and tried again. "Theron."

"I'm here." His warm palm captured mine, and our fingers laced together.

Just his nearness, his presence, lit up something within me. I opened my eyes and shifted, finding myself tangled in sheets and blankets, but Theron pressed a hand to my chest to keep me in place.

"Not so fast, Your Majesty."

Your Majesty. A small part of me missed how he'd called me *princess.*

But I supposed I would never be a princess again. I was the queen now.

My eyes grew wide, and I turned to look at him. He was wearing a fresh tan tunic with a dark brown vest and matching trousers. His hair had been slicked back, and his beard was trimmed. He looked elegant and regal, although I did yearn for the musky, wild hunter I'd grown accustomed to.

"Theron," I said again, my voice urgent. "What happened? How long was I asleep?"

"You resurrected Stella." His voice was sharp. "You almost *killed* yourself, Eira."

I squeezed his hand, gritting my teeth against my impatience. "Answer the damn question, hunter."

He sighed. "You've been unconscious for three days. Stella is fine. So is Kendra. Your recently appointed courtiers are managing state affairs quite well."

I arched an eyebrow, full of doubt. "Really?"

He huffed. "They are doing as well as they can. No civil wars yet, although there have been several riots, but they've been quelled. Word has spread of Calista's deception, and many of her forces have shifted loyalties. To you."

To me. Blood and ice, I couldn't believe it. My mouth opened and closed, and a swell of dizziness overtook me. I leaned back against the pillows, gasping for breath. My tired gaze shifted to Theron, who looked at me with worry etched into his face.

"I'm fine," I said. "I'm just... still a bit weak."

"That was reckless and stupid, Eira."

I nodded feebly. "I know."

He groaned and ran a hand down his face. "I can't protect you from everything."

"You don't have to. I can protect myself."

A smile twitched at the corners of his lips. "I know that. I *want* to protect you from everything. But I can't. It's something I must come to terms with."

Warmth crept up my throat as I looked at him, drinking in his features and memorizing every inch of him, from the faint scar above his eyebrow to the tanned skin of his forearms. "I almost lost you." My voice broke on the words.

Theron sobered and leaned closer to the bed, clutching both my hands now. "But you didn't."

"Talk about stupid and reckless, Theron, what the *hell* were you—"

"You were dying," he said simply, as if this explained everything.

"But your magic…"

A sad smile played at his lips. "You did more with my magic in five minutes than I did in an entire lifetime. You wield it far better than I ever did, Eira. It's for *you*." He clutched my hand in his, his thumb stroking along my knuckles. "Do you still have it? The necromancy power?"

I took a deep breath and closed my eyes for a moment, trying to sense that presence within me. When I opened them, the faintest flicker of blue thread ignited in the air next to Theron. In a flash, it was gone.

"It's still there," I said softly. "But it's weak."

Theron sighed and nodded, focusing on our interlocked fingers.

"Theron, you were *dead*." My words caught, and heat stung my eyes. The thought of losing him—

Sorrow weighed heavily on his expression. "This kingdom needs you more than it needs me."

He had said that before, and the words made my chest ache. Resolve coursed through me, and I found the strength to lean forward and meet his gaze. "This kingdom needs *you*, too. It needs more men like you who are willing to risk everything for their people."

He smiled. "I risked everything for my queen. It was all for *you*, Eira."

Moisture tickled my eyes, and I nodded. "I know." I inhaled, my breath shaky. "I want you by my side, Theron. I want you to rule this court with me."

His eyes grew wide. "I—as *king*?" When I nodded again, he said weakly, "Eira…"

"I can't do this alone. You know that."

"You have your nobles! You aren't alone."

"And what will you do? Skulk off to your secluded cabin, isolating yourself from the world? Is that what you want?" The words were meant to be teasing, but the catch in my voice betrayed my insecurities. If that *was* what he wanted, I would let him go. I would let him be free at last. I refused to enslave him like Calista had. If he loathed court life so much, I wouldn't blame him for wanting to escape it.

Theron raised my hands and brushed his lips against my knuckles, sending a shiver of pleasure down my spine. "I go where you go, Eira. I am yours to command."

"Then, I command you to marry me."

He chuckled and shook his head, his lips grazing my skin again. "I can't."

My heart dropped to my stomach. "Oh."

"Could I be your consort instead?"

I shook my head. "I've been thinking about this, Theron. I don't want someone to merely be attached to me as my spouse. I want someone to share my power, to rule alongside me. This court needs a king. A king like my father."

"Make me your assassin. Your commander. Your advisor. Anything else. I want to serve you, but I—I can't be king."

I frowned at the weakness in his tone. "Why not?"

He shook his head. "You know me, Eira. My father led a crusade against the very people you've sworn to protect. I helped Calista slaughter innocents for years. I can't wear the crown. I'm not fit for it."

My eyes narrowed. "Who are you to decide that?"

"Do you really think the people will follow me? Even the nobles of your court despise me."

"Denton will come around."

"It isn't just Denton."

I sighed. He wasn't making this easy. "Please, Theron."

He raised his eyebrows, mischief glinting in his eyes. "Are you... *begging*?"

My face burned, and I rolled my eyes. "Are you really going to make your queen beg?"

He leaned closer and pressed a kiss to my nose. "As much as I'd like that, I just need time, Eira. This kingdom needs time. I'm not saying I don't want to marry you. Believe me, I want nothing more than to declare my love for you for the world to hear, and then claim you as my own. Over... and over again." His teeth nipped gently at my nose, and I shuddered as coils of heat twisted in my stomach.

My breath hitched as I prompted, "But?"

"But..." He drew back, and darkness crept into his gaze. I knew that darkness well. He wore it like a cloak, shrouding it around himself until he was swallowed by it. In that moment, I knew he was right. He needed time. He was a man burdened by the blood on his hands. I saw him differently, but that didn't matter. He had to see it for himself.

"But I'm not ready," he finally finished. "My heart and soul will always belong to you, Eira. But I'm not ready for the burden of the crown just yet. Let the kingdom adjust to a new queen first. Once they have accepted you, we can see what they think of an assassin for a king." His mouth twisted in a grimace.

"You aren't an assassin," I said earnestly. "Not anymore. I will *never* ask you to kill, Theron."

His throat bobbed as he swallowed. "Thank you." Something shifted in his gaze as he looked at me. "You don't have to wait for me, Eira. If it's a king you want, you should... you should..." He broke off, his eyes flaring with pain.

I squeezed his hands again. "There's only you, Theron. I

won't take another husband or lover. I will wait for however long you need. I swear it."

He exhaled in relief and nodded.

A slow smile spread on my face. "I'd even be willing to make a bargain over it."

He laughed, ducking his head. "Don't you dare. We've had enough of those."

"What, you didn't enjoy being bound to me?"

"I enjoyed it far more than I should have."

"See? We should make more bargains, then. Just to keep things interesting."

He leaned in again, and I closed my eyes, relishing his woodsy scent as it washed over me. His mouth captured mine, and I tugged on his collar to bring him closer.

Theron chuckled against my lips. "Life with you," he murmured, "will always be interesting, my queen. With or without bargains."

The Hunter

Three years later

"Watch your footing," I said, gesturing to Morwenna's feet. "Plant them firmly. If you wobble, your strike won't be as forceful."

Morwenna's brows screwed up in concentration as she mimicked my movements, her small mouth puckered. Her blunt blade swished with her movements, her footwork steady and firm.

I nodded with a smile. "Good." I turned to Gemma, her younger sister. "Show me your strike."

Gemma lifted her wooden blade, then jabbed it forward with the exact intensity I had taught her.

"Here." I drew closer, lifting her arms up a fraction. "Aim higher. Your opponent will likely be much bigger than you. And if you have the strength, *twist*." I motioned with the practice blade. "If you can wrench that weapon inside them, it'll slow them down further."

"Sir Theron!"

I looked up, finding a servant sprinting into the courtyard, a rolled-up piece of parchment clutched in his hands. I stepped away from my students and raised my eyebrows expectantly.

"Your presence is requested." The man shoved the parchment into my hands.

I unrolled it and glanced over the familiar handwriting. "She needs me right now?"

The servant huffed in exasperation. "It is the *queen*, my lord. She asked me to summon you, so I did. I did not ask questions."

"Right. Of course." I sighed, tucking the parchment into my pocket before turning to the six young girls waiting for me to continue training. "I'm sorry, everyone, but we will have to resume our lessons tomorrow."

A few of them groaned in disappointment.

"I can take over," said a familiar voice.

I turned and found Stella striding toward me, her steps lithe and graceful. She wore black leathers and had a throwing knife in each hand. After Eira had been coronated, Stella had worked with me on creating a training program to teach young girls self-defense. Now, between court duties, we alternated instructing our pupils.

I smiled warmly at her. Ever since Eira had resurrected her, Stella had been… different. More altered. She was much more somber than before, though there were echoes of her former self that emerged in moments here and there. Her hair was now silver, completely void of all color. Her eyes, once a brilliant blue, were as black as my own.

And there was something… off about her scent. She no longer smelled human. Not quite fae either, but… something dark. Something close to death.

Regardless, she had served on the Winter Court for years now. Eira trusted her, and I did, too. Bringing someone back from death was likely to change a person. I could hardly judge her for that.

Stella's fathomless eyes fixed on me expectantly, and I nodded. "Thank you, Stella."

She offered a small smile. Positioning herself in front of the crowd of students, Stella said, "All right, girls. Show me how you block."

The girls immediately sprang into action. I smiled slightly, thinking of Eira and her ferocity. These girls would grow up to be like her someday.

That was my hope.

I returned my sword to the armory and made my way up the steps to the castle entrance. My stomach was already doing backflips at the thought of meeting a guest with Eira in the throne room. Teaching fighting skills was comfortable for me. Easy. Familiar. But court politics? I wasn't sure if I would ever get accustomed to it.

There wasn't time to bathe or change, so I merely adjusted my coat and smoothed down my wild hair before climbing the spiral staircase that led to the throne room. I nodded at the soldiers guarding the doors as I walked in.

Eira stood in the center of the room in front of her throne. For a moment, I was swept away by her beauty. She wore a long, midnight blue gown with sparkling diamonds embedded in the fabric. A white shawl was draped around her shoulders, and her silver crown glistened in the faint light streaming in from the windows. Her inky black hair was twisted into a knot on the side of her head, with several loose curls framing her face. Her expression was solemn as she conversed with...

My heart stuttered in my chest as I recognized the rose gold skin and white hair.

This was Nyra, the pixie queen. She wore a vibrant purple dress that exposed her back, allowing her long, glittering wings to stretch freely behind her. Next to her was Sage, the ambassador for the pixies, who wore a golden gown that fell in shimmering waves all the way down to her feet.

The three turned to look at me as I entered. I sketched a quick bow and said, "You asked to see me?"

Eira waved her hand at me. "Drop the pretense, Theron. Nyra knows you."

I scoffed and straightened. "It's not a *pretense*. You're still my queen, even if we share a bed."

"How scandalous," Nyra said with a smirk, her all-black eyes drilling into me with an intensity that made me want to fidget.

"Riots have broken out in Jarta and Dahl," Eira said. "Pixies are being attacked, dragged from their homes and captured. We think the seelie nobles might be involved, but we can't prove anything."

My chest constricted. Eira had been queen for a few years now, but there was still discontent over a human ruling the court. Especially since she had decreed that the unseelie were to be granted the same freedoms as the seelie.

"What can I do?" I asked, spine straightening as I waited for my queen to command me.

A small smile lit Eira's face. "You can talk to them."

I frowned. "Talk?"

"Yes. It's something you do with your mouth instead of your hands. Although, I think you are skilled at using both, if memory serves me."

My face flushed, and I sputtered awkwardly, unable to provide a coherent response. Sage snorted, then covered her mouth. Nyra cackled and clapped her hands together in delight.

"I *mean*," I said, my face still hot, "don't you want me to lead forces down there?"

"I've tried that. Many times. But it doesn't seem to be making a difference."

"The seelie need someone like *them* to speak with them," Nyra said. "Eira here is a human, as is her court. I think they see it as offensive that there is no seelie emissary."

I blinked once. Twice. "Emissary?"

"Are you going to continue to parrot words back to us?" Eira asked with a long-suffering sigh.

"I'm just confused as to what you want me to do here."

Eira drew closer to me, her eyes sparkling. "Theron, I want you to be a leader."

I swallowed hard and waited for her to continue. My pulse began to thrum.

"You've been leading our court meetings for years now," she said.

"I've only been directing them."

"And you've been leading training lessons with the soldiers and civilians," Eira went on.

"That is *voluntary* and a completely informal setting."

"Not to mention the fact that you *know* the fae and their customs far better than I ever could." Eira lifted a hand and ran her fingers down my jaw, teasing my beard. "This court needs you, Theron. In an official capacity. If you're ready for it."

My heart rate quickened as I glanced from Eira to Nyra,

who was smiling slyly, then to Sage, whose eyes were wide. "You want me... to be your emissary?" I clarified.

"Yes," said Eira. "You would be my official spokesperson, traveling throughout the provinces and providing counsel."

I looked at her, my stomach wriggling uncontrollably. "How often?"

"What?"

"How often would I be traveling?"

Eira frowned at this. "I'm not sure yet. As often as is required."

The knots tightened in my chest. "I see." My voice sounded strained. I glanced at Nyra, whose smile widened.

Eira cleared her throat. "Nyra, Sage, could you give us a moment?"

Nyra's smile fell. "Damn. I was starting to enjoy his discomfort. We'll be in our rooms, then." She swept from the room, with Sage trailing after. The doors slammed shut behind them.

I exhaled in a puff of air, struggling to control my breathing. Eira's hands were on my shoulders, her expression full of worry. "What is it? What's wrong?"

"Emissary?" I said weakly. "Eira, why?"

She pressed her palms against my cheeks. "Why *not*? For years, you've refused to hold an official position in my court. You're just... I don't know, my rugged bedmate."

"I offered to be your consort!" I objected.

"I know that," she said gently. "But it's been three years. Don't you think it's time for something more?" She took a breath, her eyes suddenly guarded as she searched my face, no doubt taking in my panic-stricken expression. "Unless you don't want to? I would hate to push you into a role you don't want. I just thought..."

I placed my hands on her waist. "I am yours, Eira."

She offered me a wry smile. "I'm not questioning your love for me, hunter. I just... I thought you needed time. That if I waited long enough..." She broke off and shook her head. "It's all right. If you don't want to be in this court in that way, then maybe I can shift some things around. Keep our relationship more private so you can be a civilian instead."

My brow furrowed. "I don't want that."

"Then what *do* you want?"

I paused, considering this. In my life, I hadn't often been given the luxury of choosing my path. My father had forced me into court life early on, and then Calista had forced me to continue his work.

It wasn't until I met Eira that I'd truly felt like I had a purpose. Like I could do good things, despite my past.

"I want to make a difference," I said quietly.

"Being my emissary will achieve that," she said.

My throat went dry, the fluttering in my stomach becoming uncontrollable. "I want... to be with *you* making a difference."

Eira cocked her head at me in confusion. "What do you mean? You already are."

"As emissary, my job is to travel on your behalf, correct?"

"Yes."

"Which means we will be apart quite a bit."

She hesitated. "Yes. It will involve a lot of traveling and liaisons when I can't be there."

I shook my head. "Then, I'm afraid I cannot accept. My place is with *you*, Eira."

She dropped her hands on her thighs with a loud slap. "Damn it, Theron, I don't know what to do with you. Do you want to continue teaching villagers how to wield weapons for the rest of your life? Our kingdom is on the brink of a civil war if we can't find a way to reach the seelie nobles who are unhappy with me as their queen."

"Why do you think I'm the one who can do that for you?"

"You are the only person left in this court who knew Calista's ways. You know how she ruled, how she treated her nobles. You know what they expect of a ruler. And no matter how often I try to speak to them, they do not hear me when my mouth opens. They only hear a belligerent human princess who fancies herself a queen." Her eyes glistened with tears, and the sight was like a dagger to my heart.

"This isn't just about *traveling* on your behalf, is it?" I asked softly.

She shook her head, lips pressed together tightly.

"You need someone who *isn't* you—who isn't human—to reach out to these people."

"Yes." Her breath was shaky. In this moment, she was opening herself up to me. She was vulnerable.

She *needed* me.

And I needed to overcome this crippling fear of being a leader. For three years, I had been serving this court to the best of my ability. I'd walked the streets alongside ordinary men and women, stepping into their shoes and helping them with their burdens. I'd made suggestions during Eira's meetings with her human court, advising the best way to govern a predominantly seelie court.

I enjoyed it. Despite the nerves, despite my anxieties, I enjoyed doing work that mattered.

Eira was asking for more of me. And for the first time, I finally felt ready.

With a deep breath, I said, "You need a husband who is a full-blooded seelie fae."

Eira's mouth dropped open. "I—what?"

"You need a king by your side who will travel *with* you to these places of unrest and show you are both a united front. Fae and human, ruling together."

Eira took a step back, looking over me like she'd never seen me before. "Theron, what the hell are you talking about? Are you suggesting I go out and find myself a seelie fae husband?"

I uttered a frustrated growl, my rage igniting at the thought of Eira marrying anyone who wasn't me. I seized her and dragged her body back to mine before planting a rough kiss on her lips. She touched my cheek, her hand shaking, as I drew back and whispered, "Marry me, Eira."

Her breath hitched. "Marry you… as a consort?"

"I—I would like to marry you as… your king. As your equal. If that is acceptable to you." My face heated again, and I felt absurd and foolish for even presuming that she would still want this from me when I had done *nothing* to deserve it.

A wide smile spread across her face, and her eyes filled with tears. She pressed a hand to her mouth and uttered a soft gasp. Then, she laughed loudly. "Are you serious?"

I nodded, and she squealed with delight before throwing her arms around me. "You stupid, grouchy man, why did it *take* you so long?" She pressed a trail of kisses from my lips to my chin and up and down my jaw. I clutched her tightly, relishing the way her body seemed to mold against mine. Never would I tire of the way we seemed to fit perfectly together.

"Is that a yes?" I muttered between kisses.

"*Yes!*" she cried, threading her hands through my hair. "Yes, Theron. A thousand times yes. Be my husband. My king. My everything." She turned her head, her lips meeting mine, but slower this time. My mouth captured hers again and again, tasting her as if it were our first kiss. As if we had all the time in the world to memorize each other's lips and tongue, to claim one another in every way.

"Yours," I murmured against her lips. "Always yours, my queen."

I tasted her tears as they streamed down her face. We laughed together, arms tangled, unable to keep our hands off each other.

I knew we had an uphill battle to face. It certainly wouldn't be easy. But in the three years since she'd become queen, I had learned that nothing could be done perfectly. To me, Eira was flawless. She was everything this kingdom needed. And yet, people still found fault with her. People still expected *more* of her.

Not everyone saw her the way I did.

It had opened my eyes to how the world saw *me*. How Eira saw me.

I would never be able to earn every person's forgiveness for my past sins. But that didn't mean I couldn't make a difference in this court. That didn't mean I shouldn't try. For three years, I had strived to atone for what I'd done. While many people were amenable to accepting me, there were many who were not—and they never would be.

I could never win them over. And I had to accept that.

So, here and now, I was making my choice.

I would rule with Eira. Even if I didn't deserve it. Even if there was still blood on my hands that I could never scrub away.

Because Eira needed me. She believed in me. And I believed in her more than I believed in myself. Her light pulled me from the darkness, showing me that not all of my shadows were poisonous. I was a killer, but that was not all that I was. There was more to me than my skill with a blade.

And I was finally ready to illuminate those hidden parts of myself.

With Eira by my side.

Being resurrected comes with a deadly side effect... Read Stella's story in ***Crown of Ashes***, a Cinderella retelling!

ACKNOWLEDGMENTS

There are so many incredible individuals who helped bring Crown of Poison to life! I am forever grateful for their contributions to this story.

My beta readers, Jenni, Sara, Melissa, Tori, and Kari. You have been phenomenal, giving me exactly the critiques and feedback I need to make this story shine.

My incredible ARC team! I love your enthusiasm, and I greatly appreciate your kind reviews.

My Tuesday Tribe, for helping me brainstorm when I got stuck.

My awesome editor, Allison Rose.

Blue Raven Book Covers for the beautiful cover designs.

Poyjeee, Mage on Duty, Kuri Draws, and Samaiya Art for the stunning character art!

My wonderful Kickstarter backers. Without you, the Crown of Poison special editions never would have happened! A million thanks for your pledges.

And most importantly, Alex, Colin, Ellie, and Isabel. You are my everything.

ABOUT THE AUTHOR

R.L. Perez is an author, wife, mother, reader, writer, and graphic designer. She lives in Florida with her husband and three kids. On a regular basis, she can usually be found napping, reading, feverishly writing, revising, or watching an abundance of Netflix. More than anything, she loves spending time with her family. Her greatest joys are her children, nature, literature, and chocolate.

Subscribe to her newsletter for new releases, promotions, giveaways, and book recommendations! Get a FREE eBook when you sign up at subscribe.rlperez.com.

www.ingramcontent.com/pod-product-compliance
Lightning Source LLC
LaVergne TN
LVHW040035080526
838202LV00045B/3344